D0594987

She was the most desirable woman he had ever seen, and he ached for her.

"Please let me go," she was saying, her voice holding a note of pleading in it now, and he could not help but be amused by her change in tactics.

"I ask a price for all favors granted," he answered her insolently. "I want you to let me make love to you, kitten," he said, the devilish look in his eyes.

Gabrielle felt her throat go dry and she could not swallow for a moment. "You—you cannot ask such a thing. I—I am still a maid."

The stranger's arrogant laugh was her only answer.

GABRIELLE

Theresa Conway

A FAWCETT GOLD MEDAL BOOK

Fawcett Books, Greenwich, Connecticut

GABRIELLE

© 1977 Theresa Conway

All rights reserved

ISBN 0–449–13916–6

Printed in the United States of America

10 9 8 7 6 5 4 3 2 1

To my sister, Laura
with love

PART ONE

Paris—1809

Chapter One

Gabrielle de Beauvoir breathed in the smells and sounds of the teeming, bustling city of Paris with her usual air of suppressed excitement. Below her, a group of young students on their way to classes glanced up at the enchanting vision of the slim, lovely girl standing there half-naked, and shouted bold compliments and urged her to display more of her charms. Blushing in confusion and aware of the immodesty of her chemise, which displayed the upper slopes of her small, upthrusting breasts, Gabrielle quickly retired into the still-darkened room, fearing that at any moment her aunt would come rushing up the stairs to her room to scold her for her improper behavior.

She sighed, for her Aunt Louise was forever lecturing her on this or that propriety which she was sadly lacking, taking every possible moment to inject a reprimand directed at Gabrielle's dead father who had been an abominable rakehell before he was thrown from his horse at a hunt, suffering a broken neck. André de Beauvoir, the Marquis de Molisse, had been dead nearly three years now. How ironic that his illustrious name had survived the gruesome Revolution in France only to fall prey to the most mundane of accidents.

Gabrielle realized, of course, that somewhere in that disapproving heart there must be some love for her only niece, for why else would Aunt Louise have bothered to care for her and taken such pains to ensure that she had an education?

She heard footsteps on the staircase and braced herself for another lecture, but to her surprise, Aunt Louise burst into the room with a look of elation on her face. "Gabrielle my *chérie,* you will never guess how lucky, how truly lucky we are today!"

"What has happened?" Gabrielle questioned, schooling herself against the rising tide of her excitement, for if she knew her aunt, she also knew that many of that lady's most elevating moments were spent exulting over the birth of some baby, or a new gown, or even a day without rain so that she needn't worry about muddying her new slippers.

"I have found us a patron!"

"A—patron?"

"Yes, yes!" the woman nodded her head as though she were jerked by invisible strings, "a grand patron who is very rich—rich enough to enable you to attend a convent to further your education—although I daresay at sixteen you are a little too old to be attending one."

Gabrielle's brows drew downward in a little frown, as she struggled to piece together her aunt's story for her own understanding. Finally, she gave up and asked her point-blank what she was talking about.

"Do not be ill-mannered, child," Aunt Louise spoke pointedly. "M'sieur le Marquis de Chevalier, an acquaintance of Bonaparte's, has offered to become your guardian as well as protector to both of us. He was a great friend of your father's, and I can only say I'm surprised the offer did not come sooner after André's death. But no matter, now 'we need not worry about the future. Don't you see! You will have the opportunity of being presented at the emperor's court!" She clasped her hands together in unbridled glee; Gabrielle had never seen her so animated.

"But how—" she began uncertainly, wondering if she should question her aunt further.

"You needn't worry, child. I have made all the necessary arrangements with the marquis, and he has agreed that it would be most advisable to present ourselves at his hôtel immediately. Thank goodness, we need not reside in this straggly house one moment longer," she added, gazing around the small attic bedroom with a sniff of disdain.

"But this was my father's house!" Gabrielle protested.

"Yes, and what did he use it for? Women and drink and gambling. How he ever had the decency to leave it to you in his will—" The woman's dark eyes snapped with outrage. "But no longer will I have to be reminded of his debauchery, for M'sieur de Chevalier has wisely advised me to put it up for sale." She cast a sideways glance at her niece, noticing the distressed look on the girl's face. "You should be happy, my dear," she commented in a gentler tone. "Think what this can mean for you. Someday, perhaps, the marquis will have the opportunity of making a splendid match for you with the oldest son of some wealthy noble. You will never have to scrimp and save as I have done these past three years, striving to make ends meet and appear respectable in the bargain."

"But Aunt Louise, I was never aware that we were in such dire straits. We live in the country house during the hottest part of the summer and return here to Paris in the fall as we are doing now. You never once mentioned to me that our funds were running out."

"I didn't want you to know how bad things were, my child. There was no point in worrying you since there was no remedy and certainly nothing *you* could do."

Gabrielle found herself confused and somehow uneasy about this turn of events, but certainly there seemed little choice for her now. "When—when shall we be leaving here?" she asked finally.

Her aunt's breath exploded in a little puff as if she had been holding it, and Gabrielle felt her plump arms encircle her. "There, now, that's my girl. You must see that I am really only doing this for your own welfare." She patted her shoulder awkwardly. "I have already charged the servants with packing our things into trunks, and the marquis will be here in an hour to escort us personally to his hôtel. So hurry now and dress.

Gabrielle nodded, shaking off the moment of depression. After all, if this marquis were a friend of her late father's, it might be nice to be able to talk with him about

André de Beauvoir. A thought came to her mind, and she turned to her aunt who was already nearly out the door.

"Aunt Louise, you did not say: is M'sieur de Chevalier married? Has he no children?" She could have sworn that her aunt blushed briefly.

"He is a widower with a sole heir. His son is in the army now, though, and when he does visit, he does not stay long."

Gabrielle smiled at her aunt's discomfiture. Did it mean that she was perhaps nourishing more than gratitude towards this very obliging marquis?

Turning to the tall pier glass, Gabrielle critically surveyed her reflected image—a young girl, not yet a woman, with a slender body and a lovely face. Her breasts, she noted with considerable satisfaction, were not heavy and pendulous like some of her friends', but small and tightly rounded, tilting upwards slightly as if the pink tips were forever trying to peep over the neckline of her chemise. Her waist was willow-slim and supple and flared nicely into her graceful hips and thighs.

Her reflection smiled back at her, and she noted the flawless, peach-tinted cheeks, the determined chin, and the smooth-lipped mouth that was just short of generous and revealed perfect white teeth when she smiled. Her nose was straight and short with a careless dusting of golden freckles across its bridge to testify to her blondness. Her hair was certainly worth noting: almost a honey-blond, it glistened with reddish tints and looked so glowing that it reminded her of a campfire. Set under delicately arched brows were eyes the color of violets with no trace of grey in them. Oh, they could darken to near-black when her temper overcame her, but their color was as fresh and true as the little velvet-smooth flowers that grew in the flowerpots on the windowsills. And, framed by amazingly long lashes, they reminded her of amethysts set in gold.

More than once, her aunt had told Gabrielle that her mother had had eyes that very color. But look how little help they had been to that poor woman! Aunt Louise admonished Gabrielle not to set such store by her good looks, for they would surely fade as she got older. And then what would she have left but a remembrance? This was the reason she had insisted on lessons for her niece "in spite of their considerable cost." She had never acknowledged how proud she was of her niece's accomplishments, but Gabrielle had overheard her talking of them to anyone who cared to listen.

But, for all her beauty and intelligence, Gabrielle had been introduced to very few men. When all her friends were giggling over their latest beaux, one of them relating her adventures in a hayloft with some well-endowed shepherd boy, Gabrielle would struggle to keep the color from her cheeks and wonder at their boldness. Then she would think that perhaps she was too backward, but how could one cultivate the artistry of a coquette when one was given no opportunity? The stable boys' eyes promised a boldness that caused her involuntary shivers, but her aunt's sharp eyes never let her out of her sight long enough to permit such promises to become reality.

And the men who visited the country house were mostly old widowers who sometimes drooled unconsciously into their wine cups as their lasvicious eyes wandered over the girl's throat and bosom. At such times, Gabrielle felt almost sick and experienced only relief when their visits ended.

When Aunt Louise would announce their return to the capital, Gabrielle had to restrain herself from throwing her arms around her neck, for at least there were things one could do in the city that made one forget about the absence of suitors.

Her best friend, Isabel de Montfort, lived in Paris; and although Aunt Louise labeled her a bold little baggage, Gabrielle knew the girl more deeply and realized her true good nature and spontaneous affection. Outrageously, Isabel admitted that her first entry into the realm of love had been initiated by a sergeant in Napoleon's army, but it had been a wonderful experience. And indeed, it must have been, if one could judge by the steady stream of young men who called upon her now.

Gabrielle pushed thoughts of her friend out of her mind for the moment as the slamming of trunk lids and the hurried tone in the servants' voices reminded her that the marquis would be here shortly. Certainly it would never do to show her gratitude by compelling him to cool his heels in the sitting room.

She pulled a soft, blue gown over her head and settled it over her figure. The neckline was scooped fashionably low, and there were tiny puffed sleeves and a sash tied snugly beneath the breasts. She heard her aunt calling for her below, and with a final touch of rosewater at her throat and breasts, she hurried downstairs.

Gabrielle sat down on a chair, clasping her hands in her lap and feeling the tide of excitement flow up towards her throat. It would be wonderful to be able to attend balls and soirées with her friend—properly chaperoned, of course—at the neighboring hôtels and even at the Palace of the Tuileries itself! Perhaps she would meet some very nice young man who could be induced to be her escort. Of course, Isabel could be counted on to provide someone suitable to her tastes, but whether or not Aunt Louise would approve was another matter.

Her mind traveled pleasantly in this line of thought until her aunt's voice, anxiously fluttering, announced that the marquis had arrived and commanded her to ready herself to receive him. Gabrielle hadn't recognized the strain she was under until the marquis swept grandly into the room at the heels of one of the scurrying servants. For a moment she could only stare at the richness of his finery; then, at her aunt's indrawn breath, she curtseyed as sedately as possible. A warm hand on her shoulder half-lifted her up, and she looked into dark, laughing eyes in a face framed by dark, gleaming hair. She judged the marquis to be a little more than forty and thought him a fine figure of a man.

"Good day, Mademoiselle de Beauvoir—or may I call you Gabrielle?" His lips touched her hand as he squeezed it heartily. "It will be a pleasure to allow myself the luxury of launching you in society, my dear. And let me assure you that when your aunt told me how pretty you were, she truly failed to do you justice."

His gallant speech caused a blush to suffuse the girl's cheeks, but she murmured her thanks, casting a hasty glance at her aunt who was gazing at M'sieur de Chevalier most anxiously. As if aware of the girl's uneasiness, the marquis turned his attention to her aunt, bowing over her hand and talking pleasantries until even her aunt's cheeks grew slightly pink. At thirty-eight her aunt was still good-looking, with the appearance of a gentle, attractive, middle-aged woman.

She is truly taken with him, Gabrielle thought, pleased, and yet worried lest her aunt be deceived by the obviously worldly nobleman. After a few moments, one of the servants came to the door to announce that the packing was finished.

"Good. I have taken the liberty of bringing along a cart, driven by one of my servants. With the help of some of your own menservants, he will be able to load the cart without delay. Meanwhile, let me escort you two lovely ladies back to my home, for I am positive you can hardly wait to view your new lodgings."

He extended a velvet-sheathed arm to each lady and together they stepped from the room into the strangely deserted-looking hall and out into the sunshine of a fine September morning. The open carriage that awaited them was smartly outfitted in blue and gold livery, and the marquis gallantly helped the ladies in.

Once comfortably seated, he signalled for the driver to start up the horses, and Gabrielle revelled in the fresh breeze that fanned her face and lifted her hair. They chattered about unimportant things—the weather, the Emperor Napoleon's good health, the former Empress Josephine's loveliness even in the face of her divorce. Gabrielle's mind was only half-engaged with what the other two discussed, for she was engrossed in viewing the bustling activities of the world's second largest city.

They passed the market place of the Pont Neuf and the raucous cries of the fishwives and tripe sellers mixed with the sweeter notes of the young flower sellers. With untiring fascination, Gabrielle watched the antics of the jugglers and the tightrope walker, who were performing in the large square to the applause of the admiring populace. They trotted through narrow streets lined with refuse, the smell of which caused her to wrinkle her nose in mingled pity and disgust.

Finally they ventured out into the Rue du Faubourg St.-Denis and stopped in front of an imposing edifice of grey stone which stood three stories high with a wide courtyard fronted by a five-foot wall of white brick. The Hôtel Chevalier stood, in spite of its expansive front court, quite close to its neighbors on either side, similar buildings of the same grandeur. Gabrielle caught herself staring speechless at the palace and realized that the marquis was studying her in amusement.

"It is so grand," she murmured inanely, feeling unsure under his speculative gaze. "I cannot believe this is to be my home."

"It will be your home for as long as you wish," he replied easily, and taking her arm he helped her out of the carriage.

They entered the hôtel and Gabrielle mentally exclaimed over the richness of the furniture, the wall hangings, the carpets. Everything was so lovely and in such exquisite taste. She felt sure that in another moment someone was going to pinch her and she would wake up from the delightful dream world. But no, they had mounted the staircase now and were being shown into their respective suites, and still Gabrielle found she was not dreaming.

"I trust you will find your rooms suitable, Gabrielle," the marquis was saying amiably. "Unfortunately, as you can see, this balcony window looks directly into the bedroom of our neighbor, but he hardly ever uses the house—travels a great deal." As if to assure himself of his neighbor's absence, the marquis walked to the balcony window and pulled aside the long damask curtains, peering out in a manner that suggested he was slightly nearsighted. He stood for a moment thus, as if watching or waiting for something, but then shrugged and turned aside, smiling at the questioning look on Gabrielle's face.

"Your neighbor and you—are not friendly?" she asked uncertainly.

He laughed. "Quite the opposite, my dear. The captain and I get along together very well." He bowed and went out into the hall, where Aunt Louise was admiring some of the portraits that hung there.

Once her two elders were gone, Gabrielle flitted about her bedroom, touching the softness of the lemon-yellow counterpane, the hand mirror with its border of pink-tinted seashells, feeling the luxury of the real Turkish carpet underfoot. Besides her bedroom, there was also an adjoining sitting room, a large closet which was, she suspected, for her maid's use, and to her immense delight, a tiny bathroom, tiled in pink and white and with a huge copper tub.

Oh, what luxury this was! She kicked off her slippers and dug her stockinged toes into the carpet, revelling in its texture. She tried out each of the three dainty-looking chairs, then sank blissfully onto the bed, uncaring as to the state of her gown.

As if she had chosen just that moment to come in, the maid returned with an admonition that her dress would be horribly wrinkled if she insisted on lying down in it. Gabrielle would have felt affronted by her impertinence if the warning had not been made in such a kind voice and with such a wide smile.

"Are you to assist me personally?" she asked, obediently rising from the bed and shaking her skirts.

The woman nodded. "For the time being. Actually, the housekeeper will be retiring in a few months, and I am to be elevated to her position, so we will be looking for a younger girl to suit you. My name is Pauline."

Gabrielle circled the room and came to stand by the same window where her patron had stood some minutes before. "I expect M'sieur de Chevalier will require me for dinner tonight, Pauline. Please choose something you think would be suitable."

The maid curtseyed and began to open the wardrobe trunks which had been set in the room, beginning to hang gowns away and unpack slippers and handkerchiefs.

Curiously, Gabrielle drew the draperies back from the window and gazed at the opposite balcony which couldn't be more than ten yards away, trying to peer through the closed windows into the dark interior of the house itself. She gave up presently but still wondered about her new guardian's neighbor. The captain, he had called him— probably of some vague outpost on the French frontier. Wasn't the marquis' son in the army too? It would be nice, she admitted, to have a soldier for an escort to some of the balls and parties, and she hoped that one of the unknown men would arrive home in time for the Christmas gaieties.

Chapter Two

It was well past nine o'clock and Gabrielle glared at the small china clock on the nightstand as if willing it to disappear. She had been up late last night at a small party given by a close friend of the marquis. Her patron had insisted she call him Alexandre; after two weeks the strangeness had subsided, and she felt towards him the way she would regard a long-lost uncle. After all, if her aunt's languishing looks meant anything, he might very well become just that one day.

She must have drunk too much champagne at the party, for now her head ached dully and she only half-remembered struggling coyly out of M'sieur Burchand's amorous embraces. Really, that young man was diligent with his unwanted attentions.

She turned away with a sigh from eying the clock and

buried her head in the pillow, wishing she could go back to sleep and escape this abominable headache. But such was not to be, for a quick knock, followed by Isabel's light laugh, bade her lift her head and regard her friend wearily.

"Goodness, Gabrielle! Still in bed, *chérie*! How can you bear to miss this beautiful morning? Crisp October air, says Maman, is the best thing for a headache. I assume by the way you're glaring at me that you *do* have a headache?" Isabel pulled off her gloves and hat and threw them on a chair, coming to sit on the bed and pat Gabrielle's hand. "Poor dear, I know you're not used to wine. You know I tried to keep you from indulging, but that odious rascal, Pierre Burchand, kept filling up your glass until I had the unpleasant sensation that he was going to try and claim your maiden's virtue last night." She glanced casually at the younger girl. "Umm—you are still intact, aren't you?"

"Isabel, sometimes I don't know whether I should laugh or get angry with you! Do you think I would let that man touch me?" She shivered involuntarily. "His hands are faster than a pickpocket's—and up to just as much mischief!"

Isabel laughed, at which Gabrielle begged her to stop, holding her aching head between her hands.

"I'm sorry, Gabrielle. Believe me, I do sympathize with you. Of course, Pierre and I would do better than you and he, but he seems to prefer the untouched ones." She grimaced comically and Gabrielle tried in vain to suppress a giggle.

"Isabel, what would I do without you?" she said affectionately.

The other girl shrugged. "Be bored, I expect." She walked to the dressing table and studied her wind-flushed cheeks and patted the smooth, dark coils of her hair. "What I came for, Gabrielle," she said idly, moistening her lips with her tongue, "was to ask you to go shopping with me. I've heard of this marvelous new designer who is all the rage."

Gabrielle's brows flew up in some surprise. "But you just ordered three new gowns from Madame Marie, the day before yesterday!"

Isabel pouted and tossed her head saucily. "I know, I know, but M'sieur LeRoy is reputed to be the best in the business now. Josephine, our dear empress—for I still think of her so, despite that horrid divorce—allows him to dress her. So, of course, we must not be laggard, Gabrielle. Besides, I must have a new gown for my engagement party." She glanced slyly at the other girl's happily surprised face.

"Isabel! You're teasing me . . . ?"

Isabel laughed and threw her arms around Gabrielle, who laughed with her. "Yes, it's entirely true, my friend. I still cannot believe I am to be a married woman! My parents only announced it to me this morning."

"But—but, who is it and—when is it to be?" Gabrielle asked her excitedly.

"The engagement party, darling, is set for Christmas, which is only two months away, so let us go and see this M'sieur LeRoy so that he will have ample time to make us our dresses. Of course, you will be maid of honor," she added smoothly, enjoying the delighted look on the younger girl's face.

"Wonderful!" Gabrielle clasped her hands together, forgetting her headache entirely. "But, Isabel, you sly puss, you will not answer my question, will you? Who is it?"

"Get up and ring for your maid. I'll tell you while you're getting primped."

Gabrielle obeyed, choosing a gown at random. She reflected for a moment that perhaps Isabel was not as happy with the choice of bridegroom as she might have been had she herself been able to choose. She eyed her friend covertly as the other commenced trying on each of Gabrielle's rings and bracelets to while away the time while Gabrielle was being dressed.

"The Duc de Gramount!" The name was shot out like

a cannonball, making Gabrielle nearly jump out of her seat.

"The Duc—?" She puzzled over the name. It was unfamiliar to her, and she looked questioningly at Isabel for further information.

"Henri Lenoir, Duc de Gramount," Isabel amended. "He owns lands in the south of France, quite close to Marseilles—extensive, I believe. At least that's what my father says. Of course, he *would* say that."

"But *who* is he?" Aimee asked.

"He is a captain under General Murat; in fact, his regiment is with the one commanded by your dear benefactor's son, the Comte de Chevalier. In case you didn't know, they are both fighting on the Austrian front—very brave men, so my father takes pains to insist, although it is probably truer that they drink and wench in the sacked towns, waiting for their men to take the next one."

"You are saying, then, that you do not approve of this match?" Gabrielle speculated, her eyes trying to define the look on the other's face.

Isabel shrugged. "The duc is reputedly attractive enough. He is a soldier and supposedly a good one, so it is most probable that we will not see much of one another after we are married. That will suit me fine, I can assure you. I'm afraid I've developed a taste for lovers that my husband would find hard to tolerate were he with me all the time."

"But, Isabel, once you are married, surely there will be no more lovers. I mean, wouldn't it ruin your reputation, your husband's honor, if you were to—?"

"Gabrielle, really, you should know by now that scandal these days merely enhances one's social position. Besides, my husband is one of those men who enjoy war, and my affairs will not interest him one whit."

Gabrielle was dressed and they were descending the stairs after dispatching a message to the maid to deliver to her aunt. "And when is the wedding date, then?" she asked.

"The wedding is set for June, of course, as that is maman's favorite month."

"June of next year," Gabrielle thought dreamily. The months would probably fly by. She would be seventeen in April, and perhaps by then she, too, would be making plans for a wedding.

They set out in the chaise, enjoying the leisurely ride, nodding to acquaintances as they passed. On entering the dress designer's shop, they caught their breath at the sight of the exquisite satins, silks, *peaux-de-soie,* and laces heaped on the shelves that lined the inner room.

In no time, they were greeted by M'sieur LeRoy himself, and their measurements were taken by two young seamstresses who went about their work with the efficiency of those used to the impatience of their elite clientele. Materials and designs were chosen with painstaking care by the grand fashion designer whose face had lighted up when he was informed that the emperor himself might be in attendance at the forthcoming festivities.

"Isabel, surely you were stretching the truth when you said the emperor would attend the bethrothal party?" Gabrielle inquired excitedly when they were seated once again in the carriage.

Isabel shrugged. "Why shouldn't he come to witness the marriage of one of the oldest names in France?" she asked haughtily.

"Perhaps because he cannot boast the same distinction," Gabrielle returned drily.

Isabel glanced at her. "Then he will at least send a present," she commented in a tone that brooked no refusal.

The two settled back in their seats. Gabrielle gazed out the window after a time and saw that they were passing the Rue Montmartre. The Hôtel Chevalier was not far, but she did not want to go home yet. She was still too caught up in the excitement of the morning.

As if sensing her thought, Isabel sighed. "I really am starving, Gabrielle. I didn't eat a thing before I rushed over to tell you the news—and you didn't, either." She threw a positively wicked glance at her friend before continuing. "Let's stop at one of those new little cafes where they sell hot chocolate and tea and pastries. Oh dear, my mouth is watering already!"

Gabrielle gazed askance at the girl. "You cannot mean it, Isabel. Your father would be outraged and would bellow something terrible if he found out. And Aunt Louise —I shudder to imagine what she would think!"

"Oh, they aren't that terrible. Justine de Larges and I have already visited one, and no one tried to accost us or leer at us. We went in, ate a roll, and came back out, just like that. We both felt marvelously dangerous with all those dandies and loose women about."

Gabrielle, against her better judgement, was finally talked into going—but just for a few minutes, she said adamantly.

"To La Petite Fleur," she said sharply to the driver, who mumbled something indistinctly but did as ordered.

"Your aunt will be told the minute we return," Isabel observed drily, and Gabrielle nodded.

They waited, with suppressed excitement, as the carriage slowed in front of a cheery-looking establishment, painted green and gold and nearly bursting with customers.

"Oh, God, there's no room to move an inch!" Isabel exclaimed, biting her lip in exasperation.

"We can go to another one, or wait a bit," Gabrielle suggested.

They decided on the latter course and sat, eyes wide, as they watched the painted women, resplendent in gowns cut to show the tips of their breasts and so sheer as to leave nothing to the imagination. There were a few sailors, some soldiers from the city militia, and a dozen or so prosperous-looking merchants, discussing business around enclosed booths. The rest of the company comprised two or three expensively dressed women and a handful of rakishly outfitted young men, who boldly handled the prostitutes. After a half-hour had passed, most of the merchants had left to return to their shops for the afternoon's business. Some prostitutes had also retired from the scene, escorted by soldiers and a few of the dandies.

Inwardly, Gabrielle was thankful that the three well-dressed women were still there as well as a couple of quiet-looking gentlemen who must be professors at the Sorbonne. Boldly, Isabel descended from the carriage, motioning to her companion to do the same.

Gabrielle, still a little reluctant, followed her into the shop. At their entrance, the remaining dandies looked up, saluting them with their insolent smiles, but the girls bustled over to one of the empty booths, careful to keep their eyes on the cafe owner who hurried over to take their orders.

"Ah, ma'm'selles! My cafe is indeed honored by your presence. I might hope that you will come again and bring more of your friends, please. Maître Rosambeau is an honest man and one who seeks only to please his customers."

After this little speech, he took their order for hot chocolate and sweet pastries, returning quickly with their food.

"What do you think?" Isabel inquired between mouthfuls of the sweet confection she held in her hand.

"Rather exciting, but really not so bad once you're inside," Gabrielle conceded, attacking her portion vigorously.

They had finished the last few sips of chocolate, but before they could catch the owner's attention to pay their check, a slight stir in the room caused both girls to look up at the doorway where a tall man was just stepping into the cafe, leading two other men to a table close to their booth. The three men were accompanied by a woman, whose slanted black eyes, small stature, and yellow-tinged complexion told them that she was an Oriental. She was careful not to look at any of the gaping, wide-eyed men who were staring at her as if she were a freak. Once she looked up, and Gabrielle caught the gleam of contempt and disgust that was reflected in her eyes.

After the new arrivals were seated, Gabrielle beckoned

to Isabel. But the other girl shook her head, a half-smile on her lips. "Isabel, you mustn't stare at her!" Gabrielle reproached her nervously, aware suddenly of a feeling of tension in the room.

"I'm not," Isabel replied huskily. 'But Gabrielle, just look at that man!"

Unwillingly, Gabrielle turned her eyes to study the apparent leader of the strange group. Certainly, he was tall and well made, with wide shoulders and a broad chest that looked out of place encased in the expensive cloth of his coat. His hair was not quite as dark as Isabel's, more of a deep chestnut that complimented the deep-brown tan of his complexion and made the white of his teeth startling when he laughed, as he was doing now at some sally from one of his comrades.

"Don't think she's a whore, Rafe, my lad, but she's a-starin' at you as though she'd welcome a proposition, that's for certain," Gabrielle heard one of the men say. In the next instant, she found eyes so deeply green, so utterly dark green as to be almost black, gazing boldly at her with an accompanying insolence held barely in check as the man smiled lazily.

Quickly, a blush suffused her face and she looked away in acute embarrassment. Dear God! Those men thought she was a prostitute, of all things! She could see the contemptuous glance of the Oriental woman in her mind's eye, sweeping over her, seeing her as being no better than herself.

"Isabel," she nearly hissed at her companion, "let's leave, for pity's sake, this instant!"

Isabel shrugged airily. "Goodness, Gabrielle, they're not going to rape you on the spot! And even if they were," and she smiled her most wicked smile, "it might not be so terrible."

"But Isabel, we're making a spectacle of ourselves!" Gabrielle returned, helpless against her friend's self-assurance.

Before Isabel could answer, they both were drawn to the commotion ensuing as two swarthy-skinned sailors

swaggered recklessly over to the table of the three men
and the Oriental woman.

"Did you pick up that woman on one of your sea
raids, Savage?" one of the sailors leered drunkenly.

His companion laughed no less drunkenly. "Yes, she
looks like good booty, although one never knows how
clean she would be, considering—" They moved closer
to the woman, who remained with her eyes downcast, refusing to play their game.

The leader, the tall, dark-haired man, smiled with
pitying mockery, even as his hand strayed to the pistol
that was stuck in his belt. "You must be mistaken," he
commented indolently. "Please be so kind as to remove
yourselves to another table."

"Goddamn it, Savage!" roared the first sailor, his fists
clenching. "Don't try to palm me off. I know too well
who you are. I was on the ship, *Marina,* that you crippled
so badly off Martinique; we barely escaped with our
lives."

"My sympathies," the man called Savage rejoined,
playing idly with an imaginary string on his sleeve.

The sailor seemed about to burst in his rage, and the
other sailor, suddenly aware of the danger in the man's
still, self-assured presence, attempted to calm him down.
"Now, now, Folere, we could be mistaken. I'm sure this—
gentleman has been telling the truth. Let's go now, your
wife will be wondering where you are."

Gabrielle held her breath, fully expecting the other
sailor not to heed his friend's warning. But to her intense
relief, the mention of his wife seemed to bring the sailor
to some semblance of calm. Shrugging off his friend's
hand, he made his way uncertainly to the door, pausing
only to glare at the man's back.

"No matter," he muttered. "The next time we meet,
Savage, I'll not hesitate to run you through!" Then he
walked out the door, to the relief of everyone present,
who immediately went back to their wine.

"Did you hear that?" Isabel whispered. "He's a pirate!

I wouldn't doubt it for a moment by the look of him. Oh, but isn't it all exciting!"

"Very exciting," Gabrielle retorted, "especially if someone had been killed!"

"Oh, that sailor was all wine and bluff—anyone could see that," Isabel said in her worldly manner.

"Well, I hope you've had enough excitement for one day. Let's do go home now."

"Oh, all right. But remind me never to invite you to a cafe again, Gabrielle. You're not in the least adventurous," Isabel complained, retrieving her shawl from the back of her chair and settling her hat back on her head.

They paid for their food and began to make their way carefully past the tables, taking care not to glance curiously at the tall, dark man who was now apparently engrossed in conversation with his friends. As they were about to brush by his table, a young ruffian, quite drunk, reached out laughingly for Gabrielle's skirt, catching a bit of the material in his hand. Isabel went on, not realizing that her friend had been momentarily detained.

More irritated than afraid, Gabrielle gave her skirt a small tug but failed to dislodge it from the boy's grasp. With a stronger tug, she pulled at it, and, as the boy loosened his hold to return to his glass of wine, the effect of Gabrielle's exertion released the material so quickly that she lost her balance, coming up sharply against the opposite table. A pair of strong, brown hands were about her waist in a moment. One moved upward in a sliding movement and caught hold of her just beneath her breast, and Gabrielle, attempting to steady herself, looked into those same green eyes that had gazed at her so insultingly.

The sailor moved out of his chair with a lithe movement that was so swift it startled her, and then his arms were somehow tightening a little on her, and the firm, sensuous mouth curved into a smile.

"Are you all right?" he said in a voice that held a trace of an accent.

She nodded, feeling his hands still holding her and her

flesh warm where they rested. The next instant, though, he released her.

She hesitated for a long minute, then hurried as though to escape, still hearing his mocking laughter in her ears. If he were a pirate, she thought furiously, chances were he would have a price on his head and the police would catch up with him soon enough.

Chapter Three

November had passed, grey and overcast, a month that Gabrielle had always disliked because of its slowness in anticipation of the Christmas holidays. Her aunt had stressed the importance of deportment, especially after the incident at the cafe, and Gabrielle had been restricted in her outings with Isabel. Of course, the latter was caught up in her preparations for the ball, and Gabrielle could imagine how delightfully busy she must be.

Finally Alexandre paid a personal call on the de Montforts, expressing his wish that they join him for luncheon the following day. Gabrielle was estatic with joy, and at the lunch table she went over every detail of the ball with Isabel.

That night, Aunt Louise visited her in her bedroom, and Gabrielle was told that Alexandre and her aunt had decided to announce their own betrothal quietly after the Christmas festivities. Privately, Gabrielle was not at all sure of her own reaction to this news, but she marvelled at the obvious change in her aunt, who had softened visibly. Even so, there was a tinge of disappointment to her aunt's happiness.

"Charles, Alexandre's son, does not approve of the marriage," she confided, her face betraying her deep embarrassment. "He has written his father several letters enclosing his ideas on the exact reasons why I am 'entrapping' him in marriage—money, social position, and other things that demean our love and trust for one another. Gabrielle, I want you to know that none of that is true and that, although I will admit that the prospect of wealth and security was what attracted me to Alexandre in the beginning, these considerations are not so important anymore. Alexandre is the only man who has ever been tender and protective towards me. He is the most thoughtful person in the world, as I'm sure you would agree."

Gabrielle patted her aunt's hand comfortingly. "Then there is nothing for you to fret about, is there? Since Alexandre loves you, certainly he will not worry about what his son says. It seems to me that Charles is overstepping himself anyway, presuming to advise his father on the choice of a wife."

Aunt Louise shrugged, and she seemed to draw some comfort from the words. "You are absolutely right, of course, but I would hate to be the wedge that might drive Alexandre away from his only son. Charles would never forgive me for that, and I have a feeling that Alexandre would also be grievously wounded by such a development."

"You mustn't feel that way. Perhaps Charles will get over his aversion to the marriage before the time arrives for him to come home from the field. He sounds more like a sulky, spoiled child than a man twenty-three years old."

Aunt Louise sighed, passing a hand over her forehead. "Alexandre confided in me that Charles did not have a happy childhood. It seems that his mother, Alexandre's first wife, Hélène, took hardly any interest in the boy. For that reason, he began to distrust all women, and he has a cruel streak in him at times that is a little frightening even to his father. It would be best if he would remain in the army since it is the only kind of life he can enjoy, but he is to be the witness for the Duc de Gramount as you will be for Isabel at their wedding."

At the prospect of seeing this repulsive-sounding man at the betrothal ball, Gabrielle grimaced in distaste. "Well,

I shall have to put up with him for Isabel's sake," she thought quickly and tried to focus her concern on her aunt's problems which truly seemed too pressing for a prospective bride.

Two weeks of Christmas passed happily enough and everyone in the house became gay and spirited in preparation for the betrothal celebration that was getting nearer every day. Gabrielle almost forgot her aunt's anxiety until they received a letter relaying the message that Charles had decided to return from the campaign early and would be home some time in the third week of December.

Her aunt looked very pale at the news, but Gabrielle could hardly let the knowledge dampen her enthusiasm, for her new gown had arrived that very day and it was as breathtaking as she had hoped it would be. The bodice was cut very low, almost indecently so, just skimming her breasts at the halfway point and covering the pink tips against the chill. The sleeves were full, and they exposed her shoulders, making them look like marble against the softness of the velvet. The bodice was caught beneath her bosom in a wide, silvery gauze sash.

The betrothal party was only ten days away, and she knew that she would rank favorably among the other pretty, sophisticated women who would be attending. Isabel exclaimed that she would be extremely jealous if Gabrielle turned her fiance's eyes away from herself, but Gabrielle assured Isabel, laughing, that her rose satin gown would look breathtaking.

Gabrielle mentioned the subject of Charles in an offhand manner, watching for Isabel's reaction.

The latter wrinkled her nose. "He is rather crude in social settings, from what I've heard, but Henri insisted on naming him as his witness, and of course, I had no choice in the matter.

"But do you think he would do something to stop the marriage between Alexandre and Aunt Louise?" Gabrielle asked anxiously.

Isabel shrugged as if to indicate that the matter was really trivial. But she doubted that Charles would do anything so foolish as to anger his father, especially since the marquis could easily have his army commission revoked.

Gabrielle looked doubtful but decided that Isabel would only become irritated at persistent questioning.

The days went by too quickly, and Gabrielle saw her aunt's nervousness increase. Alexandre comforted her, but even he seemed somewhat more withdrawn.

On the morning that Charles was to arrive, there was an unusually heavy snow that blanketed Paris in a shroud of crystal whiteness. A very young maid, Chloë, had taken over as Gabrielle's servant, and she was extremely adept at fixing the heavy tresses of her shining hair. She arranged Gabrielle's hair in a simple chignon for the day and dressed her in a silk gown of soft lilac. Gabrielle had chosen the gown, hoping to make a favorable impression on Charles for her aunt's sake.

The clock on the mantel chimed two o'clock and Gabrielle caught the sound of crunching snow as a carriage rolled into the avenue before the house. She dared not go to the sitting room until she was summoned as she did not want to embarrass her aunt or Alexandre should this prove to be a distressing moment.

A soldier's boots rang hard on the tiled floor and a deep voice inquired quickly, "Where is my father?" The voice held a tone of ruthless command; its owner was used to being obeyed in any event, and the servant squeaked that the marquis was in the sitting room with Madame de Beauvoir.

"That adventuress! Tell him I will see him alone in the library, then!" Charles bellowed, and before Gabrielle could think what to do, he had opened the door to the library and swept in, shaking the snow and ice off his army cape.

For a moment, they could only stare at one another, he seeing a lovely young girl, obviously a trifle anxious, and she taking in a young man of medium height with blond hair, lighter than her own, and puzzled grey eyes.

She cleared her throat, amazed at this flesh-and-blood antonym of her nightmares, but she did not know what to say.

He closed the door, fully at his ease, watching her with a mixture of amusement and irony. After a moment, his brows drew downward, and he took a step toward her. "Well, you must be the niece, Gabrielle de Beauvoir. Am I not correct?"

Stung by his tone of exaggerated arrogance, Gabrielle drew herself up a little and tried to keep herself from glaring at him. "Yes, m'sieur. But you will excuse me for not addressing you so knowledgeably, for I do not know you, nor have we been introduced," she murmured, not troubling to keep the bite from her words.

He laughed unpleasantly. "Oh, but ma'm'selle, I am quite sure you must know exactly who I am, for your whole future may depend on me. My eyes do not deceive me when they note the anxious air about you." He seated himself in a chair, not bothering to ask her permission. "I am told that my father is waiting for me in the salon with your aunt. I haven't the faintest idea why she would choose to be present at this important family reunion, as it will only prove an embarrassment to her. I'm positive she must have told you I consider her nothing more than a scheming adventuress who, finding my father an easy mark, could not resist but to hold out for marriage."

Gabrielle's face went crimson with mingled rage and embarrassment. "How dare you speak of her in that tone of voice and with such words of stupidity! Obviously you have not chosen to read any of your father's letters informing you of my aunt's good and kind nature, nor have you managed to learn the simple rules of etiquette, m'sieur. I do hope all of the officers are not as uncouth as you are!"

His eyes flickered over her for an instant. "And I hope, ma'm'selle, that I am not expected to be the elegant nobleman for the likes of a child like yourself. I have a strong feeling that we will not meet again soon, ma'm'selle, except where necessity dictates. So I would request that you excuse yourself from my presence."

"I am not one of your snivelling aides that you can order around, m'sieur. I'm afraid you will just have to get used to me unless you wish to take your meals in the seclusion of your own rooms. Good day, m'sieur."

Gabrielle walked as sedately as possible from the room, not daring to look back at him to watch the effect of her words. She hurried to her own rooms, fighting back the tears of frustration and anger that threatened to spill over at any moment.

Chloë found her a few minutes later, dabbing at her eyes with a scented handkerchief and brushing away the tear stains on her cheeks. "Oh, ma'm'selle, you have been crying!"

Gabrielle nodded, not wishing to explain.

"I know why ma'm'selle is so sad. I heard the angry words of M'sieur le Marquis and his son in the library just before I came up and Madame Louise was weeping in the sitting room. Oh, I don't understand what has happened, ma'm'selle. Surely the marquis will not send you away, will he?"

Gabrielle shook her head. "He will not send us away. He loves my aunt very much, Chloë. But I'm afraid that the son does not share his view, and he is not as courteous as his father."

Isabel dropped by on the eve of her party, her spirits bubbling and excitement shimmering from the top of her fur-trimmed hat to the tips of her heavy walking boots. Almost immediately, as they entered Gabrielle's bedroom, Isabel swept around to face her friend, eyeing her closely. "All right, what has been happening around here, my dear? I've heard everything: a story that you and Charles had a bitter fight after rubbing each other the wrong way, and the equally disturbing tale that he refuses to escort you to my betrothal ball. I've been in a state all morning and would appreciate your enlightenment at once, if you please!"

Gabrielle stared at the other girl, striving for words to explain the fiasco of Charles' homecoming. Finally, bit by bit, the whole distressing truth came out, after which Isabel plopped in a cushioned chair, her hands up in the air.

"You mean to tell me that he was that rude to you and spoke of your aunt that way? I don't blame you one bit, Gabrielle, for I most certainly would have done the same. But—" and she glanced at the other with her familiar grin, "I think I would have made sure that he did not leave the house in such an angry mood. I mean, couldn't you have gone to his rooms to see him and have done your apologizing there in a way that would simply melt him, my dear? You do understand my meaning?"

Gabrielle nodded miserably. "He would never give me a chance to get near him."

"That is nonsense, after all. He has to stand by you during the marriage ceremony, and there is absolutely no way that I am going to change my mind and pick a 'more suitable' girl for my maid of honor."

Gabrielle smiled her gratitude, then frowned thoughtfully, her eyes watching her friend carefully. "Perhaps your brother could escort me to the party, Isabel. He—"

The other shook her head vehemently. "I wouldn't give that devil Charles the satisfaction of knowing he has you cowed. You're a woman grown, for Heaven's sake! I'm satisfied that you have the ability at least to behave as though nothing happened between you and Charles at the ball tomorrow night. He will call for you around eight o'clock. I'll tell Henri to arrange it." Isabel laughed wickedly. "Poor Charles! He will be smoldering when he finds that all his plans are thwarted. And certainly there is nothing he can do about the marriage of your aunt and the marquis. Impossible as it may sound, he will be getting married himself some day and will hardly be seen around here, anyway."

Chapter Four

"You're sure you don't want us to wait with you?" Aunt Louise asked nervously, adjusting her long satin gloves.

Gabrielle shook her head. "Of course not. You and Alexandre go on, and I'm sure it won't be long before Charles arrives to escort me."

Aunt Louise bit her lip for a moment, thinking, then shrugged her shoulders. "Well, I suppose it wouldn't be a good idea for me to be here when Charles arrives. But you are sure you will be all right?" Her eyes went over her niece swiftly.

Gabrielle smiled, attempting to hide her own anxiety, and willed her hands to stop trembling as she hid them in the folds of soft velvet. "Of course, and if Charles decides to play the boor and not come for me, it would be just as easy for me to walk over to Isabel's house. After all, most of the snow and ice has melted, and—"

"You will do no such thing, Gabrielle. If he does not come for you, you will send a messenger to the de Montforts, and I will return to escort you myself," interrupted Alexandre, just then coming in from seeing to the carriage.

"Yes, please do not walk over there alone, my dear."

"All right. I promise that if Charles does not arrive by a quarter past the hour, I will send a messenger to you."

Alexandre smiled, satisfied, and extended his arm to Aunt Louise. Together they went out the door, and after they'd gone, Gabrielle turned into the library, wishing that she had a little more courage.

She studied her reflection in the mirror, pleased with the coiffure that Chloë had arranged for her. Her hair

35

was piled in large curls on top of her head, exposing her slender neck. She had placed a silvery fillet around the curls and it drew attention quite effectively to the glossy thick tresses that shone with warmth in the light of the fire. Her eyes looked larger than ever in her pale face, and their violet color was almost unreal. The dress was, she admitted, cut very low. It skimmed her upcurved breasts a bare inch above the tips, and the gauze sash tied snugly beneath her bosom accentuated her breasts' firmness.

She glanced at the clock but saw to her dismay that it was nearly eight o'clock. She *had* given her promise to Alexandre that she would not wait. A little restless, she thought of calling Chloë to check minor details in her gown, and she slipped out of the library to the stairs. At the landing she saw Pauline calmly checking for dust on the balustrade.

"Why, hello, ma'm'selle. I had thought you already gone with your aunt." Her eyes grew sharper. "Are you not well tonight, ma'm'selle?"

"I'm fine, Pauline, thank you. It seems that my escort is late."

Gabrielle proceeded up the stairs to her room after directing a departing nod to the servant. Aimlessly, she wandered over to her vanity and peered at the reflection cast back from the gilt-edged mirror. She took a perfume bottle and dabbed a few more drops on her neck and in the décolletage of her gown. Then, setting it down, she walked over to her window.

There was still some frost that formed a pretty pattern on the glass, and she traced it dreamily with her fingers, her eyes seeing nothing in particular as she gazed out at the serene stillness of the night.

But suddenly, as though her mind was only reacting, she focused on the dim light that shone from a candelabrum in the room directly opposite hers. She straightened quickly and rubbed at the frosted window in order to see better. Yes, there was a light, although the rest of the house opposite was still shrouded in darkness. How odd, she thought, puzzled that her guardian had mentioned nothing about his neighbor being at home. But of course, the marquis had been preoccupied with his son's behavior for the past few nights. She watched the room curiously for a few moments until a dark shadow passed in front of the window and stood there, seemingly watching her.

For no reason that she could think of, Gabrielle felt a shiver pass through her, and she withdrew quickly in behind the curtain. Certainly she had not been very polite, spying into another person's bedroom. But then again, could the shadow belong to a burglar? Why else would the rest of the rooms be unlit?

She waited some seconds before peeping out again from behind the curtains. But to her disappointment she found that the candles had been blown out and she could no longer see anything. She supposed that the light could have been a servant's tidying up before his master's return.

In any event, she noted that the clock on her night table was showing ten minutes past eight o'clock, and she was bound to send a message to Alexandre immediately, or else Isabel would be most upset.

Hurrying a little, she went downstairs and proceeded to the library where she had left her scarf and gloves. Upon entering the room, she found herself drawn up sharply by a figure most elegantly attired in dress uniform, seated comfortably in an armchair.

"M'sieur Charles! I—I—" she stammered in her abrupt confusion.

His face did not change its marble-set expression as he rose and bowed correctly. "Good evening, ma'm'selle. Are you ready to leave?"

Gabrielle felt her cheeks grow hot, realizing that her curiosity upstairs had prevented her from hearing his entrance. She had obliged him to wait, no doubt setting his temper further on edge. "Of—of course, I—"

"Good. Might I suggest, then, that we leave now, or I'm afraid we will be unforgivably late."

She nodded, swallowing the lump in her throat, and picked up her gloves and scarf, while he, with a magni-

tude of unconcern, held out her cape for her. She soon
found herself outside and bundled into the carriage, her
escort seated opposite her, his face turned away as though
he found the window infinitely more entertaining than
her presence.

Cautiously, she made an attempt at conversation. "You
must forgive me for keeping you waiting, m'sieur. I did
not hear your arrival. No servant announced—"

He turned to her quickly, allowing his temper to flare
for a moment. "Do you think I have to be announced in
my own home, ma'm'selle?" he questioned, his voice tight
with anger.

Gabrielle did not reply, realizing that her attempt to
draw him into conversation was futile. He would only
badger her for her discourtesy. Suddenly the beautiful
dress had lost some of its magic for her, and she felt
unsure of her own loveliness. He seemed not even to
have noticed her attire, and his eyes dismissed her coldly.

She sat quietly, galled at his silence and glad that the
ride to the de Montforts was not long. They arrived to
find that a number of guests had preceded them.

Upon entering the wide hallway, Gabrielle found her
aunt eyeing her with some relief, and then Isabel hurried
over to draw her into the welcoming line. A servant took
her cape and gloves, and she smiled softly at the compliments she received from Isabel's father and brother. There
were others who certainly appreciated her, and she would
take great care to keep a distance between herself and
her escort.

The guests began arriving in force now, and Gabrielle
was busy for a long while smiling and allowing her hand
to be kissed, exchanging pleasantries with friends, and
murmuring polite phrases to the people she did not already know.

Finally, when the last of the guests had arrived, the
company went into the huge ballroom, which was lit
splendidly with blazing candles in every corner. Evergreen
and pine boughs were strung everywhere, and even a few

bunches of mistletoe hung in conspicuous places. The musicians began to play, and Gabrielle found herself swaying delightedly to the music in Alexandre's arms.

"Is everything all right between you and Charles?" he questioned.

She smiled. "Perfectly. He has ignored me most of the evening, and I like it much better that way." She related how she had kept him waiting, and the story brought a smile to Alexandre's lips.

"A military man is not used to waiting on women, Gabrielle, my dear."

She danced most of the dances, stopping now and then to visit with acquaintances of Alexandre's and friends of her own. She danced a lively tune with Henri, an old-fashioned roundelay that caused her breathing to quicken and a few curls to tumble delightfully from her coiffure. Afterwards, he brought her a cool drink and was proceeding to entertain her with stories of the front, when Isabel rushed up, her cheeks red with exertion.

"Goodness! Stealing my fiance out from under my nose, Gabrielle!" she laughed, her dark eyes snapping with excitement.

Gabrielle laughed graciously, protesting her innocence. But she was secretly relieved that Isabel had rescued her from the Duc de Gramount. He was terribly bold, the type of man that Gabrielle had always associated with the military.

She stood for a moment with her back leaning slightly against the pillar where Henri had led her, still a little breathless and watching the dancers with evident enjoyment. To her utter amazement, she looked up to see Charles bowing deeply before her, an unspoken question in his gaze. She curtseyed formally and wordlessly, and Charles swept her out onto the dance floor. For some reason, Gabrielle found his hand at her waist annoying. It was certainly not that he held her too tightly. On the contrary, she recalled Alexandre holding her more closely than his son was doing. But he held her almost gingerly,

as if he were loath to feel her flesh. His hand that held
her own was damp with perspiration, a fact she attributed
to the heat of the room under the blaze of candles.

"Smile, ma'm'selle, we are passing our friends," he
suddenly spoke between his teeth, and Gabrielle saw
Isabel and Henri laughing and talking with a few other
people, but glancing almost casually at herself and
Charles.

She smiled reflexively, annoyed as her partner's hand
tightened a little on hers.

"You must look as though you're enjoying yourself,
ma'm'selle. It wouldn't do to have Henri think we are
still spitting at each other."

They finished the dance and a few moments later,
Pierre, Isabel's brother, bowed before her. Gabrielle hurriedly accepted his offer to dance.

"You have outshone all those other wax dolls who
smile woodenly and accept any offer a man makes to
them," he said to her after the dance was ended.

Gabrielle thanked him for the compliment, and he took
her into the dining hall where tables were laden with food
that was virtually untouched. Gabrielle accepted a glass
of wine.

"Perhaps you should eat something, Pierre," she suggested hopefully, attempting to direct him to the mound
of cold ham as she watched him twice refill his own glass.

He shook his head. "No, Gabrielle. Tonight is my
sister's engagement ball, and I think I should drink liberally to the occasion. A headache in the morning will, no
doubt, make me regret my decision. But the night is still
young, and, who knows, perhaps one of those wooden
dolls will share my bed tonight." He gazed woefully out
towards the ballroom. "And now, ma'm'selle, I must return to the field of battle." He bowed a bit clumsily and
walked away, the wine glass held firmly in his hand as
though it were a banner.

Gabrielle glanced at the clock in the hall as she passed
it on her way back to the dancing and saw that it was
close to one o'clock. Suppressing a yawn, she hesitated

at the threshold of the room, searching for Charles'
blond head. As she expected, he was talking with a group
of men, all wearing uniforms and airing their views on
the war.

"Mon dieu, I will never get him away," she thought,
irritated because she knew he would enjoy her having to
wait for him. Someone asked her to dance, and she accepted out of sheer caprice, even though her feet were
beginning to ache and her annoyance made it impossible
to enjoy the dance. She continued dancing for a quarter
of an hour until, passing the group of soldiers, she succeeded in catching Charles' eye.

Instead of excusing himself as any gentleman would,
he smiled arrogantly at her and continued the conversation. Stung, Gabrielle finished the dance in a grim mood,
much to the chagrin of her unfortunate partner.

The time began to drag on. It was not until after three
o'clock, when only a very few guests remained and she
was seated wearily in a chair, that she saw Charles making
his way slowly towards her.

"I am ready to leave, ma'm'selle," he informed her
curtly.

Gabrielle felt like screaming at him, telling him to go
to the devil for all she cared. But with an effort she
calmed herself and rose to walk next to him into the
hall, complimenting Isabel on the success of her party.

She shivered as Charles went to get their carriage, the
chill of the outdoors hitting her like an awakening blow.
It seemed endless moments before he returned, blowing
on his ungloved hands.

Contrary to his earlier mood, Charles relaxed, stretching his legs out in front of him and pushing his cape back
a little. "Did you enjoy the evening?" The question was
as icy as the weather.

"Yes, yes, I did," Gabrielle replied, determined not to
let his demeanor dominate her. "And you?" she inquired.

"I have never liked too much frivolity. I can remember,
when I was a child, my mother going to endless parties
and balls. I grew to hate the thought of her going out."

"If you hate such gatherings so much, you should have told me. I would not have had you escort me no matter what anyone might have demanded."

He looked at her, and his gaze was so cold she wanted to shrink away from it. "It was a duty. A soldier never shirks a duty—no matter how disagreeable."

"Do you mean that taking me to the party was so disagreeable? Let me assure you that I took great pains to stay as far away from you as possible all evening." Her voice rose with disgruntled vanity.

"And do you imagine I enjoyed being badgered into escorting you because Henri listened to the pleas of that vain little bitch whose reputation for bed partners precedes her even to the battle front!" His own voice cracked with rage. "If I had had my way, I would have gone to one of the little inns along the river bank and enjoyed the company of a warm-fleshed whore tonight. Instead, I am obliged to escort a young woman whose dress cries the tart, but whose face remains as innocent as some tarnished angel's. I can only suppose that you wear your many lovers' victories a bit more easily than your good friend does her own conquests.

Striking blindly in her fury, Gabrielle felt her palm sting against Charles' cheek. "How dare you say such a thing!" she half-screamed at him, breathing hard. She made as though to strike him again, but his hand came out to catch her wrist, the fingers biting painfully into her soft flesh.

"A whore does not strike the prospective customer," he laughed hoarsely. "I suppose you're an adventuress just like your aunt."

"M'sieur, you forget yourself," she went on, a little more breathless with the pain, but still defiant. "Would you break your future cousin's arm?"

"Cousin!" his voice was hardly more than a whisper. "A harlot for a relative—"

Completely outraged, Gabrielle drew herself up as well as she was able. "I do not enjoy your continued use of such words to describe me. I swear that I am not what you think and that no man has ever—"

"No man has ever touched you? Is that what you expect me to believe?" he flung at her. And suddenly he thrust her away from him as if he had sickened of her. "You lie with such sincerity, ma'm'selle. Surely you can do better than that?" His voice was tight with sarcasm. "I have had nuns in cloistered convents scream those very same words at me, and I have found too many times that even such holy women have spread their legs for a man!"

Gabrielle, still rubbing her throbbing wrist, looked at him with disgust. "You have raped a nun, m'sieur, so I can only suppose that nothing is sacred to you. Is that how you embellish the 'sport of war,' as you call it?"

She knocked hard on the panel, obliging the driver to stop. "I will return the rest of the way home on foot. I would not wish to detain you from your other pleasures." She drew her cloak around her like a cocoon of dignity. "It would please me very much if you and I were not obliged to meet again. But circumstances being as they are, I suppose that is too much to hope for. Nevertheless, I will not subject my person tonight to any further insult from you."

After quitting the considerable warmth of the carriage, Gabrielle shivered in indecision for a moment as she watched the vehicle move down the street. She was thankful that at least the footwalk that ran along the fronts of the houses was virtually free of ice, and she began to make her way with little difficulty. She passed several imposing edifices, all nearly alike, before she came to the right number. Stamping her feet, she blew on her gloved hands and was about to call for the gatekeeper, when out of the corner of her eye, she saw a shadowy movement to her right.

A figure slipped into the gate of the house next to Alexandre's, and Gabrielle remembered seeing the light in the lone window earlier in the evening. Could this be the person who had been inside the house before? She listened for further footsteps but heard nothing. Finally, taking her courage in both hands, she approached the neighboring gate carefully, seeking to reassure herself that there was no one there. As she rounded the stone pillar, a cry nearly escaped her, for she could see a wavering light in one of the second-story windows of the house. So, the shadow had gone into the house—but for what purpose? Her curiosity pulled her forward, but her common sense told her that now was the time to call for the gatekeeper and to hurry into the safety of her own home. She backed away from the gate, her foot treading suddenly on brittle ice that cracked loudly even as it caused her to slip backwards and lose her footing.

Almost before she had hit the ground, a tall, dark shadow loomed up in front of her, scaring her nearly witless.

"What are you doing snooping around here? Who are you?" The voice was deep, arrogant, and somehow strangely familiar with the faintest alien accent in the French. The man bent to pick her up, setting her on her feet effortlessly.

"I—I live here," she managed between chattering teeth, nodding her head towards the other gate.

For a moment, she could sense the hesitation in the man whose hands remained on her shoulders. Then a low whistle came clearly through the crisp, chilly air, and he released her. "Be on your way then, wench," he admonished her gruffly.

Gabrielle was only too eager to obey and hurried back to the gate, calling for the keeper with an urgent note in her voice. Old Antoine, his face a mask of surprise, shuffled to the gate to let her in, but she avoided his questions and hurried up the drive to the house.

Everyone was asleep, and she made her way with as little noise as possible to her own room, finding that she was breathing hard and that her heart was beating like a drum beneath her bodice. On an impulse, she approached her window and drew back the curtains. A silhouette was etched against a dim light in the window opposite her own, and the figure seemed again to be watching her. With a mixture of fright and anger Gabrielle let the curtain drop.

Chapter Five

Charles did not make an appearance in the house the next morning, a fact that caused Gabrielle considerable relief. She was dreadfully tired and had caught a cold. Certainly she did not feel up to another confrontation with a man who seemed to enjoy causing her temper to flare. She hoped he would not stay too much longer, but would rejoin his regiment with all due speed.

Unfortunately, such was not to be the case, as Aunt Louise informed her the following day. Still fighting the sniffles, Gabrielle had elected to stay in bed and was reading a novel when her aunt came in carrying her lunch tray. Gabrielle put the book aside, realizing that she had not been concentrating on the words but was allowing her mind to continually stray to the strange meeting with the shadowy figure the night before.

"Feeling better, Gabrielle?" her aunt asked her.

Gabrielle was not deceived by her aunt's false cheerfulness and asked if anything was the matter.

Aunt Louise looked utterly crestfallen as she told her niece that Charles had requested a leave of absence from his troops through June. "This upsets our marriage plans considerably, and Alexandre wants to postpone the ceremony until this summer."

Gabrielle felt pity at the tired look in her aunt's face. "I'm sure he thinks he is doing the best for all concerned. After all, it will only be for six months—"

"But Charles could turn his father against me in six months," Aunt Louise cried bitterly, her fingers tightening around the handle of her teacup.

Gabrielle gazed with surprise at the desperation in her aunt's face. "But surely you and Alexandre love each other too much to let the time of waiting come between you," she said, hoping to comfort her.

"I'm not getting younger, Gabrielle, and Charles is his father's only son."

Gabrielle looked with renewed concern at the distraught woman. "I think you are making entirely too much of this. In the next six months, perhaps Charles will gain a better understanding of his father's feelings toward you."

"No, he hates me. He looks on me as the usurper of his mother's position."

Gabrielle could find no more words, as her aunt seemed bent on believing that Charles would somehow find a way to destroy all her plans. She would have liked to speak to Aunt Louise about her strange experience of the night before but felt that she would hardly be an ideal listener under the circumstances. Who could she confide in, then? Alexandre? No, he too was probably under emotional strain. Charles was the least likely candidate. There was no one except for Isabel, and telling her somehow would make the whole thing seem foolish. No, she would not tell anyone. After all, the man had not hurt her. Perhaps, as she had thought before, he was merely a servant come to open the house for his returning master.

January and February flew by. Gabrielle seldom saw Charles, although he was living at home now. He took his meals out or with his father, and Gabrielle was too unsure of her own position to protest the arrangement. She noticed her aunt's increasing anxiety and the despair that was written on her face.

March brought a surprisingly early spring, and most of the flowers in the garden had begun to bloom by the end of the month. Gabrielle watched her aunt and sensed that she was still unhappy. True, Alexandre still seemed considerate towards her on the occasions when Gabrielle saw them together, but those occasions seemed to be fewer and fewer. Gabrielle finally had to face the unpleasant suspicion that her first assumption—that Alexandre was too worldly a man for her aunt—was, perhaps, the truest picture of the situation. Surely, if a man loved a woman as much as Aunt Louise believed herself loved by Alexandre, he would not allow anyone to come between them. But then, Gabrielle could never remember hearing Alexandre actually telling her aunt that he loved her. True, he was attentive and kind to her, but that did not ensure a person's love. It was clear that Gabrielle would have to take Isabel's advice and speak to Charles herself, no matter how galling the experience might be.

Well, she would humble herself enough to request an audience with Charles. And what more perfect time than the following day, when Alexandre had promised to escort her aunt to a picnic given by Napoleon in the country in order to introduce his new Austrian empress to the court. Charles would not be attending as he had other matters to occupy his time in the Austrian Consulate. Determined to see the thing through before she lost her nerve, Gabrielle penned a brief note to Charles requesting that he see her the following afternoon and gave the note to Chloë to hand to his personal valet.

The next day, Gabrielle dressed with special care, wearing a pale pink gown of watered silk, and had Chloë dress her hair most becomingly. She would be seventeen in two weeks, she reminded herself, a woman grown, as Isabel had remarked. Certainly she would be able to break through Charles' icy exterior if she tried hard enough.

Anticipated excitement caused the color to bloom in her cheeks and her eyes to sparkle provocatively. At precisely two o'clock, she went into the garden where she expected Charles to join her shortly. It never occurred to her that he would refuse to speak with her, would actually be rude enough not to send her a note of apology.

She was brimming with humiliated rage by the time she heard his carriage in the drive a little after three o'clock, and she waited until she heard his booted footsteps on the stairs before entering the house from the garden. Her anger blinding her to caution, she stormed up the stairs to his room and knocked sharply on the door.

"Yes, ma'm'selle." The valet looked at her with smug insolence, as though at any moment he would slam the door in her face.

"I wish to speak to M'sieur Charles," Gabrielle got out, and before the surprised valet could realize what she was doing, she pushed the door open and stepped inside.

Charles, clad in shirtsleeves and breeches, his boots still dusty, looked up from where he was standing by the armoire.

"M'sieur Charles is on his way out," sputtered Jean, casting a sheepish glance at his employer.

"He will talk to me first. Please leave us." Gabrielle stood tense in the middle of the room, unaware of the becoming blush in her cheeks and the incredible deepening of her eyes. Her breasts rose and fell with her increasing fury, and she thought she would scream at the valet if he didn't leave the room.

"You may go, Jean. I'll call when I need you." Charles sat down calmly in a chair, crossing his booted calves and gazing with speculative interest at the truly beautiful spectacle Gabrielle afforded him. As before, he did not ask her to sit.

"Well, Gabrielle, it seems you are determined to speak with me, no matter that we have nothing to say to one another."

Taking a deep breath to control her rage, Gabrielle walked to the window, taking a position directly opposite her opponent. "I have come to discuss the way you have been treating my aunt and me," she began, her eyes on his face.

"I have no idea why," he responded, tapping his fingers against the arm of the chair with an air of boredom.

"You know perfectly well that your discourtesy towards us both has caused us to feel like strangers here—"

"A fact that does not displease me in the least," he

answered disdainfully. "In all honesty, I hope you and your aunt will see fit to vacate these premises for good."

"Your father, himself, told me that I could consider this place my home for as long as I wish," Gabrielle reminded him, her breath catching a little in her throat. "Where would we go, m'sieur? For, as you must know, your father persuaded my aunt to sell the house my father left to me."

"I believe there are convents that would welcome two new novices," he replied, watching her agitation increase.

Gabrielle pressed her hands together, her eyes surveying the room in distraction. The interview was not going at all as she had hoped. "But why—how can you be so—so unfeeling?" she questioned. "I have never harmed you, nor has my aunt. She only wishes to marry your father out of love. She—"

"Enough of love, ma'm'selle." Charles rose abruptly from his chair and came closer to her. "You women are so adept at spouting the praises of an emotion that cannot exist in the world today. I think you confuse love with lust, Gabrielle, the feeling a man has for a woman who can excite his senses but leaves his mind untouched."

Before she could utter a word in protest, Gabrielle felt his arms catch her roughly against him, and his mouth was kissing hers, forcing her lips open as he increased the pressure of his arms until she felt crushed like a rag doll. She could not fight against him for she was imprisoned too tightly, and he was bending her backwards as easily as he would a sapling. Forcing his mouth away, she saw his eyes like cold steel, looking into hers, and she shivered at the harshness of his laughter.

"This is lust, Gabrielle, the feeling that causes me to bruise your fragrant body even as I bestow the age-old symbol of love on your lips. Lust is the emotion that makes me desire to spread your sweet, white thighs and bury myself in you."

Gabrielle felt as though she would faint, and she knew for certain that she would fall if he took his arms from around her. In another moment, his mouth had swooped down on hers once more, invading her mouth with his tongue. His hands had moved from her arms to her neck, and she felt them caressing her skin. A shudder passed through her body.

With a tremendous effort, she tore her mouth from his and cried out at him to let her go. His immediate compliance startled her so that she had to clasp the frame of the window ledge in order to prevent herself from falling.

"How—how dare—" she began breathlessly, seeking to regain her composure.

"I've taught you a lesson, Gabrielle. You see, I'm afraid that your feminine wiles and smiling promises are lost on me, my dear, for, as most women I've known will assure me, I have no heart; only a brain that can ferret out their lying thoughts and the words that cover their true purposes. I suppose, in your extreme vanity, you thought you could win me over to your thinking if you bestowed a few of your favors on me, if you allowed me a discreet kiss or two, perhaps, even risking a more indecent caress, all in the name of your aunt, of course."

His mockery made the blood boil in her veins again, and she returned his gaze with a lofty pride as she drew herself up while adjusting her gown. "You are mistaken if you think I would stoop so low. You are correct in your assumption that what I do I am doing for my aunt's sake; but even for her I would never welcome your disgusting hands touching me as you did. Nor do your lips give me any pleasure, let me assure you. I think, perhaps, you would do better to look for your pleasures in the gutters of the beggars' quarter, m'sieur."

His laugh grated on her nerves, and she flinched involuntarily as his hand caught her arm. "You deceive yourself, Gabrielle, if you think I was trying to give you pleasure. But let us drop the whole subject. I must get ready for my engagement this evening, and you have only succeeded in wasting my time."

He turned away from her, dismissing her abruptly. Completely crushed, Gabrielle walked to the door, realizing that she had only put her aunt and herself into a more tenuous position by irritating their antagonist even more than before.

By the time her aunt and Alexandre had returned from their outing, Gabrielle had calmed herself sufficiently to greet them without revealing her inner turmoil.

"Alexandre, I should like to speak with you," she said, hoping her voice sounded casual enough.

"Certainly, my dear. Come to my study."

"Alexandre," she began, after taking the proffered seat in front of his desk, "I'm afraid that I have some rather unpleasant news to tell you."

She watched as Alexandre lowered his hands carefully on the desk, really looking at her, an unspoken question in his eyes. Gabrielle went on to relate the event that had taken place in Charles' room, admitting that she had been foolish to go there, but declaring that her desperation had driven her to try anything. She omitted the hateful kiss, but finished by saying that Charles had told her he would be only too glad for them to leave.

She paused for breath, watching his reaction closely for any clue to his inner thoughts. But he gave none, only nodding for her to go on.

She continued, "In short, I have decided to put the question directly to you, Alexandre. Do you want us to leave? I don't think that you realize what a toll this pressure has taken on my aunt's health, and perhaps everyone's purpose would be served better if we took up residence elsewhere, at least until Charles has rejoined his regiment."

Almost absently, Alexandre agreed, his eyes still on her face. Gabrielle felt the first cold fear begin in the pit of her stomach as she saw his facial lines tighten perceptibly.

"But where do you propose to take up residence, Gabrielle? Where will you obtain the money?"

The coldness in her stomach rose up and threatened to stifle her voice, but she replied, "From the money my father left me as well as the money left from the sale of his houses."

Alexandre stood up and took several turns about the room, his brow furrowed in thought. Finally, he came to stand in front of Gabrielle, his face downcast. She swallowed hard, but met his gaze steadfastly.

"Gabrielle, you have put me in a very embarrassing situation, I'm afraid. You have no money," he ended.

"What—what do you mean?" she asked him incredulously.

"I'm not as rich as you might think," he began. "Oh, yes, I keep up this house and all appearances in front of my peers, but to do this I use means that may or may not be considered totally lawful under the circumstances." He sat on the desk in front of her, as if struggling to make a decision. "Gabrielle, first I must tell you that I am extremely fond both of you and of your aunt, and I want you to believe that my intentions were not to hurt Louise if I could possibly avoid doing so. I'm afraid I shall have to be somewhat brutal with you, my dear; but the simple truth is, I offered my patronage only on the condition that you and your aunt turn over all your capital to me."

"But no one asked my permission!" Gabrielle cried, aghast and amazed at this flagrant violation of her personal rights.

"You are not of age, of course, and so your aunt signed the necessary documents as your legal guardian."

"But there wasn't enough money in what she brought to you to pay for your style of living all these months," Gabrielle objected, feeling as though she were grasping at straws.

"There was enough to finance a certain project I had in mind, Gabrielle—enough to get me started in a profitable, a highly profitable business. But I needed the capital right away, and at that time my credit was not good enough to borrow it."

"You mean you were virtually penniless?" Gabrielle cried in disbelief, gazing around the room as if to assure herself of its rich appointments.

He smiled indulgently. "Not completely. I had the stipend I receive from the government as well as the inheritance my father left me, an inheritance sadly dwindled through the price of Charles' commission in the army."

Gabrielle stood up slowly, hardly believing what he had just been telling her. "You mean," she demanded breathlessly, "that this was all a little scheme of yours—a trick to find a means of obtaining the money you needed? I suppose my aunt was just the one you required —alone and not very smart in the worldly ways of a gentleman like yourself!"

Alexandre reached over to pat her shoulder, but Gabrielle drew away, not ready to be comforted.

"Calm yourself, my dear. You have a roof over your head, don't you? And a promising position in society. Despite the evil thoughts you have about me at this moment, I swear that I have every intention of paying you back your money with interest. The documents are all held safely by my banker, as your aunt can most certainly assure you."

"But," and now Gabrielle was aware of the desperation in her voice, "you don't realize how Charles—how he hates our being here. He resents our presence and more and more I feel like a servant in this house. I cannot continue living like this; nor can my aunt, who, unhappily, thinks she is in love with you."

She was gratified to see the embarrassed flush come to his face. "I deeply regret toying so flagrantly with your aunt's tenderer emotions, Gabrielle, but Charles has made me see the folly of marrying her. If I marry, I must marry a woman who can bring money into the family."

"And hasn't my aunt already done so?" Gabrielle questioned, her voice vibrant with emotion.

Alexandre would not look at her. "I have told you that I will pay you back your money as soon as it is possible to do so. Believe me when I say I do not particularly enjoy taking advantage of two helpless females."

Gabrielle gazed at him from beneath lowered lashes. "But tell me then, Alexandre, what business it is that drives you to such despicable paths? Are you engaged in something that does not smell so rosy as its profits do, were the case taken to the courts?" She watched with satisfaction as a new wariness came into his face.

He searched her expression for a long time, then silently sat down in a chair opposite her, beckoning her to do the same. "I have decided to be honest with you, Gabrielle, not only because I cannot help but admire your courage, but also because I feel it is the only gentlemanly thing left for me to do under the circumstances."

Gabrielle seated herself and clasped her hands together, waiting for him to speak. He looked directly at her as he began, and she listened with considerable interest to what he had to say.

"The business I am involved in, Gabrielle, is smuggling. Yes, I can see from your face exactly what you are thinking—a treasonous offense against Napoleon's embargo. I am well aware of the danger in such a business venture, but I could not resist the prospect of profit. You see, my dear, I suppose I am somewhat of a gambler. A close associate of mine told me that he would put up half of the initial expenditure if I would supply the other part. The money from your father's will and the sale of the houses in Paris and the country provided my share. All that was needed was to find a ship with a captain willing to take the risks involved. My associate succeeded in finding one, an American, who seems more a privateer than a legitimate businessman. We decided to rent the house next door in order to serve as our offices and a place to store goods."

Gabrielle stared at him, interrupting pointedly. "I remember seeing someone in the house the night of Isabel's ball. That's it, isn't it? He's your American captain. He was there that night in the house."

Alexandre bowed his head. "I did not see the necessity of informing you of the truth when you came to live here. I had hoped, in fact, to be able to repay the money quickly and settle your account without undue fuss. But then, naturally, I had not imagined that Charles' animosity for you and Louise would require me to become involved in this damnably messy explanation."

Gabrielle found that she had relaxed suddenly, as though by simply trusting her enough to tell her the truth, Alexandre had once more gained her confidence. He seemed to sense her calmed emotions.

"I apologize once again, Gabrielle, for the way I so wantonly used your inheritance, but I must stress I will pay you back as soon as this last business venture is finished. I cannot go on with it any longer."

He drummed his fingers lightly on the desk top. "Since Charles is now going to be at home until June, I cannot take the chance of his finding out about all this. Charles' devotion to Napoleon and the Empire is such that I know he could not condone my action no matter what the profits were." Alexandre looked with a sudden sharpness at the girl. "I do not understand Charles' reaction toward you, Gabrielle. You are poised, charming, and very beautiful. In fact, you remind me a little of Charles' mother. Hélène had hair almost the color of yours and the same sense of vitality that you carry with you."

"Perhaps Charles did not love his mother as much as you seem to think," Gabrielle suggested quietly.

Alexandre shook his head. "He worshipped her. Unfortunately, she would not, or perhaps she could not, return his love. Her life was too full of the court and the gay whirl of social activities—I hardly saw her myself. When she died, she had become almost a stranger to me."

They were both quiet for some moments, until Alexandre stood up.

"I am going now to talk with your aunt. I will tell her the truth," he added. "I believe she is strong enough to accept it."

"Will you tell her about the—the smuggling?"

"No, she did not know what the money was going to be used for when she signed the documents. There is no need to tell her now."

As Gabrielle watched Alexandre leave the room and make his way up the stairs, she thought of Charles' satisfaction at the news, and her hatred of him grew.

Chapter Six

It was late afternoon of the following day when Isabel decided to make a surprise visit to her friend. She swept confidently into the main hall of the Hôtel Chevalier, bursting with energy and eager to swap confidences with Gabrielle.

To her surprise, she found Gabrielle in the sitting room, her eyes tearful as she dabbed abstractedly at them with a linen handkerchief.

"Good God! What has happened, *chérie*?" She sat down sympathetically, prepared to listen to a recounting of some distressing episode that could be easily solved.

"Aunt Louise is—is leaving today." The words tumbled out as Gabrielle continued trying to stop the flow of moisture onto her cheeks.

"Leaving? But then, where is she going?" Isabel prompted, studying her fingernail speculatively.

"She is leaving for the Convent of Ste.-Agnes in Lyons."

"A convent!" and Isabel raised her brows in mock dismay. "Whyever would she want to do that?"

Gabrielle revealed that Alexandre had called off any plans of marriage.

"You mean, she's going to shut herself off from the world because of a little disappointment like that?" Isabel scoffed practically. "If she'd start eating again and take a little more time with her looks, she could get another man quite easily—I'm sure of it."

Gabrielle attempted a forlorn smile. "But she really cared for him, Isabel. I think she had been expecting this blow for some time, but it was still a shock to her, especially since Alexandre was the first man she really believed in."

56

"But is she really going to stay there for the rest of her life?"

Gabrielle shrugged. "She vows she will. She says she doesn't want anything more to do with Paris or men."

Isabel laughed shortly. "I'm sure we could all say that at some time or another." She stood up, waving her hand airily. "In any case, she is to leave today, and you will be alone with Charles and his father—a rather scandalous arrangement, don't you think?" she inquired, her face anything but innocent.

Gabrielle laughed. "Of course, Isabel. I shall be hard put to keep up with both of them hopping in and out of my bedroom, won't I?" she answered, meeting her friend's challenge with bravado. She smiled to herself. "You do have a way of lifting me out of my despair, Isabel my friend. Do you ever take life seriously?"

Isabel sighed and gave Gabrielle an uncompromising look. "I understand more than you think, Gabrielle. And if you ever feel that the cards are stacked too high against you, just send me a message and I'll be over to rescue you in an instant."

Gabrielle thanked her friend and, after seeing her to the door, walked slowly up the staircase, dreading these last moments with her aunt. How should she possibly comfort her? What could she say?

At her knock, Aunt Louise's voice called out for her to come in. "I'm just finishing with my packing, Gabrielle," she informed her, looking up from the depths of a deep trunk. Seeing her niece's tear-stained face, she said kindly, "Don't worry about me, my dear. Alexandre and I had a very long discussion, and I think he was honest with me. I can forgive him now to some degree. He made me see that what I truly desired was human affection and companionship and, perhaps, I could find it elsewhere. That is why I have decided to go to the Convent of Ste.-Agnes. The good sisters help to run the hospital there, and I think my energies will not be wasted."

"But are you going to take the vows of sisterhood then, Aunt Louise?"

The woman shrugged. "I cannot say. It is enough for now that I am leaving here. I hope that you will be well cared for, my dear, and I will pray for you."

"Charles is a strange man, Aunt Louise. I do not know how he will act after you are gone, but Isabel has told me that I can stay with her if ever the need arises."

The older woman turned to the girl and gave her a long, steady look. "Do not run from friend to friend, my dear, as I have done all my life. It seems I have always lived on someone else's charity. I was either the spinster aunt or the unmarried sister. It is not a life I would wish for you, Gabrielle."

Later that evening, Alexandre arrived to escort Aunt Louise to an inn where she would catch the post chaise that would take her to Lyons. He had confided to Gabrielle that afterwards he planned to go into the city for a business meeting, with an associate, and she wondered if this were the meeting in which he would tell the man that he was withdrawing from the smuggling venture.

After they had gone and all the farewells were said, Gabrielle went back into the house, pausing to enter the library in order to select a good book for an evening's reading. Upon entering, she stopped short to observe Charles seated in a chair, a cheroot in his mouth.

"Good evening, Gabrielle."

"Good evening, Charles," she replied lightly.

"Your aunt has left, I believe?"

Gabrielle nodded, feeling the lump begin to form in her throat. "Yes, she has gone. I—I suppose you're satisfied now," she murmured bitterly, walking past him to select a book from the shelf.

He laughed shortly. "If it wasn't for this damnable headache, I would have escorted her to the station myself."

"I'm sure she was most fortunate, then," Gabrielle returned acidly. She sensed rather than heard him rise from the chair and move closer to her.

"I suppose you and I will be alone tonight," he said easily, laying a hand casually on the shelf above her head as he stood in front of her.

Gabrielle did not deign to answer, wondering what sort of cat-and-mouse game he was playing with her now.

"You're not afraid of me, are you, Gabrielle?"

"Afraid of you, Charles? That's absurd. I feel only loathing towards you."

His hand on her arm, turning her towards him violently, caught her by surprise and she found herself gazing up into his face, which had turned a dull red.

"I think, Gabrielle, that we should be truthful with each other. You are a guest in my house, a person who, if I had my way, would be put out immediately. Unfortunately, my father feels some responsibility for you, but I can assure you that I will not miss a chance to make life miserable for you. I'm quite sure that after some time you will think it a wise idea to follow your aunt to her haven in the arms of religion."

Gabrielle attempted to take her arm from his grasp, but it was as though a vise had clamped painfully down on it. His face was threateningly close to hers, and she shrank away from the hurting mouth that she so clearly remembered. But he did not kiss her, and after a few more minutes, he released her arm. Gabrielle left the room without a backward glance.

The rest of the evening passed without incident, and Gabrielle hoped that Charles had gone out for the night. She went to bed but found sleeping fitful.

It was very late when she was awakened by a clamor outside. Loud voices reached her through the open windows, and one of them sounded very much like Charles, obviously very drunk. Her contempt for him increased. He was not even gentleman enough to hold his liquor. She listened idly for a moment, her ear catching the sound of another voice with a slightly foreign drawl.

"No need to wake up the whole neighborhood, Chevalier. The wound's just a scratch."

Wound? Gabrielle quickly rose from her bed and slipped a nightrobe over her gown. Good God! What had Charles done now?

She hurried down the upstairs hall and paused for a

moment at the landing to look down in the hallway just as the two men came inside. There were only a few candles still lit, and it was hard to make out the face of the man with Charles. She could tell he was tall, but the brim of his hat shielded his features even as she saw him look up at her.

"You there, move your legs, girl, and tell me where to put this man. He's been stabbed in the shoulder."

Gabrielle smothered a gasp and, without thinking, obeyed the man and swiftly descended the steps, guiding him to the downstairs study where he laid Charles on the couch. Gabrielle flew about the room lighting the candles until a fairly bright blaze of light illuminated the room. Her eyes went first to the spot on Charles' coat, a dark brown mark with a center of bright red.

"What—what happened?" she questioned breathlessly as she struggled to pull the fabric back from the wound.

"A young lady of the evening stabbed him. She said he was trying to kill her." The words were uttered matter-of-factly.

"Was she arrested?" Gabrielle asked, hoping the stranger could not see her flaming cheeks.

She could feel the man's shrug. "I'm sure he wouldn't want the publicity, miss."

Gabrielle continued fumbling at the coat, her fingers somehow nervelessly ineffectual. She saw the strong, brown hand close for an instant over hers.

"I'll get it. You go bring water and a cloth to wash it out."

She hurried to fetch the needed articles from the kitchen, and when she returned she found the man had taken off Charles' coat and shirt, leaving his upper torso bare. She could see the ugly, puckered flesh at the shoulder, steadily oozing blood.

She thought that she was going to gag but forced herself to remain calm, wrinkling her nose as she passed the bowl of water wordlessly to the other man. He had not taken off his hat or coat, and Gabrielle was too busy sponging the wound to look at him.

"*Mon dieu*! What has happened?"

Gabrielle turned with a sigh of thanks to see Pauline hurrying to the settee, where she took over the washing of the wound.

"You go to bed, ma'm'selle. I will see to this."

By now a small knot of servants were looking in on the room curiously, and Gabrielle hurriedly shooed them away, explaining that M'sieur Charles had had an accident and that they need not worry.

"Gabrielle! What's wrong? Charles!" Alexandre pushed past her and gasped at seeing his son stretched out on the couch, his face blanched and perspiring. "I will send for a doctor," he muttered and turned to go when his eyes fell on the other man, who was leaning indolently against the back of the couch now, watching the events with an unhurried gaze. "Savage! What—what are you doing here—with Charles?"

Gabrielle turned from the doorway and met the shock of those cool green eyes that semed to pierce her completely.

"Your son, Alexandre, seems to have gotten himself into a scrape over some prostitute down on the quai. She ran out screaming that he had tried to strangle her." He shrugged casually, his voice indifferently amused. "Rather messy business, but as I happened to be in the same locale, I took it upon myself to see him home."

"But—what was he doing there?" Alexandre questioned him dazedly.

The man cocked a darkly arched brow, and his smile could only be called mocking. Alexandre turned red, but further explanations were cut short by a long moan from Charles as he tossed restlessly under Pauline's administering hands.

Alexandre bent over his son, the concern on his face easily evident. He called to the sleepy-eyed majordomo and ordered him to send immediately for a physician.

Gabrielle, a little apart from the rest of the group, turned away. She felt no real pity for Charles, but she hated to see anyone in pain and hoped the doctor would

arrive soon. She felt too tired to try to explain to herself
that Alexandre seemed to be acquainted with the man he
had called Savage—the very same man she remembered
from the time she and Isabel had visited the coffee house,
La Petite Fleur. She recalled someone calling him a
pirate then, and the murderous gleam in his dark eyes had
seemed to confirm the opinion.

She had forgotten the impropriety of her attire and
was unaware of the stranger's eyes appraising her through
the thin silk of her gown. The half-hour had chimed before the doctor made his arrival, coming in briskly with
an air of confidence that immediately eased the tension
in the room.

"Thank God, you've arrived, Clary! My son has been
stabbed."

The doctor impatiently brushed Alexandre's hands
away. "I think it would be better if you had him moved
to his own rooms so that he can rest more easily. I will
make my examination of him there."

Alexandre signalled two footmen to carry Charles up
the stairs to his bedroom. The doctor followed with an
easy tread. Alexandre accompanied him up the stairs, and,
one by one, the servants went back to their beds,
grumbling over their young master's thoughtless actions.

Gabrielle remained in her chair, leaning her head back,
her eyes closed. She would have thought she was alone
except for the feeling of someone's eyes on her, and she
opened hers to meet those of the man called Savage.

In that first moment of surprise, she noted his tall, lithe
figure, the wide shoulders, and powerful thigh muscles that
strained against his fashionable tight breeches. His face
was brown from the sun, and the lips were firm and
sensual, curving now in a slightly insolent grin as he surveyed her. Gabrielle blushed at her own impolite scrutiny
and stood up, preparing to go back to her bedroom.

"Don't leave me yet, kitten," he said quietly, the tone
of his voice almost caressing.

She turned towards him, her eyes questioning. "I'm
sorry. I suppose someone should thank you for what you

did tonight," she murmured softly. "I'm sure Alexandre will want to thank you himself in the morning, but as you can see, he is most anxious for his son's health."

His smile deepened, and he strode towards her with a soft, pantherlike stride as though he were barely holding himself back from springing at her. The force of his masculinity struck Gabrielle with a sudden awareness of her clinging gown.

"Please forgive my attire," she began, the pink of her cheeks deepening.

"On the contrary," he answered her with sarcasm in his voice, "I approve. I only wish I had been introduced at the cafe."

A blush suffused her face at his mention of La Petite Fleur, for she remembered that at the cafe he had thought her a lady of the streets. "I—I am Gabrielle de Beauvoir, M'sieur de Chevalier's ward. And you, m'sieur?"

He bowed negligently. "Captain Rafe Savage, miss."

"I am sure, captain, that you must be very tired. Let me show you to the door."

"Why, kitten, you're not going to run away from me, are you?" He moved still closer to her, and Gabrielle felt as though she couldn't move away from the look he gave her, an indecent look that spoke confidently of his virility. "I seem to recall your interest that day at the coffee house."

"Please, captain, do not bring that up. I—I am sorry for staring so rudely at you that day."

"I don't mind in the least being stared at by eyes the color of yours, kitten. Beautiful eyes," he commented and came close enough to touch her.

Gabrielle's mind was screaming for her feet to move, to run away from this man and the strange attraction he seemed to hold for her, but she could only look at him helplessly.

Suddenly, with a fluid movement, he pounced on her, his arms holding her in a powerful grasp as he bent her backwards against him, his mouth closing on hers with the expertise of a master. His swiftness left her numb with shock, and she was helpless to resist the onslaught.

His kiss went deeper, and it seemed to last forever as he forced her lips apart and took possession of her tongue. Her breasts were crushed against the hard steel of his chest, and she felt dimly the motion of his hand as it crept upward to tug at the material of her gown. I cannot breathe, she thought, feeling dizzy and trembling at the same time. He took his mouth away from hers only to bend downward, his lips making heated imprints on the flesh of her throat. His hands had pulled the gown from her shoulders, and with a sense of shock, Gabrielle saw her naked bosom. He was murmuring something against her flesh, and she struggled with the sense of unreality that was enveloping her.

"You must forgive my impetuousness, kitten. But, unfortunately, I was interrupted in my own expectation of pleasure this night by the accident caused to your patron's son. It seems, though, that you will do very well, very well indeed."

His laugh mocked her, and Gabrielle felt as though an icy bucket of water had been thrown over her. She struggled in earnest against his encroaching mouth and arms.

"You—you uncouth villain!" she managed breathlessly, pushing against his chest with all the force she could summon. "You compare me to those filthy sluts who take money for their pleasure. Let me go, you pirate!"

He caught her arms easily enough, and she could see the hateful amusement in his eyes. "Without your perfumed hair and clean clothes, sweetheart, I swear I would not have known the difference when you let me kiss you just now. Tell me, kitten, are you angry because I took you like a whore, or because you acted like one."

Gabrielle blinked in mingled fury and shock, pushing him away even more vigorously. "I hate you! How dare you presume to speak to me like that! Let me go, or I shall call the police and have you thrown in prison, you arrogant pirate!"

"That is the second time you have used that term in

referring to me. Would you like to see how a pirate treats a spirited wench, milady?"

He lifted her off the ground, and she was held suspended for a moment, her legs dangling helplessly. Then he lifted her easily so that she lay against his chest, unable to do anything but glare defiantly at him. Her hair had tumbled from its pins and spilled luxuriously over his arm, its silky texture catching the glow from the firelight. Her eyes were luminous and a dark violet, her cheeks flushed becomingly from her exertions.

He thought at that moment that she was the most desirable woman he had ever seen, and he could feel the ache in his loins demanding satisfaction. What impulse had led him to start this love play? he wondered in private amazement. She was beautiful but certainly not worth risking his neck if she did succeed in calling for help.

"Please let me go," she was saying, her voice holding a note of pleading now, and he could not help but be amused by her change in tactics.

"I ask a price for all favors granted," he answered her insolently.

She gazed at him stubbornly, her mouth shaping into an irresistible pout. "It is granted in advance," she finally got out, "but you must put me down immediately."

He stood her on her feet, holding her firmly with one hand so that she could not escape. "I want you to let me make love to you, kitten," he said, the devilish look in his eyes.

Gabrielle felt her throat go dry, and she could not swallow for a moment. "You—you cannot ask such a thing. I—I am still a maiden," she murmured, blushing hotly.

His arrogant laugh made her shudder. "Such information is supposed to disarm me, no doubt," he went on. But as though his mood had suddenly changed, she heard him saying, "It is late, kitten, and I think that such designs as I might have on you would be wasted at this hour. Please be sure that I will collect my price at another

time, though." He released her and strode swiftly out of
the room before she could even collect her thoughts.

She stood for a moment hardly breathing until she
heard the slam of the front door and the sound of his
heels crunching the graveled court yard. The tears were
gathering in her eyes as she made her way up the stairs,
still shaking from her experience. The man was dangerous,
a rogue who needed to have the insolence whipped out of
him, she thought. But, she reminded herself with some
shame, he had been right when he pointed out that she
had let him kiss her. What was the matter with her?

Chapter Seven

It was early the next morning when Gabrielle was
aroused from sleep by a soft knocking on her door.
Chloë, who was laying out clothes for her to wear that
day, hurried to answer it.

Alexandre peered around the door, looking somewhat
relieved to see Gabrielle blinking sleepily at him.

"What is the matter, Alexandre?" she questioned him,
barely troubling to conceal the yawn that escaped her.
"How is Charles this morning?"

"Better, under the circumstances, but he still has a
slight fever." He moved away as if to leave her room so
that she could dress, but affecting an afterthought, he
turned back and fixed her with a level stare. "I suppose
you saw—you saw Charles' rescuer to the door last
night?"

Gabrielle's eyes widened, and she could not help the
slight color that came to her face. "Captain Savage stayed
for only a short time and then left," she managed.

"You introduced yourselves, then?" he asked, pressing
her for an answer.

She nodded noncommittally.

"I find it rather strange, but," and he cleared his throat, "I received a note earlier from Captain Savage asking if he might call on you."

Gabrielle felt her body stiffen. "Of course you declined, didn't you?"

He shook his head, at which her heart sank. "Under the circumstances, and as he expressed a wish to look in on Charles, I could not do otherwise than say yes. After all, I do owe him something for his actions last night."

His actions last night! Gabrielle shuddered, remembering the power and strength in those long-fingered hands and broad shoulders. She decided to face Alexandre squarely with her suspicions.

"You know him from somewhere else, don't you?" she asked him.

It was Alexandre's turn to flush, but he nodded as though he realized that it would do him no good to lie. "Yes. It is quite a long story, Gabrielle, but suffice it to say that I know he is a man with few scruples and no loyalties. He is an American—I believe his family comes from Virginia in the United States."

"And he is the one whom you called your American captain—the one who is involved with the smuggling—the one who was in the house next door the night of Isabel's ball!" Gabrielle exclaimed suddenly, as everything fell into place. She turned in amazement towards Alexandre. "Of course! But didn't you tell me that you were withdrawing from the smuggling?"

His nod was vigorous. He realized that there was no point in dissembling before her. "Yes, I had a meeting with my business associate last evening to discuss exactly that. He was expecting Savage later on, so I am positive he too knows I am out of it."

Gabrielle frowned, her mind working. "And so he turns up at the convenient moment when Charles is in trouble. He brings your son here and then manages to obtain your permission to see me. You said yourself, Alexandre, that this man has no loyalties and no principles. Do you think—might he be thinking of blackmail?"

Alexandre's face sagged visibly. "He couldn't be—he couldn't."

"But yet, he knows that you were funding part of the business. He realizes what you have to lose, and if the profit was as good as you told me, perhaps he thinks you can afford the price of his silence."

Alexandre did not answer for a long moment. "In that case, I must play his game," he finally muttered. "I cannot risk the scandal and Charles finding out. You will not tell Charles anything of this. Do I have your promise?"

Gabrielle gave it halfheartedly, thinking it was rather too late for that now, and at the same time wondering if the price that Savage would set was higher than Alexandre would be able to afford. How could she be civil with him, let alone allow him to call on her with the knowledge that had just evolved? And how could Alexandre have given him permission to see her? She looked for a moment at the man, seeing, in a flash of understanding, the weakness that assailed him. She must have time to think.

After Alexandre had left, she called Chloë back into the room. "I want to wear something especially nice," she informed her, rising from the bed.

Chloë brought out a lettuce-green gown of cool batiste trimmed with a froth of white lace at the neckline and hem. She dressed Gabrielle's hair simply with a green fillet tied around the untidy curls and added a long sliver of silver chain at her throat. Gabrielle surveyed herself in the mirror with a critical air and was satisfied with the effect. At least Captain Savage could see she was a woman in command of her feelings and not some giddy, nightgown-clad fool.

It was as she was coming downstairs and into the hall that she heard the outer bell. Instead of waiting for a servant to answer it, she opened the door herself.

Deep green eyes appraised her with that maddening touch of insolence as the lips curved into a mocking smile. "Good day, Miss de Beauvoir."

Gabrielle struggled to regain her composure.

"Why, Captain Savage! I'm—I was only just going up to my room with a—a headache."

His smile deepened, and she noticed the grooves on either side of his mouth that heightened the impression of recklessness. "May I come in?" he continued, and Gabrielle realized that she was holding the door as though to slam it shut on him.

Embarrassed, she swung the door wider. "Do you wish to see the marquis? I'm afraid he's not here right now, but I will gladly give him your greetings, m'sieur."

He laughed deliberately, walking easily into the hall and closing the door softly behind him. "On the contrary, I have come to see you. Is that so hard for you to believe?"

He was mocking her, taunting her, and Gabrielle felt her anger begin to build up unreasonably.

"Frankly, captain, I do find it hard to believe as I am quite sure my feelings towards you have been expressed—"

He was walking past her into the sitting room as though he was accustomed to entering wherever he pleased. "May I sit down?"

Gabrielle, her face quite flushed now, hid her clenched fists in the folds of her gown. "Does it matter if I say yes or no, as I'm sure you will do what you wish anyway?"

He sat down, his eyes running over her figure as minutely as though he were ready to fix a price on her. She steeled herself for an ordeal as she seated herself calmly on another chair.

"Well, captain, you said you wanted to see me?"

"I'm here to invite you to a dinner party."

"Really? Well, you must forgive me, but—"

"I'm sure you will want to attend, as there will be quite a few personalities from the court. Perhaps even the new empress will be there."

Gabrielle's mouth formed a round "O," and for a moment she could not think what to say.

"Does it surprise you that I walk in royal circles?" he questioned, and she could tell he was laughing at her.

"Yes, as a matter of fact, it does, captain, as I can only see that you are an American with no connections here, a man who commands a ship that—" She stopped abruptly, afraid that she would let him know how much she knew of his projects.

"Go on, please," he said, his voice deceptively silky as he leaned forward.

"Projects that may or may not be wholly legitimate," she finished, feeling suddenly as though she were walking on treacherous ground.

He sat back in the chair again. "I didn't realize that my projects concerned you enough to warrant your own investigation, but now I remember that you did accuse me of being a pirate the last time we met."

Gabrielle swallowed and nerved herself to present a composed face to him. "I remember that those men in the coffee shop called you a pirate and—and there was an Oriental woman with you then."

He laughed outright. "So, you would believe a pair of unlikely sailors, and just because I had a woman who was not of our descent you thought I must be a pirate. Really, I did give you more credit for intelligence, kitten. Did it ever occur to you that that woman could be my mistress?"

Gabrielle flushed deeply. "I never gave it any thought, as my interest in you is hardly large enough to fill a thimble," she said, barely controlling her anger.

"Now, be honest with me, kitten," he goaded her, the smile teasing her with its sardonic indolence.

"Don't call me that!" she burst out. "I suppose you call every woman you know by such familiar endearments!"

"Not every woman," he answered her softly, disarming her for a moment before she could whip up her anger again. "I think, kitten, you try too hard to dislike me."

Goaded past endurance, Gabrielle stood up and gave him a scathing look. "It is not hard to dislike a man who resorts to smuggling to fill his coffers," she threw at him, and then, horrified at her disclosure, she saw the devilish look close over his features.

"First a pirate, and now you accuse me of smuggling." He seemed to think it over for a moment. "I think that perhaps you know too much about me, kitten, and it might prove ill for me if I didn't do something about ensuring your silence."

For a moment, Gabrielle felt terrified. Then she realized that, as usual, he was mocking her apprehension. In her fury, she threw caution to the winds.

"And don't you think it would give me some pleasure, seeing you in jail where you belong, Captain Savage? Smuggling, as you must know, is a treasonous offense in these times and—"

"—and your guardian is no less a party to it than I am, kitten, but you forget that for a man like me, a pirate as you insist, treason is a word that signifies nothing. I am an American, if you recall, and I have no ties here, whereas your guardian would be ruined if the authorities were to find out how he makes a profit."

Gabrielle remained silent for a moment, realizing that she had acted childishly and now must hold her temper. Of course, now he would tell her what he wanted from Alexandre—how much money it would take to silence him. Everything that had come before was only leading up to this moment, and she hated him for making her sit there in suspense while he played with her like a cat with a mouse.

"I am sure, mademoiselle, that you understand how important it is to your guardian that you not inform on me, for that would necessarily drag him into unpleasantness."

She averted her eyes from his lazy smile and willed herself to remain calm.

"This may come as a surprise to you, my sweet, but I am already quite wealthy for a man of only twenty-five years. My family has owned land in Virginia for a hundred years or more, and in that time, we have built up quite an extensive import operation, all legitimate."

"So, then, you are so wealthy that you must break the law to back your shipping operations?" she asked, her own voice betraying sarcasm.

He shrugged. "That is a long story, but it is enough to say that I am considered the black sheep in the family and have always done things my own way, whether those means involved breaking the law or not. For your information, my smuggling adventures have been looked upon quite highly by the islanders in the West Indies, as it is their only means of obtaining goods from your country. You might even say that I am regarded as something of a hero," he said, but there was no trace of smug self-importance in his voice.

Gabrielle refused to be baited. They were both sitting silently attempting to gauge one another when Gabrielle heard Alexandre's voice in the hall. She started, her eyes going to the door in alarm.

"You must not—" she began, turning back to the man who lounged composedly in the chair.

"Gabrielle?" Alexandre was at the door, the smile on his face turning to a look of concern when he saw his visitor. "Savage! What—what are you doing here?"

The captain bowed. "I am trying to obtain your ward's approval to my suggestion that I escort her to a dinner party this evening." He gave Gabrielle a look of sardonic confidence. "Have you decided yet, mademoiselle?"

Gabrielle bit her lip in vexation, furious that he had backed her into this corner. Barely able to get the words out calmly, she replied, "I would be happy to attend with you, captain."

"I will return at eight o'clock, then." He bowed to her, and she curtseyed briefly before leaving the room.

Once in her own room, she recalled that he had not brought up the subject of pricing his silence but had made a point of having no need for the profits obtained from smuggling. Had he been trying to impress her? she wondered. Vehemently determined not to enjoy herself in his company tonight, she rang the servants' bell for Chloë.

"I will be attending a dinner party with Captain Savage this evening, Chloë. I will need something suitable to wear."

"Yes, ma'm'selle, but of course, the new gown from M'sieur LeRoy would be the only one worthy of the occasion."

Gabrielle had ordered the gown especially for the bridal

dinner to be held at Isabel's house on the evening before the wedding. LeRoy had made it of the softest watered silk, in a color of deep lilac that complemented her eyes. It fairly floated around her as she walked. The bodice was cut extremely low, and the sleeves were actually nothing more than bits of rolled fabric adorned with crystals—they rested on her shoulders like straps. It was a daring gown, and Gabrielle smiled to herself picturing the look of amusement on the captain's face if she wore it. After all, it would be an invitation, wouldn't it! But not to the captain, she thought firmly. She would wear it, if only to tease him. She refused to think of the consequences, confident that she could handle anything.

"Yes, the new dress, Chloë, by all means," she agreed.

Chloë helped her into the gown after she had bathed and her hair had been dressed. It fit her almost like a second skin, matching the curves of her breasts and hips. Her bosom was exposed most daringly and the color of the dress made her skin seem almost translucent.

"It really is too indecent," Gabrielle commented, frowning at the alarming expanse of flesh that was exposed. "I shall take a shawl."

At exactly eight o'clock the carriage arrived. Gabrielle could hear the captain's laughter in the hall as he spoke with Alexandre. How could he be so pleasant with Savage, when all the time the American is planning to play such a terrible trick on him! she thought furiously. Savage simply had no principles. She adjusted the shawl around herself, aware that the lace did little to conceal the ivory-gold of her skin. She walked down the hallway, taking a deep breath at the stairway landing before descending to the main foyer where both men were looking up at her, Alexandre with an agreeably entranced look on his face, and Captain Savage with that infuriating air of appraisal.

"My dear, you look beautiful, like a butterfly with gauze wings," Alexandre said, kissing her hand as he saluted her beauty.

"Thank you," Gabrielle said, smiling. She felt the captain's hand at her elbow, steering her out to his carriage.

"Savage, I put her well-being in your care tonight." Alexandre's voice held a note of warning in it.

"Have no fear, her well-being will be my utmost concern," Captain Savage retorted, not even turning his head.

When they were seated in the carriage opposite each other, Gabrielle was suddenly aware of the consummate power of the man, and she realized with some force that she was completely alone with him. She noticed that his own clothes were very fine. He wore a navy blue coat that deepened his eyes and an ivory waistcoat over his white linen shirt. His trousers matched the vest, and his knee-boots were polished to a slick black shine. She tightened the shawl around her as though for protection.

He laughed mockingly. "Oh, my poor little kitten. I suppose you expect me to pounce on you in the carriage. An intriguing idea, I must admit, but I would hate to tear that lovely gown."

Gabrielle blushed hotly. "I expect nothing from you, captain, except that you escort me to this—this party of yours. Once there I will gladly leave you to your own devices."

"Oh, yes, I had forgotten that you were accompanying me under duress. Does it not occur to you that the noble M'sieur de Chevalier is using you to protect himself from what he thinks might be a possible attempt at blackmail? Most women would not be so obliging, unless, that is, they did not hate the perpetrator as much as they insisted." He laughed again with insolent boldness.

"And so, you do have blackmail in mind!" Gabrielle pressed him, her mind catching instantly at the word she had dreaded to hear.

He shrugged. "Why should I be interested in obtaining money from the marquis when I keep assuring you that I have quite enough to satisfy me?"

She bit her lip thoughtfully. "If you are being honest, which I am still inclined to doubt, then why am I here with you now?" she demanded.

He laughed even harder. "But that is exactly my point,

kitten. Could you bring yourself to be in my company for a whole evening unless you held me in some favor?"

His self-assured sarcasm burned her, and she wished she could just jump out of the carriage and show him exactly how little he mattered to her.

"Of course, I cannot deny my interest in you, kitten," he continued, studying her. "I have high hopes that it will climax in something quite—shall we say—pleasant for both of us."

"Oh!" she knew her face had reddened at the implication in his words. But he was lounging carelessly in his seat now, apparently tired of the game. His lack of interest only heightened her humiliation. He had made her out to be secretly longing for him to make love to her, and he openly admitted that he would look forward to just such an episode, but no more so than with any other desirable woman. He really was loathsome, and she vowed that if he ever tried to lay his hands on her, she would scratch his eyes out.

They were both silent for the rest of the ride, she inwardly fuming at her own weakness, and he watching her discomfiture with amusement. When the carriage stopped, Gabrielle did not wait for him to help her out but jumped down from the step herself, nearly twisting her ankle in a crevice. He caught her arm easily enough, forcing her to his side as they entered the well-lit house from which music and laughter were pouring into the street. At the door, Gabrielle searched the salon, hoping to see someone she knew, but found that everyone there was a stranger to her.

"Oh, Rafe, you devil! I thought you had decided not to come." The lilting voice belonged to a woman whose dress completely revealed her breasts through the sheer material. Her flaming red hair and sparkling green eyes proclaimed her a beauty, and the size of the jewels at her wrists and throat hinted that she belonged to Napoleon's court.

Captain Savage was bowing to the woman, and she simpered, leaning toward him so that even Gabrielle could see well into her dress. Her own unease increased when the captain pulled her towards him to be introduced, and she was aware of the narrowing of the woman's eyes.

"Let me introduce Mademoiselle Gabrielle de Beauvoir. Gabrielle, this is Madame Martine Cavounnais. She will be your hostess this evening."

Gabrielle curtseyed; the name rang a bell somewhere in the back of her mind. Hadn't a Madame Cavounnais been the emperor's mistress for some months before the new Austrian empress had arrived?

"How nice to meet you, my dear. Philippe, do come over, darling and meet our new arrival. Ma'm'selle de Beauvoir, this is my cousin, Philippe Aubremont. Philippe, you know Captain Savage."

A fair-haired young man walked confidently over, his eyes sliding over Gabrielle in a way she found particularly irritating.

"A pleasure, ma'm'selle," the man was saying, bowing over her hand. He took her arm and led her into the room, making introductions to many people, some of whom she knew by name. She glanced once at Captain Savage, but, as he was seemingly engrossed in what Madame Cavounnais was whispering to him, he did not notice.

"Oh, my dear, you must let me see your gown. Monsieur LeRoy's touch, I can tell." A woman was commenting on her dress, pulling the shawl from around her shoulders.

Gabrielle clutched at the garment a little forlornly and watched as a servant took it away to be put with the other capes and cloaks. She managed to thank the woman for the compliment and saw that perhaps her dress was not so dangerous as she had first thought. Surely all of the other women's bosoms were at least partially exposed, and Gabrielle felt a little proud of her breasts, which rose high and firm, nestling pertly in her bodice.

The talk was barely distinguishable among the noise and music, and the heat was already causing her to perspire a little. She felt obliged to do her best and listened with feigned interest to idle chatter about life at court.

She looked up now and then to see the captain encircled by a knot of admiring women who listened breathlessly to his bold but amusing conversation.

Gabrielle found herself wishing he would stay by her side. She did not fit in with these people. After what seemed like hours, dinner was announced, and Gabrielle turned thankfully for Captain Savage to escort her to the table. But he was already leading the hostess inside, and Gabrielle found that Aubremont was bowing to her and offering his arm. She took it with some spirit, determined that Captain Savage's lack of interest was not going to spoil her evening. After all, she had to admit that she had as much as told him in the carriage to keep his distance.

She found herself seated between Aubremont and an elderly gentleman who, despite his age, seemed to have a gift for intelligent repartee. He kept her fascinated through much of the meal as he talked knowledgeably about the Russian front, the Americas, and his estates near Marseilles.

She would have forgotten about Aubremont if he hadn't insidiously slipped his hand beneath the table, next to her thigh. "I thought you'd forgotten me," he said by way of explanation when she gave him an outraged look.

Gabrielle would have answered with a biting reply, but she caught herself, remembering that she was a guest and this man was a relative of the hostess.

"My small talk is, perhaps, not as interesting as M'sieur Duvall's, but I can assure you that my prowess on the dance floor is unequalled, ma'm'selle. After dinner, I insist on enjoying the first dance with you."

Gabrielle accepted him, although her response was probably not as enthusiastic as he would have wished. But she did not like his eyes that roved continually over the bodice of her gown. She was annoyed enough to slap him but again reminded herself to hold her temper.

She looked down the table where Captain Savage was engaged in lively conversation with his hostess and one or two others. She caught the white gleam of his teeth as he smiled when Madame Cavounnais put her arm possessively on his sleeve. It promised to be quite difficult to arrange for Captain Savage to return her home, Gabrielle thought.

After dinner was over, Aubremont hovered close to her, never missing an opportunity to fill her empty glass with more wine, which caused her to drink more than she was accustomed to. When the music started, his arm slid easily about her waist and he guided her out to the dance floor. The music was really lovely, and Gabrielle leaned back in his arms and allowed him to swirl her about the polished tiles, conceding that he was a first-rate dancing partner.

She danced with several men during the evening, and she refused to let her eyes search for her escort. It was quite late, after midnight, when she saw him on the other side of the ballroom with the hostess. Martine looked quite flushed as the two walked together about the room, and Gabrielle felt a sharp pang of anger as she guessed at the cause of her disarray.

Her disgust heightened as she watched them dancing together—nearly pasted against each other, she thought. She took the proffered wine from Aubremont who had returned to her side and downed it in one gulp, causing herself to cough until tears sprang to her eyes. Aubremont followed the direction of her eyes and smiled to himself.

"Ah yes, you've noticed how my cousin monopolizes the captain's time, ma'm'selle. Rather insulting to you, I'm sure, but my cousin is a ruthless woman, and I'm afraid she cares very little about other people's feelings. She usually gets what she wants, and I doubt that Captain Savage will be an exception."

"I agree," Gabrielle replied. "But I really don't care what she wants, be it Captain Savage or anyone else. Shall we dance again?"

She was surprised at her own boldness but attributed it to the effects of the wine. She was feeling a little warm, and when Aubremont led her towards the garden outside, she didn't object, although she leaned away from him when he would have put his arm around her. She wished she had thought to bring her shawl outside, as the April night was a trifle chilly.

"A beautiful night," Aubremont commented idly, his hand toying with the leaf of a juniper tree.

Gabrielle breathed deeply, hoping to clear her head. "Yes, it does feel good to get out of the stifling atmosphere in there."

They walked further into the garden, Gabrielle's senses dulled to the warning of intimacy. They sat down on a bench, and she allowed him to take her hand.

"A beautiful night," he repeated, "but not so beautiful as you, my lovely Gabrielle."

He turned towards her, and Gabrielle knew that he was going to kiss her. Ordinarily she would have been repulsed by his forward manner after knowing him such a short time, but in her present mood of anger and carelessness, she offered her lips silently, feeling almost gratefully the warmth of his arms around her shoulders. His kiss did nothing to her, only creating a pleasant anticipation as his mouth moved to her temple. Contrarily, though, she sensed that her partner was becoming a bit heated from the experience, and she decided it would be best to stop him while she still held control over the situation.

Gently she brought her hands up to push him away, but she found that he resisted her unspoken demand while he took her lips again. She freed her mouth in annoyance.

"M'sieur Aubremont, please! I wish to be taken back inside now."

"In due time, ma'm'selle. But now I have other things on my mind which require the privacy of just such a space as this."

He would have clasped her harder against him, but Gabrielle struggled out of his grasp, agile as an eel.

"Please, I—"

"Quiet," he spoke sharply. "Do you think I'm some

ninny that you can lead by the nose as my cousin does so skilfully with her paramours? I gathered from your actions that you would enjoy an intimate moment with me."

"Well, then, you have judged wrong, for although I find your company pleasant, m'sieur, I cannot bring myself to more."

Gabrielle was shaking a little, whether from the cold or the anger he had instilled in her.

"I see—a mere dalliance, then. Perhaps you hoped that your Captain Savage would see us walk out here and be moved to jealousy. Well, ma'm'selle, I'm afraid that he is well taken care of by the beautiful Martine, and your jealously guarded virtue will grow old waiting for him."

Stung, Gabrielle glared at him, her humiliation all the greater as she recognized the innuendo in his words.

"He is not *my* captain, m'sieur."

He laughed shortly. "Oh, don't bother to dissemble, ma'm'selle. It's not worth it. I've seen what the man does to women with his damnable good looks and bold manners. You're just like the rest of them, unfortunately."

Gabrielle stamped her foot in irritation. "I am not like the rest of those silly, twittering women," she cried out. "I abhor the man, but I was obliged to accompany him tonight. If I never had to see him again, I would count myself blessed."

"Then why do you resist me?" he put in slyly, reaching for her.

Gabrielle twisted away from him. "Because your manners are repulsive, m'sieur. I barely know you. How can you expect me to—" but she could not finish the sentence when he caught her again in his arms, his mouth pressing against her, effectively choking back further discussion. His hand explored her breast beneath the neckline of her gown and Gabrielle raised her hands once more to push him away.

"That is quite enough, Aubremont." The deadly seriousness of the voice caused him to move back quickly.

Gabrielle stared at Rafe Savage, whose eyes gazed back at her filled with mockery.

"I believe the young lady no longer wishes your company."

For a moment, Gabrielle thought the other man would spring at Savage.

"I believe that this is hardly your business, Captain Savage. Don't you think you have enough to handle just entertaining my cousin? Surely you would leave some of the other women for the rest of us." His words were biting with rage.

A suggestion of a smile appeared on the captain's face. "As you say, Aubremont, there are other ladies inside who would be glad to put up with your bad manners and your fumbling attempts to please a woman. I suggest you go and find one."

The younger man's face with livid with rage. "You go too far, Savage. If I but had my sword, I'd run you through for your insults!"

"You'd best be glad you do not have one, m'sieur, for I would be obliged to kill you in short order." At the words, uttered in a quietly menacing tone of voice, Aubremont seemed to recoil.

"I—I suppose I could forgive your interference, then, but—but I—"

"Why don't we ask the young lady what she would prefer to do?" Savage interrupted and turned towards Gabrielle, whose face was glowing with embarrassment.

She looked at both of them in an agony of humiliation and then turned to rush back into the house. Oh, I hope they both kill each other, she thought, feeling tears of helpless anger gathering in her eyes. She must—she must go home.

She walked almost blindly into the room and nearly bumped into Martine, who caught her arm almost casually. "My dear, whatever happened out there? Are you all right? When Rafe saw you walk out the door with cousin Philippe, he said he thought he'd best see that you were safe. I suppose he feels responsible for you. After all, you're only a child."

"I'm fine, thank you, madame. There—there was no need for the captain to worry on my account. If you will just call a carriage for me and have a servant fetch my shawl—I think I'd like to go home now."

The woman released her arm and went to find a servant. Gabrielle dabbed at the moisture in her eyes as she waited in the huge hall, hoping the servant would hurry and direct her to a carriage. To her chagrin, instead of a servant she perceived the figure of Rafe Savage coming towards her. Behind him, a frown marring the beauty of her face, trailed Martine.

"But Rafe, darling, you cannot be leaving so soon. Why I thought that, perhaps, you and I might—"

"I'm sorry, Martine, but I do have a responsibility towards Mademoiselle de Beauvoir."

"Since when have you felt a responsibility towards any woman? Rafe, please—"

Gabrielle felt embarrassed to be a witness to this naked pleading. She tried not to see as Savage bent down to the woman and bestowed a kiss on her full lips even as his hand caressed her flagrantly.

"Tomorrow, then?" she heard the woman whisper huskily.

He laughed but would not commit himself, and Gabrielle wondered if the beauteous Martine had finally found a man who could not be wrapped around her little finger.

She felt him standing behind her and turned. "I would not take you away from your pleasures, captain. I assure you that I can get home alone." She thought of the night she walked home after Charles had insulted her in the carriage.

"Perhaps, kitten, but I prefer to leave, myself, and found you a likely excuse."

"Oh!" How easily he can anger me, she thought, and wondered why he persisted in doing so.

He took her arm and walked with her to the carriage.

Before she quite knew what he was about, she felt his arms around her, lifting her into the vehicle as easily as though she were, in truth, a child.

"I think you've drunk a little too much wine—thanks, no doubt, to young Aubremont, the lecherous pup," he said, settling down next to her.

"I'm not drunk, Captain Savage," she assured him, still smarting from his earlier slight. "Besides, I'm sure M'sieur Aubremont could take lessons from you when it comes to seducing young women!" Privately she admitted to herself that she did feel tired and a trifle light in the head.

She leaned against the side panel of the carriage, trying to keep as far away from her companion as possible. She did not close her eyes, though, fearing that he would mistake her action for acquiescence. Instead, she found herself remembering parts of M'sieur Duvall's dinner conversation, especially those stories related to the Americas.

He had made several voyages during the late Revolution, helping to stock the Americans' provisions against the British forces. She had wanted to ask him if he had ever heard of the Savages in Virginia, but had decided against it. He had drawn brightly colored pictures in her mind of naked Indians swooping down on settlers and he extolled the splendor of the port cities and the novel way of life in the United States. Duvall had especially liked the city of New Orleans, mostly because of its French flavor and design.

The sound of carriage wheels coming to a noisy halt on gravel woke her from her doze, and she felt ashamed that she had allowed herself to fall asleep despite her previous resolution. Her mind was still blurred, and she blinked her eyes at the sudden dim triangle of light from the open door of the house. In another moment, she was lifted in strong arms and taken inside the house.

"Please forgive me for falling asleep, Captain Savage, but I can assure you that I am quite awake now. You can put me down, please."

She focused on his face that seemed suddenly too close to her own. His mouth drew up on one side in an insolent grin, but his eyes held a gleam that she could not quite fathom. It frightened her, and she insisted that he put her down at once. She was surprised to find him carrying her up the stairs and into the hallway that led to the bedrooms.

"Captain! Please put me down. I'm quite able to put myself to bed, thank you! Chloë!" Her voice rose a little with her increasing nervousness. Where was that girl! And Pauline! Gabrielle gazed about her a little wildly and finally realized that she was not in her own home. "Where—where am I?" she questioned the man who still held her even as they entered a large, dimly lit room where the fireplace was sending out a comfortable warmth.

"You are in a friend's house, kitten—a friend who conveniently agreed to let me stay here while I am in France."

"And, pray tell me what I am doing here?" she demanded as he finally let her feet touch the floor.

His brow arched lazily as his eyes stripped her. "You made me a promise one night, kitten, on which I have decided to collect." He waited as the realization showed in her eyes, a realization followed by horror at his intentions.

"What are you saying! You—you can't bring me here like this and—and—"

"Make love to you?" he interrupted helpfully, calmly taking off his coat and cravat and laying them across the back of one chair. "Why not, my sweet?" He sat in the chair, preparing to take off his boots, and Gabrielle could only watch, paralyzed with fear and disbelief.

"You would save me from the attentions of lesser men—like M'sieur Aubremont—!" she began, venom in her voice.

"Only to save you for myself, kitten. Did you think I would allow that dandy to take for himself what I have fully intended to have since the first time I laid eyes on you?"

She was speechless, her mind refusing to function clearly. He stood up, unbuttoning the front of his shirt.

"I suppose you have been through all this a little earlier with Madame Cavounnais," she spit at him, backing up as he came toward her, his shirt unbuttoned to the waist.

He laughed sardonically—almost brutally, she thought. "Do I detect jealousy? Then I am indeed flattered, kitten. But, for your own information, Martine did not get to that point this evening, although she tried her damnedest."

"I'm surprised she would even have to try," Gabrielle commented, hoping for a little more time. She glanced quickly around the room and measured her distance from the door. He caught her look and reached for her, catching the edge of her shawl and pulling it off her shoulders.

"I'm a seaman—remember, kitten—and men like me do not have much time. I want you, Gabrielle, and I mean to have you—now!"

"You're—you're despicable!" Gabrielle cried breathlessly, stepping behind a chair. "You just can't carry me off and—and rape me!"

"And why not? If you will recall, when we discussed the possibility of blackmail, I assured you that I have no need of money." He moved closer to her even as he spoke. "My price for silence is not gold, kitten—it's you!"

She gasped and made a dash for the door even as his hand closed around her arm, jerking her to a sharp halt. He seemed content, for the moment, to hold her at arm's length, and despite her considerable pulling and twisting, Gabrielle knew she would not be able to escape his hold. If only the effects of the champagne were not so apparent in the slowness of her reflexes, she felt sure she could have escaped him—another reason to curse M'sieur Aubremont, she thought bitterly.

After her struggles finally slowed and then ceased altogether, they stood looking at each other silently, she with furious despair in her eyes and he with a lazily arrogant smile playing about his mouth.

"Are you finished with your display?" he questioned, laughing at the spark of outrage rekindled in her eyes.

"I ask you to consider your actions, Captain Savage," Gabrielle began, striving for calm, "for I can assure you that if you persist, you will pay for this—this disgrace!"

His left brow quirked upward. "Really? And what penalty must I pay, sweetheart?"

"Imprisonment, m'sieur, or worse! I—I have friends." She uttered the words on a rising note of hopelessness, aware that he was pulling her closer to him.

"My beautiful little siren, I shall be gone by this time tomorrow. My business here in Paris is finished and I am on the early morning coach to Brest to catch my ship, the *Vixen*. It only remains for me to deal with you, kitten."

Beside herself with rage, Gabrielle glared at him. *"Deal* with me! You speak as though I were some last-minute detail that you must take care of. Why, if you are leaving so soon, must you force your attentions on me? Go and find someone who would be glad to give you a suitable farewell."

He laughed again as his other arm took possession of her waist, pressing her lightly against him. "Kitten, you astound me. I have always gone after a challenge, a trait I inherited from my father, I suppose, and it has always served me well in the past. Enough talk, though. Time grows shorter, and I am impatient."

He calmly proceeded to unbutton the back of her gown, holding her against him so that her struggles were, for the most part, useless.

"Be still, kitten, can't you see that I'm trying my best not to rip this gown? But, if you continue, I'll have no choice but to tear it off you."

"Must you live up to your reputation?" Gabrielle inquired bitingly, hating him so much at that moment that if she had had a knife she would not have hesitated to kill him.

She sought to twist out of his grasp as he backed away a little to push the gown from her shoulders, but in the next instant, her dress had slipped down around her ankles, and she crimsoned at the picture she must make to him in her chemise and petticoat.

Uttering a cry of despair, she felt his hands pulling at the thin silk of her chemise until it tore with a forlorn little sound, leaving her breasts naked to his gaze. Gabrielle hurriedly crossed her arms over her bosom, but found that her position only made it easier for him to strip her completely. Finally, she found herself standing before him completely nude with his hands resting lightly on her shoulders.

"I hate you! I hate you!" she cried out, tears of embarrassment and rage spilling unheeded down her cheeks.

She thought she would die from the look of savage passion he gave her as he disposed of his shirt, throwing it carelessly to the floor. He took her in his arms, pressing her so hard against him that her breasts were flattened against his chest. The feel of the crisp, dark hair against her skin made her shudder, and she tried harder to pull away. His thighs were hard against her legs as he arched her backwards and moved his head down to kiss her. His lips were demanding and almost brutal as his kiss deepened, and Gabrielle knew she would fall if he didn't continue to hold her. She heard a soft whimpering deep in her throat and hated herself as he laughed softly against her mouth.

He kept on kissing her as he picked her up effortlessly and moved with her to the bed, the covers of which were turned down in blatant invitation. He laid her on the cool sheets as he straightened to take off his belt and breeches.

Gabrielle lay rigid with mingled fear and incredulity, but when she realized that he was quite naked, she gave a small shriek and made as if to scramble out of the bed. He sprang on top of her, knocking the breath out of her for a moment, and in horror she felt his flesh on hers.

"You—you must stop!" she pleaded when she managed to find her voice, her eyes widening in fear of the unknown.

His answer was to kiss her again, his hands moving possessively over her body as though to acquaint himself with it and commit its curves to memory. Gabrielle clenched her teeth and pulled her mouth away, her hands forming fists to beat on his shoulders and back. His victorious laugh only made her angrier, and she tried to draw up her knees to throw him off. But he was too strong, and her struggles only seemed to excite him further.

"Calm down, kitten, and I promise you I'll be gentle," he murmured, his mouth nibbling at her ear, and bestowing small kisses down her jawline to her throat.

"Never!" Gabrielle cried furiously. "I'll not submit like some tame cow, you hateful beast!"

He sighed softly and Gabrielle shrank as his hands seized her breasts in a movement that was brutal. "Then it is to be rape. I had hoped you would see reason, perhaps even be willing."

He shrugged and lowered his mouth to her breasts, toying with the pink tips until Gabrielle begged for him to stop. He disregarded her pleas, and she felt the treachery of her own body as her nipples rose and tautened. His tongue traced their outline slowly, maddeningly, until Gabrielle heard a low moan begin in her throat and felt a strange warmth spreading in the pit of her belly.

Horrified at the unexpected reaction of her body, she sought to quell its awakening, but his hands persisted as they stroked her thighs, and his mouth would not leave her bosom. She arched reflexively underneath him and heard him laugh again softly, his hands parting her knees as he settled himself against her.

A slow, steady throb seemed to fill the length of her body and center in her belly as Gabrielle listened to Savage's rapid breathing in her ear. He moved upward on her, fastening his lips once more on hers. And this time Gabrielle found herself accepting his kiss, returning it with a fervent passion that she seemed powerless to stem. Her mind screamed at her to stop, to think logically, but her body moved of its own accord, seeking with breathless curiosity the moment when she would be completely a woman.

He sensed the change in her emotions and redoubled his efforts until she was moaning with pleasure, her hands moving over his back with light, feathery touches, her eyes closed in an attitude of surrender. She started as his fingers moved up her thighs and found her center, working their magic so completely that her legs seemed to turn to jelly. She was too warm, and she tossed her head from side to side, her mind beseeching him to satisfy this excited anticipation that was nearly too much to bear.

"Captain—" The address seemed ridiculous now. "Rafe, please," she whispered. She looked up to see his face above her, the eyes black with desire as he gazed at her silently. "Please," she repeated, moving her hips against him, ashamed of her invitation but not able to stop it.

He smiled with the familiar mockery. "Please? Why, kitten, I only suspected the fires in you, it seems. Tell me what you want." He was taunting her.

"I—I don't know."

"Yes, you do, kitten. Tell me."

Gabrielle struggled against the humiliation, hating him for bringing her to this. "Don't tease me," she whispered, glad of the darkness that hid her blushing cheeks.

Still he continued to play with her, bringing her back again and again to the peak of excitement until she felt exhausted.

"Stop it! You're—you're being cruel!" she shouted at him, beginning to fight again.

She took him unawares and landed a crackling slap against his cheek. He stiffened against her, his body flattening until it felt like a slab of iron on top of her. His hands caught hers and pressed them back behind her head.

"Let me go! I hate you!" she spat at him.

"You hate me, but your body invites me to continue,

kitten. Damn, but I can feel how moist you are, how ready," he mocked her.

"You—you did this d-deliberately, to—to humiliate me," Gabrielle was crying now, hating herself as much as she hated him. Tears wetted the pillow as she turned her head away from his lips.

He forced it back and took her lips with unexpected savagery. "You'll get what you want, kitten. Sheathe your claws, my love."

Gabrielle felt his knees between her thighs, forcing them wide, as he poised himself for a moment, then drove into her. A startled cry escaped her as she felt the pressure within her, building up until she thought she would burst.

"You're—you're hurting me!" she cried, her body once more rigid with shock.

"Just for a moment. Relax, my sweet."

He continued his attack, and Gabrielle felt a slow pain grasp her between the legs along with a sudden moistness, even as he buried himself deep within her. They lay unmoving for a moment, Gabrielle gasping for air as her breasts rose and fell rapidly. His head lay on her shoulder and his body began to move again. Gabrielle tried to move away from him, her thighs clenching from the unaccustomed ache.

"No, no!" she pleaded.

"It will be better now," he murmured in her ear, his movements becoming more rapid.

An unbearable tension began building up within her, and Gabrielle waited breathlessly for release, sighing deeply as it finally came. It was true, she thought grudgingly, there was no more pain, just a tiny ache as he continued to move, building up to his climax.

He brought her back to that now-familiar anticipation, and she arched her back, moving her hips, meeting his thrusts until the release came again, for him, too. She lay back, her muscles relaxing as she closed her eyes in her pleasure. A long moan escaped her, and she felt his mouth on hers again.

"Contented?" she heard him say, a trace of insolence in his voice.

She refused to be drawn to the bait and remained silent, letting him have his way with her as he caressed her slowly and expertly. He slipped to her side and pulled her against him, her face turned into his shoulder.

Suddenly she felt terribly sleepy and totally exhausted. She felt his lips in her hair but was too tired to fight him any more and snuggled closer to his hard, lean frame.

Chapter Eight

Gabrielle awoke slowly the next morning, curling herself tightly and then stretching out luxuriously as she allowed herself a huge yawn of well-being. But her sense of comfort did not last long as the memory of the previous night gradually crowded into her consciousness—that, and the slight tenderness she still felt in certain areas of her body.

With growing panic, she opened her eyes wide and searched the room for any signs of her erstwhile companion. But, to her intense relief, she saw no one in the sparsely furnished room. She remembered now that he had said he was leaving on the first post to Brest, and so he must have slipped away before she awakened.

She was surprised he had not disturbed her sleep, for she could easily imagine the smug look of satisfied victory on his face. She cringed from the picture, nearly letting herself sink into self-pity. How she hated him! The physical evidence of his victory had stained the sheets a dark brown, but that she would not allow herself to think of. Still, it annoyed her to think that she had submitted so passionately to his demands. A dangerously clever man, she had to admit, for he had turned her surrender into a sensual passion of need, if not a complete willingness.

The humiliation caused her cheeks to burn and she buried her head in the pillow, only to take it out again at the sound of uneven footsteps in the hallway outside the door. Had he come back? She bit her lip in an agony of embarrassment, pulling the sheets over her shoulders. She could not endure another meeting with him! She waited, watching as the handle turned slowly and the door opened.

"Ma'm'selle!" Chloë stood, blinking in disbelief at the sight of her mistress.

"Chloë! What—what are you doing here?" Gabrielle half-whispered, wondering if she was dreaming.

Chloë's eyes took in the rumpled bed covers and the other evidence of the night's activities. She gulped audibly. "Oh, ma'm'selle. I—I, that is, a note was delivered to the house early this morning. A boy brought it to the door, and it said that I should come fetch you at this address."

"And—and what is this address?" Gabrielle demanded sharply.

Chloë blinked again and looked at the other girl oddly. "Why, it is right next door to M'sieur Alexandre's house. You mean, you did not know?"

Gabrielle struggled to keep her composure in the face of the maid's stare. Damn that man! Damn him for playing such a despicable trick on her! Her increasing anger effectively wiped out any remaining embarrassment, and she thought of calling for the police to track down the rogue. But the futility of such a gesture struck her immediately, and she did not want her name bandied about in public as being a woman raped by a callous American pirate. She blushed at the thought and realized, with a wealth of bitterness, that the captain was no fool—how he must be laughing now!

She slipped out of the bed, careful not to reveal the bloodstained mattress. Her ruse, though, was fruitless, and she knew the maid was well aware of what had happened.

"Oh, ma'm'selle!" Chloë sighed, clapping her hands delightedly. "You and the handsome captain!" She glowed as she helped her mistress into her chemise, which was sadly torn along the neckline.

"Chloë! You will say nothing of this to anyone else. Do you understand?"

"Of course, ma'm'selle. I daresay, M'sieur Alexandre would be furious, would he not? But, of course, when the captain returns to ask for your hand—"

Gabrielle turned to her so swiftly that the maid took a step backward.

"The captain will *not* be returning, Chloë!"

Chloë was taken aback by her mistress's vehemence. As soon as they had returned home, Gabrielle said, her voice breaking slightly in a nervous little rush, "I want you to go back to the house next door and take the sheets from the bed and bring them back here. Also, take this dress I have on and—and destroy it along with the sheets."

Gabrielle saw her maid's eyes grow round. "Oh, no! ma'm'selle, the dress is much too beautiful—and expensive! Surely, you cannot—"

"Chloë! You will do as I have requested!"

The maid hung her head and took the gown from her mistress as soon as Gabrielle had taken it off. Immediately, Gabrielle called for a bath and she was soon covered with bubbles, hoping that the soothing, scented water would take her mind off the previous night. She rubbed at her skin until it was grew pink from her roughness. She scrubbed her breasts, unmindful of the hurt. Hadn't they betrayed her last night? She washed her hair vigorously, seeking to rid it of *his* odor of tobacco and leather and man's sweat.

Stubbornly, she lifted her chin, hating the knowledge that *he* had been able to walk away from their brief encounter without qualms, without fears, without memories.

How dare she let herself wallow in this pit of self-pity and self-hatred—she would not give him the satisfaction!

Gabrielle stepped out of the bath and rubbed herself with the soft, fluffy towel the maid had left for her. She would simply not go to pieces. She had too much pride for that, surely.

But her pride was sorely tried at the return of Chloë, who came into the room, looking at her doubtfully, her hands held behind her back as though she would hide something from her.

"What is it?" she demanded, her voice sharper.

Chloë shook her head slowly, and Gabrielle saw that her cheeks were bright red with embarrassment.

"What is it?" she demanded, her voice sharper.

"Oh, ma'm'selle, I—I did as you told me and went back to the house to take the sheets from the bed and—and under the pillow—I found—I found. . . ."

"Yes?" Gabrielle prompted although she already knew that she did not want to know.

Silently, the maid brought out her hands and opened them, revealing ten brightly glittering gold pieces that seemed suddenly to swim before Gabrielle's eyes. So, he had paid her for her services like any other cheap, dockside prostitute, she thought in agony. And to be shamed, thus, in front of her own maid was nearly too much to bear.

Her small laugh was filled with bitterness as she waved the money away. "Keep them, Chloë. So you see how things really are between the captain and me," she said, her voice heavy with humiliation.

"Oh, ma'm'selle, it was cruel of him to—to cheapen such a—"

Gabrielle motioned her to silence. "I'm afraid, Chloë, that the captain does not care much for sentimentality, nor even for respect or consideration."

Listlessly she chose a gown from her wardrobe and prepared herself to go downstairs. She was well aware that she must make an appearance today, for Alexandre would be anxious to hear how the evening had turned out. She would have to count on Chloë's silence and hope that she, herself, would be able to act with some semblance of normalcy. She descended the stairs, hoping to catch Alexandre alone. Such was not to be the case, for to her dismay, Charles was with his father.

"Good morning, my dear," Alexandre smiled at her, coming over to raise her hand to his lips. He tried to study her face, but Gabrielle carefully veiled the expression in her eyes. "I trust you enjoyed yourself last night?"

Gabrielle nodded silently.

"I must confess, my dear, I—I was worried about you," he went on. "I believe it was quite late when you returned home, for I fell asleep waiting for you."

"Yes, it—it was quite late, Alexandre. There was no need for you to wait." Gabrielle felt her mouth tremble ever so slightly. She knew Charles was watching her surreptitiously, and she wished now to escape.

"I'm pleased you had an enjoyable evening," Alexandre was continuing nervously. "I—I must admit I had my doubts as to Savage's integrity, but it seems as though I underestimated your ability to handle him, child."

Every word he uttered seemed to send barbs deeper into her, and Gabrielle shifted on her feet, uncomfortable in the face of Charles' continued staring.

There was a sudden, complete silence in the room as Alexandre could find no more pleasantries to say, and Gabrielle's throat was too dry for her to contribute anything else to the conversation. Charles, his eyes never leaving her face, moved over to where she had seated herself on a chair.

"I'm sure M'sieur Savage was sufficiently charming, father, to keep our guest entertained throughout the evening."

Gabrielle did not comment at this unexpected utterance, nor did Charles seem to expect any.

"I'm curious, though, as to why you allowed him—a stranger—to escort you to a dinner party, Gabrielle. Surely, you were a trifle hasty in your—selection of evening partners?"

Alexandre cleared his throat a little nervously, and Gabrielle could not keep from blushing. She exchanged a glance with the older man, then met Charles' level stare, wondering why he was badgering her this way.

"Captain Savage is—is a friend of your father's, Charles. He saved your life the night you were stabbed."

"A friend of my father's, you say? How curious that an American sea captain would be on friendly terms with a marquis of France, wouldn't you agree, Gabrielle?"

Gabrielle stared at him, wondering, with a chill of premonition in her heart, if Charles had somehow found out about the smuggling. How could he? Unless—unless he had overheard a conversation between herself and Alexandre? Or, perhaps he had come across some papers in his father's desk? There was nothing for her to say, and she waited in trepidation for his next probe.

"Charles, I can't think why you are cross-examining our guest," Alexandre put in suddenly, striving to keep his voice under control. "She must be tired from her late night out."

Charles hesitated and turned a look of ill-disguised disgust on his father. Gabrielle held her breath, hoping not to be witness to a confrontation between father and son in such a personal matter. Quickly she stood up from her seat and made a small curtsy of departure.

"I—I have a few things I must attend to," she said by way of explanation, and she made a hurried retreat from the room, unmindful of Charles' knowing laughter or the look of consternation on Alexandre's face that seemed a portent of things to come.

Chapter Nine

It was fortunate for Gabrielle that she was so caught up in the preparations for Isabel's wedding that she had no time to brood on what had happened to her, nor on

Charles' increasingly curious attitude towards her. At times he seemed genuinely interested in her activities. Yet he also seemed to be watching her like a cat, waiting for the right moment to spring the trap.

With a determined effort, Gabrielle had shaken off any melancholy memories of her night of seduction with Rafe Savage. After all, she reminded herself steadfastly, he was gone now and she would certainly never see him again. She had not told Isabel about the experience, realizing that Isabel had much too much to contend with already. If she had not been so busy, she might have guessed at the change in Gabrielle for Isabel had an uncanny faculty for ferreting out the truth. But as it was, Gabrielle was thankful that for the moment Isabel guessed nothing.

June burst into full flower, bringing with it a lazy heat and balmy breezes that were hardly conducive to making all the preparations for a grand wedding. But Gabrielle set about with considerable vigor helping Isabel and on the morning of the wedding, she awoke with excitement.

She rang for Chloë and stretched languidly, eyeing the clock to check on the time. The wedding was arranged for twelve noon and it was now a little past eight o'clock. She would have to get up presently for her bath. She glanced at the dress she would be wearing today and sighed with pleasure at the artistry of M'sieur LeRoy. The gown was a shimmering silk, in a soft shade of spring green that rippled through its diaphanous folds like a shaded woodland stream. The décolletage was low and squared with a double row of Belgian lace ruffles edging it, and there were tiny puffed sleeves. A wide sash ran beneath the breasts and tied coquettishly in the back, its ends trailing just below the hemline. There was a train fastened at the waist which would be taken off for dancing.

She gazed out the window, filled with gladness that this was going to be a beautiful day.

Nothing could go wrong on such a day, and the thought brought her comfort and a sense of well-being that had been missing until now.

"Ma'm'selle looks truly beautiful this morning. I am much afraid that you will outshine the bride," Chloë said.

Gabrielle laughed. "Oh, no, Chloë. Isabel will be more radiant than I this day, but I do feel wonderful. I think I shall want some of that heavenly perfume that Alexandre presented to me last night. Pour some in my bath water."

As Chloë obeyed, the room was filled with the delicious scent of honeysuckle and roses, and Gabrielle lay for almost an hour in the tub, luxuriating in the scented warmth. When she was finished, Chloë toweled her dry and slipped her chemise over her head. Its silkiness caressed her skin, and Gabrielle wriggled sensuously, pulling on her silk stockings with practiced hands and tying the embroidered garters with a flourish.

She sat at the dressing table as Chloë worked patiently on the thick coils of her hair, brushing it so that it shone like burnished bronze. She arranged it high on her head, sprinkling brilliants with careless abandon in between the curls. Only the bride would wear her hair down this day, and Gabrielle could picture Isabel's dark, shining tresses, curling softly at her shoulders. Yes, she knew Isabel would make a beautiful bride, and the thought came to her, unbidden, that Isabel would be beautiful even though her body had known many men. Another thought followed—that she herself was lovely, too, and that knowing a man did not necessarily make one old and ugly. The conclusion gave her strength and the beginnings of inner peace.

The drive to Isabelle's house was short, but even before they reached it Gabrielle felt a light film of perspiration like a veil on her arms and shoulders. She wiped her skin with a handkerchief and alighted from the carriage to hurry into the comparative coolness of the house.

Isabel was upstairs, putting the finishing touches to her toilet, for once nervous and unsure of herself.

"Oh, my hair," she wailed, tugging ineffectually at it with a brush. "Gabrielle, you know how it tangles in this heat."

"Calm yourself, for goodness' sake, Isabel, or you'll be weeping down the aisle," Gabrielle interjected, secretly amused at her friend's unusual lack of composure. She could not imagine Isabel as anything but her calm, cool self. But then she supposed marriage did that to one. She said as much to Isabel, while the latter bit her lip in exasperation as she attempted to pin a large white camellia in her dark hair.

"Oh, you can say that," she said, in answer to Gabrielle's comment. *"You're* not the one getting married, but just you wait, Gabrielle. Some day, it will be you in this position, and I won't offer you an ounce of sympathy."

She cast a sober look at the other girl, her eyes going moodily over the shining coils of hair, the gleaming whiteness of her shoulders, the tiny waist. "And look at you! Standing there as unruffled as I should be—and, what is worse, looking lovelier than ever! Gabrielle, I should positively hate you if you were anyone else!"

Gabrielle laughed good-naturedly and picked up the brush the maid had set down. "Let me brush your hair for a moment. It may soothe you and, besides, you know perfectly well that Henri will have eyes for no one but you today."

With two maids working swiftly and competently, Isabel was soon dressed, and both girls were safely ensconced in their carriages on their way to the church. They arrived at Notre-Dame with some minutes to spare, although the courtyard was already crowded with cabriolets, carriages, and hired chaises. Isabel pointed excitedly to a large, imposing carriage that bore the imperial eagle.

"The emperor," Madame de Montfort noted calmly, "I knew he would come. After all, they say he tries constantly to conceive a son on his Austrian broodmare. But who would pay homage to the boy if his father did not honor the ancient blood in his court."

As maid of honor, Gabrielle was expected, along with three other young ladies of good family, to hold Isabel's

long train. It would take that many attendants to keep
the enormously long, heavy material straight, and Gabrielle trembled with pride as she lifted a portion of the
satin in her hands while Isabel readied herself to walk
down the long aisle.

The two girls looked gravely at one another one last
time before walking out into the huge church. Gabrielle
felt herself very nearly on the verge of tears, and she
reached forward spontaneously to hug her friend.

Music, laughter, and the buzzing of conversation lasted
far into the evening at the home of the de Montforts.
Commoners and simple folk tried to peer in the windows
if they could manage to slip past the guards at the gate
and struggle between the closely packed carriages. They
could hardly believe their eyes as they gazed first at the
lovely, bejeweled ladies and gentlemen of the court and
then at the splendor of the decorations which included
fresh flowers everywhere, even strewn aimlessly on the
dancing floor—and a huge, sparkling fountain of wine
that shone ruby-red under the light of a thousand candles.

All these pleasant images stayed in Gabrielle's mind
as she and Alexandre seated themselves in their carriage
for the drive home. It had been a perfect wedding. She
had not lacked for dancing partners and had noted the
unusual enthusiasm on Charles' face, attributing it to the
presence of his commanding offcer, Murat. He had seemed
to watch her throughout the dancing but had made no
attempt to be seen with her. The look on his face could
almost be called conspiratorial, she thought, and she felt
an odd shiver pass through her.

Riding home with Alexandre, Gabrielle was contented.
She had received a letter from her aunt, informing her
that she had decided to take the vows of poverty, chastity,
and obedience with the good sisters. Somehow, Gabrielle
could not quite visualize her sturdy aunt as a nun devoted
to God and good works, but she accepted the decision
with something like relief, glad that Aunt Louise had
found something that would give meaning to her life.

Alexandre seemed to be watching her thoughtfully. "Happy, my dear?"

Gabrielle smiled. "Yes, I'm so glad that Isabel's wedding turned out to be perfect. It was all that she deserved."

As soon as they returned home, Gabrielle excused herself to go up to her room. She had only been there a few moments when there was the noise of several horses in the courtyard and sounds associated with a soldier's boots and guns. Gabrielle looked out the window curiously, then hurried downstairs in sudden inexplicable alarm.

Alexandre was in the foyer and as their eyes met, she read the expression of fear on his face. "What is it, Alexandre?" she asked, her voice rising.

The majordomo had already opened the door, and six uniformed officers marched into the hallway where they bowed smartly. The officer in charge, a thin-faced man with a long nose and cruel lips stepped closer to Alexandre who stood as though about to be sentenced.

"M'sieur de Chevalier? Permit me—Lieutenant Michel Rué. I have come to inform you of your immediate arrest in the name of the emperor of France, against whom you have participated in treasonous acts. I must tell you that we are prepared to deal with any resistance."

Alexandre bowed his head. "Allow me to fetch my hat and cape, lieutenant." He started to leave the room, btu the officer's voice stopped him.

"Your ward, one Ma'm'selle de Beauvoir, will accompany you, marquis, as she will be necessary in the questioning."

"But she—she has nothing to do with it, I can assure you. She would be no help at all, lieutenant."

The officer motioned to one of men to follow Alexandre upstairs. "I have my orders," he said briefly.

Gabrielle, wide-eyed and trembling, thought she must be having some sort of nightmare.

"Please, ma'm'selle," the lieutenant was indicating that she should ready herself.

"But—but where are you taking me?" she asked with difficulty.

Lieutenant Rué half-smiled, but there was no humor in the sadistic twist of his lips. "Why, to the conciergerie, ma'm'selle."

Gabrielle gasped. "To the prison!" she repeated in disbelief. "But I have done nothing. We have only just come back from—"

"I am aware of your whereabouts earlier today," the officer cut in impatiently. "I can assure you, we were instructed to avoid any scandal to the de Montforts."

Gabrielle stared at him for another moment, but at his nod, she hurried to fetch her cape and scarf. Several soldiers waited outside and Lieutenant Rué dispatched them to surround the house and grounds with quick, clipped instructions. He and the six officers escorted the carriages, one of which would take Gabrielle to her destination and the other to carry Alexandre.

Gabrielle's heart sank when she realized that she would not have an opportunity to be alone with Alexandre. With a terrible dread she knew that this arrest had resulted from the authorities' somehow finding out about the smuggling business. But why she had been taken she didn't know.

Once they arrived at the prison, Gabrielle was led immediately through a doorway and into a large room that served to house the guards on duty. She followed a woman who appeared from another doorway and ushered her into a small, dark cell whose only window was so small that only a sad trickle of light could seep through to the inside. The stout metal door was shut with an ominous creaking, and she heard the key turn in the lock.

Once her eyes had become accustomed to the semigloom, Gabrielle could make out the bare essentials of the cell—the narrow cot, whose mattress was in a sad state of decay, the chamber pot, whose odor was worse than anything she had ever smelled, and a low stool that was placed in front of a table.

She felt tears gathering in her eyes. This was much worse than she had thought it would be, and she wondered if she could endure it for even a few hours.

After a wait that seemed like days, Gabrielle watched the thin blade of light go out in the window of the cell, and the darkness closed in around her. She could hear faint scurrying sounds and almost screamed when a small furry thing ran over her slipper. She huddled herself on the stool, feeling a desperate urge to run to the door and beat her fists on it and demand to be let out. But she knew that no one would come to her aid. It seemed they intended to keep her here for the night.

Gingerly, she walked to the cot and made herself lie down on it, feeling the metal beneath the mattress, cold and hard as stone. She slept fitfully, hearing the continued scampering of the rats and hoping they could not find her on the cot.

She awoke with her head aching and shivering from the cool moistness of the cell. The delicate fabric of the gown she had worn as maid of honor was no protection, and she wished she had thought to change. But then, how was she to know that she would have to spend the night in this awful place!

After some hours, the door was opened carefully and one of the guards pushed a tray of something towards her. Confused, Gabrielle stopped him.

"But why are you bringing me food—when—when I shall be leaving today?" At his lecherous grin, she shrank back. "I will—I will be leaving today, won't I?"

He shrugged. "Perhaps, perhaps not. They might forget you're here."

"Forget? But what about the man who was arrested with me?"

"They've called him before the tribunal—for smuggling." The man laughed and spat, missing her hemline by inches.

Gabrielle's hand went to her mouth. So—they *had* found out! But—but how? Alexandre had told her some time ago that he was quitting the operation. How had the authorities found out? Someone had informed on him! But who?

She must wait—wait until this was over, and then she would be able to find out what was going on. The officer had said that he was going to arrest her for questioning, so they would surely be calling her soon in order to interrogate her. Then she would be able to find out why they were keeping her here.

In the meantime, she must keep herself from falling apart in this black hole. She snatched at the tray on the floor. The contents nearly made her sick, but she forced herself to eat the greasy soup and the hard bread.

More days passed, so many that Gabrielle lost track of them, wondering if her mind were becoming unhinged. She could hardly believe that she was still locked up with no word either of Alexandre or from anyone who might be worrying about her. She forced herself to remain as calm as possible, but it took all her strength of will not to fling herself against the door and scream at the top of her lungs. When—when would she be told why she was being held here? And when would she be released?

Chapter Ten

At the rasping of the key in the lock, Gabrielle looked up dully, her mind barely registering the shadowy figure that stood in the doorway to her cell. She had been in her cell a whole month, and still no one had told her of Alexandre's whereabouts.

"Get up, girl. Lieutenant Rué wants to see you now."

Gabrielle struggled to fight down the nausea that engulfed her as she stood unsteadily on her feet. The guard grasped her arm roughly and pushed her out of the cell and down the hall, back through the guard room, and into the lieutenant's office.

"Ma'm'selle de Beauvoir, please be seated." The lieutenant motioned her to a chair, and Gabrielle took it silently.

"I can assure you, ma'm'selle, that I deplore such treatment as our prisoners must receive, but our accommodations are old and funds somewhat lacking." His thin face broke into an apologetic grin that did not reach his eyes.

"However much I do deplore these conditions here, there is nothing that can be done about them, so let us get on with the matter at hand."

"My release," Gabrielle said. She was surprised at the croak that was her voice.

The lieutenant's colorless eyes measured her as though he were taken aback by her lucidity. He folded his hands deliberately on top of his desk and set his mouth in a hard line.

"I'm afraid, ma'm'selle, that you are not at liberty to return to M'sieur de Chevalier's house." His eyes went over her, making her wince with their probing.

She could find nothing to say to him, nothing that could possibly convey her misery and humiliation. She noticed that he was nodding to someone—the woman who had led her to her cell upon her arrest.

"Berthe will take you to where you can bathe and change into a clean gown in order to appear before M'sieur Gall. If you will follow her, ma'm'selle?"

Gabrielle hesitated, wondering who this M'sieur Gall might be, but she was too tired to think about it for long, and she followed the woman to a cubicle where a tub of water was steaming. The woman placed a folded towel on a stool and waited for Gabrielle to undress so that she could take away the torn remnants of her gown.

Gabrielle immersed herself in the water with a pleasure so keen it brought tears to her eyes. She scrubbed herself thoroughly, only just finishing when she heard Berthe's footsteps coming through the door once again.

Berthe pulled back the screen and handed her a clean dress. Gabrielle quickly slipped the gown over her head, feeling the scratchy material against her skin; there was no chemise to be worn with the garment.

She followed the woman back to Lieutenant Rué's office, where he stood impatiently, his hand drumming loudly on the desk top. When he heard their footfalls, he seemed to brush at his uniform nervously.

"Follow me," he said abruptly to Gabrielle and led her into another room. As soon as she entered through the low door, a large black bag was thrown over her head, startling her so that she did not even cry out. Something hard hit her alongside the head, and she whirled down into blackness even as she felt someone catching her limp body and flinging it over his shoulder.

"For Christ's sake, man! Did you have to hit her so hard? Now she's got an ugly lump at her temple which isn't going to raise the price any!"

Drifting back to consciousness, Gabrielle heard the man's voice, and it seemed to her so familiar that she moved without volition towards the sound of it. The bag had been removed from her head and she felt rough hands examining the knot at her temple. She flinched as they pressed down on the lump.

"Well, no matter, get what you can out of her." The words were uttered without mercy, with no feeling at all.

The early morning sun lit up the harbor of a bustling city as Gabrielle looked out of the window of the carriage she had been confined to for two days' travelling. A man jumped down from the seat and helped her out, prodding her in the back towards a large, square building that looked to be some sort of warehouse. They passed through a door that someone unlocked from the inside.

"Good work, Turpin. M'sieur Gall has been waiting for this one. He will see you in his office and make payment for your employer." The man who spoke indicated that she was to follow him, and he led her to a bare, small room where he told her to sit quietly on a stool. He clapped his hands twice, loudly, and two enormously tall men with shaved heads entered the room and stood on either side of her so that she felt dwarfed between them.

She waited anxiously, not daring to look up at either of her two sentinels.

"Gabrielle de Beauvoir?"

The voice came from behind her, and Gabrielle was so startled that she jumped up from the stool and turned her head in the direction of the voice before two pairs of strong hands pressed her back to her seat. A tall, dark-haired man walked in front of her, his fingers brushing his chin as though trying to make up his mind about something.

"Do you know where you are?" he asked her swiftly.

She shook her head, then looked up into his swarthy face. "I've been told nothing." She hesitated, then plunged on. "Please, please, m'sieur, you must tell me what this is all about. I was held in prison for a month—"

"A month? I suppose he thought to gentle you. People, especially women, are notoriously easier to break once they have tasted the hell of a prison cell. The idea that they might be sent back there causes them to do anything to escape such a fate. Have you not found this out for yourself, ma'm'selle?"

The question was uttered softly, but Gabrielle had the distinct impression that it was meant as a threat. "I—I don't know what you're talking about. All I know is that no one would tell me where Alexandre is or what has happened to him. No one has told me anything."

"Then I will tell you, ma'm'selle. My name is Julien Gall and my profession is a lucrative one—I deal in slaves, ma'm'selle, slaves of all kinds. You are in my warehouse in Marseilles, and you have been sold to me."

"Sold!" Gabrielle's eyes widened in incredulity. "Sold like a—a slave. But, surely, there has been some mistake. I am Gabrielle de Beauvoir—my father was a marquis of France! I am under the protection of the Marquis de Chevalier! You cannot do this to me!"

"I'm afraid that it has already been done," he answered quietly.

"By whom? Who would do such a thing? Why?" The questions were piling up inside her head, and she thought she might scream with the frustration and fear. Who had the right to sell her to this slave trader? Hadn't she been arrested by the authorities in order to be questioned about the smuggling venture? Surely Lieutenant Rué would not have the authority—or the audacity—to have her sold to this man without a trial! Why would he have done it? She had done nothing. Nothing!

She was aware that the two giants were holding her arms now on either side, pulling her up from the stool so that she could stand in front of the slave trader who was looking at her with a practiced eye. She hated the expression of inhuman interest on his face that told her so clearly she was not being looked at as a woman but as a piece of merchandise.

He nodded casually to the two giants, and in a flat voice he commanded: "Strip her."

"Oh, no!" she cried out and proceeded to struggle against this final outrage. The two guards, expert at their job, held her firmly, but not so hard that they would leave marks on her flesh. It was a simple enough task to rip the gown from her body, and, as she had been given no underclothing, she was instantly naked to his gaze, her dress crumpled in a pile around her ankles.

She shrank from his probing glance, pulling back to the limits of her arms as the two men continued to hold her, not looking at her, like twin molded statues. Julien Gall's hand reached out to feel the smoothness of her skin, to test the weight of her proud, young breasts, to trace the line of her hip.

He clapped his hands twice and the two giants pulled her, protesting, from the room and down a dark hall that led into several other rooms. She was thrust, still naked, into a room by herself. She did not have long to wait before the door was opened and Julien Gall stepped inside without his two assistants.

"I will arrange your passage on one of my ships." His voice was the same, flat and uncaring. "You and some fifty others will be put on board the *Lillias* to be sold at port somewhere in the West Indies, possibly Jamaica or Cuba."

"I have no taste for being sold like—like an animal!" she lashed out in despair.

He shrugged. "That is your misfortune, ma'm'selle."

He moved towards her, and Gabrielle backed away, hardly daring to put her fears into thoughts, for the look on his face was unmistakable. He was going to take her—sample the cargo for himself, she thought in a rage. She cried out, but it was too late, and she choked back a sob as he pushed her backwards to the bed.

PART TWO

The Pirate

Chapter Eleven

On October 15, Gabrielle and some fifty other women were taken aboard the ship, the *Lillias,* a cargo vessel. It would stop first in Haiti, and then on to the English port of Jamaica where she and the others would be disposed of like contraband bales of hay or barrels of salt pork, she thought bitterly.

After the first two weeks, when the newness had somewhat worn off, Gabrielle took little interest in the running of the ship, although she still marvelled at the dextrous agility the sailors displayed when trimming the sails and shinnying up the tall masts. During the women's exercise periods, she would gaze out at the sea and think of what lay ahead for her. She would stroll quietly in the line of women, joyful to feel the sun on her face, the breeze in her hair, before she must go back down into the hold of damp wood and unbearable stench which served to house the women with the rest of the cargo.

Gabrielle was grateful for the attraction she perceived in Jacques Andrès, the ship's physician, for it was evident that he enjoyed her company. She found herself looking forward to his visits; he would talk to her when she came above board, and he even risked the stench and the insults he would receive when he came down to the hold.

He tried to tell her something of the islands, advising her that as they neared the Caribbean the weather would begin to get hot and laughing at Gabrielle's incredulity. It was nearly November, she would protest, but she realized that as the days went by it did, indeed, seem to be warming up. And with the additional warmth, there came another torment for the women, for the hold became almost an oven during the day, and the captain had to increase the exercise periods or risk losing more of his cargo to the heat. The hold was washed down with bucketfuls of water, which rose in steam from the boards, making an even worse hell for the prisoners.

Gabrielle looked forward to her usual walks with the other prisoners—anything to get out of the hold, which was as hot as an oven by midday. She was glad to feel the wind fanning her hot cheeks and looked with delight at the deep blue-green of the sea where a school of brightly striped sea bass swam by, followed by a pair of dolphins that jumped high in the air and arched gracefully back into the water.

Dr. Andrès joined her often during these exercise periods, and it was on one of these occasions, as the two stood side by side at the ship's railing, that another nightmare began.

"Ship sighted to port!"

The cry from the crow's nest alarmed Gabrielle, and she saw the look of concern on Jacques' face as he gazed out to sea.

"Bearing fast. Three-masted and sleek! Twelve guns on her!"

The cry was followed swiftly by another. "Second ship to starboard—sixteen guns!"

Gabrielle could feel the sudden tenseness flowing through Jacques' body and communicating itself to her own. She looked in the direction the sailor had indicated and was able to see a speck on the horizon, and then another, both of which seemed to loom larger every second, until she could make out the three spindly masts on the two ships' decks.

"She's a pirate vessel—a privateer, as they like to call themselves," Jacques whispered beneath his breath, indicating one of the ships.

She heard a sailor agreeing. "Sailing under letters of marque they've made up themselves, no doubt."

"Oh, Jacques, what will they do?" she whispered.

He put his arm around her shoulders and hurried her to the hatchway and down the steps. "They most likely will want to see if we are carrying anything of value," he answered briefly once they were in his cabin.

She watched, not understanding, as he pulled the bed-clothes down and let them spill over the bunk.

"If they do come aboard—" and he stopped, noticing the increased fear in her eyes, "if they do," he repeated, "it is better that they do not find out there are women aboard. I want you to be safe, Gabrielle. Crawl under the bunk and make yourself as small as you can. I'll throw the blankets over it so that they hang down and cover you, if someone should look in here."

"Oh, Jacques, you don't really think they would. . . ." Gabrielle's voice faltered, and she looked up at him for reassurance.

After she had crawled under the bunk, she heard his footsteps and the closing of the door. She strained to hear more, but all seemed deathly quiet. She could only listen with growing anxiety to the pounding of her own heart and the labored breathing that she could not control. It was dark underneath the bunk, and she was pressed, out of necessity, close to the side of the ship. It seemed she had lain there for hours, and her legs felt as though she would suffer cramps if her position were enforced much longer.

Then, suddenly, with a frightening explosion, a cannon roared and a ball ripped through the side of the ship. Gabrielle, with her ear to the floor, could hear shouts and cries coming from the hold of the ship and felt a rush of pity for the women in the hold. Captain Gaston must have stationed several men below to pump out water should the hold begin to fill up. With a fateful clarity, she realized that she, too, would die if the ship went under.

The explosion was followed by another cannon ball and then another. She heard the creaking of the mast as it toppled to the deck and then the shouts and screams that issued from the deck. She felt sick at the thought of human bodies crushed beneath the stout oak of the mast.

A sudden, shuddering bump testified that the enemy ship had drawn alongside. The privateer crew must be boarding the *Lillias*. In the next minute, she felt all her hopes leave her as she heard the clash of sabers and the explosions of pistol shots. The pirates were not even going to give the crew a chance to surrender! She heard the frantic footsteps above her and wondered what was going to happen next.

More booted feet sounded above her—and then poured through the hatchway and down to the hold. The uproar was at its height, and she could not make out who the screams were coming from. Muskets fired and metal clashed and men cried in agony. She could hear the women in the hold screaming against reports from pistols.

Gabrielle huddled against the wall, nearly out of her wits with terror. She heard men bawling orders to other men and quick footsteps coming up from the blackness of the hold. They were transporting the cargo from the hold of the *Lillias* to their own ship, she guessed, but the fate of the women prisoners she did not even think about. She continued to listen to the never ending footsteps that descended and then ascended from the hold. Every time they passed her door, she tensed for the inevitable opening of it. She waited for agonizing minutes, still straining for the sound of a familiar voice, despite her certainty that she would never hear another one again.

Perhaps they only came for the cargo and have decided to let the crew go, she thought. But her hopes died quickly as she caught the smell of burning wood. It took her several seconds to realize that they were burning the ship!

Within minutes, the smoke was thick within the cabin and, in panic, she struggled from underneath the bunk and, coughing and choking, raced out the door into the hatchway which was already full of dense smoke. She dashed up the steps and looked back, realizing that they must have started the fire deep in the hold after the cargo had been emptied. Women's screams, curses, and agonized calls filled her ears, but it was too late to save any of her fellow prisoners.

On deck, she looked around dazedly, her eyes sick with

horror at the sight of men strewn about the deck, maimed, dead, and some still living, but so horribly wounded that it would be a mercy when the smoke choked them to death. She looked in vain for Jacques and ran up to the poop deck, dodging the hands of a greedy pirate whose jaw had slackened in surprise at the sight of her.

On the bridge, she could see a black-clothed figure barking orders to the lingering pirates, his sword still held lightly in his hand, deeply stained with blood. She continued to search the ship for Jacques, stepping over bodies and shrinking in horror as hands reached feebly for her. She dashed the tears from her eyes, tears that were caused as much from the smoke as her sorrow, for the black clouds were spilling out from the hold with increasing volume. There was not much time left before the ship would be swallowed forever by the sea, and she with it.

At last she spied the beige breeches and leather jerkin that Jacques had been wearing when he hid her under the bunk, but now they were spattered with blood. He was lying against the railing closest to the privateer whose name she could barely read through the haze of smoke— the *Golden Serpent*. A sea serpent that had brought fear and death and disaster, she thought in impotent rage.

She knelt beside Jacques' prone body. For a moment he did not recognize her, and as gently as she could, she wiped the blood-tinged spittle from his mouth with a piece of her petticoat. His eyes focused with a determined effort, and she saw the sadness filling them at the sight of her.

"Punctured lung," Jacques said breathlessly. "It's no good, Gabrielle. Save yourself!"

Gabrielle fought back the urge to scream at him that there was no place for her to hide now—no place that was safe against the enormous ocean that would be their final grave. She stroked his hair with a trembling hand and willed herself not to break down into useless tears.

"It's all right, Jacques," she murmured.

She crouched next to him, waiting for death. A sound caught her ear and she glanced up to see the man in black she had observed before on the bridge passing near her.

With brimming hate in her eyes, she glared at him, her head held proudly back on her neck. "Let him kill me now," she thought, "so that I need not fear the end any longer."

With the deep contempt that only the dying can hold for their tormentors, she spat at his feet. "I commit you to the devil!" she cried out at him.

He stopped suddenly to turn and look at her, and Gabrielle thought he truly did look like the devil himself with his black hair and jet-black eyes. With the smoke billowing about him, he could have been Satan within his lair, she thought cynically.

He laughed hoarsely at her. "Would you wait here to be roasted, my lovely?" he asked in English, and suddenly he had bent down to her and was catching her around the waist.

She struggled in outrage as she found herself held tightly against him. He caught at the grappling rope that was curled around the mast rigging, and, still holding her tightly, he swung himself across the widening expanse of water and landed, catlike, on his feet, allowing her to drop ignominiously to the deck.

"A good feat, captain," said one of his crew sourly, "but what do you propose to do with the woman?"

The man laughed again and caught her up in his arms. "Do with her? Why, I intend to bed her, what do you think?" he mocked the other.

Gabrielle blushed hotly and struggled vehemently in his grasp.

"Looks as though the lady has other plans," another of the crew laughed.

Gabrielle was caught between two powerful emotions: horrified disbelief that these same men, who had committed others to death such a short time before, could laugh so freely, and her intense loathing of this captain, who was fondling her boldly before the avid eyes of his crew. She still could not believe that she was not actually going to drown on the fired ship, that she had been snatched, so to speak, from the yawning orifice of death on the whim of a pirate.

"The captain has never yet been bested by a wench," another man said, winking at his leader who, with no more words spoken, walked with a struggling Gabrielle to his cabin on the bridge and plopped her down unceremoniously on his bed like a sack of booty.

He hooked his thumbs in his belt and stood with his legs apart, eyeing her with that unwinking black gaze that seemed to take her in from head to heels. "Be glad I rescued you from that burning ship, little dove.

"I cannot be grateful to a man who is a pirate and kills innocent men and women. I only hope that you have the decency to put me ashore at the nearest port."

His laugh jarred her nerves. "How very obliging that would be," he agreed. "I'm sure, my lovely, that you are not in the slightest aware that I seldom take any prisoners from a quarry ship. A woman's tears have been wasted on me too frequently for them to be of any consequence. But I must say, your outraged pride caught my eye, and I told myself that this once I would break my own rule—for your sake."

"Oh!" Gabrielle raged on, her eyes flashing. "Then I am to understand that you also murder innocent women without compunction. Perhaps you even add children to your heroic list of conquests!"

He shrugged. "Tell me, spitfire, how comes it that you are a passenger on a cargo ship? Such a vessel is hardly recommended for its luxurious accommodations. Were you, perhaps, the captain's mistress?" His dark eyebrows lifted sardonically at the haughty look of disdain she gave him.

"I am no man's mistress," she threw at him hotly. "I was—I was obliged to leave France quickly and I—"

He laughed at her sudden reticence. "I begin to understand now. So you are a fugitive! How you escaped the hold is a puzzlement, but what had you done to deserve such punishment as deportation? Stolen the purse from a stuffy old shopkeeper? Or have you gone after bigger game?" He turned away from her. "I'm afraid that you were too swift in commending me to the fires of hell, my fine lady. It's a shame, too, for I was hoping to gather a large ransom for your safe arrival."

Gabrielle proudly threw back her head. "I am Ma'm'selle Gabrielle de Beauvoir, daughter of a marquis of France. My family is dead, m'sieur, so it makes no difference to anyone if you kill me. But for Heaven's sake do it now so that I will not have to submit to your disgusting pleasures."

" 'Disgusting pleasures'?" He glanced boldly at her. "Why, such thoughts never entered my mind," he said smoothly. "I had more in mind to tie you to one of the cannon and have you whipped for your waspish tongue!"

Gabrielle's eyes widened, then narrowed, darkening perceptibly. "Do what you will and be quick then. But before I die, I would like to know the name of the man I shall curse with my last breath!"

He bowed and smiled dangerously at her. "You have the extreme good fortune, ma'm'selle, of speaking to Jean Lafitte!"

Chapter Twelve

"Land ho!"

Gabrielle craned her neck in order to see anything of the narrow stretch of purple that she could distinctly make out now on the horizon. She drew away from the aperture and paced about the room in nervous agitation.

Jean Lafitte had kept her locked in his cabin for over a week while the ship had set its course for the port of New Orleans and, more specifically, for his headquarters, as he called it, in Barataria Bay. He had dined with her a few times but had not attempted to force himself on her in any way, and she had been surprised and extremely relieved when, upon awakening each morning, she still found herself quite alone in the big bed. Of course, he was in and out of the cabin many times during the day, usually with his Italian navigator or American first mate. She had realized that his crew was made up of an odd assortment of all nationalities.

His threat to have her flogged had never been repeated, but she found his total dismissal of her almost as irksome. She would still awaken at night, sweating, her mouth open in a soundless scream, as she fought off a nightmare from the firing of the *Lillias*. She had wept bitterly, and her resentment grew against the perpetrator of the deed.

She wondered what plans Lafitte had made for her and told herself that at least she was going to be kept alive. She had found out through eavesdropping and piecing together bits of information gleaned from the navigator, Antonio, that Lafitte's whole purpose in pirating the cargo vessel, or any cargo vessel, was to sell the merchandise for his own gain at a low price in New Orleans, where the people flocked to his auctions. Antonio had even told her that they took a great many black slave ships in order to sell the Africans at bargain prices in places where the selling of slaves had been outlawed. If the merchandise were in prime or near-prime condition, Lafitte stood to make four hundred dollars from the sale of each male slave and up to three hundred and fifty dollars from each female.

Gabrielle was sickened at the talk of dealing in human merchandise, for what kind of leniency could she expect from such a man? She had learned that Jean Lafitte and his brother, Pierre, lived much of the time on Grande Terre island, in spite of its name a very small island located at the mouth of Barataria Bay some forty miles south of the city of New Orleans. They made numerous trips to the city in order to dispose of cargo and see to the running of their warehouse just outside the town. While there, they walked about as bold as you please, in broad daylight.

"Those women think Lafitte is a devilish handsome man," Antonio confided, "and they nigh throw themselves at his feet."

Gabrielle found his words hard to believe. Surely everyone knew he was a pirate and a murderer, didn't they?

Antonio shrugged, commenting that in this wild, new country, it really didn't make much difference what a man did for a living.

Gabrielle still refused to believe that any decent, law-abiding citizen could actually consider piracy a "decent living." She asked, curiously, if Lafitte was a married man, at which the navigator shook his head sadly, relating the tragic story of his captain's wife's death from childbirth during their escape from the slave-held city of Port-au-Prince in Haiti. According to Antonio, Lafitte wasn't very much interested in women and, in fact, was strangely indifferent to them.

Now, as the echoes of "Land ho!" filled the ship, she felt a new courage and resolve growing within her. She would escape from this Jean Lafitte and make her way to New Orleans, and the city would hold her future in glittering hands. She gazed out now, with eyes brilliant with excitement, as they neared the island, which she could see quite clearly in the distance.

She could hear Lafitte shouting orders to the crew as the ship turned towards a small pass that seemed hardly wide enough to allow the ship passage. The channel lay between two islands, one of which Gabrielle was sure must be Grande Terre; she could see other, smaller ships tied up against its shore. As they passed between the two islands, she held her breath, for surely the strait was not more than a quarter of a mile wide. But the ship glided through easily enough, and soon they had rounded the corner and Gabrielle saw that they were in a wide bay that was protected from the Gulf of Mexico by the two islands they had just passed.

The ship turned, and she could see the island of Grande Terre, which was bustling with exuberant activity, surprising her with all the people who seemed to be squeezed onto the small land mass. She could count several, possibly more than thirty warehouses, and there were fenced enclosures that reminded her incongruously of animal pens but seemed to serve as places to imprison the slaves, some of whom she could see, crouched in the dust. There was a structure that looked like a haphazardly erected fortress and numerous other dwellings. It was quite a thriving community.

Away from the island, she could catch glimpses of prize ships and large brigs that must belong to the other crews that Antonio had spoken of. He had told her that Lafitte actually had several lieutenants under him. His brother, Pierre, was one of them, although Antonio had complained that Pierre was more interested in food and women than hard work.

Gabrielle felt a lump of fearful excitement in her throat as the ship dropped anchor and she heard calls coming from the shore. She paced nervously and waited impatiently in the cabin, hoping that Lafitte would arrive soon to take her ashore. But would he take her ashore? she wondered suddenly, rushing to the window to look out at the crew, who were hurrying to the side to descend into long boats that would be rowed to the island.

She did not see Lafitte, and she wrung her hands in her skirt to lessen her tension. She could hear loud yells and cheering from the people on the island and thought, with disgust, that such a man did not deserve a hero's welcome. What would they have thought, she wondered, if they had been aboard the *Lillias*?

She jerked her head up at the sound of approaching footsteps, rising quickly to her feet and passing her hand through her hair. Lafitte stood, unsmiling, in the doorway, his eyes measuring her for a moment.

"Come with me," was all he said, and Gabrielle hurried after him, glad to be out of the cabin.

They went out on deck, where Gabrielle could see several men bringing up cargo from the hold of the ship.

She noted a solidly built man with broad shoulders and a strong, aquiline nose that reminded her a little of Lafitte, making his way towards them. He seemed perhaps two or three years older than Lafitte, who Antonio had already informed her was twenty-eight years old.

Lafitte saluted him, smiling. "Renato! Has everything been quiet while I've been gone?"

The man he addressed nodded his head, his eyes going to the girl beside his comrade. "Everything has gone well, Jean. With this cargo the warehouses here will be packed to bursting. We shall have to begin making the journey to New Orleans to transport some cargo there. I'll have to send word to Sauvinet to send out notices for the sale. But—" and he nodded towards Gabrielle, "—it seems, my friend, that you have brought home something with which I am at a loss to know what to do. Is she yours?"

Jean Lafitte shrugged at the question. "I'm afraid I made the mistake of rescuing her from one of our prizes, Renato." He smiled ruefully, and the other man laughed.

"Ah, Jean, don't tell me you have finally fallen under the spell of a female. Impossible—everyone will say so. And your brother, Pierre—I have the feeling that he may want her for himself as soon as she's cleaned up a little."

Gabrielle's face was mutinous as she glared at the stranger, and if it had not been for a restraining hand on her shoulder, she would have tried to claw his face.

"A spitfire!" Renato proclaimed in delight. "Ma'm'selle, may I present myself? Renato Beluche, at your service."

He bowed in pretended gallantry, and Gabrielle sprang out from under Lafitte's hand and tried to pummel Beluche's face with her clenched fists. Shrieking French at him, she felt two strong arms encircle her waist and lift her off her feet, so that she was dangling helpless, above the ground.

Lafitte shook her roughly. "Calm down, spitfire. I won't have you leaving your nasty marks on my friend here. Renato, do you still want her?"

The other man still smiled despite one red blotch on his cheek where a fist had found its mark. "A tigress only makes the inevitable a bit more spicy," he remarked, allowing his hand to brush against Gabrielle's bosom, which was just now heaving with mingled anger and loathing at the unspeakable way they were treating her.

Lafitte set her back on her feet and then pushed her toward the side of the ship where she could see a long boat waiting for them. Beluche, after giving her another engaging grin, slipped over the side and into the boat. Gabrielle's foot groped for the rope ladder and found it as she descended the side cautiously, feeling her way from rung to rung. Beluche's arms were waiting for her in the boat, and he obligingly helped her to a seat after pinching her derrière.

Gabrielle merely gave him a look of disdain, although she longed to finish the job she had started on board ship. She watched as the slim, lithe figure of Lafitte climbed down easily, and then the men in the boat began rowing them towards the island.

Before Lafitte could alight from the boat, a veritable swarm of men and women descended on him, patting his back, shaking his hand, the women bestowing kisses on his face and neck.

One particularly beautiful girl, who could not have been much older than Gabrielle, leaned towards him deliberately and kissed him full on the lips. Her coffee-colored skin gleamed in the afternoon sun and her dark eyes flashed haughtily over Gabrielle's person as she dismissed the newcomer with a lowering of her lashes.

Lafitte seemed not to notice and caught Gabrielle's hand to bring her forward from the boat. "Pierre! Pierre! Where is that rascal of a brother of mine?" he demanded of the crowd.

Everyone laughed, and some of the women preened saucily. "Probably in bed getting another one with child!" one woman laughed.

Lafitte laughed too and dragged Gabrielle toward the partially erected shell of a large house. With the crowd following curiously behind, Lafitte knocked on the door and demanded that his brother come out and greet him immediately.

From within the building, a small scream of embarrassment issued and the crowd pressed inward, laughing even harder at some joke that Gabrielle could not understand until the door was opened and a heavier, more bearlike replica of Lafitte lumbered out, clad only in a hastily buttoned pair of breeches, his hair tousled and his face curiously distorted on one side as though from some temporary paralysis. He was not unhandsome, but when he looked at her his eyes seemed almost to cross owing, perhaps, to the disfigurement of his face. Gabrielle gasped as she stepped back against Jean Lafitte.

Pierre Lafitte looked at the girl his younger brother had brought back with him and immediately felt a tightening in his groin. "Where did you find such a little beauty, Jean?" he asked, catching her chin in one huge hand. "God, but you have all the luck."

"Don't worry about the girl, Pierre. I might give her to you if you like her. But get yourself dressed while we inventory the goods I've brought back with me. They're worth considerably more than this little cat."

He pushed Gabrielle toward the girl who had given her the look of dismissal before. "Julie, see that she's cleaned up and presentable."

Gabrielle found herself pushed along to a small building where the girl bade her get inside and hurry up about it. Once within, the girl looked daggers at Gabrielle.

"Who are you? Where do you come from?" she demanded, her arms folded across her bosom.

Drawing herself up, Gabrielle eyed her in exactly the same manner. "I am Gabrielle—Captain Lafitte took me from a ship he had—had destroyed." She struggled to keep the sobs from reaching her throat.

The girl looked even more narrowly at her. "You mean that Jean rescued you from a captured ship?"

Gabrielle nodded, suddenly feeling completely miserable.

"What is he going to do with you, then?"

Gabrielle shook her head. "He has not informed me of his plans for me. I wouldn't doubt that he plans to kill me," she said soberly, remembering the regret in

Lafitte's voice when he had told Beluche about his rescue of her.

"Hmmph! Jean knows the value of a pretty woman too well to kill you. He might give you to Pierre or one of his other lieutenants or—" and here her eyes gleamed maliciously, "—he might have brought you as a lady's maid for me."

Gabrielle looked around at the slovenly room. "Why would he bring you a lady's maid?" she asked sarcastically.

Julie drew up her hand to slap her but decided against it. "You don't really think I live in this hole all the time, do you?" she said. "Why, I have beautiful quarters in New Orleans where I live in the style suitable to my station."

"And just what is your—station?" Gabrielle inquired smoothly.

The girl flicked imaginary dust from her sleeve. "Why, I am Jean's mistress, of course. He bought me at the quadroon ball only two months ago for just that purpose. My rooms are more beautiful than you can even imagine," she continued in the same vein as before. "And, although Jean does not come to see me often—" she bit her lip at the slip she had made. Then, shrugging, she went on airily. "Jean is not a man like others. He is busy with so many things he does not have too much time for—lighter matters."

Gabrielle would have laughed in the girl's face if she hadn't felt so miserable. Well, she was relieved that the pirate already had a woman with whom to amuse himself. But, and she shivered, would she prefer the older brother to the younger? Dear God! Better to be a lady's maid to this jealous bitch. At least she would be ensconced in New Orleans, the better to make her escape.

The girl was calling to someone to bring clean clothes. "Come. We can go down to the beach and bathe. You really are dirty, you know," she pointed out cuttingly.

Gabrielle followed her out of the house, relieved to see that the earlier crowd had dispersed to help with the new cargo. They walked down the dusty street and then turned onto a winding path that led down to an isolated cove where a beach of fine white sand shone like drops of crystal.

Gabrielle could not help but be awed as she looked at the emerald green of the ocean as it lapped lightly against the shimmery beach. Not far away she could hear the shouts and orders as men unloaded the long boats and made their way back and forth between ship and shore with the prize booty. She hesitated at undressing so close to where they were unloading, but the water did look inviting and she saw that Julie had already divested herself of her clothing and was romping in the water, splashing herself to cool her skin.

Gabrielle finally made up her mind, and, lifting the hem of her dress, she brought it over her head and stripped off her chemise, kicking away her shoes as she ran, head first, into the cool water. A wave hit her full in the face, and she tasted the salt in her mouth as she tried to clear her eyes. She coughed and gagged, then stood up to gain her bearings. She had never been in the ocean before, and she felt strangely exhilarated as she splashed water over her arms and shoulders. She submerged her hair, watching delightedly as it spun away with the current like golden seaweed. She swam a little further out, glad of the chance to exercise her muscles, which had been turning soft with her enforced inactivity.

"Hurry up!" Julie was crying out petulantly. "I didn't mean for you to have so much fun."

Gabrielle laughed exuberantly and dunked herself beneath a wave, ignoring the girl. Oh, it did feel good to have so much freedom, she kept thinking. She would have continued to frolic in the sea, but she found suddenly that her arm was caught in a viselike grip as she was literally pulled out of the water.

She was about to utter some scathing comment to the girl, but, peeking out from beneath her strands of wet hair, she found herself looking into those same jet-black eyes that she despised. They were in waist-deep water, and Jean Lafitte was wet up to his belt buckle—and very angry.

Silently, he pulled her with him to the shore, where Gabrielle looked around frantically for something to cover herself with, painfully aware of her complete and defenseless nudity. Lafitte, though, barely looked at her, and she would have thought he was unaware of her femininity if his hand had not moved from her arm to her waist, where it moved up briefly to caress the curve of one perfectly shaped breast.

"A very dangerous thing—to come down here to bathe, spitfire," he said. "All the men will be down here very shortly to wash the grit of battle from themselves."

Gabrielle sent a suspicious look toward the other girl, who would not meet it as she sullenly began to dress herself.

"Julie, why did you bring her down here?"

The girl's dark eyes were rebellious. "What would you care if the crew saw her naked? Let them have her! By the look of her, it wouldn't take them long to finish her off, and then you'd be rid of her!"

Gabrielle's eyes widened as she understood the merciless streak in the other girl.

"Get dressed," Lafitte said to Gabrielle, giving her a little push towards the stack of clothes in the sand.

She did so hurriedly, and silently the three of them marched back up the path to the settlement. Lafitte took her by the hand and led her towards the fortress after harshly ordering Julie back to the little house. Stumbling a little, Gabrielle grabbed at his arm to steady herself, and she felt the tightening of the muscles beneath his sleeve. He was taking her back to the place where she had seen Pierre, and she wondered if he had decided to give her to the other man.

"Sally!" A young white woman came to the door in answer to Lafitte's call. "Sally, I want you to watch over this little hellcat. I know I can trust you to see that she is fed and dressed in something that suits her."

"Of course, Jean, but you—you do not want. . . . You don't want Pierre to. . . ?"

"He won't touch her unless I tell him she's his. Now, I've got work to do and can't be bothered with this thorn in my side." He walked briskly out of the door, leaving Gabrielle standing next to the girl who seemed rather placid and was certainly extremely pregnant.

"You are Pierre's wife?" Gabrielle asked her politely.

The girl smiled. "No, of course I'm not. His wife, Françoise, died some time ago, and Pierre has no intention of tying himself down again."

"Oh, I—I see," Gabrielle muttered inanely, but she didn't really see. What kind of place was this where the men seemed to service any woman they wanted and then sailed away to plunder some unsuspecting ship?

The girl led her inside and motioned her to sit down at a long table. "I was just fixing soup for Pierre and Jean when they return from their work," Sally commented. "Let me give you some now. I know you must be hungry."

"Thank you," Gabrielle said, her nose twitching at the delicious smells that were wafting from the pot on the hearth.

"You have just arrived on the island?" Sally asked.

Gabrielle nodded. "Lafitte took me from the ship *Lillias.* We were bound for—for Jamaica."

Sally was silent for a moment, considering. "Were you the only one who survived?" she asked gently and her direct question caught Gabrielle off guard.

"Yes!" she gasped, trying to recover her poise.

Sally patted her hand. "Please don't cry. You're alive, and you have not been treated too badly, I hope.

"Were you—were you brought here, too?" Gabrielle asked her hesitantly.

"I was not brought here from a ship. I was born here. This island used to have just a few shacks that comprised a small fishing village. When Jean first came here, all the people thought he was some lunatic whose thoughts of grandeur would land him in the calaboose. They were wrong. Jean was not, as some thought, an illiterate numbskull, but an educated, refined man who, when one sees him in New Orleans, meticulously dressed and completely polished in his manners, would seem like some wealthy plantation owner in the city on business. And so he is on business," she said. She seemed to recollect herself and then stared sharply at Gabrielle. "He has never . . . that is, you're the first woman he has ever brought back with him. . . ."

Gabrielle leaned towards her. "But that is why I am so confused," she said. "Everyone keeps telling me that he is not interested in women. Is there something wrong with him?"

Sally shook her head. "He was once married to a lovely young girl—"

"Yes," Gabrielle interrupted. "One of the crew members told me that she died during childbirth."

Sally nodded. "Then you know as much as I. I think he fears getting involved with another woman so deeply. He must have loved his Christina very much."

The two young women finished eating in silence. Afterwards, Gabrielle sat in front of the hearth, drying her hair and wondering how she had come to this point where she could sit calmly in a stranger's house, the prisoner of a pirate captain on his island fortress.

It was late in the evening when the two women heard the sounds of men's voices and heavy footsteps. Peeking out the window, Sally signalled to Gabrielle to get out more dishes.

"They have brought others with them. A meeting of the lieutenants," she explained shortly.

The door was flung open, and Pierre entered, his eyes immediately seeking out Gabrielle as she hurried to put out more plates and get out of their way. The next man was Renato Beluche, who smiled at the sight of the girl and winked knowingly at her. Behind him came two men who were unfamiliar to Gabrielle, but whose Italianate looks caused her to shudder in apprehension. One man was dark and squat with a deep slash scar across his face that left him with only half a nose. He reminded her of a deformed monkey, and she disliked his dark eyes when they roved silently over her. The man with him was dark also, with liquid dark eyes and a fierce-looking mustache, although he was taller and less heavy than the first man. He smiled dimly and somehow he reminded her of Lieutenant Rué, with the same cruel expression in his eyes.

Jean Lafitte was the last to come inside, and Gabrielle watched his face for some expression when he saw her. But to her relief, he seemed just as disinterestedly casual towards her as before.

"A long, hard day, my friends," Pierre laughed, drinking noisily from his cup. "Time to rest, make love to a good woman." He eyed Gabrielle deliberately, but she would not look at him as she replaced the pot on the hearth.

"You've brought a valuable cargo with you this time, Lafitte," the taller of the two Italian men spoke up. "Have you decided how we are to split it?"

Lafitte carefully broke a biscuit that Sally had laid on his plate. "The usual way, Gambi. That is acceptable, is it not?"

The other nodded, but his eyes slid craftily to the shorter man.

"I wish to be frank," that one said. "Shall we send the women out?"

"Chighizola, you are not going to tell me you are dissatisfied with our arrangement, are you?" Lafitte asked him.

"Well—I believe that giving you a fourth of everything. . . ."

"You imply that I do not deserve a fourth, Chighizola?" Jean asked, looking at him directly for the first time as the sudden and immediate tension in the room was communicated to everyone present.

"We will certainly concede that you work for it, Lafitte," the man said quickly, looking to the taller Italian for approval, "but Vincente and I only receive a sixth, and we work just as hard as you do."

"How many ships have your crews brought in in the last month, Louis?" Jean went on. "I believe the last count was five. Personally, I have brought in twice that number and Renato has brought in four."

"We have no quarrel with Renato," Gambi said harshly. "What we cannot understand is how your brother can receive a sixth of the take when he does nothing but add to his harem and grow fatter on chicken fricassee and gumbo."

Pierre's bull-like face took on the color of the coals in the hearth, Gabrielle thought, as he rose from his seat, his swift movement causing his soup bowl to be upended and the contents spilled into his lap. Sally hurried to clean up the spilled soup.

"For Christ's sake, woman! That soup is scalding!" Pierre yelled at her, barely missing her cheek with a sloppily aimed blow. "Get me another bowl, and be quick about it!"

"Go into the other room, Gabrielle," Sally whispered to the girl, obviously afraid that Pierre's wrath might find her a more suitable target.

Gabrielle did as she was told, disappearing into a room that must be Sally's sleeping quarters. She closed the door behind her and sat in the chair in one corner until the meeting was finished. She heard the endless droning of voices as the men continued talking, some angry, others seeking to placate. Much later, Sally told her to get undressed and slip into bed.

"The men will be awake all night. You may as well get some sleep," she explained.

Chapter Thirteen

Gabrielle gazed absently out the window to where Lafitte lazed in the rope hammock, a cigar in his mouth as he listened to his brother, Pierre, who sat in a chair next to him. She was sewing a ruffle on one of his shirts,

and every time she stuck the needle in the snowy shirtfront, she pictured herself plunging it into Lafitte's chest
instead.

It had been four days since he had brought her to
Grande Terre, and still he had done nothing about her. He
had never told her his plans for her, and he barely spoke
to her at all, unless it was absolutely necessary. At times
she would catch him watching her almost covertly, an
enigmatic expression in his dark eyes, but he would look
away when she met his gaze. It troubled her, not knowing
what would happen to her, and Sally, knowing how the
question preyed on her mind, gave her plenty of work
to do.

Gabrielle's sewing talents were held in extremely high
esteem by all the women, and Gabrielle thought she must
have repaired at least twenty gowns in the short time she
had been on the island.

Pierre had not attempted to press his person on her
other than at mealtimes, when he was careful to sit extremely close to her. She had learned that he spent most
of his time in New Orleans and was thankful that she
would not have to put up with his irritating attentions
much longer. Jean sat at the head of the table, apparently
taking no notice of his brother's irritating habits.

So Gabrielle had silently seethed for four days, wondering when something would happen to change the dull
pattern of living. Even as she thought this, a young boy
came scampering up to the yard, his dirty face bright
with excitement.

"The *Tigre*, Cap'n, the *Tigre*! She's coming in!"

Both Lafittes stood up expectantly and ran down to
the shore. Gabrielle stood with Sally on the doorstep and
watched as the 120-ton brig rounded the strait and
downed anchor. Shortly, three or four longboats were
lowered into the water and filled with men. She could see
the Lafittes and Beluche on the beach, their hands extended in warm greeting as a short, swarthy man stepped
from the lead boat and nearly crushed Lafitte in his burly
arms.

As with Lafitte's return, it seemed as though everyone was on the beach to welcome yet another hero. There were cheers and acclamations as everyone talked at once about the success of this man's mission. This, Gabrielle thought, must be Dominique You, a well-known pirate who was, she understood, as yet uncommitted to a complete affiliation with Lafitte.

Gabrielle stepped back inside the house as she saw the men approaching. She looked up from the chair where she had rescued her sewing when she heard their voices and received an impression of flashing black eyes, a hawk nose, and powder-burn scars on the left side of the man's face, which made him seem truly ferocious. His eyes were fixed on her for a moment, and a voice like a lion's rang out.

"And where did such a likely-looking miss come from? Pierre, don't tell me you've added another one to your bevy of ladies." Dominique You strode over to where Gabrielle sat, and with both hands holding her helpless, he placed a very wet and noisy kiss on her mouth.

Gabrielle wiped her lips with one hand as soon as he released her, at which the man roared with laughter.

"So, she doesn't like old Dominique, heh? I suppose you prefer the more pristine lips of fine Pierre here?" He slapped his thigh as Gabrielle's face turned rosy.

"She's not Pierre's woman," Jean Lafitte said quietly, seating himself at the table.

Dominique's eyes brightened and his mouth formed a snort of surprise before he slapped the slighter man on the back and whispered something in his ear. Lafitte's laugh grated on Gabrielle's nerves, and with a swishing of skirts she got up from her chair and moved away from the table. How dare they make sport of her! She could not bear this much longer.

For a moment she did not register the voices of the men as they turned back to business and Dominique You informed Lafitte of his booty. But she froze suddenly when she heard him inform the captain that he had brought back five women whom he'd taken from a ship bound from Spain for Mexico.

"Gorgeous beauties they are, too, my lads, though I doubt you'd interested, Jean, with that remarkable-looking wench you've acquired. Is she English?"

"French, but she speaks English like a native."

"I see. In that case, I give you my blessings, my friend."

Gabrielle heard Pierre's voice, a little excited as he questioned Dominique about the women he had brought back with him.

"Five of the prettiest señoritas you could have asked for," Dominique proclaimed. "If you like 'em dark, that is. Velvet skinned and clear-eyed. A mother and her four daughters from what I can tell."

Without looking at him, Gabrielle could picture the look of lustful interest on Pierre's big face, and she felt sick with revulsion.

"I suppose we could hold them for ransom," Jean was saying idly, his voice betraying little interest as he toyed with a penknife.

Dominique nodded thoughtfully. "We could, but it might take months before we were paid off. *If* we were paid off, that is. The señora's husband was killed in the foray, and one of the daughters was married—her husband was lost, too. From what I gathered, they had been on their way to Mexico to settle down for good—mayhap they were running away from the authorities in Spain."

"Are you saying that a ransom note would be no good?" Jean asked.

The big man shrugged. "Not likely."

"Well, then, what do we do with them?" Pierre asked with increasing excitement, leaning over the table. "I would really like to see them, Dominique, if it's all right with you."

"Of course, but we must settle what's to become of them, my friends, before any other action is taken."

Jean stood up. "Well, it matters little to me what you two decide," he began. "The island is getting crowded as it is without adding to the population with captured prisoners. Then, too, women always cause fights among the crews." His words were practical, uttered without feeling.

"You'll not kill them?" Gabrielle could not help her rash cry. She could not believe the coldness of the man.

He looked at her angrily. "Be quiet, wench. Must I remind you that you, yourself, are on this island through my good graces? Keep your nose out of matters that don't concern you."

The other men gave her looks that mixed appreciation with caution. Without another word, she returned to her room. A few minutes later the door was pushed open roughly and Lafitte stood in the doorway, half-glaring at her. Past him, she saw that the kitchen was now empty, the others having already taken a hasty leave.

Lafitte closed the door carefully behind him and lounged against it for a moment as though to calm his temper. Gabrielle stared back at him.

"That is positively the last time you will be allowed to cross-examine me in front of my own lieutenants." He straightened from his position against the door. "I do not in the least like anyone to interrupt me, much less express disapproval of my opinion when such an expression is not asked for," he continued slowly. "I will remind you for the last time that the only reason you were not thrown to my crew upon our arrival here is because I chose to keep you safe. Can you even imagine some thirty men using you, wench? Can you imagine how long you would live before you no longer had the strength to scream anymore—before you became unconscious—and then died?"

He watched as her eyes grew wider and her lovely mouth trembled with fear. "Please remember, you are not here to express any opinions on the conditions of our profession." He moved to leave the room, then turned to her and added in a softer tone, "I will come for you tonight. I have only waited this long because I was anxious for You's return."

After he had gone, Gabrielle rose shakily from the chair and began to pace the room. "I will come for you

tonight." The words went round and round in her brain.
What did he mean? Was he going to make her watch the
horrible festivities of the evening? Was he going to force
her to see the degradation of the Sapinsh women, just to
teach her a lesson? Or was he coming for her for himself? The thought made her grow cold. Although she was
technically no longer a virgin, the thought of this villain
seeing her body, doing things to her that she only dimly
remembered now, made her mouth go dry with fear.

As the evening drew near, Gabrielle found herself becoming ever more nervous. It was twilight before a young
boy came to the door, his elfin nose sniffing the smells
issuing from the kitchen.

"Cap'n Lafitte says he'll not be to dinner tonight." The
boy relayed the message, then stood hesitantly in the doorway until Sally called him in to share their meal, an
invitation which the lad quickly accepted. As the three
ate, conversation turned to the "booty" from You's ship.

"The women have been assembled on the beach.
There's a huge bonfire to be lit, and then the men'll have
a go at 'em."

Gabrielle stared at the boy, who could be no more
than eleven years old. He continued to eat with total
unconcern, munching the steaming carrots as though he
hadn't eaten in days. He went on jabbering happily between mouthfuls about the other prizes that You had
brought back: a chest of gold, yards of silk and lace,
finely made arms. Gabrielle barely listened as she pushed
her half-finished plate away listlessly. When the boy had
finished his meal, he thanked the two women politely,
then hurried out the door, presumably to watch as the
bonfires were being lit. It was now quite dark outside, and
Gabrielle helped Sally with the dishes to keep her mind
away from the beach.

"How—how can you be so calm when you know what
is happening to those defenseless women?" she finally
exploded in a rush. Even as she spoke, a scream
punctuated the chirping of the crickets.

Sally looked levelly at the other girl. "Be glad," she said quietly, "that you are here with me."

"Glad! Oh, yes, I am considerably beholden to Captain Lafitte for sinking the ship I was on, for bringing me here against my will, for letting me stagnate here on this horrible island! If I had never seen his face, I think I should count myself the luckiest of women! I hate him! I hate him, do you hear?" She was nearly screaming the words at the other woman.

"Such bravado!" Gabrielle whirled to see Lafitte himself standing in the doorway, his black eyes flashing with some emotion. "What an odd way for you to express your thanks that I saved your life."

"You—you didn't save my life," Gabrielle threw at him, nearly on the verge of hysteria. "You destroyed it!"

He stood deathly still as he picked at a nail almost too calmly. "Then, are you saying that you would prefer to have died on the cargo ship with the others?"

"Gabrielle!" Sally warned, "think what you are saying!"

Gabrielle turned her back on the woman, "Yes! Yes!" she cried out. "I would rather be dead than remain here."

"Very well, then." Roughly, Jean Lafitte grabbed her hand and started pulling her behind him as he made his way down the path that led to the beach.

Gabrielle could hear Sally's imploring sobs, and she felt the gravel scraping her bare feet. She heard the chirping of the crickets, the loud laughter of drunken men mingling with low moans and shrill screams. She could feel the moistness of the air on her face, the slight chill in the December breeze on her arms. Like a brand of iron, she felt the hand of Lafitte nearly crushing her fingers as he dragged her towards the sounds and the light on the beach. Her head was dizzy with smells, sounds, and feelings. As she realized where he was taking her, what he had decided to do with her, she felt fear in her throat squeezing the breath from her body.

"Oh, no! Oh, my God, no!" she cried, trying to wrench her hand from Lafitte's grasp. No, she didn't really want to die, not now, not like that!

He stopped momentarily on a small knoll, and Gabrielle's horrified eyes took in the scene of bloody carnage on the pristine sand. She shut them tight but could not block out the screams and pleas.

"You cannot do this!" she yelled at him, desperately kicking out with her feet and trying to loosen his hold on her.

"Be quiet!" he hissed and pulled her along again.

Hysterically, Gabrielle pulled and twisted against him, but he was stronger than she, and she remembered Sally's warnings—too late. Dear God, she couldn't go through with this—she couldn't be mauled and savaged and torn to pieces by a dozen men who were so drunk they hardly knew what they were doing.

In her state of horror, she did not realize at first that Lafitte was taking her away from the terrible scene. Not until she heard the voices of the men growing dimmer did she attempt to crush her own hysteria. Broken shells hurt her feet, and she stumbled on loose clods of earth as Lafitte pulled her down a small hill to a private little cove. She felt warm sand underfoot and looked dazedly at the bright moon in the sky, the darkness of the water, the brightness of the sand.

He let her hand go. "Do you still want to die, Gabrielle?" His voice seemed very far away, and was that truly anger she detected in its tone?

She pushed her tumbled hair out of her eyes and attempted to look up at him through sudden tears. "No, no! I don't want to die! I don't want to die!" she repeated brokenly, covering her face with her hands.

He pulled her to her feet and lifted her in his arms. He will hold me under the water until I cease to breathe, she thought. As he lowered her, she braced herself for the shock of icy water but felt soft earth beneath her and opened her eyes to stare up at the sihouette of his head hiding the moon.

He was bending down to her, silently, slowly, and Galbrielle held her breath, wondering what he was going to do. The touch of his hand on her cheek unnerved her so that she jerked her head away from him and tried to struggle to her feet. He pressed her back firmly on the sand, and she felt his leg over both of hers, holding them down as his hands caught her arms.

She turned her head to avoid his mouth, but he followed her so that he fastened his lips over hers. Her whole body shook with reaction and the dawning sense of the nearness of his body to her own. His hands left her arms to pull with growing impatience at her bodice. Another moment, and she shivered when his hands caressed her breasts, even as he went on kissing her. Her lips felt bruised when he lifted his head, her eyes were brimming with tears and her ears were suddenly filled with his warm breath and the sound of soft murmurings in French.

Eventually, her body began to respond to the half-forgotten sensation of caresses, and then there was nothing but his mouth on hers, his hands on her skin, and the sand at her back. Warm tremors rose from her thighs to her breasts as he continued to embrace her. The sea breeze was suddenly cool against her perspiring skin as he removed the last of her clothing.

Involuntarily, she drew her thighs tightly together and raised her hands to ward him off. Silently, he caressed her belly and hips until she relaxed and allowed herself to drift pleasantly along on the rising tide of anticipation. She began to feel that dimly remembered core of heat in her belly which seemed to radiate to her whole body until she was returning his kisses with equal fervor and pulling him down to her.

She started as she felt something hot and alien probing at her thighs and, for a moment, she struggled again, coming back to herself. "No, no," she murmured. She couldn't let him do this to her. She couldn't! He was a murderer, a pirate, a man with no morals—how could she let him make love to her like this!

But now it was too late, and he was not to be denied. His teeth bit at her nipples and his hands came down to part her thighs with a strength that she could not fight.

She could feel one hand on each of her thighs, digging into the soft inner flesh as his weight pressed down so that he could drive deeply into her. She cried out with initial surprise and hurt as he drove again and again until he was all the way inside her and his hands moved up to hold her shoulders.

His thighs were strong and he moved within her, faster and faster, making her head roll from side to side as she fought her body's reaction. No use! Despite her hatred of what he was, instinct drove her legs upward to clench tightly around his hips, aiding his movements as she arched her back and left herself open to him, like a budding flower whose petals were spreading one by one. She was crying and gasping for air, hating herself and him for her own act of betrayal against those of the *Lillias* who had died at his command.

My God! she thought, if she were honest with herself, she did not want to think of that now. She did not want to think of anything but this man and his flesh inside of her flesh and this soaring feeling of excitement that was carrying her faster and faster towards its climax.

Her fingers pressed into his strong back and his lips worked against hers until, finally, everything seemed to explode at once, and a soft scream was torn from her throat. They lay together, exhausted, he breathing deeply and she glad of his arms around her, holding her tightly against him.

"I knew it would be like this," he murmured after a few moments. He licked her neck and she sighed. "Raped by a pirate," he went on, chuckling a little. "You can see, I hope, what a pleasant experience it can be, spitfire."

Privately, Gabrielle was still amazed and a little frightened at how easily she had shed her inhibitions with this stranger—this pirate—whom she did not really know. Certainly there could be no hope of anything permanent with the corsair, for hadn't she seen how Sally and the other women were treated by their men? On the island the women were used to assuage a hunger, a basic need. If there were marriages, they were treated lightly, and most of the men still assumed the license of the bachelor.

Gabrielle moved out of his arms and sat up suddenly, reaching for her clothing. Lafitte caught her hand.

"Stay with me a little longer, Gabrielle. I will be lonely without you."

"But—but it is late—and Sally will be wondering. . . ."

"Does it matter?"

Gabrielle was silent, and he drew her down beside him once again. She felt his hand in her hair, twisting it idly, and she wondered if he guessed at her reason for wanting to get away. Could he sense her embarrassment, her confusion over her own passionate response to him?

Lafitte turned her face so that he could look at her. "You are the most beautiful woman I have ever seen, Gabrielle. It's not just your physical attraction, but something else—an inner quality that I find lacking in so many women. It was this that I sensed on the ship, and this also kept me away from you. I did not want to know a woman who might be able to bind me to her." He paused for a moment as though expecting her to answer him.

Gabrielle could think of nothing to say. Certainly she had no wish to hold him in her power—she felt nothing more than a pleasant sense of appeasement now as she lay next to him.

Practically, she couldn't help but think that after this episode, perhaps he might allow her to leave Grande Terre and go to New Orleans. It made sense to her that if he was worried about her influence over her, he would wish to be rid of her.

"I'm—cold. Could we get up now?" she whispered.

He held her for a moment longer then reluctantly release her so that she could dress herself. She felt his eyes brooding on her. Perhaps, even now he was thinking that he should let her go, she hoped.

After he had put some order to his clothing (she realized, with a slight feeling of distaste, that he had not troubled to remove his shirt or breeches), he grasped her hand as before and led her back up the path. Gabrielle could still hear the yells and shouts of the men on the beach, but there were no more screams from the women. With a dawning sense of sickened realization she knew that the women were probably dead or too weak to resist anymore. Even as Lafitte had been making love to her in the cave he must have known that his men were destroying those prisoners. Perhaps, she thought, risking a guarded look at her companion, she had best not underestimate this man.

At the door to Sally's house, he released her and waited until she had slipped inside.

"Wait for me. I will join you later," he said, and his tone was commanding again.

Gabrielle shivered and watched as he left her, knowing that he was going down to the beach to check on the condition of his men. The thought continued to gnaw at her mind that here was a man who held human life very cheap. Despite his markedly special interest in her, she would have to be very careful not to anger him past the point of endurance, for she very much doubted that, even for her, he would make any exceptions to his own hard rules.

Chapter Fourteen

Gabrielle lay face down on the mattress, wondering sleepily whether she should get up now or wait a bit longer, hoping that perhaps one of the women would come over for conversation. Lafitte was gone, had been gone for almost two months, after settling her in the new house that was only recently completed.

It was hard at times for Gabrielle to believe that she would be eighteen years old in April and that she was, virtually, a prisoner on the island, since Lafitte had left strict orders stating that anyone responsible for any attempts to escape would have his hands cut off. The warning made Gabrielle's flesh squirm, and whenever Lafitte's hands claimed her body in the bed they now shared, she was only just able to keep herself from shuddering wtih revulsion. They had had only five days together before he left on another voyage, which filled Gabrielle with nothing but relief, and she hardly looked forward to her master's expected return sometime in early March.

Sally's baby had been born—a small, red-faced boy who did nothing but cry and demand to be fed. Gabrielle declined to hold the baby any more than necessary, for every time she looked at the tiny face she saw the lecherous round visage of his father, and the thought filled her with disgust. Sally had gone to another man. He was kind and much older than Sally, but she assured Gabrielle she was completely content.

Pierre Lafitte had obtained a lovely, young quadroon, well mannered and a little shy, whose name was Marie Villars. She made cautious friends with Gabrielle, feeling a kindred spirit with this other young woman who served her own master's brother.

Gabrielle was patient and helpful with the girl, but she couldn't help despising her placid contentment with her lot. Marie explained to Gabrielle that she had gone dancing at the Quadroon Ball every Sunday night for six months; her mother was in hopes that she might find a rich planter for her protector. When Pierre made an offer for her, the mother was speechless with joy that one of the famous Lafitte brothers wanted her daughter.

Gabrielle could easily see why Pierre took to the young Marie, whose golden skin shone luminously in the evening light and whose great liquid eyes were like twin pools of blackness in her oval face.

She questioned Marie curiously on the custom of the Quadroon Balls, and Marie, always willing to gossip, told Gabrielle about the beautiful golden-skinned women in their expensive damask and satin gowns and the fine

jewels that sparkled around their necks and dangled from
their ears.

She told her quite candidly that Jean and Pierre had
attended a number of the balls, and many of the girls had
set their caps for the younger brother. But Jean preferred to frequent the gaming room that adjoined the
ballroom.

"All the dandies of New Orleans attend these balls,
dressed in their stiff, white ruffled shirts and suits of
tightest broadcloth," Marie giggled. "Of course, my
mother sat with the rest of the matrons, along the wall,
all looking very dignified in their silk turbans. I used to
be a little afraid of her, she seemed so regal and then
I found out that she had served one of the richest men
in New Orleans when she was younger and as beautiful
as I."

She chattered with a kind of poignancy about the
liveried black servants who carried the great silver trays of
cordials among the guests while the strains of violins and
guitars filled the room.

"But what do the wives of the planters say to all
this?" Gabrielle wondered. "Don't any white women ever
attend the balls?"

Marie's liquid eyes looked surprised. "Of course not!
Only men are allowed at the balls. Why would a woman
want to attend?"

Gabrielle shrugged. "Certainly I would not want my
husband to attend such a thing—would you?"

The other girl sighed. "Sometimes it is not what *you*
want. Although Pierre is not my husband, I am jealous
every time he journeys to New Orleans, for I know that
he will attend the ball and perhaps even sample another
of the girls. He has assured me, though, that he will
find a suitable home for my mother and my sister and me
as soon as he can, but still I fear for my position since
I know that the other girls are very lovely."

"But how can the citizens of New Orleans tolerate such
a thing?"

"It is a very old custom, Gabrielle. Most of the wives

expect their husbands to attend at least once, and some women have to accept the practice as part of their marriages." She looked frankly at the other girl. "It is too bad your skin is not a shade more golden, my friend, for then you might be able to sneak into one of the balls and pass for an octoroon. You seem so curious to see one, but they would never let a white woman inside."

Gabrielle turned away from her. "It's not that I'm so curious to attend one, Marie," she said a little severely. "It's just that I wonder what attracts the men to them. I think it is scandalous that those poor young women should be paraded before married men to be mauled and petted as though they were animals for hire."

Marie laughed. "Oh, but they do not consider it such. Only when they grow too old to spark a desire in men, only then do they begin to worry about their futures. For in such cases they will have to marry men of their own race or, perhaps, men from a class beneath them, in order to survive."

"How unfortunate to be cast down from the luxury of their accustomed standards," Gabrielle said bitingly.

Marie nodded, choosing to ignore her obvious sarcasm. "Fortunately, black men do not consider it dishonorable to marry a woman who was the mistress of a white man, even when she has two or three of his children to care for. Maybe they believe it is a sign of their own desirability when such a woman turns to them for marriage. Our men—they are sometimes very stupid," she finished, and there was a note of bitterness in her voice.

They did not talk of the Quadroon Balls after that. Now, as Gabrielle turned restlessly in her bed, she thought about Marie Villars with compassion, realizing that she, too, must fear the day when her beauty would fade and Pierre would grow tired of her. Of course, Gabrielle could not understand what the eighteen-year-old girl saw in the heavy, older man. But Marie insisted that Pierre pleasured her considerably, and, above all else, he provided her with security.

"Still sleeping, Gabrielle?" It was Marie's voice coming cheerfully from the kitchen as she walked into the bedroom. "Get up, get up! Don't you know the ships have been sighted this morning in the Gulf? Our men will be home soon, and you are still abed. Jean will surely think you a lazy wench and replace you, if you're not careful."

Her lighthearted patter brought a distinct flush to Gabrielle's face as she thought of the welcoming Jean would demand from her. How she wished to get away from here! As Marie continued talking, Gabrielle felt as though she would like to gag her.

The early-March breeze was still chilly, and she hurried with her bath, eager to slip into the warmth of her lettuce-green muslin gown, another gift from her lover—probably taken some from poor woman's sea chest.

As Marie helped her into the cotton chemise and adjusted the lacing, Gabrielle decided to take all of her courage into her own hands and tonight—when the timing was right (and she gulped nervously at the thought) —she would ask Lafitte to take her to New Orleans with him for a—for a shopping excursion! Yes, that was perfect! After all, he was well aware of her extreme dislike for wearing the spoils of his plunder. Surely he would not refuse her!

"You look beautiful," Marie declared without malice when Gabrielle had finished dressing.

"Thank you, Marie. I—I only hope that Jean thinks so."

The girl laughed. "He is a complete fool if he does not fall head over heels in love with you," she assured her, but the words only brought a dread into Gabrielle's heart.

No, she did not want him to love her. He could not love her, for if he did, she knew that he would never let her go. But she was silent to Marie about her thoughts, knowing the girl would never understand her passion to leave.

Together they walked down the sandy path that led to the beach and waited with the others for the arrival of Lafitte and his lieutenants. Lafitte's ship was the first to round the turn, and Gabrielle had to admit that it was a magnificent schooner. It was followed by You's ship and Beluche's.

The people on the beach began shouting and waving almost hysterically, and Gabrielle realized that winter without their leader had been hard on them. Now she was swept on toward the shore by the surging tide of people, for they could see the longboats being lowered into the water as the sailors filled them and began rowing to shore.

Lafitte was in the first boat that touched land, and his dark eyes searched the mob of faces for her. His eyes found hers, and their gazes locked for a moment as she perceived the look of relief that changed his sharp features. Behind her, she could feel hands pushing her forward, the mistress ready to greet her master.

She would have held back, but, remembering her earlier resolution, she let them pass her from hand to hand until she stood within arm's length of Lafitte. He smiled at her and let out a whooping shout as he gathered her up in his arms and kissed her full on the mouth, so that everyone else laughed and shouted approval. Breathless from his kiss, Gabrielle let her head drop back into the crook of his arm as she stared up into those eyes that searched her face hungrily.

"Did you miss me, Gabrielle?" he whispered.

Her throat felt tight as she strained to answer him. "Yes." The word exploded softly on a puff of breath, and his smile widened as he hugged her tighter against his chest.

Putting her on her feet, Lafitte addressed his people, his face flushed by his personal victory as well as the good news he held. "We have been successful," he shouted to the crowd. "Seven ships among us and enough gold and silver to give every man a goodly share. We'll have a feast tonight, if you ladies will be good enough to start the cooking and spread the tables."

In a frenzy of titters and giggles the women hurried to do as he bade them. Meanwhile, the men began talking

excitedly among one another, and Gabrielle followed the
rest of the women with Marie tagging behind her.

"Oh, Gabrielle! You must be the luckiest woman in the
world! Did you see—did you see the way he looked at
you?"

Gabrielle stopped and stared at the girl. "What—what
do you mean? He was glad to see me, as all the men are
glad to be home. It's too bad Pierre never goes away
except on a short trip to New Orleans, or you would see
the same glow in his eyes," she ended, laughing a little
nervously.

Marie shook her head vehemently. "No, no! Jean
looked at you the way a man does who understands that
his fate lies with one woman. He is made for you, Gabrielle. Don't tell me you couldn't feel that?"

Gabrielle longed to slap the girl's grinning face, but her
hands were shaking so badly that she hid them in the folds
of her skirt. He can't be in love with me, she thought
wildly, he can't be! Dear God, he won't ever let me go!
Oh, why, why did he have to choose me from among all
the others? She hurried into the house.

"You don't mind if I help you with dinner?" Marie
asked cheerfully. "Pierre's not due back from New
Orleans until tomorrow, and I don't have anything to do."

"Of course I don't mind, Marie," Gabrielle replied,
desperate to hide the anxiety she felt. "Jean—will not—
he won't be home for hours."

Marie giggled. "By the look in his eyes, I'd say his
trousers should already be near to bursting," she sighed.
"I doubt that he will wait too long."

"Marie, I really wish you wouldn't talk so," Gabrielle
begged her, tying a clean white apron over her gown.

"Oh, I'm sorry, Gabrielle. Sometimes I forget that you
are a lady of quality and not used to the things I have
been surrounded with since I was a child."

Gabrielle whirled around, her face a mask of surprise.
"How—how do you know that?"

Marie shrugged. "Pierre told me how you came to be
on the island, of course, but I can tell, too, by the way

you talk and walk and other little habits—your insistence on bathing, for one. Don't you know that all the other women think you are a little bit crazy to want to bathe every day?" She tittered smugly as though mimicking them.

"Well, you mustn't worry about my past, Marie," Gabrielle assured her with a trace of bitterness. "Here on Grande Terre, I am no better than anyone else."

"Ah, ha! And you long to be," Marie whispered softly, tying another apron around her waist.

Gabrielle looked at her carefully before replying in the same tone of voice. "You're right, Marie. I cannot imagine growing old on this island and—and I am almost eighteen years old—"

"There are many aristocratic women in New Orleans who would give anything to be your age again, and there are just as many young girls who would give the same to have your beauty. You are young, lovely, and intelligent, Gabrielle. Do you truly think I am silly enough to believe you would want to stay on this island? I'm surprised you haven't tried to escape before now."

"Escape! Marie, I think of nothing else! But how could I try such a thing when you know I would need help— and you also know what would be the fate of my accomplice."

"And there is where your upbringing will trip you up again and again, my friend. You have not been taught that life is always a matter of the survival of the strongest and that you must care little about those you leave behind."

Gabrielle felt a lump in her throat, and she could not believe that Marie was talking to her this way. All along, she must have known about her and divined her feelings, but Gabrielle had been too wrapped up in her own miserable thoughts even to guess at the sharp intelligence behind those languorous dark eyes.

"And now," Marie continued a little more hesitantly, "you are afraid that if Lafitte truly feels love for you, you will never be able to leave here."

Gabrielle was practically speechless before the girl's utter candor.

"Gabrielle, you're so silly, really," Marie went on. "Don't you see that Lafitte only makes himself more vulnerable the deeper he lets himself feel for you? If you only had a little less of the lady in you, and a little more of the wanton, you could probably wrap him around your little finger."

"No, no, he is not easy to bend," Gabrielle corrected her. "You don't understand, Marie, how cruel he can be. I saw what he did to the crew of the ship I was on—to the women prisoners! He is not a man to be easily tricked, whether or not he loves a woman."

"Oh, foolish Gabrielle! Think a little less instead of letting your intelligence smother your emotions."

Gabrielle shook her head, still not willing to believe it would be that easy. Perhaps Marie really thought that Lafitte would be easy to control. And although she might be right, up to a point, Gabrielle could not imagine Lafitte taking her to New Orleans with her baggage and setting her down comfortably in the nearest hotel lobby, wishing her good fortune, and walking out of her life.

"And then again," Marie's voice broke through her reverie, "is Jean Lafitte all that bad?"

"What do you mean, Marie? He's a murderer, a thief, a smuggler, a man with no morals!"

"There are many men in New Orleans who have killed others in order to defend points of honor, many fine, upstanding members of the community who buy what Lafitte has smuggled in without a thought as to where he got the goods. Are they any better because they shut their eyes and ears to his true nature, thanking themselves that they have made a good bargain? As for morals—how dull the world would be if all men went to church on Sunday and never indulged in a little reckless gaiety. What about the adulterers in your own homeland, Gabrielle? What about the dalliances and clandestine romances that result in murders and tears and recriminations?"

"Are all those other girls like you?" Gabrielle asked

wonderingly. "I begin to see why the planters find your Quadroon Balls so enticing."

For the first time, she smiled genuinely, with an honest affection, at the other girl. "Forgive me for underestimating you, Marie."

Marie flushed. "I'm only glad to be your friend, Gabrielle," she replied, then cocked her head. "You know, you look even prettier when you smile like that. Your dimples show."

The two young women laughed together and set about fixing dinner. Gabrielle realized that Marie hadn't solved all of her problems, but she had forced her to take another look at her own attitude and had strengthened her resolution to escape.

By the time all the food was eaten, it was well into late afternoon and the sun was already casting long shadows on the ground. Lafitte, with his two lieutenants, sat a little apart from the rest of the group with two clerks who were busy writing on their tablets as Lafitte went over the long lists of goods in the ships.

Gabrielle, sitting a little to the right of them, leaning her shoulders against a small knoll, listened with half an ear to their talk. But something Lafitte said made her straighten up suddenly, her face revealing her excitement.

"Of course, I shall have to leave for New Orleans tomorrow to set up an auction date with Sauvinet. The word will get around soon enough. We can't keep these goods here or the warehouses will be bulging at the seams."

The other two men agreed and after a little more conversation Lafitte cast an impatient glance at Gabrielle, then stood imperiously before her, extending his hand. "Enough talk," he said quietly. "I long to be welcomed home by my woman."

Gabrielle placed her hand in his and felt his hold tighten as he pulled her to her feet. She noticed that several of the others had paired off and were drifting down along the beach in order to find more private places.

Trembling a little, she followed Lafitte as he pulled her along to the house he had finished building for her. At the threshold he picked her up in his arms and pressed a deep kiss to her mouth before slamming the door shut behind them and taking her to the bedroom. He laid her on the bed and tore at his clothes hurriedly before divesting her of her own garments.

For a moment, he lay beside her on the bed, both of them naked, just holding her in his arms. Gabrielle could feel his ragged breathing against her hair, and the beat of his heart mingled with hers as her breasts were flattened against his hard chest.

"This is good," he murmured, kissing her eyes and ears, moving slowly down to her throat before burying his head against her bosom.

Despite her rationalization that she was only complying so as to get from him what she wanted, Gabrielle soon found herself kissing him back and caressing him as he lowered his body onto hers. His hands smoothed her thighs and swept over her hips as though he could not get enough of her. He took her forcefully and with a passion that left her moaning softly. There was perspiration on her face and body, and his flesh was slippery against hers. His mouth and tongue drove her crazy, and a cry of astonishment escaped from her throat in the darkness, causing him to smile at her response. It seemed he would never get enough of her, never stop driving into her flesh, and she surrendered herself to a world of sensual pleasure until, finally, he lay spent beside her, his breathing gradually returning to normal.

"Dear God, how I have dreamed of this night, this moment, all these weeks away from you," Lafitte murmured softly, his hand lightly teasing her still-upright nipples. He turned to his side and propped his head on one hand. "To tell you the truth, spitfire, I was mightily afraid you might not be here when I returned."

Still steeped in languor, Gabrielle would have liked to brush his mouth with her finger and kiss his chin lazily, but she forced herself not to give in to such a display. "How could I escape?" she questioned him seriously.

He reached down and kissed her bruised lips softly. "I'm glad you had thought of no plan," he answered her ambiguously. "Then, too, upon seeing you, I was surprised that I did not find you growing bigger with child."

His words made Gabrielle shiver, and she pulled away from him fearfully. He pulled her back possessively and was gentle with her as his arms held her against him.

"Does such a thought frighten you, Gabrielle?" She did not answer, and his arms tightened. "It does not please you, does it—to think that I might plant my seed in you?"

His hand forced her face towards him, and in the semi-darkness he thought her eyes looked like sparkling amethysts. God, but she was the loveliest thing he had ever seen!

"Having a child," Gabrielle murmured as though to herself. "A child—the responsibility—frightens me." She stumbled over the words. "Out of wedlock, isn't that being selfish and cruel to the child?" She was thinking of Sally and her infant, but as soon as she said the words she regretted them, for she could feel Lafitte stiffening in resistance to her implication.

"I have told you before, Gabrielle, a man like me, in my position—"

"Yes, yes, I know. I'm—I'm sorry," she hurriedly got out, her fingers now coming up to close his lips. Since she could not retract the words, perhaps she could use them to fan his vanity. "Forgive me for being a—a selfish woman."

His arms relaxed a little, and she allowed herself a small sigh as she snuggled closer to him. Already she could feel him becoming aroused again as his hands moved slowly over her back and buttocks.

"I—I suppose I do get a little bored here," she began haltingly, then taking her courage in her hands: "I was hoping—that is, I wanted to ask you if—if it's not too

much trouble, that is—could you, would you take me to
New Orleans with you, Jean?"

He pulled away from her abruptly and sat up. "To
New Orleans?" he said suspiciously, and Gabrielle's heart
beat faster with her heightened fear.

But, despite her raging emotions, she put her arms
around his neck and widened her eyes provocatively. "Oh,
please, Jean! Please take me with you! It would be such
fun for me, and I could shop just a little, and you—you
could show me all the sights, and—oh, it would be
wonderful, just this once! Please," she ended, smiling
even though her face felt stiff and her mouth tasted bitter
from her lies.

His hands began to explore her body once more, and
she felt the familiar tingling begin again.

"Please, Jean," she whispered again, fastening her lips
on his.

He kissed her deeply, then pulled away to look into
her face. "All right, all right, you little vixen. I'll take
you with me." His expression was veiled, but he grinned
as he saw the dazzling smile she bestowed on him. "I
suppose it is worth it."

"Oh, yes!" she cried out, her heart singing within her
as she gave herself to him without reservations. "Oh,
yes, Jean!"

Noting her complete surrender, Lafitte redoubled his
efforts, and then they were locked together once more,
oblivious to the sounds of laughter and revelry that drifted
softly through the open windows.

Chapter Fifteen

"Mama! Just look at that handsome devil!" a slim,
young octoroon girl whispered to her dour-faced mother
from behind a fluttering fan. "Lord, if he asks me out
into the garden, I shall probably faint with excitement!"

"You'll do no such thing, girl!" replied the stout matron. "You'll act like a lady, or I'll take a switch to your backside when we get home. Now quit your simpering. My guess is, a stallion like that isn't looking for a giggly girl on his arm!"

The girl agreed, but couldn't help another nervous giggle escaping her bejeweled throat as the man turned and looked in her direction. She held her breath as the full impact of dark, emerald-green eyes met hers. Their boldness as they swept over her figure made her step backwards, closer to her mother, as though for protection.

Rafe St. Claire, newly arrived in New Orleans from Richmond, Virginia, smiled to himself, his sensually molded lips curving into a mocking salute to the girl. She was pretty enough, he thought, to keep him well occupied for the rest of the evening—if, that is, he could manage to get her away from that frowning duenna of a mother.

He had just arrived a week ago from Virginia where he had filled his ears with the ominous rumblings of war by talking with his father and those members of Congress who elected to risk their reputations by conversing with the black sheep of the St. Clair family. It always amused him to answer their personal questions with as many outrageous lies as they would swallow.

After a while, though, the relatively peaceful existence at Clairemont, his father's plantation manor, preyed too much on his nerves, and he decided to seek stimulation elsewhere. The stodgy society of Washington City was part of the reason that he had left home three years before. The men wanted to talk of nothing but politics or other equally dry topics, and the women would not allow their emotions to override their cumbersome etiquette.

He missed the gaiety of Paris, the adventure of smuggling goods under the very noses of French and English blockaders, who knew him as Captain Savage. He longed to experience again the freedom of a place not completely bound by rigid codes. So, he had left Clairemont without any farewells, bent on escaping to the more raw, more booming, more adventurous young city of New Orleans.

He looked up an old acquaintance from Virginia, Leigh Owens, who had moved to New Orleans some five years before, and through him learned of the Quadroon Balls, which were held every Sunday. Leigh offered to take him to one, and Rafe, naturally, accepted. Liaisons with girls of mixed blood were not uncommon among the gentlemen of Virginia and the idea did not in the least shock him.

Now, as he eyed the bevy of beautiful, golden-skinned young women whose dark, laughing eyes reminded him of some of those Parisian beauties, he found himself mentally picturing their perfectly formed young bodies against the white bed sheets of his hotel room. Leigh, who had been watching his friend covertly, came up alongside him.

"Enough time for those beauties later," he informed him, laying a hand on his shoulder. "Come with me to the gaming tables in the other room. You'll enjoy the stakes as well as the play. Have you brought much money with you?"

"Enough," Rafe said lightly, "although most of it is still tied up in my bank in Virginia. If I'm to stay here very long, I suppose I should have my account transferred to a bank here in the city."

He followed his friend into the gaming room with its green baize tables and let his eyes roam silently about the various personalities occupied in the different games. He noticed a large, heavyset man at one table, his arm placed quite familiarly around a young woman of color whose own face revealed the prolonged suffering she had endured. The man hiccoughed drunkenly, belched, and rubbed his stomach with one huge paw before transferring it to the bodice of the embarrassed young girl and then back to the gaming table to throw down more coin.

Leigh, following the direction of his gaze, laughed. "That is Pierre Lafitte, Rafe. Even though he looks like nothing more than a drunken sot, he is probably one of the wealthiest men in the Louisiana Territory, thanks to the daring exploits of his noteworthy brother, Jean Lafitte. You've heard of them?"

Rafe shrugged. "I've heard a little of Jean Lafitte," he said, his dark brows making sardonic crescents in his sun-browned face. "What I've heard isn't anything to enhance a man's reputation."

"True, but Lafitte could hardly care less. He's intent on building some sort of pirate empire out there on that island of his. He's just the sort to do it, too, by the look of him. The people here in New Orleans don't know quite what to make of him. Many of the businessmen are concerned about the effects of his smuggling on the commerce of the city. Legal trade suffers because of the smuggled goods Lafitte can bring in at much lower prices. The governor of the territory, William Claiborne, has tried to take some action against Lafitte and his men, but nothing seems to get through to these fun-loving Creoles."

"And where does that gross buffoon fit in to his brother's scheme?"

"He's useful. Comes into New Orleans to gather information, spreads the word on upcoming sales, takes orders for black slaves. Pierre's a natural-born promoter. Jean Lafitte's much better at doing the dirty work."

Rafe nodded, watching as the man called Pierre Lafitte, coming to the end of his money, proceeded to stumble away from the table in the direction of the double doors that led out into the garden, his arm still firmly wrapped around the mulatto girl. With a shrug, Rafe walked over and took Pierre's place at the table, placing a modest bet.

Within two hours, he had scraped up enough to quadruple his original stipend and was becoming bored with the ease of winning. Leigh had already gone to another table, lost heavily, and retired to the music room to select a partner for the dancing.

Rafe scooped his winnings together, dropped the money into his pockets, and strode back to find his friend. The music was soft and delicate, the partners sparkling on the

dance floor as he stood just inside the archway, watching
with amusement. He turned to scan the other side of
the room and nearly bumped into a pert young girl who
was passing through the archway. Her dark eyes looked
up gaily into his, and he remembered her from before
as the nervous, giggling young girl he had noted upon
entering the building.

"Your pardon, mademoiselle," he said in French, bowing from the waist, but not troubling to keep the mockery
from his smile.

The girl flushed but stood her ground. "Excuse me,"
she murmured in the same language. She hesitated, wondering how bold he required her to be before he would
accept her invitation to dance.

"If you would allow me the next dance?" he inquired,
making it easy for her. He noted the look of pleasure
on her small face and once again pictured her lying back
against the pillows, her crimson-tipped breasts pressed
flat beneath his hands.

He took her arm and led her out to the dance floor,
pressing her slim waist with one hand while the other
took possession of her fingers. These curled gently in his
own, and she did not seem to mind when he brought her
closer to him. They danced in silence, their eyes on each
other, and he could easily see the eagerness reflected in
her face.

He danced with her toward the open French windows
leading into another part of the garden that surrounded
the building on three sides. And, as she looked to see
if her mother were watching, he whisked her outside onto
the small terrace. He did not wait for polite conversation
but dispensed quickly with formalities by taking her in
his arms and pressing a masterful kiss to her soft, full
mouth. His lips traveled down her throat to the upper
swells of her full breasts, and he pulled the bodice downward to capture one of those crimson points he had
imagined only minutes before.

The girl's breath was coming faster, and he half-laughed
to himself, congratulating his own instincts on selecting

this particular girl. It would be ridiculously easy for him to lead her into the tall shrubbery and tumble her on the new grass.

He was doing just that, his hand pulling on hers to lead her down the steps into the seclusion of the garden, when a sharp tap on his hand made him release her and turn around. He found himself staring into the enraged face of the girl's mother, her white teeth flaring in her black face, her wide-cleft nostrils bristling with her displeasure. The girl was already weeping, and he could see the strong red mark on her cheek where the mother had already planted a swift but vicious slap.

"What do you think my daughter is, m'sieur? Some whore you can lead into the night air for a brisk fling in the grass? Some ten-dollar slut who opens her legs for anybody? You've made a mistake, then, for my girl is still a virgin and intends to remain so until a gentleman comes and asks *me* for permission to set her up in style. I'll not have my daughter whelping a little half-white bastard in the streets without the protection of its father!" The force of the woman's ire was so great that she would have struck Rafe if he had not caught her hand in his.

"Keep your little virgin, you ugly old bitch! But may I remind you that she was not unwilling, and your claim as to the state of her hymen could be grossly exaggerated." He made a mocking bow to the speechless woman, then sauntered away, leaving the hapless girl to face her mother's wrath alone.

Once back in the dancing room, he searched for Leigh and signalled to him abruptly. His friend excused himself from the lovely girl he was with, his eyebrows indicating his puzzlement over Rafe's savage frown.

"What's up?" he questioned him.

"I've had enough of these fancy whores, Leigh. Take me where I can get a woman who knows how to pleasure a man without leading him on."

Leigh grinned. "You've found out how terrible these old dragons can be, eh? Never underestimate the power of mother love, Rafe."

Rafe's mocking smile deepened the grooves in either cheek. "I doubt that I will ever do so again, Leigh, nor the power of greed. This place stinks of it. Let's go."

Obligingly, Leigh led him out onto the street where he hesitated while he thought of a place that would fit Rafe's description. "Madame Renée's is the perfect place," he said finally, snapping his fingers. "It's on Royal Street too, not far from your own lodgings."

"For Christ's sake, man! Why didn't you take me there to begin with?" Rafe laughed.

The two men hailed a carriage and were shortly set down in front of a fashionable-looking residence whose shutters were tightly drawn. They walked to the front door, rang the bell, and waited until it was opened by a sprightly, half-caste maid whose eyes ranged knowingly over them.

"Yes, sir?" she inquired of Rafe, her red tongue passing speedily over her very white teeth.

"We've come for entertainment, Claudine," Leigh laughed, stepping into the circle of light.

The girl, upon recognizing him, smiled warmly. "Why, of course, Mr. Owens. Please come in and sit down. Madame Renée will be so happy to see you—and your friend."

She led them into a large candle-lit parlor where a variety of girls lounged in semierotic postures, their dresses cut low over ample breasts and their skirts hitched obligingly over well-turned calves. Madame Renée, a woman of plump proportions, hurried over to them, her hands outstretched in greeting.

"Mr. Owens! I declare I'm so happy to see you—and on a Sunday! Why, you know that's our slowest night, what with those cursed balls they have. You'll have your pick, sir, and you know my reputation for taking in only the finest girls." She looked at his companion. "Oh, my goodness, and you've brought a friend. How thoughtful of you! Girls, girls! We have company."

The girls settled themselves in more decorous positions,

although a few left their ankles exposed and leaned over
to allow their breasts to show beneath their bodices.

A dark-eyed, dark-haired, olive-skinned woman stood
up from her chair and sauntered over to Rafe, inquiring
if he wished a drink or perhaps a cigar. He laughed and
whispered something in her ear, causing a catlike smile
to come over her Spanish features.

"Of course, señor. Rosa is the best in all of New Orleans," she said huskily.

Rafe nodded and his white teeth gleamed at his own
smile. "Then, if you will show me the way, Rosa?"

The girl took him up the curved staircase and into a
long hallway on either side of which there were several
doors. She opened one and led him into a comfortable
room, pointing out the enormous, canopied bed that was
set in the very center in a blatant invitation to the prospective customer.

Rafe wasted no time in haggling over prices but quickly
opened the girl's robe to reveal her full-blown body, the
tips of her breasts erect with her excitement. His hands
captured them easily, and he pushed her backwards onto
the bed where she waited for him to disrobe. Her dark
eyes fastened on his throbbing manhood, and she laughed
in anticipation, her white teeth flashing as her mouth
opened wide to receive all of him. She rolled him over
onto his back and continued her ministrations, her deft
hands caressing his buttocks and legs, her long black hair
streaming over his heaving belly.

"Christ!" he said between his teeth, and she took her
mouth away, replacing it with the soft, enveloping warmth
between her thighs. She bit at his chest and shoulders
until he caught her chin strongly in his hands and brought
her mouth up to his. They kissed long and hard, and
then he rolled over her and pinioned her to the mattress,
driving with masterful strokes within her, causing her to
cry out with exquisite pleasure and pain.

"Dios!" she cried out, her legs writhing around his
hips and clenching over his strongly-muscled back. She
caught his tongue between her lips and sucked at it while

her seeking fingers moved downward over his buttocks until they found that dark, moist place they sought, driving him crazy as they worked urgently to match her own need.

Finally they released their tensions, and Rafe stroked inside of her with lessening urgency. Then he slowed and stopped, lying against her sweating body, his breath coming fast, as he listened to her gulping for air.

After a moment, her hands touched his face softly. "You like Rosa, señor?"

He grinned. "I like Rosa very much," he affirmed, turning his head toward her breasts.

Chapter Sixteen

It seemed to Gabrielle as though they had traveled four hundred miles instead of only forty in the last three days. Her body ached from the unaccustomed ride on the mule, and she was tired of the humid, treacherous bayou land that held too many dangers.

The small caravan had headed straight for the large warehouse outside New Orleans that Jean Lafitte had acquired nearly four years before in order to store goods for his auctions. The warehouse stood near the levee, and seeing its bustling activity Gabrielle soon forgot her weariness as the long flatboats were unloaded by red-shirted men depositing every conceivable size of box and crate along the dock.

Lafitte had ordered her to sit down on a big crate that stood just outside the wide doors of the warehouse where he and his men, assisted by dock negroes, worked to unload their cargo. It was a time-consuming job, so Gabrielle had plenty of time to marvel at all the activity on the levee.

Blacks squatted on sidewalks with baskets of yellow

oranges, hawking their wares in strangely soothing sing-song voices. There were banana sellers and vendors displaying honey-flavored cakes that made Gabrielle's mouth water with their spicy aroma. Ginger beer cooled in big tubs of cold water that were guarded by two blacks who had a thriving business on this unusually warm day.

As Gabrielle sat, her hands clasped in her lap, she could not help but think how incongruous it was that she, the daughter of a marquis of France, should be sitting on a levee in this half-savage land of America, looking for all the world as though she were part of it.

And this existence, this life that she was leading now—the mistress of a pirate, the plaything of a brigand—how Isabel would laugh at the irony of it, and, Gabrielle thought with quick wistfulness, how easily Isabel would settle into such a life. She had always had that ability to adapt easily to things that surrounded her.

Watching her covertly, from the corner of his eye, Lafitte saw the look of thoughtfulness on her face and wondered what she was thinking—he had little doubt that she would try to escape him while they were in the city. He was filled suddenly with an inexplicable dread, a haunting knowledge that she would never truly be his. Grimly, he let his eyes roam over the perfection of her features, the youthful swell of the beautiful breasts beneath her snug bodice, the way her hands lay, with unconscious grace, in her lap. He had behaved like a fool, he thought, allowing himself to feel anything other than a healthy lust for her. He should have taken her to New Orleans the first opportunity he had had—in order to lose her. But as surely as he knew that she was not meant for him, he also knew that he would not let her go without a struggle.

Gabrielle, unaware of Lafitte's thoughts, was trying to brush the past from her mind, and she concentrated on the panorama in front of her.

"Good afternoon, ma'm'selle."

Gabrielle turned to see a rather short, paunchy, middle-aged man bowing to her, his round face looking almost cherubic as he grinned widely.

"Good afternoon, m'sieur."

He quickly took possession of her hand and kissed it elaborately. "Charmed, ma'm'selle, indeed. Permit me to introduce myself. I am Jean-Baptiste Sauvinet, completely at your service."

"Sauvinet! You rascal! I hope you're not trying to lay a claim to my young friend there," came Lafitte's voice, a tinge of warning in it.

Sauvinet recovered from his surprise quickly and extended a hand to the other man. "Lafitte, as always I am completely attuned to you in matters of taste. But tell me, where did you get her?" And then in a lower voice, "Is she for sale, for God's sake?"

Lafitte laughed and grasped the older man by the arm. "You sly businessman. As always, Sauvinet, I am astonished by your duplicity. Indeed, she is not for sale. This is Gabrielle de Beauvoir—my companion."

Sauvinet was silent for a moment. "Lafitte—you! I daresay all those tempting young Creole girls will tear their hair out in a fury when they find out the fox has been snared at last."

"Jean-Baptiste, you must have been drinking too much rum this fine day," Lafitte interjected goodnaturedly.

The businessman shrugged. "I'm certainly not too drunk to see the fine merchandise you've brought in, lad. Egad! Did you pillage the fleet of the king of England?"

"Even better than that, my friend. Come inside and let me go over the lists with you. As always, I depend upon your discretion in getting the word around to the right people."

"You can rest assured it will be done. And what date did you have in mind for the auction? I'm afraid that Claiborne is getting rather domineering about the whole thing, as you no doubt have heard that Louisiana is being considered for statehood. As governor of the Louisiana Territory, Claiborne stands to land quite a plum if we go into the United States."

Lafitte nodded, his brows lowering. "He struts like a puffed-up cock in his palace," he growled, "but thank God we have the citizens opting for us. Christ, he can't fight the entire populace of the city! Everyone knows there are too many factions now, what with the French quarter, the Spanish sector, and the new Americans pouring in."

Sauvinet nodded. "It's a mess that I wouldn't like to be responsible for. But show me your wares, partner, and let's tally up the prices."

The two men went inside the warehouse, and Gabrielle was once more left alone on her crate, wondering what kind of businessman it was who would take up with a pirate in order to gain a profit. A little less than an hour later, Lafitte returned to her.

"Come on, it's getting late, and I thought you wanted to see something of the city. Would you like to go to the theater tonight?"

Gabrielle smiled, instantly as excited as a child. "Oh yes, how wonderful!"

The carriage took them to a cozy little cottage of brown stucco where Lafitte informed her he kept apartments to serve him when he was in the city. A shy-looking black boy greeted them at the door, and, once inside, Gabrielle marveled at the good taste of the decorations. "You are not quite the barbarian that I had thought," she murmured lightly.

He smiled at her. "I am glad you enjoy such things, Gabrielle. But then, I suppose that is your birthright, is it not?" He was deliberately goading her, she knew, but she refused to lose her calm.

He proceeded to show her through the house. In the bedroom a large rosewood armoire stood in the farthest corner, and, opening it, Gabrielle found a woman's wardrobe, all the dresses cleaned and pressed, as though waiting for anyone to wear them. The thought rankled her, and she would have refused to wear anything that the closet contained if it weren't that she was so looking forward to going out.

After a lengthy debate with herself, she pulled out a white satin gown that looked to be about her size. "I suppose I can do a little hasty pinning if necessary," she commented idly, pressing the gown against her as she looked in the glass.

She caught Lafitte's dark eyes on her and flushed. "Why don't you take your bath, fix your hair, and do whatever else must be done to make yourself ready. I have a little business errand to attend to, and I shall be back in two hours.

He left without touching her, and Gabrielle couldn't help uttering the sigh of relief that escaped her. A few minutes later, a young black girl knocked on the door, and soon afterward Gabrielle was luxuriating in a tub of scented bathwater, letting the aches and soreness be soothed away.

"Ah, this is Heaven," she murmured to herself, letting the sponge drip water over her smooth breasts as she held it in the air. Was it really worthwhile to attempt to escape from all of this? Yes, she thought fiercely, remembering that she would also be escaping from Grand Terre and the pillaged ships and screaming prisoners.

The black girl helped her into a silk chemise that she found in one of the drawers as well as real silk stockings that felt odd on legs so used to going bare. The gown needed very little in the way of alteration, and very soon she was posing in front of the mirror, studying the effect of a rope of pearls in her shining hair.

The shimmering white material of the gown was a perfect foil to her peach-tinted skin, which had acquired a touch of gold from her exposure to the sun. Her small, perfect breasts pushed upward at the neckline. Her arms were bared up to the tiny, puffed sleeves, and the skirt of the gown fell in graceful folds from beneath her bosom where it was tied with a garland of silken daisies. LeRoy couldn't have done better, she thought.

When Lafitte returned, he found her waiting for him, tapping a Chinese-print fan that the maid had found in a chest. Lafitte, himself, was already dressed in a black broadcloth suit, and she could see from his slow appraisal that he thought her very lovely. He took her out to the waiting carriage.

"All of this," and Lafitte indicated the gown, the fan, and the carriage, "suits you extremely well, Gabrielle."

Gabrielle smiled, lifting her head proudly, and her violet eyes flashed with tempered arrogance. "Of course, what did you expect?" She realized that, once more wearing the clothing she was accustomed to and moving within the kind of surroundings she had grown up in, she was gaining her self-confidence as well as a certain air of relaxed assurance. Lafitte could not fail to notice the subtle transformation, and he sat watching her speculatively from beneath the lowered brim of his hat.

When they arrived at the theater, Gabrielle felt her heart begin to beat faster at sight of the throng of people in attendance. Many of them glanced up at sight of Jean Lafitte and called out hellos in a familiar manner.

An usher seated them at one side of the stage in a small box that afforded a generous view of the hubbub below. Gabrielle gazed with eager interest at the ladies in their glittering jewels and feathered headdresses and the men who strutted like overdressed peacocks as they wound their way through a myriad of smiling faces, flirtatious eyes, and sighing bosoms. Truly, there was an odd assortment here, for in the farther corners she glimpsed the painted faces and gaudy costumes of the prostitutes and their escorts.

"Well, what do you think?" It was Lafitte leaning towards her, allowing himself a generous view down the front of her bodice.

Gabrielle tapped him on the wrist with her fan. "Really, I don't quite know what to think, Jean. I could almost be back in Paris, and yet—" Before she could finish, the curtains to their box were swung open with a flourish, allowing a young man and a woman to enter.

"John! You, at the theater! My eyes must be deceiving

me," Lafitte burst out, clasping the man's hand heartily. "But I thought you detested these plays," he went on, smiling.

The man bowed to Gabrielle and indicated his friend. "Lord knows I do, Jean, almost as much as you, but Denise insisted we come tonight. She says the actors are very good, and everyone is talking about the play. I was powerless against her feminine wiles." He grinned at Gabrielle, who was looking on in curiosity.

Lafitte introduced everyone. "Gabrielle de Beauvoir, I would like you to meet John Randolph Grymes, one of the best attorneys in New Orleans, and his friend, Ma'm'selle Denise Almond."

Gabrielle smiled in acknowledgement, finding her hand taken in a firm grasp and kissed appreciatively. "Charmed, I must say, Miss de Beauvoir. Forgive me, Jean, but if I hadn't looked up and noted this vision sitting next to you, I daresay I wouldn't have persuaded Denise to climb the stairs."

After a little more repartee, Grymes was taking his leave with an invitation that they call on him at their convenience. "Lord knows I only see you when you're in some kind of mess, Jean," he said with a teasing note in his voice.

"You're quite right, John, but I'm afraid we shall only be staying in New Orleans for a few days at most. You can be sure, though, that I shall certainly make a point of calling on you the next time I find myself up here for a longer stay."

"And you must not forget your devastating companion," Grymes returned.

Lafitte smiled, but Gabrielle felt her gay mood slowly evaporating as she digested the full meaning of his words. "The next time we are in New Orleans." She felt suddenly as though she would like to fly from the box and run—run anywhere to escape from the man at her side. She tried to conceal her anxiety and turned her face to gaze somberly once more at the crowd. Her situation

was not made any easier when Lafitte reached an arm
possessively around her shoulders.

"I think John was quite taken with you, my sweet.
What did you think of him? You know, he is really one
of the best attorneys in the city, probably even in the
whole territory."

"I can only wonder how such a man would be acquainted with a pirate," Gabrielle answered tartly, shaking herself free of his encircling arm.

The smile left Lafitte's face, and his brow furrowed.
"I thought you were enjoying yourself."

She didn't reply, afraid suddenly of his mood. The
silence grew between them until she was saved by the
beginning of the overture. She kept her eyes on the stage
as the performance began promptly at nine o'clock. She
was acutely aware of Lafitte's burning gaze on the back
of her neck and found that she could not become involved
in the play. His eyes seemed to be trying to burn a hole
in the base of her skull, she thought, but she kept silent,
realizing that by the flippant utterance of those few
words she had placed him once more on his guard.

Now, now when she wanted to win him by winsome
smiles and flirtatious glances, to ease him into trusting
her just long enough to escape him, she had bungled
by allowing her temper to overcome her reason. Why,
why must she be so impulsive? she thought in exasperation.

When the intermission came, she steeled herself to
risk turning around to face Lafitte. His black eyes met
hers with no sign of softening.

"I—I was hasty in my words before," Gabrielle began
slowly, as she took a deep breath. "I suppose I was feeling homesick, and—"

"Please, my dear, you do not have to take the trouble
to lie to me. I believe we understand each other."

Her brows lifted. "Understand each other?" she
prompted, at a loss.

He nodded. "Of course. Your feelings toward me are
anything but loving. I am not such a fool but that I

can see that," he said bitingly. "So we must face the truth of this relationship. I am, as you say, the pirate, and you, Gabrielle, are my kept woman. A very simple and satisfying arrangement."

Gabrielle's face flamed scarlet at his words, and she pulled open her fan to hide her blushing cheeks from inquisitive eyes. "I dislike having such words applied to myself," she whispered in affront.

He smiled grimly. "But you wanted the truth, did you not? All right, I admit to being a pirate—well, let us say a privateer at the very least, and you, well, you must be truthful enough to admit your own profession."

She flashed him a glance of anger from above the top of her spread fan. "I will certainly not admit to any such thing," she whispered vehemently, working the fan with swift irritation. "A woman who is forced against her will to stay with a man—"

He was watching her with a crafty look on his face as though waiting for her to say the words that would sink her into the abyss, and she hesitated, realizing that this man held her life in his hands.

"Perhaps we had better take our leave now," Lafitte suggested softly, a slightly menacing note in his voice.

Gabrielle shook her head, afraid suddenly to be alone with him. "If you please, I should like to see the end of the play," she said, dropping her eyes from his gaze.

He shrugged his shoulders. "As you wish."

It was over too soon, Gabrielle thought, as she applauded without enthusiasm. Beside her, Lafitte stood, offering her her cloak. Settling it carelessly on her shoulders, he led her from the box and out into the narrow hallway. They descended the stairs to the milling throng below.

Her unease did not subside when they seated themselves in the carriage. Lafitte did not speak, and Gabrielle creased and recreased her handkerchief nervously.

When they arrived at the cottage, he escorted her silently to the bedroom, but when the black girl made as though to help Gabrielle undress, he ushered her out of the room with an oath. Gabrielle shivered, hoping to maintain an air of cool disdain as she threw the cloak and fan onto the bed.

"Jean," she began, "I am truly weary. Perhaps it would be best if we—"

"Ma'm'selle," he interrupted in a cutting tone, "I hope you are not suggesting that I go off somewhere and leave you to yourself tonight? After all, you are my paramour, are you not? Or are you becoming greedy?"

Gabrielle looked up at him blankly, her hand to her lips.

"A woman must always have money to tempt her virtue," he said cuttingly, coming towards her. He brought out several gold pieces from his coat pocket, shoving them roughly beneath her nose.

Gabrielle looked at the money in horror, a distant memory returning to her of ten gold pieces winking in the palm of her maidservant, deposited under her pillow by a man as payment for her "services." She flung her hand out and knocked the money onto the floor, a look of disgust on her face.

"Your money will not buy me!" she cried out at him, retreating behind a table. "Your actions have been unforgivable. I—I must say that I was certainly beginning to think that you were somewhat of a—a gentleman, despite your despicable profession, but after tonight, you cannot think you have done anything to confirm that shaky opinion!"

He laughed loudly, throwing back his head and showing his white teeth. "Ma'm'selle, you are priceless!" he said, still laughing. "The very picture of outraged innocence, which can so carefully hide the nature of a courtesan. Perhaps you should think about joining those actors we saw on the stage tonight, for you, surely, need no script."

White with indignation, Gabrielle pointed to the door. "You will please leave me," she said.

He shook his head, still chuckling, as he began to divest himself of his coat, shirt, and boots. Gabrielle watched, thunderstruck, and determined that he should not have her this night after his verbal abuses. Dressed only in breeches and stockings, he trod softly towards her, his black eyes gleaming in the candlelight.

"No!" she cried, running from him. But there was no place to go, for he effectively blocked any avenue of escape.

His hands tore the silk from her body hurriedly and with no regard for her shrinking flesh. When she was naked, he stared at sight of her slender, golden body before him. Roughly, he pulled her to the bed, and without preliminaries he possessed her in haste. The act left her aching and unfulfilled. He continued to lie atop her, nearly crushing her into the mattress, and Gabrielle struggled to roll him over, angry and frustrated. He finally rolled to one side but kept his leg and arm thrown over her body so that she could not even rise from the bed.

Once more in the night he took her without compassion or regard for her feelings, leaving her once more bruised and tearful. Oh, how she hated him for his cruelty! She would escape from him at the very first opportunity, she thought, clenching her fists. He thought he could possess her and treat her like dirt. Gabrielle de Beauvoir, the girl who had been presented to Napoleon himself! How could she have sunk so low! Remembering the kisses and caresses she had so warmly given Lafitte on those other occasions, she crimsoned in shame. What had happened to her? How was it that God had decided to deal her such a cruel blow?

She began to weep, shedding tears of self-pity that shook her with their intensity. She was at the mercy of the brigand, who neither loved her nor even cared for her.

Beside her, Lafitte bent over her sleepily. "What are those tears for?" he asked with little tenderness.

Gabrielle bit back fresh sobs and refused to answer him. His hand closed painfully over her left breast, drawing a gasp from her lips.

Truth to tell, Lafitte thought to himself, he felt very bad about his performance tonight. But she had wounded his pride, dammit! Didn't the wench think he could have as much as anyone else? She was so damned beautiful, and he was furious at the thought that he could have all this loveliness within his grasp and yet not be sure of her. Damn! The girl would drive him crazy if he didn't think of some way to keep her out of his sight for a time.

If he could only keep her somewhere where he wouldn't have to worry about her running away—didn't the little fool realize that New Orleans was no place for a young, beautiful girl to be alone? Bigger fish than he would gobble her up soon enough, he thought, and many of those would have little, if any, concern for her personal welfare. He could keep her at Grande Terre, but he couldn't be sure she would not try to escape despite the many dangers involved. He could picture her exquisite face drifting, white, in the pools of quicksand, or in the treacherous swamp waters—worse, there were the alligators lurking in evil menace in the shadows. If only he could keep her here in New Orleans, safe from such horrors, he thought. But where?

Certainly not here in this house, but—and his face suddenly relaxed in the darkness and he tightened his arm unconsciously about her now-still form. Yes, the first thing in the morning, he would have to pay a call on his good friend, Renée.

Gabrielle was seated at the breakfast table when she heard the front door open and Lafitte's voice greeting the black boy.

"Ah, I see you have eaten already," he said, entering the room and kissing her lightly on the mouth as though nothing had happened between them to disturb his accustomed manner with her.

Gabrielle nodded curtly, more than a little embarrassed after last night's episode. "Yes, it—it was very good. And—and yourself?" She gazed steadfastly out the window, refusing to meet his gaze.

"I've already been to the old Absinthe House. I breakfasted with friends there. I had some business to attend to before returning here." He laughed as though in fond recollection.

"It's all very easy, I suppose, for you to be amused," she put in bitingly. "But please do not expect me to join in your good humor. I'm afraid my—my feelings have altered considerably towards you after last night."

He frowned. "Is that some sort of refusal, spitfire?"

She stuck out her chin in defiance, and her violet eyes sparkled with temper. "I will not be treated like a—like a common—common—" she broke off and turned away from his black gaze.

"Did you say, spitfire, that you are not a common whore? Then, my dear, are you an uncommon one?" His laugh was totally devoid of levity, and Gabrielle could not meet the angry look in his eyes. "I have been debating for some time just what to do with you. Believe me, I realize that you will not hesitate to try to escape me, and, frankly, I cannot understand why I don't let you do so. But, unfortunately for both of us, there is a very strong attraction that you continue to hold over me. The only feasible solution I can see is to secure you in a jail." He smiled at her outraged look. "No, no, my lovely, not the menacing old calaboose in the square. I mean a silken prison of such luxury that you should be thankful that you have such an obliging master." His eyes narrowed. "Madame Renée, then, has kindly consented to keep you for me."

At the look of puzzlement on Gabrielle's face, he explained. "It's the best brothel in the city of New Orleans, my dear. Didn't you just scream at me that you were no common whore? Well, this is not a common whorehouse. Many of the finest men in New Orleans frequent it, including Governor Claiborne himself, I'm told. Madame Renée's is the perfect solution, you see, for she guards her girls as jealously as a lover. She offers everything from young virgins to quadroons so beautiful you would think they were white."

"What—what are you saying?" Gabrielle whispered faintly, her eyes wide in her strained face.

He laughed cynically, deliberately hardening himself against the stirring picture she presented to him. "In a word, I am installing you in one of Madame Renée's better suites, exclusively for my use on those occasions when I am in New Orleans."

Gabrielle's eyes glittered with outrage. "I am to be set up as your—your mistress in a brothel! How can you be sure you will be the only man I see?" she taunted him, her voice icy. "After all, you are gone for months at a time, as I well know. How can you be positive that I will be there when you return?"

Lafitte admitted to himself that he couldn't be positive, but he was betting on Madame Renée's greedy hands, for he had promised her an outrageous sum to ensure that this girl would not be touched by anyone else. He sent a swift glance toward the young woman who sat opposite, blazing defiance at him now, and he felt a pang of regret that things could not have been different between them. If only—but he quickly, determinedly, shook his head to clear it of such thoughts. No, the best thing would be to get her with child, and quickly. Mothers, he knew, were less apt to fight when the welfare of their children was at stake.

"You may take anything you wish from the closet upstairs," he indicated harshly. "But make it quick, for I have other matters to attend to."

"I will not take anything obtained by your lawless pillaging," was her haughty answer. "I would not even wear this gown if propriety did not demand that I not walk naked on the street!"

"Very soon, spitfire, you'll have little use for such propriety," he returned softly and called for the carriage to be brought to the door.

Trembling with anger and humiliation, Gabrielle shortly found herself crossing the threshold of Madame Renée's house, Lafitte's hand tight on her arm. Madame Renée herself greeted them in the front parlor, a room that was, to Gabrielle's considerable surprise, tastefully decorated in soft blues and greens. The madam was dressed very

conservatively at this time of day in a high-necked gown
of stiff damask that did little to enhance her overly en-
dowed figure.

"Ah, the terrible pirate of the Gulf," Renée smiled as
she extended her hand for Lafitte to kiss. "Who would
ever think that such a man would be conducting so unusual a transaction, eh, my friend?" The woman turned to
look speculatively at Gabrielle, who could not help flush-
ing at the obvious inspection. "Don't be afraid of me,
my dear. I'll take the very best care of you, which is
more than the streets of this city can offer. You know,
you're really very lucky. Captain Lafitte has told me a
little about you, and I think that you will find we are
a very civilized group here."

Gabrielle did not deign to answer. Renée turned back
to Lafitte and beckoned him into another room.

"Come with me, captain, and we will conclude our
business. Meanwhile, I'll have Claudine take our new
resident to her room." She rang a tiny silver bell, causing
a pretty mulatto girl to appear at the doorway. "Take
Ma'm'selle Gabrielle to her room on the second floor,
Claudine."

The maid curtseyed, and Gabrielle realizing there was
no use resisting, followed her silently up the stairs. There
were no other girls about, and Gabrielle concluded that
they must all be asleep at this time of day. Claudine led
her to a room at the far end of the hall and opened it to
reveal a nicely furnished bedroom, papered in a soft print.

"Have you any baggage?" the girl asked her in English.

"No, I have nothing except these clothes I am dressed
in," Gabrielle replied.

Gabrielle heard the distinct click as the door was
locked, and she sat hopeless on the bed after first inspecting the room to see if there were any other exit.
The one window was barred by wrought-iron grillwork,
and Gabrielle surmised that she was truly a prisoner
within the confines of this room. Dear God, she would
die of boredom within a month.

After a while, she heard a soft tapping at the door,

followed by the sound of a key turning in the lock. The door was opened timidly by a girl who looked no more than twenty. "Hello."

Gabrielle barely acknowledged her greeting with a slight nod.

"You are Gabrielle, are you not?"

Another nod.

The girl broke into a dazzling smile that transformed her plain features into a look of total sweetness. "I'm Dolly Ames. I have the room right next door." She pointed to the wall and then walked in and seated herself on a chair.

Still a bit nonplussed, Gabrielle continued to stare at the girl, who was dressed only in a light silk robe that left little to the imagination. She had round, blue eyes and a wealth of auburn hair that floated softly about her shoulders in pretty dishabille.

"You—you live here?" Gabrielle questioned finally in order to break the silence.

"Yes. I also work here. I'm one of Renée's girls," Dolly offered with a complete absence of embarrassment. She appeared to study her pearly, polished nails for a moment, then cocked her head to one side as she studied Gabrielle. "You are very pretty," she announced finally. "You'd probably do very well here—I mean, of course, if you wanted to make it a permanent thing."

"I—I wasn't brought here for that," Gabrielle said firmly, hoping to draw the line between this girl and herself, if only for her own feeling of self-respect.

Dolly waved her hands in understanding. "Oh, of course. Renée has already informed everyone that you are an exclusive resident. My, my. However did you capture that exciting man, anyway? It must have been thrilling for you."

Gabrielle shuddered inside but kept her outward demeanor cool as she shrugged with nonchalance. "Not really. After all, he's just a man—like any other."

Dolly laughed. "Spoken like a sister!" She stood up and extended her hand. "Come now. Renée asked me to bring you down to dinner. Everyone is dying to meet you."

Gabrielle hung back a little. "Must I go downstairs? I mean, I really don't—"

"You'll be all right. Really, the girls are all very nice, except Rosa, who's a Mex and as catty as you'll ever see. Steer clear of her and you won't have any worries."

Dolly pulled at her hand and, resigned, Gabrielle followed her down the hall and downstairs to a huge dining room towards the back of the house. She noticed that Claudine and another girl were lighting candles in two spacious rooms that were connected by an archway and whose furnishings were lavish in bright reds and golds. The "meeting room" she thought distastefully.

In the dining room, there was plenty of food spread out on the table, and about ten girls were digging in with hearty appetites. All talk stopped as she made her appearance beside Dolly on the threshold.

"Ah, there you are, Gabrielle. Please forgive us for starting without you. I hope you will enjoy your meal." Renée ushered her to a chair beside her, and Gabrielle took it hesitantly, careful not to look up at the curious faces who were all staring at her. "Girls, please remember your manners," warned Renée, casting a wary glance around the table.

The talking resumed after a few stilted hellos, and the clatter of knives and forks mixed with the aroma of excellent Creole food. But Gabrielle ate very little and sincerely wished herself back in her room alone.

The girl to her right was a stunning redhead with languorous green eyes and a voluptuous figure, partially revealed by her lacy robe. "I'm Catherine," she told her between mouthfuls. "My room is just across the hall from yours." She giggled a little. "I hope I don't keep you awake at night. Renée says I'm one of her best girls, and she—"

"That's enough, Catherine," Renée interrupted, noting Gabrielle's reddening cheeks.

Catherine pouted prettily. "Well, for goodness' sake, it's not as if she doesn't know what it's all about!"

Gabrielle cast a grateful look at her benefactress.

Renée said, "I'm afraid, Gabrielle, that you're just going to have to get used to the girls' way of talking and dressing. It is part of our business—and it's a profitable business. None of us here is ashamed of the way we make our living."

The other girls agreed, to the accompaniment of titters and giggling.

"I'm sorry," Gabrielle murmured, "but I'm not used to—"

"But I thought you were Jean Lafitte's mistress!" said a girl. "Surely you must know how to make a man desire you if you were lucky enough to catch him!"

Another round of laughter greeted this statement. Gabrielle said nothing, her face reflecting her embarrassment.

"You act so innocent," came another voice, disgruntled. "Perhaps that is how you caught the pirate's attention, eh? Did you have to steal him from another woman?"

All eyes turned to the end of the table where a striking, dark-haired woman sat, her liquid eyes watching Gabrielle with calculated indifference. "I tell you this, bright-haired one, if I ever thought you would steal a man from me, I'd slit your pretty throat."

"Rosa! Hush! Good Heavens, do you want to scare the child? Of course she's not going to go after any of your men. She'll stay put in her room during business hours—strict orders, my dears."

Rosa refused to be quieted. "Oh, yes, but how long will that be? How long before she opens her door 'just out of curiosity'? I tell you, if she even looks at one of my customers, I'll—"

"Oh, shut up, Rosa! We all know you're jealous as a tigress over that handsome Mr. St. Claire of yours. My God, after you're done with him, it's a wonder he can still walk out the door," Dolly replied saucily, sticking her tongue out at the other girl.

Rosa's eyes glittered. "You remember, Dolly, what happened to you when I caught you showing your legs to him?"

Involuntarily, Dolly winced and held her arm, where Gabrielle could see a long, white scar that ran from her shoulder to her elbow, obvious even through the enveiling robe.

Rosa laughed. "So you did learn your lesson. And I'm glad this new one knows, too, now."

"I can assure you that I have no intention of sticking my nose out of my—my room at any rate," Gabrielle told her in a level voice, feeling as though she should justify herself in the face of this other woman's disbelief. "My door is locked. How could I get out?"

"Locked? All the time?" a sympathetic voice murmured.

Madame Renée's face hardened a trifle. "I'm afraid that those are my orders from Captain Lafitte, girls. So, until I have some proof that our new boarder won't be attempting to escape, I shall, for the moment, comply with his wishes."

Gabrielle felt completely defeated. It seemed even more humiliating to be labeled a virtual prisoner in front of all these others. She noted the smile of satisfaction on Rosa's face and swallowed hard to keep the tears from her eyes.

Chapter Seventeen

A week passed without any incident, and Gabrielle found that she was becoming more and more used to observing the unusual habits of the girls—their daytime sleeping hours, the infectious laughter and ribald humor, their form of dressing. Her sleep at night was still disturbed by laughing, shouts, singing, and deep men's voices calling and cajoling, but she hoped she would soon grow accustomed to these noises.

Most of the girls were friendly in accordance with their natures, and even Rosa, after a few days, behaved cordially towards her.

At length, Madame Renée condescended to leaving her door unlocked, for as Gabrielle pointed out, there was no place she could go. Lafitte had informed Gabrielle on his last visit that he was leaving immediately on more business and would be gone for a few weeks, news that drew a sigh of relief from Gabrielle, who had not been looking forward to another meeting with him.

There was a general joke among the girls at Renée's that very soon they would have to initiate their unwilling guest into the "sisterhood."

"Oh, yes!" Catherine cried, clapping her hands with unbridled glee one night at the table. "We could use dear old Mr. Sawyer for a guinea pig!"

Rosa snorted in disgust. "You mean that old man—what good can he do? His loins are filled with cold water!"

"You would be surprised," Catherine returned primly, folding her lips and glaring at the other woman.

The others burst into laughter at this remark. "What about that young man that seems to favor you so much, Margot? Mr. Bryan—the one who is here every Thursday night precisely at ten o'clock for his weekly purge," called one girl.

The girl called Margot shrugged. "Not him—in one minute, and finished the next," she remarked, causing more fits of laughter.

"Oh, but what about the dashing Mr. St. Claire?" Dolly asked, her sharp gaze on Rosa, who immediately darkened with anger.

"I've warned you once," the Spanish girl hissed, half-rising from the table.

"All right, all right, girls, that's enough of your silliness. Eat your dinner and get dressed. It's nearly seven o'clock now, and we'll have some very irritated customers if you don't hurry," intervened Renée, clapping her hands for silence.

The meal was finished and the girls left to go to their rooms to change. Left alone, Gabrielle hesitated and then walked toward the middle parlor, curious to see just how the evening would be conducted. There she found Renée busily laying out cigars and bottles of the best wine and bourbon, careful to put the cut-glass decanters well back from the edges of the tables. The candles were lit and seemed to cast a rosy glow over the deep plush of the red loveseats and gold chairs, the luxury of the wine-red carpet which, Renée told her, had come at considerable cost all the way from New York. A gracefully curving staircase spiralled up to the second floor, connecting with the hall where the girls' rooms were. Gabrielle had always used the back staircase, and she marveled privately at the exquisite grace of the white grillwork on the front stairs' balustrade.

"What are you doing here, child?" Renée asked as she turned to find Gabrielle standing in the middle of the room, admiring the ornate work on the curio cabinet.

"I was just looking," Gabrielle remarked, smiling at the woman as she passed her hand over the softness of a linen tablecloth.

There was a worried expression on the older woman's face, half-understanding and half-disgruntled. "You best hurry upstairs now, Gabrielle," she said softly. "The gentlemen should be arriving any minute."

Gabrielle nodded and left the room, unaware that Renée was watching her and shaking her head anxiously.

During the days that followed, Gabrielle found herself drawn quite inexplicably to the parlor in spite of herself. She didn't know that she was simply displaying the natural curiosity of the young and "innocent" towards the lives of "ladies of pleasure," and instead she felt ashamed of her feelings and tried to suppress them.

It was, of course, inescapable that one day she would

be caught. The girls were, as usual, getting dressed, and Gabrielle had taken to helping Renée set out cigars and brandy for the gentlemen guests. She was wearing a gown borrowed from Dolly, a pale blue froth of a dress that was too tight in the bust for the other girl. It fit Gabrielle very well, and she delighted in its swirling folds. It was a Saturday night, the busiest time of the week, so that there was an unusually large amount of liquor to be set out.

"Please finish for me, Gabrielle, and light the candles afterwards—those against the mirrors," Renée asked her, checking the porcelain clock and hurrying upstairs to don her own attire for the evening.

Gabrielle set the exquisite decanters in strategic locations around the room and lit the taper from one of the table candlebra in order to light the remaining candles in holders attached to either side of the new gold-plated mirror that had arrived just the previous morning from Savannah.

Claudine rushed through the hall to open the door, urging Gabrielle to hurry on with her work and get upstairs. But Gabrielle took no notice of her as she carefully lit the ten candles on either side of the mirror. The effect was truly breathtaking, and as she looked at her reflection in the mirror, it exhibited a misty effect that was quite becoming.

"Oh, ma'm'selle, how lovely you look tonight," she mocked her reflection.

"How lovely, indeed," boomed a man's voice directly behind her.

Turning so swiftly that she nearly dropped the taper, Gabrielle flushed with annoyance at the sight of the eavesdropper, a tall giant of a man whose reddish hair and beard seemed to flame in the light of the candles. Out of the corner of her eye, she caught sight of Claudine disappearing down the hall to answer another bell.

"Here, let me take that away from you. The way you're shaking—look's as though you'll be setting this place on fire in another minute," the man commented genially, his fingers brushing her hand as he took the taper from her.

He put out the candle in the sandpot and took her arm to pull her down beside him on the loveseat. "You're new here, aren't you?" he said conversationally, his hand moving casually around her shoulders.

Gabrielle's throat felt constricted and she could only nod, her eyes wide and jewel-bright.

He chuckled amiably. "I thought I hadn't seen you before. You're a pretty thing. Where're you from?"

"P-Paris," Gabrielle whispered.

"Really!" he returned, pressing his thigh against hers. "This is your first night, then?"

"Yes, I mean—that is, I don't really—"

"Oh, now don't worry about anything, sweetheart. I'm gentle as a lamb with a girl, and if you're worried about the money, well, I might look like some big, country oaf, but I—"

"Oh, no, I'm not worried about the m-money," Gabrielle gasped.

Two other gentlemen entered the room and looked in her direction with interest. Dear God, where were the girls? She heard the swishing of petticoats and looked over to the staircase where Rosa stood, looking at her with mocking amusement. With a silent salute, she made her way down the stairs and into the room, catching the arm of one of the two new arrivals.

"What's the matter, sweetheart? You're as skittish as a nervous filly. I told you Jim West wouldn't hurt a fly, much less a pretty young morsel like yourself." He edged closer to her, his eyes searching beneath the neckline of her gown.

"I'm afraid you don't understand, Mr.—Mr. West," Gabrielle began, in a reflex action putting her hands against his chest. "I've never—"

He slapped his thigh and smiled widely. "An unplucked one!" he surmised incorrectly, patting her shoulder with understanding. "I didn't know there were any left in New Orleans. Just you sit here, sweetheart, while ole Jim gets us both some brandy—that'll loosen you up a bit." He left her with a look of regret, his mouth barely brushing her temple.

By now, most of the other girls had arrived, and, while Jim West was having Sara pour him two brandies, Dolly hurried over to where Gabrielle sat almost frozen with shock.

"Good God, Gabrielle! What in the world are you doing down here? And with Jim West, of all people! He's such a bear when he's crossed—and where he is, his nemesis will soon be, if he's not here already—that would be Mr. St. Claire, of course, and if he even looks at you, Rosa will have your hair!"

Gabrielle looked in the direction of Rosa's tinkling laugh and saw her seated on the lap of a skinny-looking fellow with stringy dark hair. "If that's Mr. St. Claire—" she began, laughing shakily.

Dolly shook her head. "You dolt! Of course that's not him. But never mind about that now. You've got to figure out how you're going to slip out of Big Jim's notice so I can smuggle you back upstairs."

Jim West was already making his way back across the room, smiling and nodding to some of the other girls.

"I—I could pretend to be sick," Gabrielle whispered.

Dolly frowned, but nodded swiftly as Jim West came up.

"Dolly, darling, I hope you're telling your new resident here only nice things about me. You know I'd do the same for you, baby." He settled himself in the loveseat obviously looking for Dolly to excuse herself and move away.

"Jim, you know I'm in love with you," Dolly joked, frowning a little at Gabrielle as a signal to begin her act.

Clutching her stomach, Gabrielle bent over and began moaning. "Oh-h-h. Oh dear, I—I feel so sick all of a sudden," she groaned as realistically as she could, not daring to risk looking at West for his reaction. She felt his arm go around her, lifting her up so that he could look into her face.

"You know, you are a little flushed, sweetie. Maybe you'd feel better if I took you up to your room," he offered, his eyes glinting. "It is a little stuffy in here."

"Oh-h, no, Mr. West. I couldn't bother you. . . ."

"Bother?" His brow lowered quizzically. "Why it's no bother, my lady. I could lift you up in one hand."

"Jim, I'm afraid she looks sick enough to vomit," Dolly interjected, putting a hasty hand against Gabrielle's forehead. "I'd better help her upstairs right now. I think she needs rest—you know, her first night and all, she's probably a wreck of nerves. I think Renée started her out too fast." Dolly was saying anything that came to mind, and Gabrielle felt her breath leave her as West stood up and swept her into his big arms.

"Well, you can at least let me carry the little thing up to her room," he growled irritably now.

Anxiously, Dolly followed the pair upstairs and down the hall to Gabrielle's room, where West laid her down as gently as an infant on her bed. Gabrielle continued to emit groans, clutching her stomach and clenching her fists until she truly felt a little sick.

Once he had deposited her on the bed, West gave her a solicitous kiss on the forehead and brushed her bosom regretfully with his hand. "I do hope you feel better, miss. Maybe if you shake off your nerves later in the evening, you can join me downstairs again. I'll be looking for you."

He left the room, and once they heard his footsteps receding down the hall, Gabrielle and Dolly looked at each other with mingled apprehension and relief.

"Oh, my God, Dolly. Did you hear what he said about later on? What'll I do?" Gabrielle implored, sitting up nervously.

"You just get your nightgown on and get into bed for now. He'll forget all about you after a few more drinks and a little dalliance with one of the other girls. He's really fond of Catherine, and I'll tell her to work on him as a favor to you. She will be glad to oblige." Dolly started to leave the room, then turned. "You've got to admit, Gabrielle, you did bring it all on yourself. I wonder—" she stopped and shrugged. "Oh well, at any rate, I'll lock the door myself and put the key in my room. That way if good old Jim decides to pay you a midnight visit later on, he'll just have to settle for one of the other doors." She threw her a kiss and was gone, locking the door firmly behind her.

Tense with reaction, Gabrielle got up from the bed and paced the room like a caged tigress. This was simply not going to work, she argued, keeping her here in this place. She must get out.

She heard the soft strains of the violins as the musicians began playing, the tinkling of glasses, and the laughter of men and women—it could almost have been a ball at Napoleon's court, she thought incongruously.

Resolutely, she shed her gown and slipped into the softness of her silken nightwear. She left the two candles burning on her vanity, thinking to let them burn themselves out in the night. She fell asleep almost as soon as her head hit the pillow.

A violent knocking on her door dragged her from her dreams. Could it be morning already? She felt as though she had hardly slept at all, and glancing at the window, she could see that it was still pitch-dark outside and the candles had barely burned down from their earlier positions.

"Open this door, sweetheart. I know you're not sick! Open it!" The bellow belonged to a man, and Gabrielle came awake swiftly, completely alert as she recognized Jim West's voice.

What had happened? He sounded drunk and in no mood to be tricked again. Then she remembered, with a sigh of relief, that Dolly had locked the door—and surely the man's bellowing would rouse the rest of the house. Gabrielle had every confidence that Renée would know how to handle the situation. Even now she could hear Catherine's voice, softly urging him to come across the hall to her room.

"Jimmy, darling—come on now. I've been waiting to bring you up here all evening, lover," Catherine purred.

"Goddammit! I'll not be treated like a half-witted adolescent! I mean to have that girl tonight whether she's new in the business or not! Now you get back downstairs and to your business, Cathy. I'll attend to mine." The door seemed to shudder from the weight of his fists as he continued to bang on it.

"Jimmy, honey, why don't we—"

"Christ almighty! Cathy, I don't want to hurt you!"

Gabrielle shivered uncontrollably, too paralyzed to move. She watched in fascination as the door began to groan and bulge at its hinges. Dear God! He must be very drunk, she thought helplessly.

"Open up, damn you! I'll not be tricked, girl!"

With his final mighty shove, the door splintered and fell apart, and in the next instant, Gabrielle was looking at the scowling visage of a man who was not about to be denied a second time.

"Good," he smiled, moving towards her. "You're already cozy in bed. Just a minute, sweetheart, and I'll join you."

By now some of the girls and their partners for the evening had been aroused and were gathering in curiosity outside in the hall. They can't just let him rape me—they can't just stand there and watch, Gabrielle thought feverishly. She heard Renée's voice when the woman came running down the hall.

"What in the world is happening here? Catherine, where is Gabrielle?"

By now, West had moved to the bed, and Gabrielle felt his hand grabbing at her nightdress, heard the protesting sound of the cloth tearing at her bosom.

"Gabrielle! Mr. West, what are you doing?" It was Renée, stepping into the room, her eyes taking in the wrecked door and dilating at the physical proof of the man's strength. "Please, Mr. West, if you will just come downstairs with me, I'm sure we can work something out for you. Miss Gabrielle is not feeling well tonight. I, myself, insisted she remain in her room."

"She'll remain here, that she will," West answered her grimly, peeling the remains of Gabrielle's nightgown from her cringing flesh. And then in a different voice, "God, you *are* a little beauty! Christ, who are they saving you for?"

Gabrielle found her voice with difficulty. "Please, please, Mr. West. You—you cannot do this."

"Why not?" the man demanded, grabbing her chin in one hand and pressing the soft flesh of her face between his strong fingers. "You're a whore, same as the rest of them, aren't you? A high-class one, but still there for any man who'll pay your price. I told you before, baby, I'll pay whatever you ask." His voice was growing thicker and his eyes could not get enough of her partially exposed body. "Get out of here. I'm a paying customer," he growled at Renée who was hesitating at the foot of the bed.

"Catherine, get help. Hurry, girl! Get some of the men downstairs. Find St. Claire; maybe he can reason with him. Move, girl!" Renée said quickly, hurrying back out to the hall.

The small gathering at the doorway was dispersing slowly, some of the men loath to leave the sight of the beautiful girl in the bed. Gabrielle felt a rush of disgust in her throat at their hanging tongues and glazed eyes. Animals! All of them! watching as though this were some kind of circus.

For an instant, she caught sight of Rosa's glittering black eyes. There was a look of anger in them, and then a man passed in front of her and moved stealthily into the room. Gabrielle closer her eyes as West's hands pushed the bedcovers away from her, leaving her completely exposed to his lustful eyes.

"Oh, no," she whispered, as she felt his mouth against her breast.

"West! What the hell are you doing?" The words were uttered with a curious, calm amusement as though the owner of that voice thought the whole thing an enormous joke. "I don't think the little girl appreciates your ardor, my friend."

Gabrielle felt West's hot mouth move away from her, felt his whole body turning. "St. Claire, this isn't your business! You've got your woman now, go pleasure her. I've a mind to teach this one that no one plays a trick on Jim West."

"Jimmy, boy, she's a cold fish. Poor little Cathy's waiting out here for you to warm her up. I've never thought you to be so stupid."

Gabrielle felt the man's body tightening with anger. "Stupid! What're you talking about? This one's worth ten times that little bitch!"

"Jimmy, Jimmy—you'll never win the ladies' hearts by such foolish statements. Think, will you, for a moment, and try to lift that whiskey-soaked brain of yours out of the gutter."

"Goddammit, St. Claire! That's just about enough!" West roared, springing from the bed to jump at the other man.

Through half-blurred eyes filled with tears, Gabrielle watched as the two figures met in the middle of the room, the one so big and bearlike, the other tall and lithe, moving with the grace of a panther as he sidestepped neatly, causing West to fall to his knees from the force of his propulsion. God, if they don't hurry and do something, these two will kill themselves, she thought.

The opponents circled each other warily.

"St. Claire, I'm telling you for the last time!"

"West, I'm afraid if you don't get out of here right now, one of us is not going to leave." The words were cold, merciless, and Gabrielle shivered at their emotionless quality.

"Why, I could kill you with my bare hands," the bigger man shouted, lowering his head like a bull, so thoroughly angered now that nothing short of a bullet could have stopped him.

From his boot, West unsheathed a long, wicked-looking

knife, and, following suit, the other man did likewise. They continued to circle for a moment, each looking for a break in the other's defense.

"You know this isn't over no whore," West spit out. "You've been itching for this for a long time, looking for an excuse to start something, St. Claire."

The other man laughed coldly. "This is as good an excuse for killing you as any, West. You've become stupid and boastful in the past few months—you're no good in this any more."

West's answering laugh was nasty. "Ah, come on, St. Claire, we both know you've hated me ever since you found me and that pert little slant-eyed fluff of yours in the hay together."

Gabrielle watched for a stiffening, some reaction from the other man, and saw none.

"She's gone now," he replied softly. "She killed herself after confessing her faithlessness rather than risk my scorn. I'm sorry she did that, West. She should have been here to see you die tonight."

Something in the man's voice must have pierced the thick fog of whiskey in West's brain, for he started to sweat, and he stumbled on the bedclothes. "Now wait a minute, St. Claire. You're not going to pin the whole blame on me! Why her tail was so hot for me—"

"Shut up!" the other man's voice bit through the words. He made a feint for the man, and his knife found the fleshy part of an arm, knocking West backwards and spinning him up against the vanity. The two candles were knocked to the floor, and Gabrielle watched in terror as the eager flames began licking at the dry carpeting and the scattered clothing. In a few minutes, the fire had groped hungrily toward the draperies at the window.

"Fire! Fire! Hurry, get water!" someone shouted from the hall, and Gabrielle saw the others fleeing.

She would have run, herself, but the two figures barred her way to the door, and she crouched with fright against the side of the bed.

The two men locked arms, then parted and locked

again. She could hear the heavy breathing, the grunts of pain, the crack of bones as hands pushed against the fingers that held the shining steel of death.

The fire was surging in a fury towards the bed, and Gabrielle pushed her body up against the wall, pleading silently for the combat to end. Haphazardly, she draped what was left of her nightgown around her. The heat fanned her face, and the smoke was becoming thick in the room. Both men were gasping for air, and they, too, knew the imminent danger that threatened.

Suddenly, St. Claire began pushing West backwards with sharp, chopping stabs of his knife, relentlessly forcing him back towards the inferno of the window. West, beaten both by the other man's skill and his own whiskey-fumed brain, tripped heavily on the overturned vanity and caught himself at the point where the window ledge had been but now was no more than a gaping hole filling with black smoke. He stood poised for the briefest second, an infinitesimal moment in space, before his weight caused the remaining damaged wood to break, and he was flung out through the window.

Gabrielle thought she could hear his agonized scream as though he were a great distance away. She slumped to the floor, sprawling, only half-conscious now from lack of air. Her eyes were smarting from the smoke so that she could hardly see the figure of the man that ran towards the door, then stopped, turned, and came back towards her, scooping her up over his shoulder. Her head bumped against his back sharply, and something wet and sticky smeared her cheek as she tried to fight off the bursting red lights in her head.

They descended the staircase that led through the kitchens, and Gabrielle could hear the sounds of confusion coming from the front of the house. They were in the courtyard now, circling the house through the side alley. The fresh air seemed to tear through her lungs as she gulped great swallows down her sore throat.

She wanted to tell the man to put her down now. She

knew he must be hovering on the verge of exhaustion, but no sounds could come from her stiff, dry throat, and her head was aching with a vengeance.

As they neared the front of the house, she could hear the firebell and more voices buzzing and calling out orders. The man shifted her from his shoulder and settled her more comfortably in his arms in front of him, pressing her smoke-blackened face to his chest. Through layers of fog, Gabrielle could hear the voice of a woman she thought was Renée, talking and screaming, near hysteria.

"Gabrielle, Gabrielle! Oh, thank God, you've got her out alive, St. Claire. I wouldn't give much for my neck if Lafitte found out she had died in all this mess. Oh, my poor girls! Nowhere to go now. Oh, my God, my God!"

Gabrielle could feel a sudden stiffening in the man's arms. "You say she belongs to Jean Lafitte?" he asked in a rush of suppressed anger.

"Yes, yes. And he paid me in gold to keep her safe. When I think—" and Renée was running around in circles once more.

Through swollen eyes, Gabrielle could make out the distraught woman as she ran from one person to another, checking on her girls, making sure everyone had escaped injury, shouting shrill orders to the volunteers who had manned the fire brigade, nearly tearing her hair out in her nervous frustration. Gabrielle would have smiled if her lips hadn't been so dry and her tongue so parched.

All she wanted was a drink of water and something to stop the pain that she now felt centered in her chest as though a great weight was pressing down on her, inhibiting her breathing. She was being lowered to the ground as gently as possible, and, instinctively, she clung to her rescuer's hand, loath to be left alone.

"P-please," she whispered between short gasps, "don't leave m-me."

Her eyes struggled to focus on the sun-browned face that gazed down at her, but her vision was blurring fast and she could only catch a glimpse of it. For a moment, in the light of the fire, his eyes, looking so intently down into hers, glinted like green ice. She cried out in sudden, swift surprise, fighting the distant memory, then fell back into the dark chasm that awaited her.

Chapter Eighteen

"But who is she?" a male voice was asking, and its easy warmth penetrated the hazy fog that seemed to be surrounding Gabrielle's brain.

She felt warm and snug and so relaxed that she couldn't have lifted a finger if she had had to. The sheets were soft beneath her, and the pillow seemed to be made for a person to sink her head in, to lose track of time in the relief of sleep. She really didn't want to wake up—hoped that whoever it was discussing her would go away and leave her to the comforting darkness.

"She's Lafitte's mistress, I've been told," came an answering voice, drawling and arrogant with a touch of harshness underlying its tone. "What should I do with her, Leigh? Do you have any suggestions?"

"Jean Lafitte's mistress! Christ!" the other man whistled softly. "You're playing with fire, don't you think, my friend? Mrs. MacDonald informed me that the physician said the girl was healthy enough—just overcome by the smoke. Why don't you let her go back to Renée's temporary quarters, and I'm sure Lafitte will come and take her back."

"I'll give her back to her lover soon enough, Leigh," answered the second man indolently. "But first I'd like to sample her charms myself. Jesus—any wench who can tie a can on the pirate's tail must have something special about her."

"I don't know," began the other man doubtfully, and

Gabrielle heard no more as she allowed the blessed calm of sleep once again to overtake her.

Something made her awaken from her dreams, and Gabrielle opened her eyes wide in that first instant of consciousness. She beheld nothing more than a darkened room with the only light coming from the partially opened window that allowed a few moonbeams to scatter on the floor.

She turned comfortably in the wide bed and came up instantly against another body lying beside her. Panic overwhelmed her at first so that she gasped out loud and hovered for an instant on hysteria, her mind rushing back in time to the horrible moment when Jim West had stripped off her nightgown and had looked with such lecherous intent at her unprotected body.

My God! What was she thinking? Jim West was dead! Where—where was she? Who was this beside her? Questions flew furiously inside her head while her heart seemed to stop beating. She struggled through memory to piece together what must have happened to her since the fire but found that she had no recall of events after that.

Carefully, so as not to wake the unknown partner in her bed, she pulled away towards the edge and sat up, attempting to make a mental note of her surroundings. She could not see much in the inky shadows of the night but could make out the outline of a closed doorway some few feet away. Perhaps she could reach the door without awakening whoever it was beside her and go on from there.

So swiftly and silently that she did not even hear a movement—an arm reached out to grasp her around the waist.

Gabrielle stifled a scream and turned her head to try to pierce through the deeper darkness of the shadow beneath the covers.

"Who—who are you?" she whispered shakily, aware of the tightening of the arm against her naked flesh.

No answer came back to her, but the arm increased its pressure until she was drawn back against her will towards the middle of the bed. A gasp escaped her as she felt naked flesh against her own.

"Who are you? Where am I? You—you must let me go!" she demanded breathlessly.

Still the shadow said nothing. She was drawn down against the mattress, an arm still about her waist. She was almost afraid to struggle—afraid to shatter the silence of the figure next to her. It was almost as though she were still asleep, caught in the mists of the dream like a fly trapped in a spider's web. Struggling would do her little good and might even hasten the moment of terror.

She was lying prone now, her body pressed lightly against warm flesh—a man's body, hard and unyielding, shaping her softness against it. She lay unmoving, her eyes staring up at the ceiling, her emotions strained nearly to the breaking point.

Lips—warm and seeking—pressed against her temple, then moved slowly down her face. She strove to move her face away, but the arm at her waist moved up to cradle her head and keep her still. She could not get away from that mouth that moved closer and closer to hers, moving softly and surely, planting soft kisses on her skin that, despite her fear, made her shiver.

The mouth slid upwards from her neck and fastened on her lips, shaping them, molding them so exquisitely that they parted without her conscious volition. She tasted his tongue on hers, a faint aroma of good brandy filling her mouth as he forced her lips wider, pressing them back against her teeth while his tongue worked magic somewhere inside her head.

The kiss seemed to last forever, and she thought she could not stand it any longer—could not endure the breathless, wondering, incredible moment with this man whom she did not even know, could not even see.

A hand moved down her neck to her shoulder, and the fingers were warm and knowing on her flesh. They grazed her breast, drifted lazily over the swell of her bosom, brushed the tender spot underneath her arm where her breast blossomed from her side. Fingers traced the line of her breast from her side to the stiffening point, circling the nipple with slow, teasing movements that tautened them to sharp peaks of desire.

Gabrielle gasped as the mouth finally left hers, and she took in quick, short breaths as though she were fighting the urge to slip into unconsciousness. Her whole body felt light and tingling, quivering with sensations that were sweeping over her in a succession of waves that she was powerless to stop.

Lips and tongue teased her breasts and sucked gently at the nipples so that she answered the urge to bring her own hands up to press against his head, feeling the soft thickness of his hair. Her fingertips brushed the nape of his neck where the hair curled slightly, then pressed downward to trap his lips to her bosom.

But he needed no urging, his movements still slow and masterful so that she bit her lip in order not to cry out with a sudden, blind need for fulfillment. She no longer cared who he was, or where she was, or that he was a stranger to her. God! She wanted a man's body—wanted to feel him inside of her—wanted to release the unbearable tension that was building up within her.

She moved her hips impatiently and heard his soft laughter, muffled slightly against her flesh. His hands brushed the tightened muscles of her stomach as his lips continued to caress her breasts, then moved further down to find the smoothness of her thighs.

Gabrielle abandoned herself to his caresses, parting her thighs without resistance when his fingers asked for entrance. Her breathing was quick and gasping, her eyes were closed now in an attitude of surrender, her body was arched to a fine-tuned pitch, waiting for the moment of release that was coming closer now as she sensed the rising excitement in her partner.

His hand caught one of hers and brought it down to where he wanted her to touch and stroke him. Her other hand curled against his neck to bring his lips back to hers, and she kissed him passionately, pressing her body against his and bringing him closer to her.

Even as they kissed, he was pressing her down, deeper into the mattress, and bringing his body over hers, positioning her as he cupped her buttocks in his strong hands. She waited, breathless and perspiring, poised to receive him as her arms clasped him closer.

His thrust was deep and sure, the stroke of a man expert in the matter of women and aware of his ability to pleasure them. Gabrielle moaned softly as she felt him within her body, and her hands slid down his back. She could feel the burning in her belly, spreading outward to her breasts and thighs, demanding to be quenched.

He moved against her, and she answered his strong thrusts with a quivering eagerness. His movements were enticingly slow, almost teasing her, so that she pressed harder against his back and arched her body to keep him inside of her.

Both of them were breathing hard now, and his movements increased until Gabrielle felt the passion welling up within her, ready to spill out. His lips possessed her mouth once more as they neared the climax of their lovedance, and she thought she would never get enough.

A startled cry of sensual ecstasy escaped her parted lips, and her eyes flew wide with wonder at the exquisite pleasure that flowed through her body as they came together in a rush of passionate desire.

She wanted to say something, to tell him how much he had shaken her, how wonderful had been their coming together like this with no words spoken. But she could say nothing.

As his movements slowed and finally stopped, she felt his lips kissing the tears from her cheeks, and she was surprised at the moisture, hardly realizing that she had been crying. She sighed deeply and kissed him once more, content as he continued to lie atop her, his flesh pressed so intimately to hers.

I must ask him again who he is, why I am here, she thought to herself. I must find out why he made love to me like this, without telling me. . . . She smiled and in a few moments was asleep once again.

The man knew when she fell asleep by the evenness of her breathing, and he allowed himself a congratulatory smile. "Remember this, kitten," he whispered softly, "when you find yourself in your lover's arms again." He moved away from her, but for a moment he felt an unfamiliar rush of emotion steal into his mind. Angrily, he shook it off and got up from the bed.

Gabrielle awoke to bright sunlight. Wrapped in the cocoon of pleasure that she had experienced the night before, she allowed herself a yawn and stretched her arms above her head, sitting up to look around the room in which she found herself. There was nothing extraordinary about it—except that it definitely had the air of being a man's room.

Curious as to the identity of her shadowy lover, she slid from the bed and went slowly towards the armoire, hoping to find some clue amidst his clothing. She had opened the door when a sharp, hissing sound caught her attention and made her turn quickly.

"Rosa! What are you doing here?" The words spilled out as much in surprise as fear as Gabrielle eyed the wickedly gleaming dagger that was held tightly in the girl's hand.

"She-devil! Temptress! I knew you were evil luck for me when I first saw you!" Rosa spat at her, moving inside the room warily as though looking around to make sure her victim was quite alone.

"Rosa—what are you talking about?" Gabrielle exclaimed.

"You bitch! You with your golden hair and violet eyes have bewitched my lover! Why else would he bring you here—keep you here, when Lafitte has been looking everywhere for you?"

"Your lover?" Gabrielle put a hand to her mouth. Mr. St. Claire—the man whom Dolly had warned her about—the man whom Rosa considered her own personal property. Was he the man who had taken her last night—who had made love to her so exquisitely that even now she ached for his touch again?

"Your eyes are easy to read, bitch!" Rosa cried out in hatred. "You have tricked him into making love to you! You have tried to steal my lover away from me, and for that you will feel the kiss of my revenge. He will not long for your white body again after I am finished with you!"

Gabrielle backed away from the furious woman, realizing that in her nakedness she had absolutely no protection against the sharp blade of the dagger. Rosa followed her, her dark eyes gleaming dangerously.

"I could kill you," the woman spoke slowly as though tasting her words. "I could kill you, and no one would know it was I. But I shall not kill you! It will give me greater pleasure to scar that perfect face of yours so that he will turn away in disgust at the sight of you! Your breasts will wither and shrivel, your belly will be hard and ridged with scars that will mar its smoothness!"

"Rosa! What—what are you saying?" Gabrielle began. "I swear to you that I—"

"Shut up, bitch! You will lie to save that fine, white body of yours—only to use it again to entice him!"

With a sudden, swift movement, Rosa lunged forward and Gabrielle dodged quickly so that the knife barely missed her shoulder. She pivoted quickly, aware that Rosa had already regained her balance and was circling her again awaiting the chance to strike with deadly purpose.

"Rosa, please listen to me!" Gabrielle pleaded. "I have no idea why this man chose to bring me here! I—I was ill after the fire and I—"

"Lies, lies! They will do you no good!" Rosa shrieked and drove forward once again.

Gabrielle sidestepped, but not in time to keep the knife from grazing her arm, causing a tiny trickle of blood to seep slowly through her skin. She gasped at the sudden, stinging pain and noted the smile of cruelty that shaped

Rosa's mouth. Her black eyes glittered, and her tongue darted out to brush her lips as she circled once more for position.

Watching her, Gabrielle could see no mercy or understanding in the closed countenance. The woman was mad, insane with jealousy, and her rage would only be extinguished when her horrible plan had been carried out!

Gabrielle backed slowly towards the bed, her mind leaping over ideas, trying to think of a way out of this nightmare. If only she could summon a servant! Anyone who would hold this mad woman long enough so that she might escape this house.

With a quick movement, Gabrielle reached behind her to the bed and swirled the bedclothes off in a frenzied cascade that settled over Rosa's head. Screams and oaths issued from beneath the covers, and Gabrielle realized she had no time to lose before the other girl would hack her way free from the blankets and come after her. She rushed out the bedroom door, running blindly down the hall and to the stairs, leaping down them breathlessly, aware of the pounding footsteps behind her now.

She reached the bottom of the stairs and saw the outside door with a sigh of relief. Unmindful of her nudity, she swung it open and came up against the well-endowed figure of a woman with flaming red hair who looked at her as though she were some lunatic to be locked up immediately.

"Well, I never—" the woman breathed, and her eyes dilated at sight of Rosa's rapidly approaching figure, the knife held dangerously in her fist.

"Stop that woman, Dominique!" came the quiet, deadly voice, and Gabrielle realized that there were two men who stood behind the redhead and that one of those men was Jean Lafitte.

Even as the Spanish woman's cry of hatred seemed to beat against her, a pistol shot rang out and the woman with the red hair began screaming shrilly. Gabrielle turned and stared at the slowly crumpling figure of the woman who would have mutilated her and saw the rapidly spreading blossom of crimson on her breast. She put her fist in her mouth to stifle the scream that was caught in her throat.

In a haze, she felt the warmth of a silk cloak thrown over her bare shoulders and drawn around her to cover her body, heard the continuing screams of the woman and the deliberate, steady cursing of Dominique You as he thrust his pistol back into his belt.

"We've got to get the hell out of here," Jean," he said hurriedly. "This is just the sort of thing that Claiborne would use as an excuse to lock you up in the calaboose. Goddammit, woman, shut up!" he turned viciously to the vocal woman and made as though to strike her.

The red-headed woman shrank away from him and steadied her sobs enough to wave the men away. "Get out of here! Murderers! You've killed—and what for? This brazen trollop who's been rolling in bed with—"

Lafitte's hand struck her swiftly across the mouth. Without another word, he turned, an arm around Gabrielle's shaking shoulders, and hurried with her and Dominique You to a waiting carriage.

Once inside, Gabrielle was only too glad to lean her head against Lafitte's chest and give way to a torrent of tears. She was aware of his stiffness, the tenseness in the arm that encircled her. Finally, when her tears had lessened somewhat, she stealed herself to look up at his dark face, seeing the set mouth and distant black eyes that would not meet her gaze.

"Jean," she began brokenly, "how—how did you know where to find me?"

He did not turn his face down to her. "I was informed of your whereabouts," he responded coolly.

"By whom? Renée—"

"Renée was not my informant," he answered. For the first time, he turned his black gaze full upon her, and she read the doubt and suspicion there. "A Mr. St. Claire sent a message to me at the old Absinthe House that he had something that belonged to me and would be obliged if I would take it off his hands. My 'property,' I think, was how he referred to you."

Gabrielle felt as though she had been delivered a swift and deliberate blow. Could this Mr. St. Claire possibly be the same man who had made love to her so exquisitely the night before?

"Did he touch you, Gabrielle? Was that woman right? Why were you there?" It was Lafitte's voice, hard and demanding as his hand jerked her chin up so that his eyes could bore into hers.

Unbearable hurt flooded through Gabrielle—to be scorned by one man so callously and cross-examined like a prisoner by another—it was too much! But she would not dissolve into tears again—she would not! Steely pride made her lift her head higher and return Lafitte's level look. She would wipe any traces of last night from her mind, she told herself firmly, as though it never had been—as though it were only a dream. . . .

"Mr. St. Claire did nothing to me," she said quietly. "Nothing. He only saved me from the fire. After that . . . nothing."

Chapter Nineteen

Gabrielle looked out of the window of the house that Lafitte had finished building on the island of Grande Terre and smiled slightly to herself as she spied Lafitte lounging in the long red hammock on the veranda, as usual smoking a thin cheroot and talking animatedly to a group of men.

That terrible day in New Orleans was like a faraway nightmare now, and she forced herself not to think of it anymore. Lafitte had silently agreed not to question her and had done his best to help brush any troubled thoughts away from her mind. He had never told her the outcome of You's shooting Rosa, nor why St. Claire had told him of her whereabouts—or how he came to know of it. The episode was part of the past now, and she had learned before that it did no good to dwell on the past.

Despite her loathing of Lafitte's business and her jumbled thoughts about his own person and her relationship towards him, she took a feminine delight in having a house for herself now. It was a sturdy place built of brick and coated with a mixture of pulverized oyster shells and plaster that gave it a whitewashed look. He had added a wide veranda that looked out towards the Gulf, and through the iron-barred windows in the Spanish style he could scan the horizon for ships.

Dominique You had finally joined his fortunes completely to those of Lafitte, and the two men had become the closest of friends. It was hard to resist the hearty bluffness of the short, dark man who was nearly as wide as he was tall, and Gabrielle would not think that there had been a time when she had witnessed his killing a woman.

The summer had passed uneventfully, and she had settled in to her life as the "Bos's" official mistress. It was now early December, and the winds coming from the south were brisker and spread a cool tang of salt air that prompted an extra blanket at night. She found through the course of the months that Lafitte was not only a superb lover but at times could be uncharacteristically gentle and easy with her so that she could close her eyes and imagine they were like any other two people. But in the morning, she must shake away such childish thoughts, for Lafitte would be brisk and businesslike, never liking to mingle pleasure with work, for he claimed it could blunt a man's good judgment.

Gabrielle knew that he was cooking up some new scheme, but he seldom spoke to her of business and she never questioned him about it. A steady stream of buyers was beginning to come to Grande Terre directly to pick and choose their slaves from the big warehouse on the island. This saved costs and enabled those who came first to get the choicest of the merchandise.

In New Orleans, Pierre still took orders for slaves and merchandise from those not brave enough or unable to make the journey to the island, and once every month or so, he would come to Grande Terre to pick up the cargo for delivery. He would fill Jean in on the news from the city.

From snatches of overheard conversations, Gabrielle had learned that the brothers were planning a bold move the very next month. This involved peddling two whole cargoes of slaves along the banks of the Mississippi River all the way to Natchez, where a sizable market was growing. Due to the distance, though, the Lafittes seldom sold merchandise directly to the citizens of Natchez, but dispersed the goods and slaves to agents.

As Dominique put it sagely, "Business is booming." Lafitte could count nearly a thousand men in his establishment, and a whole network of depots for the disposal of cargoes stretched from New Orleans north almost to Natchez and east towards the Spanish city of Pensacola. It nearly took Gabrielle's breath away when Lafitte begin to talk of the gold and silver he was amassing, and sometimes, when he seemed in a particularly good mood, she would ask him what he would do with all that money. He would laugh, shake his head, and lift her in his arms, kissing her fiercely to make her forget her curiosity.

"Dreaming again?" Lafitte's voice called playfully to her now as she leaned against the window frame. "Lord, woman, you'll be burning my dinner, with your head in the clouds all afternoon!" He laughed, showing his white teeth.

"It'll be burned anyway if you continue to jabber away as usual!" she returned saucily, wrinkling her nose as he blew cigar smoke towards her.

"I swear I'll take a whip to you before too long. The wench is sassing me like a wife!" Lafitte exclaimed, getting up from his lounging position and signalling for the men to join him in the kitchen.

Gabrielle counted four other men besides Lafitte, You, and Beluche—probably new recruits, from the look of them. She placed the tablecloth neatly on the long wooden table and set out plates, mugs, and utensils, although many of the men seldom used the latter.

"Smells delicious, wench! What is it tonight?" growled You, smacking her noisily on the cheek and leaving a wet mark that she wiped off as soon as he turned his back.

"I've fried chicken and made rice with gravy," she answered, beginning to dish out the meal on a large platter.

Renato stood next to her to take the steaming plate from her hands and pursued his lips with enjoyment. "One would think you were born a Creole the way you cook, my dear."

"Hmmph," Gabrielle retorted, her eyes sparkling. "Would that I were paid as well as the cook in the Hôtel de la Marine that you are forever patronizing. I don't doubt but that I could pay someone else to do the rest of the work!"

"What? And deprive us all of an excellent example of true female aptitude?" You put in, laughing hoarsely.

Gabrielle bristled and faced him squarely with her hands on her hips. "Dominique You, if I thought you meant that, I'd throw this gravy in your lap! Don't tell me that cooking and keeping house are the only thing you believe I'm good at!"

You winked at her craftily. "Hell, no, ma'm'selle! From what Jean tells me, you're quite good in certain other matters."

The men roared with laughter while Gabrielle turned scarlet and cast a glare towards Lafitte's amused face. He shrugged lazily and blew her a kiss of apology, but his black eyes gleamed in remembered anticipation. Put out with him for the moment, Gabrielle finished serving the meal in silence, then took her place quickly, keeping her eyes averted from the others.

The talk swerved back and forth from New Orleans to cargoes to the problems cropping up with Governor Claiborne.

"Damn! With Louisiana in contention for statehood, it looks as though Claiborne is going to go all out in his campaign against you, Lafitte!" You muttered between mouthfuls. "The man holds a personal grudge, I think, for I've heard that he has boasted repeatedly to bring you to trial and put you away for a goodly number of years in the calaboose!"

"And what, do you think, does the good M'sieur Claiborne have against you and your industrious little band here on Barataria?" Beluche, winking at Gabrielle, asked solemnly.

Lafitte shrugged his shoulders expressively. "I care little for his reasons, men, but I've heard the bastard is trying to arouse the customs officials against us. It seems our bribes have soured in their hands, and now they've turned into model citizens who are willing to obey his authority."

"I'd like to see that!" snorted one of the new men. "My brother works in customs, and he's already boasted that he can make more than double his salary by taking your money."

"Good for him!" Lafitte laughed. "Would they were all so friendly."

"Most of them are," the boy continued, "but Claiborne is putting a lot of pressure on the officials, especially with statehood in the offing."

Lafitte's eyes narrowed slightly as he seemed to size up this obviously intelligent newcomer. "And where did you learn so much, lad?" he asked quietly.

The boy blushed nervously and glanced quickly at the other men. "Well, I've had some schooling and I can read and write."

"And, from the sounds of it, you know how to use those ears of yours to good advantage," Lafitte finished.

The boy nodded. Gabrielle thought he looked like a trapped rabbit and realized that Lafitte could very easily inspire fear in a stranger with his commanding presence and snapping black eyes.

Lafitte considered for a moment and then went on,

"Well, in that case, I could use you very well in certain
errands I need done from time to time. Report to me
after dinner tomorrow night."

The boy nodded, and the rest of the meal was finished
to the accompaniment of belches and gratified murmurs of
approval. When the four recruits had been ushered out
by Beluche to be assigned sleeping quarters, Gabrielle
began clearing the table, listening to the conversation between You and Lafitte as the two of them lit their cigars.

"You know that boy who seemed so knowledgeable this
evening—he might be a good one to put in the accounting
end of things in the warehouse," You recommended absently, watching the wreaths of smoke encircle the glowing end of his cheroot.

Lafitte nodded. "Do you know his name?"

"Renato told me it was Simmons—John Simmons, I
think," You answered. "I suppose the boy is an American."

Lafitte took a puff of his cigar, then turned it so that
the glowing end winked redly at him. "He said his brother
worked in customs in the city," he went on, as though
on some specific train of thought. "If that's true, we might
be able to use the relation to our own advantage, Dominique. What do you think?"

The latter shrugged. "We'd have to have someone check
on it, of course, but I believe you might be right. After
all, if we could arrange some sort of deal between the
two of them to our advantage, it might be cheaper in the
long run."

"It shouldn't be hard to find out the hours this boy's
brother works and go from there," Lafitte continued. "But
we should tread carefully until we're absolutely sure the
boy hasn't been planted here."

"You're right there, Jean. This business is sticky enough
without getting involved in a double-cross." You's mouth
was set in a grim line.

Gabrielle listened curiously but not really understanding all of it, felt a sudden spurt of dread for the boy of
whom they were speaking. He didn't seem to be much

older than herself, perhaps twenty, and yet he could present a very real danger to these two men who held such power in their hands. Quietly, she took a seat next to Lafitte and picked up a piece of sewing.

"The picture of domestic tranquility," You laughed, winking slyly at Lafitte.

Gabrielle smiled. "Softly please, Dominique," she teased, "or you will make poor Jean think I am trying to trap him."

You roared and slapped her knee in appreciation of her jest, while Lafitte gazed at her with an enigmatic expression on his face. "How could I possibly think that, my dear, when you shout and scream at me day after day that you would like to be taken back to New Orleans?" Lafitte questioned, baiting her.

Gabrielle looked up from her work, affronted. "Jean Lafitte, how dare you accuse me of that! I have never asked any such thing. You'll have Dominique thinking I'm nothing but a shrew!"

"Then you do like it here on the island with me?" he questioned her further, but in a softer tone.

Gabrielle blushed and glanced at You. "Of course I like it here, else why should I stay?"

"I'd keep you a prisoner, if I had to," Lafitte returned, his swarthy face matching the teasing note of his voice.

"I don't doubt it," You put in. "No man appreciates losing a beautiful treasure, whether it be gold or an exceptional woman."

Gabrielle stuck her tongue out, at which You bent towards her as though to kiss her. She leaned back and he contented himself with a peck on her nose. "You should know better than to offer such a tantalizing morsel out in the open with me around," You laughed gruffly. "I'm afraid, my friends, I shall have to excuse myself. I'm beginning to feel the need for some female companionship of my own." He stood up, saluted Lafitte, and went down the sloping trail.

Gabrielle watched him go, then let her eyes focus on the bright orange ball of sun that was firing the water to crimson, feeling the cool breeze fan her cheeks and lift her hair from her temples. With a part of her consciousness, she could feel Lafitte's eyes searching her face possessively.

"Dominique was right," he commented after a time. "You really are a beautiful treasure."

Gabrielle smiled, turning her face to look at this man whom she would never understand. "You flatter me," she said lightly. "All of the gold and silver you have hidden away somewhere—surely that could bring the pirate of the Gulf more pleasure than one, solitary woman?"

"What good is treasure when there is no one to share it with, to buy things for?" he returned testily.

She sighed. "Oh, Jean, sometimes you can be so fanciful and idealistic. It's hard for me to equate that part of you with—with the other part that can be so merciless, so all-powerful."

"Good God, you're not going to say that after all these months we've had together you are still afraid of me!"

She was silent, and after a little time he stood up and bent over to lift her from the chair. He carried her silently into the house and deposited her on the bed, undressing her with slow, explicit sureness that left her body tingling in pleasurable anticipation. When he had joined her, he held her for a moment, kissing her softly on the neck and bosom.

"Tell me, spitfire," he said in the darkness, "do you think you might love me a little?"

In the pleasant haze of lust that was beginning to envelope her, Gabrielle bit his shoulder, then licked the spot in apology. "Such a silly question," she murmured in his ear. "I can only love the idealistic part of you, Jean, the romantic part. But I shall always hate the powerful part."

He thrust her away to look into her face in the dim light. For a moment, she tensed, sensing that she had said something to wound him. Then, with a small oath, he clasped her back against him and pressed her down into the mattress.

A week had passed, and Gabrielle was cleaning out the huge kitchen pantry, emitting little shrieks when now and then her hand passed over some soft, crawly thing. She was determined to keep the house as clean as she could under the circumstances.

She heard Lafitte's step and backed out of the pantry, straight into his arms. He swung her around against him, kissing her passionately. His face was smiling, and he tickled her nose with his tongue before letting her down.

"Good news, my sweet. Our venture has been successful. We've gotten rid of every slave from those last two cargoes. The profits have been fantastic!"

Gabrielle smiled, happy that he was so elated, but doubtful whether Claiborne looked on the venture in a favorable light. "Has there been any word from New Orleans?" she asked.

He shook his head. "Everything is very quiet there. I'm not sure I like it, but we're trying to get more information through Simmons' brother. I only hope we can keep the major portion of the officials on our side."

She nodded. He patted her backside and told her he'd be leaving to go to New Orleans himself, at which her face fell.

"Oh, Jean, I do hate it when you leave me here alone," she said, her big eyes troubled.

He grinned happily. "Aha! So you do miss me then, eh?" He began unbuttoning her bodice, his hands intent on capturing her breasts.

She wriggled away. "No, Jean, I'm serious. I—I wish you didn't have to go so often to New Orleans. Couldn't Pierre do everything there is to do in the city?"

He looked at her questioningly, his brows raised. "Pierre can't do it all himself. Truth to tell, he's been drinking a little too much from all reports, and is in need of some guidance from his younger brother. There's really no need to worry, since Renato is staying on the island." His eyes snapped dangerously. "Would you like me to ask our friend to spend the night with you?"

Gabrielle reddened, then put her hands on her hips and returned tartly, "No need to, as I'm sure I could do the asking very well myself, without your help." Her violet eyes challenged him, and he caught her up against him.

"If I thought you were entertaining such ideas, I'd whip you until you were black and blue and in no condition to share your bed with anyone."

She sulked for a moment. "And I suppse you go off and have your fun at the Quadroon Ball, or maybe even Renée's! You men are really intolerable at times!"

He laughed. "Accusations, now! And on top of Pierre always telling me I'm too indifferent to women. Do you know what I tell him when he twits me about having no eyes for the ladies?" Gabrielle drew her mouth down, still angry. "I simply tell him that I already have a lady, and she is all I want," he said softly.

Gabrielle looked up quickly into that dark face and sighed in surrender. "All right," she whispered, "but I will be lonely."

"And besides," he added, "I must do the thinking for all of us."

He began to laugh and plopped her down, whereupon she swung her fist, missing him completely, and glared at him until he bent down beside her, his intentions all too apparent.

"Jean, no! Not here in the pantry! What if someone should come in?"

His grin broadened. "Let them come in, then. I mean to have you now. As you say, sweetheart, we men are intolerable."

It was later that night, after he had gone, that Gabrielle prepared for bed, already beginning to feel a creeping unease that always assailed her with special force on the first night alone. It seemed like hours since she had tried to doze off, when a sharp noise brought her completely awake. Her eyes flew to the window, where she stifled a gasp at sight of a dark shadow moving across the glass. Cautiously, conquering her fear, she slipped out of bed and made her way towards the door. Seeing a heavy vase on a shelf close to her, she picked it up.

The invader was evidently taking his time with the window, hoping not to disturb her sleep, so she had plenty of time to position herself next to the window, the vase held high over her head to come down the minute the intruder stuck his head in.

Her arms began to ache with tension, and just as she thought she would scream with the waiting, the man stuck one foot through the window and then the other. He moved his head in, and, closing her eyes tightly, Gabrielle brought the vase down on his head with all her strength.

The intruder hadn't time to say a word, but quickly slumped to the floor. Gabrielle shut the window in case there were any accomplices and hurried to light a candle. A low moaning was coming from the body by now, and when she went over, armed with a heavy candlestick this time, she could see that fresh blood was matting in his hair.

"All right. Before I call for help, I will give you a moment to explain," she declared, hoping her voice did not tremble too much. She nearly gasped when she saw the face that gazed up at her, nearly as frightened as she. "John Simmons!" she exclaimed.

He felt his head gingerly, then tried to stand up and fell back against the wall.

"John Simmons! What—what are you doing? Why did you—"

He shook his head as though to clear it and seemed to be trying to focus his eyes on her. Gabrielle put the candlestick down, feeling her self-assurance come back on a quick tide of curiosity. She was certainly not afraid of a boy hardly older than herself. Besides, she had had an opportunity to observe Simmons several times in the last few days, and he seemed a very pleasant lad.

She helped him to a chair, leaving him for a moment to get something to wipe his wound. When she returned, he seemed to have come to himself, for there was a definite air of fear about him, as though he only just realized what he had done. To intrude upon the Bos's mistress was looked on as a criminal offense by any of the recruits on the island, and everyone knew Lafitte's punishment would be unmerciful.

"Please, please, ma'am, just—just let me out and I promise I—"

"Nonsense, John. I'm afraid I've put a considerable gash on your scalp, and I should at least look at it."

His eyes continued to dart about the room nervously. "I—I didn't think you'd be awake. I waited a while after the lights went out, but I guess—I'm not very good at this."

She sat beside him and questioned him slowly, "What were you trying to do?"

He bit his lip, and his eyes seemed to plead with her for mercy. "Please, ma'am, if you'll just let me leave—"

She shook her head. "I will give you my word not to inform Lafitte of this, but you'll have to trust me enough to tell me what it is all about."

He took a deep breath as though considering. "I—I was trying to get information."

"Information? Information about what?"

He took another deep breath and then plunged on. "About Lafitte's schedule—his runs. The times that he makes delivery from the island to the city. Proof of his smuggling and illegal trafficking."

Gabrielle looked steadily at the boy. "Proof for whom, John?" she asked, her eyes scanning the face in front of her for signs of dishonesty.

He shook his head, then grimaced with the pain. "I— I cannot tell you. I don't want—"

"John," she began, facing him squarely, "you're doing this for someone else. Were you sent here for that purpose—to find out when Lafitte will be delivering cargo to his depots?"

He nodded. "That, and to find out the locations of those depots."

She frowned. "So you are a spy, then?"

His eyes dropped and his silence was ample affirmation. "I must ask you again, John. For whom?"

His eyes grew stubborn and his mouth set in a determined line. "The authorities."

"The authorities? You mean Claiborne was behind this little scheme?"

He would say nothing else. Gabrielle paced the room, taking several turns before coming to stand in front of the boy. "Where are your quarters?"

He looked up. "A little way from the fort."

She made her decision. "Then you'd best get back to them before you are caught or missed. Beluche is on the island, and I have a feeling he's keeping his ears open tonight."

"But," and his face was incredulous, "but what are you going to do?"

"Nothing, for now, but I'm warning you that you are playing a terribly dangerous game, John. For your own sake, I think you should leave Barataria and go back to New Orleans before you make a worse mistake."

He shrugged his shoulders. "Back to what? My father drinks awful. My mother died when my youngest sister was born. There are seven of us trying to breathe in a house hardly bigger than this bedroom. I had to get out somehow. My brother works for customs in the city, and he stood to gain by offering my services for this. I took the offer—what else could I do?"

"Why don't you move out of the house permanently?"

"My father threatened to kill me if I didn't bring him home money every week to buy his whiskey."

Gabrielle felt a stab of pity for the boy. "Go back to your quarters, John, and get some sleep."

He nodded and proceeded painfully to shuffle out the door. "I—I know how you must hate me for doing this to the man you—you love, ma'am."

She tried to smile, but failed dismally at the effort. "I don't hate you, John. But you must be more careful in your—your activities."

After he had gone, she tried to sort out her thoughts on

this turn of events. To say nothing about this to Jean would be tantamount to assisting the authorities in putting him in prison. She would be as guilty as Simmons or his brother of breaking Lafitte's trust.

This time she did not even try to go to sleep, but watched wide-eyed as the sun began lightening the window panes. Knowing what she did, she would have to make an effort to hide her feelings from Lafitte. She could only hope that John would make no more rash moves. Try as she might, though, she could not quite shake the sense of foreboding that accompanied this night. . . .

Chapter Twenty

Lafitte returned from his journey to New Orleans in three days, but the scowl on his face told Gabrielle that the trip had not gone smoothly. She forbore to ask him about the details but kept her ears open for any information that might give her a clue as to whether John Simmons was implicated.

Lafitte called a meeting of his lieutenants and, while Gabrielle served drinks and other refreshments, the men discussed a sober turn in events.

"I'm sure all of you have heard of the little skirmish two nights ago," Lafitte began, pacing the room swiftly, his tall, black boots ringing against the polished wood of the floor. "Claiborne, it seems, has finally succeeded in arousing the customs officials, and a Captain Holmes with a company of forty dragoons was ordered to search any boat sailing the bayous." His face was dark with anger. "Forty dragoons, mind you, manning boats and sailing the bayous as though they were attached to the government!" Lafitte went on, still pacing. "I'm surprised they didn't see fit to search the boats anchored here on the island!"

You held up his hand, his voice calm. "Now, Jean, we all know you're angry and rightly so, as we are too, but we must not let ourselves be bluffed by these tactics. We've got all the luck on our side, and I've heard that the dragoons found nothing in the boats they searched."

Lafitte nodded curtly. "As you say, nothing was found and yet, how can we be sure that this harrassment won't become a continual thing? Are we to arm our skiffs like men-o'-war in order to get our goods to the people who want them?"

"A few nights sailing the bayous, and I think Captain Holmes should realize his quest is useless. If he doesn't get lost in the swamps, he'll soon get tired of the heat and the bugs," Beluche put in hopefully.

"You could be right, Renato. Let's hope so, but, for now, I want to prepare myself for an all-out attack." Lafitte hesitated and eyed his men sternly, then continued. "I am ordering fortification of the island. Cannon will be set up along the beach, and the walls of the fort will be strengthened. Every man who is not now on an assignment will help with these maneuvers. Dominique, I will put you in charge of confiscating the battery from useless ships and bringing them ashore to use in the fortifications. Renato, you will oversee the storage of ammunition and guns, preferably enough to last through a long siege. I will send a message to Pierre and remind him to keep a sharp eye out for any military maneuvers from Claiborne. Damn the man! Gambi, send one of your men to fetch one of the new recruits. His name is John Simmons. He will be a likely candidate to send with the message to Pierre, as he has a brother in customs and might be able to bring back valuable information."

Gabrielle's heart jumped at Lafitte's order. Here he was trusting the very man who could do him the most damage. Dare she tell him about the boy? No, she couldn't. She pressed a hand to her forehead. Yet, how could she do this to the man who had saved her life, who had lavished so much on her already, who had given her a home in this strange land? Dear God, why must there be such decisions for her to make? She sighed. But it was useless to question God. Hadn't she found that out already?

The rest of the winter passed with little incident, despite occasional skirmishes between the dragoons of the city and Lafitte's men.

Gabrielle breathed easier but felt that such peace could hardly last. Lafitte regarded Simmons with near-brotherly affection, for the boy was good at figure work and was required to help in the warehouses on numerous occasions. Lafitte was in contact with him nearly every day and held a certain respect for his intelligence and quickness in learning.

This closeness filled Gabrielle's heart with dread, for she could see that Simmons was becoming more and more involved with the personal activities and secret negotiations of the Lafitte brothers. The thought that he was pouring out these activities and plans to those authorities in New Orleans made her furious, and the thought of Simmons' brother and his cohorts, who took Lafitte's money on the one hand, then turned around and sold him to Claiborne, galled her even more.

Many times she had been about to inform Lafitte of Simmons' true loyalties, but something held her back. Maybe it was the fact that, through these past months, she, too, had come to know Simmons better and had taken a liking to him, in spite of herself.

It was a chilly night in March, and Gabrielle found herself alone with John Simmons for a moment because Lafitte had gone down to the beach with some of his men to check on a new cargo that Gambi had brought in. She could see that he seemed loath to leave her, and she finally sat down beside him at the table.

He laid a hand gently and quite unconsciously on hers. "You need someone to protect you, ma'am. This is no life for you—you should be one of those grand ladies in a big plantation house who has servants do everything for her. You should dress in silk every day."

She gazed absently out the window where she could hear Lafitte and his men in the distance. "You know, John, I was a girl like that once. Oh, it seems a very long time ago, but I suppose it was only—well, not quite three years ago. Strange, how memory begins to fade after a while."

They were both silent, and then Simmons moved his chair closer. "Ma'am, I hope you don't think me too forward, but if you ever need a friend or are in trouble—"

Gabrielle frowned a little and her violet eyes hardened into twin amethysts. "Speaking of trouble," she interrupted quickly, "there is something I would like your help on."

His sincere look of concern caused her a momentary flicker, but she plunged on. "I want you to tell me what information you've been able to pass on to—to your superiors."

He blanched and took his hand away as he turned his face so that she could not see his expression.

"John, you know that I care for Lafitte and that, in spite of his profession, I wouldn't want to see him trapped and brought to an ignominious defeat. I cannot stand by and watch as he puts more and more trust in you without having my heart nearly torn in half by frustration and guilt. Surely you can understand that?"

He sighed audibly and turned back to her. "I understand, ma'am, what it means to feel guilt and frustration. You see, I've grown mighty fond of Mr. Lafitte myself in the past months, and it does set ill with me to be spying on him."

Gabrielle nodded. "I can imagine how you must feel, John, but—"

He interrupted her with a wave of his hand. "Oh, but don't you worry about Mr. Lafitte getting trapped and taken to the calaboose. It's true I've given my brother a lot of information, but most of it is no good to them anyway. I take care not to give the exact day of the deliveries, or maybe set it up two days later so that he's already safe and back on the island." He grinned boyishly. "Some spy I've made, huh? But as long as it satisfies the authorities, my conscience is clear. After all, I've been saving all the money I've earned from Lafitte, and pretty soon I hope to be able to go up to St. Louis or Natchez."

"John, that's wonderful! I'm happy for you." Gabrielle got up and hugged him.

The boy hugged her back happily, and as they stood there together she felt a cold dread run up her spine, and raising her head, she saw the Italian, Gambi, looking at her with a menacing air of suspicion.

"G-Gambi, what are you—why aren't you down on the beach with the rest of the men?" she demanded, her voice weakened from surprise and the malignant force that emanated from the man.

Simmons broke away quickly and stood to one side. Gambi moved into the room with practiced ease and hooked his thumbs in his wide belt.

"Well, well, here I've come to pay my respects to the Boss's woman, and I find her behaving quite familiarly with one of the recruits. I wonder what Lafitte would say at such a display."

Gabrielle stiffened at the insinuation and eyed the man with distrust. "I'm sure Lafitte would have very little to say about it, but he might take it ill should I complain about harassment from one of his lieutenants."

The man laughed, a clipped laughter that seemed to accentuate the hardness of his eyes. "My dear girl, am I harassing you? Please forgive me. I only wanted to give you a present to show my appreciation. Lafitte was, as usual, much too busy gloating over the cargo to mind my giving it to you personally." He bowed slightly and came towards her, twirling a string of pearls that glowed with a luster all their own in the waning light.

Gabrielle's eyes did not leave the man's face. "You know that I care little for such gifts," she said, throwing back her head as he came closer.

Again that clipped laughter, and then his hands were on her throat, snapping the pearls in place. They lingered for a moment, caressing the smooth, golden flesh beneath which a pulse was beating in rapid tempo.

"Thank you," Gabrielle said stiffly, "and now I wish for you to go."

The fingers continued to fondle her, and she could hear the harsh breathing that came from his mouth. "The pearls cannot match the glow of that skin," he murmured absently.

"Take your hands off her, Gambi," came a voice quite near, and Gabrielle turned thankfully to Simmons, whose presence she had forgotten under the evil spell of the tall Italian.

"Get out, boy, or I shall have my men feed you to the sharks," Gambi snapped.

"Not before I inform Lafitte of your actions," Simmons returned bravely, stepping back a little from the anger in the man's face.

Gambi hesitated, eying the boy and then the young woman, then shrugged and smiled cruelly. "As you wish, my brave young man. It behooves me little to create a scene now amid the general jubilation upon the success of my mission, but there will be another time, better suited to a lasting revenge. I must warn you—insult an Italian, and you had better sleep with your eyes open." He nodded to Gabrielle and saluted the boy with a sarcastic gesture, then left them alone.

Gabrielle breathed deeply, her eyes looking on Simmons with distress. "Oh, John, I'm sorry. I'm deeply grateful for your intervention, but it seems as though we have both made an enemy of the Italian. He is dangerous."

Simmons shrugged in pretended bravado. "I've heard Lafitte is anxious to rid himself of the foreign scum anyway. Have no fear, ma'am, I'll inform Mr. Lafitte of the incident right away. I'm sure he will know how to deal with it."

Gabrielle caught at his arm. "I—I think not, John. Lafitte would be sure to question you further on the whole affair and—it might not be too wise to arouse his curiosity."

Reluctantly, the boy agreed, shaking his head at feminine logic.

Spring came and went, and summer was upon them. Statehood had been granted to Louisiana, and the celebrations were many and varied. In the city there were fireworks and balls and picnics, and Gabrielle listened to word of them from some of the other women on the island who had attended with various crew members. Lafitte did not like to keep his men too long on the island, away from the gaiety of New Orleans, for he knew they would grow restless and dispirited if allowed to remain idle between voyages.

She learned from Pierre that Marie Villars had been delivered of a daughter in July of that year, 1812.

"And what have you named her?" she asked one evening as Pierre sat at the table, stuffing his round face with gumbo.

"Marie has decided on Rose," he replied between mouthfuls. And then, chuckling, "And you know, she does look sort of like a little rose—all dark pink and soft."

"I would so like to see Marie and the new baby," she sighed to herself.

Lafitte, who had just come in, caught the last of her words and grinned rakishly. "Well, my sweet, if you're wanting to see New Orleans, I think it can be arranged."

Gabrielle jumped up from her seat and threw her arms around him. "Oh, Jean! Do you think I could? It's been a whole year since I've been to the city, and I do miss the excitement."

Lafitte chuckled. "I've never met a woman like you, my love. How you've stood me and this island for a whole year, I'll never understand—and not a whimper."

He gazed at her and his black eyes grew velvety soft. "And I suppose with you growing big with the little bastard in you, I'm not likely to lose you to some handsome American profiteer." He patted the gentle swell of her belly and Gabrielle blushed self-consciously, shielding her face by the fall of golden curls.

Pierre got up from the table with a crash of his chair

and rumbled over to where she stood. "Why, you little imp, here I've been crowing about my own young one, and you've been sitting there all along with your own little secret." He put his big arms around her and squeezed her mightily, taking advantage of the occasion to apply a wet kiss on her mouth. "When's the brat due?"

"The baby is due in January," Gabrielle replied, correcting him gently. "I'm just four months along and I thought that gave me ample time to inform you later." She crinkled her nose at him and leaned happily against Lafitte.

"Why, I never thought I'd see the day that my brother, the formidable Jean Lafitte, was to become a father again!" Pierre laughed, slapping his thigh. "It really does beat all."

"But what about the trip to New Orleans?" Gabrielle asked, her face aglow with excitement. "Oh, Jean, you're not just teasing me, are you?"

"Would I tease you, spitfire?" he asked, grinning. "We'll be leaving early in the morning."

Gabrielle hugged him ecstatically and hurried from the kitchen to begin her packing.

Once she was gone, Lafitte turned to his older brother thoughtfully. "I hate to admit it, Pierre," he said softly, "but I'm already feeling the pangs of fatherhood." He shook his head ruefully. "That girl has wormed her way into my blood, and now, with the child coming, I think I'm completely hooked. God, sometimes I wonder—"

Pierre laughed and slapped his brother on the back. "Jean, Jean, you're no different from any other man who's found himself falling in love."

Lafitte started as though Pierre had delivered a crass insult. "Love hardly fits into my plans," he retorted, stiffening.

"Ah, brother, I can see you're fighting yourself," Pierre returned. "This woman is different. She's one woman in a million. She's like the rose that blooms despite its surroundings. She's worth all of that treasure you keep building up." Pierre grinned slyly. "And speaking of treasure, you can't tell me you're saving that up for your old age. I've an idea that one of these days you're just going to call it quits and take your money and your woman to go off to God knows where, where no one will find you."

"An interesting notion," Lafitte responded thoughtfully as he paced the room briskly, his hands clenched behind his back. "Of course I realize that Gabrielle is the kind of woman meant for a man like me. She's worthy of a king— and would I like to be that king?" He faced his brother and his dark eyes narrowed perceptibly. "Power, remember that it is a dangerous thing, Pierre. It can turn a man's head and make him hunger for more."

Pierre sat down heavily in a chair and gazed absently into the mouth of the open bottle. He took another long pull and wiped his mouth on his sleeve. "Just remember, too, that power can ruin you, little brother."

Chapter Twenty-one

Gabrielle looked about her happily, enjoying the sights and sounds that were New Orleans. The docks had changed little in the year and a half since she'd last seen them. The black men still worked tirelessly unloading the barrels and crates from the long wooden flatboats piloted by lanky, awkward-looking Kentuckians whose bright blue eyes seemed to follow her with considerable interest.

"I've already informed Renée to put up a guest room for us," Lafitte said, bringing a smile to her lips.

"Oh, how good it will be to see her again, and the others too. You've not spoken much of them on your trips to New Orleans. How is business?"

He laughed at her and pressed his arm to her side. "Business is very good these days, what with those savages who are continually coming downriver from Natchez and the Trace. Kentuckians and Easterners who have no idea how to make a living down here. Most of them end up as gamblers or hoodlums.

"It's a shame," Gabrielle sighed, "that New Orleans can't attract decent men, or at least those who have money enough to invest in worthwhile causes."

"Most men who come to New Orleans with money are only interested in their own causes. There are some, of course, who want to help New Orleans—Claiborne, for all his faults, the Bringiers, the Dubourgs, de Marigny, St. Claire. . . ."

"St. Claire—odd, that name reminds me—"

Lafitte looked down at her sharply. "The man who saved you from the fire at Renée's."

"Of course, how could I have forgotten," Gabrielle replied, remembering the incident with a sudden clarity. She couldn't help blushing at the shadowy memory of that one night and the lover she had never seen, but she was careful to keep her voice indifferent. "So, it seems I was rescued by one of the model citizens of New Orleans."

Lafitte laughed thoughtfully. "Hardly a model citizen, my dear. St. Claire is a man who does nothing unless it is also benefiting himself. His latest venture is trying to finance overland caravans—doomed to failure, I'm afraid. Indians, crooked agents, to say nothing about damaged goods and the like. I've heard, though, that he's buying up shares in one of the bankrupt shipping companies. I'd hate to see him as a competitor—even worse, I wouldn't like to have to confiscate some of his cargo. The man is a devil to his enemies, and I heard his sword is nearly as swift as de Marigny's. Ah, now, that would be a duel to watch."

"And who is this de Marigny?" Gabrielle questioned, not really interested, but glad the conversation had turned to a different subject.

"Bernard Philippe de Marigny, Duc de Mandeville, one of the notables of New Orleans, spitfire. I'm sure that other circumstances would have found you meeting the Duc de Mandeville at a garden party or, perhaps, at one of the coming-out balls for one of the young ladies of the town.

He is, I've heard, quite the ladies' man. Inherited money, comes from one of the oldest families in Louisiana."

"How interesting. And is this pillar of society a bachelor?" Gabrielle asked in a teasing voice.

"Unfortunately, sweetheart, such is not the case. He is married to a Spanish lady, one Anna Matilda Morales, who from all accounts is a bad-tempered bitch—and with good cause, I suppose."

"My goodness, Jean, I didn't think you cared to read the scandal sheets, but you seem to be well up on much of the comings and goings of society."

"Oh, Catherine fills my ears with the gossip she learns from her little friends. The child amuses me the way she puts herself forever underfoot to cater to my slightest wish." He cast a sideways look at her. "You would do well to learn from little Catherine, my dear."

Gabrielle bristled. "And just who is Catherine?"

Lafitte laughed appreciably. "Catherine is Marie's younger sister, and just fourteen, so sheathe your claws, my jealous cat. Besides, it does my heart good to be regarded as someone's hero."

Gabrielle sniffed disdainfully. This Catherine might only be fourteen, but if she were Marie's sister, that meant that as a quadroon her mother had taught her very early the facts of life, and very likely the girl was as mature as a twenty-year-old. But then, why should the thought bother her? Gabrielle argued with herself.

As they walked down Royal Street, having declined a carriage on this perfect August afternoon, Gabrielle marveled at all the gambling houses that had sprung up and now lined the street in gay splotches of music and laughter. Her eyes took in the tall, bronze-colored Indians who reeled drunkenly through the streets, clad in nothing but breechclouts and blankets tossed carelessly over their shoulders. Quadroon girls, grimly chaperoned by their mothers, passed by, giggling and looking pretty with brightly striped tignons that wrapped their heads.

As they entered the Place d'Armes, she was delighted by the colorful promenade that formed within the square.

Old gentlemen in costumes of three generations ago with their silly bagwigs, tottered along on their canes, now and then stopping to inhale a pinch of snuff and sneeze obligingly into the crisp, cool air. There was a small procession of young girls, all of whom were dressed alike in dark clothing, walking two by two on their way to church with black-robed nuns fluttering about them like fat pigeons squawking about a covy of quail. The girls moved with downcast eyes past a group of city guards in their sky-blue uniforms, disregarding the catcalls and whistles that the men offered in appreciation. Dragoons lounged about the iron gates of the Cabildo, the formidable building that housed governmental offices—its grim façade caused a momentary shiver to run down Gabrielle's spine. Mothers clasped their childrens' hands tightly, the latter prancing and laughing with exuberant good humor. Young gentlemen, looking like overdressed peacocks, preened and strutted close to the entrance of the Church of Saint-Louis, carefully pulling back their coats to display the intricate patterns traced on their splendid vests of varied hues.

As Lafitte passed by the group, an audible hush descended for a moment while the young blades sized up this pirate of the Gulf, this man whom most of them regarded with a kind of hero worship mixed with amusement at his bravado. But who, they wondered, was the lovely young woman with the extraordinary eyes who strolled so gracefully, hand on his arm? A subdued murmuring broke out among them as each vied to catch the beauty's eye.

Gabrielle, aware of their interest, could not help but smile at the young Creoles, and she noted one young man who was not very tall, but with unusually light blue eyes in his tanned face, disengage himself from the group and walk indolently towards them. Out of the corner of her eye, she could see that very soon he would be forced to introduce himself, and Lafitte would have to acknowledge him.

"M'sieur Lafitte, your servant." The man bowed and a smile lit up his handsome face framed in dark, curly hair.

Gabrielle noted that, although he had been among the group of dandies, he did not look like a fop but had a careless assurance about him that bespoke wealth and position. With his heavy, sensual lips and humorous eyes, he looked to know his way around women. He had spoken French, and Lafitte answered in the same tongue.

"And your servant, M'sieur de Marigny." He bowed slightly, and somewhat reluctantly turned to Gabrielle. "My companion, Ma'm'selle de Beauvoir."

"Ah, a Frenchwoman! Indeed, I was sure of it the moment I laid eyes on you, ma'm'selle. Charmed, I'm sure," the man returned with a hint of laughter, capturing her hand securely in his.

"M'sieur de Marigny, I have heard of you," Gabrielle replied, smiling in her turn and wondering at the luck which would have her meet this influential man so soon after hearing about him from Lafitte.

"Ma'm'selle, m'sieur, I must insist upon sharing a drink with both of you. Do you think it might be possible—unless, of course, you are already engaged for the afternoon?"

Lafitte shook his head. "Many thanks, m'sieur, but I'm afraid that we have already promised ourselves. Perhaps another time."

Gabrielle was disappointed and realized that de Marigny could probably read her feelings in her face, as the man was watching her intently. But all he said was, "Perhaps." Then he bowed smartly and sauntered away toward a group of young ladies, escorted by their black servants. An immediate titter went up from the group, and Bernard de Marigny was nearly completely surrounded in another moment.

"What do you think of him?" Lafitte questioned her, half serious, half teasing.

"An interesting man," Gabrielle returned thoughtfully.

They continued on their way until they had passed beyond the Place d'Armes and found themselves in the French Market. This place was crowded with shoppers and onlookers, people selling everything from meats to flowers. There was a variety of nationalities among the sellers. Greeks, Indians, Spaniards, Italians, and Frenchmen hawked their wares in as many languages, and Gabrielle watched their antics. There was an abundance of fish and shrimp, and a long line of people waited patiently in front of the oyster booths where oysters were sold and served on the half-shell, to be eaten as fast as they were opened. Gabrielle declined to sample one, and Lafitte ate two, amused by her reluctance.

They passed the market and walked down one of the side streets where Lafitte pointed out the Café des Réfugiés, where, he said, refugees from Santo Domingo gathered in the afternoon and young blades congregated in the evening to watch girls perform dances to music on a small stage set up in the courtyard.

"How exciting!" Gabrielle exclaimed. "May we stay and watch?"

Lafitte laughed loudly, causing several people to turn their heads in curious stares. "No, I'm afraid not, spitfire. Only men would dare to patronize the place as just next door is the Hôtel de la Marine, which as you know is a favorite rendezvous for pirates and gamblers. I don't think you would find the entertainment to your liking, ma'm'selle." He leered dangerously at her, then winked.

Gabrielle's cheeks blushed rosy. Lafitte hailed a cab and they drove to Renée's establishment, which stood now between two other grand buildings, both of which looked to be gambling dens.

Once inside, Gabrielle began laughing and crying at once. Lafitte quickly excused himself from the embracing and told Gabrielle he would be back later that evening after taking care of some business.

"Oh, Gabrielle, how wonderful to see you again!" Dolly was saying, fondly. "And you're looking marvelous! My goodness, what is it about that island that brings such a pretty glow to your cheeks?"

"You must come and visit me sometime and find out for yourself," Gabrielle said affectionately. "I'm afraid you wouldn't care, though, for some of the men out there."

"Hmmph, they couldn't be any worse than these half-civilized pigheads from Kentucky. Those men are insatiable, and, even worse, they're always falling asleep afterwards, and they snore worse than bears."

Renée laughed. "Dolly hasn't changed, has she, Gabrielle? She still complains, but, you know, she had an offer of marriage last year and declined. Actually turned the man down, and he was rich, too! We all called her an idiot!"

Dolly made a face and crossed her arms. "Timothy O'Malley wanted a servant to cook his meals and wash his socks and warm his bed on cold winter mornings. If you call that being a wife, I'll be a whore 'til the day I die."

Gabrielle realized with a sudden spear of anguish how much she'd missed these feminine gossips.

"Oh, Dolly, Renée, I've missed you so much!" she cried out swiftly and, to her own horror, began to weep in short, retching little sobs that shook her body.

Flabbergasted, Renée took out a clean handkerchief to wipe her eyes.

"F-forgive me, I didn't mean to act like such a baby," she sniffed when she had sufficiently recovered herself.

"I think you're overtired from the journey, especially in your condition," Renée put in. "Why don't you take her up to her room, Dolly?"

Dolly helped Gabrielle with her bags. The room she took her to was very nice, and Gabrielle couldn't help thinking back to that earlier time when she had been shown to a room in Renée's establishment—but as a virtual prisoner, not a guest.

Dolly, aware of the other's thoughts, was quiet as she set out gowns and put them neatly in the armoire. "Life is really funny, just like they say," she murmured in a moment of reflection. "It can put you in the strangest circumstances and when you think nothing can possibly go right, everything seems to fit into place. Is that how it is with you, Gabrielle?"

"Except that everything doesn't always fit into place,

Dolly. Oh, I suppose I'm ungrateful, and a fool on top of that, but I just feel that something is still missing. I've been with Lafitte nearly two years, and yet I still don't know him—not completely—and I suppose I never will. There are times when he holds me and I know that no other man will feel towards me the way he does, but other times he seems just as far away as he did when I first saw him on the deck of the *Lillias*." She shivered involuntarily at the memory.

"All men are like that," Dolly put in. "They expect a woman to be theirs body and soul, and yet they are not ready to commit the totality of themselves in the same fashion. It's not fair, but—that's the way it is."

Gabrielle smiled. "You're a wise old woman, Dolly."

The latter laughed heartily. "Haven't you ever heard, my friend, that a prostitute is the wisest woman in the world? Certainly she can draw on vast experience."

A little later, dinner was announced, and Gabrielle and Dolly went downstairs. After dinner, Gabrielle returned to her room to await Lafitte's arrival. She could hear soft strains of music—violins and guitars—in the rooms downstairs, and she made her way to the window, which looked out onto the street. She could see carriages pulling up, and she watchly idly as men descended into the street to disappear under the balcony. She stayed at the window for some minutes, playing a little game in her mind, trying to guess what sort of business each man was in by his clothes. A short, stocky man dressed in a plum coat and embroidered vest must be a merchant—a tall, lanky man in sober black looked to be a clerk—a powerfully built man in red shirt and leather breeches came from the docks.

An exceptionally fine carriage stopped in front of the gambling house next door, and Gabrielle craned her neck to see out. The first gentleman to alight was tall and wore a wide-brimmed hat which shielded his face, and the second gentleman was much shorter and bareheaded. With a little start, Gabrielle recognized Bernard de Marigny. He was laughing and talking with considerable animation while his companion seemed to be listening with only half an ear and his face was turned towards the light streaming from the gambling house. She watched as the two walked into the building.

"Bored, spitfire?"

Gabrielle turned around and threw her arms around Lafitte's neck. "Oh, yes! Can't we do something, Jean? I'd like to go to that gambling house next door. It looks very nice and not at all disreputable. Why, I just glimpsed M'sieur de Marigny getting out of his carriage to go in."

Jean shook his head, still smiling. "I'm afraid not, my dear. Very few women are allowed inside, and I wouldn't want to see you disappointed."

"Jean, you're joking! Women like to gamble just as much as men," she retorted.

"Well, then, let's just say I'm not too keen on showing you off to the kind of men that frequent those places. Rich and lazy and bored, most of them. The kind that break little girl's hearts." His voice was still amused, but there was a serious light in his dark eyes. "Now, if you're a good girl, I'll take you to the Théâtre d'Orléans to-morrow night. Would you like that?"

Gabrielle bit her lip grudgingly, but nodded. "Yes," she sulked, her mouth drawn into an irresistible pout.

Lafitte was hardly one to resist, and he quickly began undressing her with a roughness that took her breath away. He was gentle, though, during their lovemaking, and afterwards he laid a hand on her stomach as though to feel the life that pulsed within.

"He doesn't move yet," Gabrielle whispered drowsily, "but soon enough you'll find yourself kicked out of bed." She laughed softly.

They fell asleep, not to be aroused until mid-morning, when a sharp tapping preceded breakfast. After eating, Lafitte ordered a carriage to take them to Marie's home, stopping along the way so that Gabrielle could purchase a complete layette for little Rose.

They rode down St. Charles Street and turned into Rampart until they came to a small whitewashed house with a decorative iron fence running the length of it and separating it on either side from two more identical houses. When the door was opened and she saw Marie smiling happily at her, Gabrielle threw her inhibitions to the winds and hugged the girl.

"Marie! How good it is to see you!"

"Gabrielle, I've so looked forward to this visit. Congratulations to you—Pierre told me the news."

Marie escorted them to the back of the house, which opened into a sunny, wide room that seemed to serve as both kitchen and dining area. At the stove a huge mocha-colored woman in a bright lime-green tignon was stirring something.

"Mama, this is Gabrielle. You remember I spoke of her many times."

The woman nodded curtly and turned back to her cooking, obviously not impressed by this woman who called herself Jean Lafitte's mistress.

"Catherine! Catherine, come out here and bring Rose with you," Marie called through an archway that led to three separate doors. One of the doors opened, and a delicate young girl approached with a blanket-wrapped bundle in her arms. Gabrielle smiled at the girl, who barely acknowledged her before turning a brilliant smile on Jean. Noting the instant and obvious affection, Gabrielle remembered Jean's words. In those huge, velvety brown eyes, Gabrielle could see an unselfish love that Jean did not discern.

"Cathy, bring the baby here. Gabrielle wants to see her," Lafitte said, placing an arm affectionately around Gabrielle's shoulders.

Immediately, the smile died on the girl's face, replaced by a sullen expression, and she brought the child silently for Gabrielle to see.

"Oh, Marie, she is precious," Gabrielle said, inspecting the tiny face with its unwinking brown eyes. "May I hold her?"

Marie nodded, and Catherine placed the baby in Gabrielle's arms. Almost immediately a loud wail arose, and, surprised, Gabrielle glanced around quickly for help. Catherine snatched the baby back and comforted it against her shoulder. "Little Rose knows you don't belong here," the girl offered without expression.

Gabrielle flushed. Marie beckoned her to the bedroom, turning to her sister. "Catherine, why don't you get something for Gabrielle to drink?"

Catherine looked mutinous, hesitated, then ran from the room in a burst of sobbing. Feeling embarrassed, Gabrielle looked helplessly at Marie.

"Pay no attention to her, Gabrielle. I'm afraid she doesn't feel very friendly towards the woman who possesses her hero's love."

"She—she loves Jean, doesn't she, Marie?" Gabrielle asked.

Marie nodded. "I suppose so, but she's only fourteen."

"Does your mother take her to the Quadroon Ball as you used to do?"

"No, Catherine has not expressed any interest in it, and since Pierre pays for all of us, there is no hurry. When this infatuation with Jean is gone. I'm sure she will consider going, if only to find a patron for herself."

Gabrielle nodded, but she felt privately that Catherine was not one to get over an infatuation so easily. In those eyes that had looked at her with misery and hate she had seen what Jean would someday recognize. Love and adoration looked out when Catherine's eyes rested on Jean Lafitte, and those two emotions were without price to a man like him—the two emotions that she, Gabrielle could not give him.

Chapter Twenty-two

Gabrielle gazed ruefully at her distended belly and counted the months mentally—nearly seven months gone and only two more months to contend with. But, according to Marie, those were the worst. She felt heavy as a cow and twice as slow as she moved about the house on Grande Terre.

Lafitte had insisted she bring in another girl to help her, and so she had engaged the daughter of one of the fishermen on the island. Janet was not lazy, but she preferred to do the tasks assigned to her with the minimum of efficiency. Gabrielle would find that she must continually watch the girl while she performed her jobs so that she, herself, would not have to go back and redo what the girl had just done.

"I'm done in the pantry," Janet called from the depths of the deep closet.

"Good. Now you must put all the food back in. What will we have for dinner tonight?"

"There's bacon, ham, and a roast in here."

"The roast. Lafitte brought it home yesterday, and we had better cook it before it fills with maggots."

Janet agreed and pulled out the piece of red meat after unwrapping it from its cloth—the sight of it caused Gabrielle to feel the bile rise in her throat. "Put it in the kettle. Hurry!" she pleaded, closing her eyes and swallowing deliberately.

Knowing her mistress's delicate stomach, Janet hurried to obey her, filling the pot with water and salting it liberally, then lighting the kitchen fire. When everything was done, she came back to where Gabrielle still sat. "If you don't mind, I'd like to go out and pick some sea oats to put on the table. Nothing is really blooming this time of year, but it would add a little color to the meal."

"I'd like to go with you, Janet, but I'm afraid I'm not feeling up to it. To think that in only two more months I'll be rid of this burden and be able to run and bend like a girl again." She sighed. "That is, if I don't stay permanently fat." She called to the girl as she was slipping out the door. "Oh, and while you are out, please stop by Mother Hanna's. Ask her for another posset for this backache. I need something to help me sleep."

Janet shook her head soberly. "You know that Mother

Hanna said she wouldn't give you another—it's not good for the baby."

Gabrielle snapped at the girl waspishly, "I don't care what she says! I tell you, get it from her, or I shall scream with pain all night and lay the fault on your shoulders. Now hurry!"

As the girl left, Gabrielle bit her lip, vexed at herself for her evil tongue. Lately she had been more than irritable, finding it harder than ever to curb her complaints and sharpness.

"Damn the bastards!"

Gabrielle hurried out of the house as fast as she could to find Lafitte on his way up the path, shaking his fists and letting out a stream of curses. Beside him, Pierre was shaking his head, his fat belly jumping at every step.

"I really didn't think that crafty fox would do it," he murmured intermittently.

"Well, he did it, but it's not going to do him much good," Lafitte vowed.

Beluche and You hurried behind the two brothers, the looks on their faces stern. Gambi and Nez Coupé followed.

"Jean—what happened?" Gabrielle asked.

He didn't answer but indicated his pleasure at seeing her after his trip to New Orleans by a hearty kiss. "Coffee, sweetheart. We've got some work to do."

The six men filed into the kitchen and sat around the table.

"Let's look at this from Claiborne's point of view," Lafitte began. "Now, on November 16, as Pierre and I were taking a small fleet of skiffs loaded with contraband merchandise through the bayous, we were surprised by Captain Holmes. Naturally, the smuggled goods were found in the convoy and were confiscated by the government authorities in the name of the United States— Claiborne doesn't miss a trick! Pierre and I were arrested, bail was set, and we were released through the good services of Jean Sauvinet. Now, the trial is set for November 29. Claiborne is going to want to speed up the process and get a conviction. Grymes will hold the position of prosecutor for the state." Here Lafitte smiled a little. "I think we can depend on Grymes to lengthen the trial until the general interest runs out. Claiborne will find himself without public backing, and we should get out of it."

"It sounds good to me, but you can count on Grymes?" Dominique asked.

"I'm sure of it," Lafitte answered.

Pierre shook his head. "Couldn't Claiborne invoke some sort of lawful procedure to speed up the trial without Grymes' help?"

Lafitte shrugged. "I doubt that Claiborne will have much to say. The tribunal will have to make those decisions, and I think I can truthfully say I don't have a real enemy on the bench. Most of the judges have bought goods and slaves from me for years. They're not going to risk losing a good source of supply just to gratify Claiborne, who is as unpopular with the general public as a fox in the henhouse. Everyone knows the Creoles don't like him, despite that very beautiful Creole wife he's taken in the hope that it will get him a foot in the door."

Dominique laughed. "Suzette Bosque is a beauty, that's for sure. I wouldn't mind getting that filly in my clutches for a few hours, but she's a smart one, too. She backs her husband tooth and nail and isn't about to lose him."

"That still doesn't assure Claiborne's position among the Creoles," Lafitte put in. "They don't understand the man, and so they are amused by his tactics."

Gabrielle, whose heart had skipped several beats on hearing this news, forced herself to remain calm as she made coffee and filled the men's cups. The men would be talking far into the night, and she settled herself comfortably in a chair in a corner.

When she awoke the next morning, she found Lafitte already dressed.

"I have two planters coming to the island today to look at merchandise," he said.

"Despite what happened a few days ago?" Gabrielle asked incredulously.

He smiled. "Remember, my dear, that men are not

concerned with anything but their own survival. I have no doubts that all of my buyers would continue doing business with me up until the day I hang from the scaffold."

"Jean! Please don't talk like that," Gabrielle said, getting clumsily from the bed.

He noted her awkward movements, and his face grew tender. "Soon this will be over," he said, coming to stand close to her. "When the baby comes, you will be your old self again and—perhaps—I will have a wonderful surprise for you."

"No more surprises, please," Gabrielle sighed, patting her stomach.

Lafitte laughed. "I think the boy will need a legal father, don't you, ma'm'selle?"

Gabrielle stopped abruptly and looked at Lafitte, her violet eyes widening considerably. "Jean, you don't mean —you can't possibly be thinking—"

"This is a dangerous life, Gabrielle, and I've been thinking that maybe now would be a good time to get out of it. You and I and the boy, together we could make a new life somewhere."

"Jean—I can't believe you're truly saying this," Gabrielle exclaimed, laughing and crying at the same time.

He wiped her eyes gently. "I can't make any promises, but I have been giving the idea much thought lately. We'll just have to wait and see."

He pressed a parting kiss to her mouth, then left the room to go to the beach in order to meet his prospective buyers when they arrived. Gabrielle watched him and felt happier than she had for months. Oh, it was too good to be true! Lafitte loved her after all, and—she was sure— with the arrival of the baby, she would be able to return that love wholeheartedly, with no reservations.

Gabrielle went out to the veranda and sat for a while on the porch, rocking gently and gazing out to the emerald sea.

"Ma'm'selle, may I join you for a moment?"

Gabrielle looked up and smiled to see Beluche coming

towards her. "Of course, Renato, sit here beside me. Lafitte is with some customers at the moment."

Beluche shrugged. "It can wait. I was only going to ask him if he had decided to attend General Humbert's birthday party."

"Birthday party? Who is this General Humbert? Jean hasn't mentioned him to me."

"The general will be fifty-seven years old on Sunday, and Sauvinet has organized a big party to celebrate. The old general mingles freely with those who might be shunned by others. He's a popular figure in New Orleans, although I've heard his temper can be worse than a bear's when he's been drinking. I'm not altogether keen on going, but if Lafitte has decided on doing so, I suppose I shall go along."

"But surely, Renato, Jean would not go into New Orleans now—immediately after being jailed by Claiborne's men!"

Beluche grinned. "Ah, but then you do not know our Lafitte, Gabrielle. Being jailed and freed on bail, then showing up a few days later on his way to a birthday party given in honor of one of the pillars of New Orleans society—surely you must know how Lafitte would relish the irony of it!"

Gabrielle smiled. "You're right, Renato. Jean would think the whole thing most amusing."

Of course, what was bound to happen happened. By the next day, news of the fiasco at the Hôtel de la Marine had seeped out to every corner of New Orleans. It was generally known that General Humbert was given to dissipation and habitual intemperance, but just how far his temper would go no one had known until now.

Someone had given a tribute to the general, who had, by that time, become quite drunk. When he heard the honors bestowed on him in the toastmaster's speech of tribute, the old general had stood up, overturning his chair and growing very red in the face. He declared, it was said, that he had been a great and worthy general and

now must not continue to associate himself with common
outlaws and pirates. He had begun a stream of terrible
oaths and denunciations that caused immediate drawing
of swords and flaring of tempers. Beating upon the table
and shrieking curses, Humbert had come very near to
being killed by the gleaming daggers of the others assembled at his own fête.

The rumors spread further that Jean Lafitte had arisen
from his chair and had held up his hand for silence, stepping close to the general who burst into drunken sobs and
fell upon his shoulder. Lafitte had led the distraught man
from the room, but those close to him heard Lafitte vow
never again to frequent the Hôtel de la Marine.

Gabrielle, hearing everything secondhand, did not dare
to question Lafitte when she saw his set face the next day.
The morning passed with him in a foul mood.

"I swear I'll set those bastards on their ears!" he
thundered to no one in particular. "So I'm only fit to consort with common outlaws and pirates while a stinking-
drunk, broken-down old general is too good for the likes
of me!"

He continued in this vein throughout the day, until by
mid-afternoon he had worked himself into a fair lather.
He snapped twice at Gabrielle, the second time very
nearly sending her into tears. He spoke sharply to both
You and Gambi, causing tempers to flare all around.

"Can we help it if a man's pride is hurt?" Dominique
wondered out loud with growing irritation.

Gambi looked positively ferocious, and when he saw
Simmons walking up the path in order to report the day's
accounting to Lafitte, he seized upon this unexpected
chance to even an old score and, so, divert Lafitte's wrath
to a better course.

"I've brought the day's accounting for your approval,"
Simmons said by way of explanation, handing a long list
to the man, and noticing immediately his foul frame of
mind.

Lafitte took the proffered sheet of paper without a
word.

"Boy! Hey, there, boy, before you go," Gambi began, his mouth shaping a cruel smile, "wouldn't you like to pay your respects to the lady?"

Simmons hesitated, not quite sure just what Gambi was up to. "I'm certain she's busy," he returned carefully.

"Come, come now, boy, I doubt she's too busy to visit with you. You're not forgetting that cozy little domestic scene I was witness to some time ago?" Gambi urged, catching him by the sleeve of his shirt.

Simmons tried to wrench his sleeve away, but Gambi held him tightly.

"Lafitte, you really should hear what I have to say. I do believe we've got ourselves a spy here."

Lafitte's head shot up, and his brow lowered in anger. "Gambi, shut your mouth before you find yourself in trouble. I've no liking for your jokes today," he answered.

Gambi, affronted, brought a hand quickly to his sword. "By God, Lafitte, you're an even bigger fool than I thought—not a man I care to call my leader. If you let a mere boy dally with your woman and then feed him information so he can spill it all to his brother in customs, then I think we should call for a change of command."

Gabrielle, her heart pounding painfully against her ribs, moved quietly to the door, her hands holding her apron tightly. Please, please, God, make him stop, she prayed.

But Gambi was thoroughly enjoying himself, taunting Lafitte, and he was not about to stop both sacrificing the boy and making a fool of the man he hated.

Lafitte stood up and started toying with the dagger at his belt. "Gambi, your accusations are of a most serious nature. I suggest that you either back them up with evidence or shove them back down your lying throat."

"Lafitte, you *are* a fool! With the truth plain in front of you! Look at him. The boy's drenched with sweat. He's shaking from head to foot because he's scared. He knows I'm telling the truth. Ask him. One of my men saw him with one of the customs officials a few days before you and your brother were caught in the bayous. A considerable sum of gold changed hands. I thought then that this

bastard was selling information to the officials, but I had
to be sure. Then, when you were arrested, I only had
to put two and two together. He's made a fool of you,
Lafitte. He's pulled a trick on you that even a ten-year-
old could have discovered." Gambi began laughing, egg-
ing him on, turning the screw deeper, until Lafitte's face
went livid with rage.

"Is it true, Simmons?" he roared, stepping close to the
boy and delivering two vicious slaps to his face.

The boy's head jerked from side to side with the force
of the blows. A thin trickle of blood appeared at the corner of his mouth.

"No, no, it isn't true! They wanted me to sell them information, but I didn't. I told them lies, wrong dates," he
muttered feebly.

Seeing the pathetic figure, Gabrielle could hold herself
back no longer. She hurried as fast as her thickened figure
would allow and grabbed Lafitte's arm. "No, please, Jean.
He's telling the truth. Don't hurt him, please."

Gambi's laugh grew even nastier. "See how she pleads
for his life. I'm telling you, Lafitte, I saw the two of them
together in an embrace. Would you have the little bitch
make a fool of you in the bargain?"

His words added fuel to the fire of Lafitte's fury, and
he pushed the girl away, into Gambi's arms. Struggling to
free herself. Gabrielle found Gambi's arms tightening
around her, squeezing the breath from her lungs.

"Quiet, bitch, the scum's only getting what he deserves,"
Gambi hissed, taking advantage of the situation to feel her
breasts.

Gabrielle kicked him furiously. "Don't, Jean, please
don't. Gambi's wrong. He—"

Her words were cut off abruptly by a heavy hand on
her mouth. She watched in horror, as Lafitte delivered
a rain of blows on the helpless boy, who did not even
try to defend himself. In a few minutes, his face was
nearly unrecognizable because of the blood flowing from
his pulpy flesh. Lafitte kicked the choking form as the boy

knelt on the sand to cough up the blood that clogged his breathing.

Tears fell down Gabrielle's cheeks and spilled onto Gambi's restraining hand. He was holding her too tightly, she thought, beginning to feel dizzy. She made a last effort to free herself and felt an agonizing pain sear her from the small of her back down her leg. "Don't, Jean. If you love me, please stop it."

But Lafitte was beyond hearing her. The accumulated frustrations and disappointments of the past few weeks were releasing a fury of pent-up emotions. He had to seek release by destroying this boy in whom he had so much confidence and trust, only to find that he had sold that trust to the very authorities who wanted to put him behind bars.

"Dominique, Renato, stop him!" Gabrielle begged, appealing to the other two men, but their hardened gazes and set jaws told her that they, too, were only too glad to find a scapegoat on whom to vent their frustrations.

"Get up, you son of a bitch!" Lafitte said, his voice hard and cold.

Hardly aware of where he was any more, the boy struggled to stand up but fell almost unconscious to the ground. Lafitte delivered a kick to his ribs, and the boy cried out in agony. With difficulty, Simmons finally managed to stand.

"Now get moving, get out of here," Lafitte snapped, pushing him towards the stretch of beach. When the boy had gone perhaps ten feet, Lafitte turned to Gambi, who was still trying to subdue Gabrielle, but with little success. "Give me your pistol," he ordered.

"No! No!" Gabrielle screamed helplessly, her eyes dilated with fear.

"I won't kill the bastard, but I'll scare the hell out of him. I doubt that he'll ever play that foolhardy game again," Lafitte returned grimly, firing two shots at the sand around Simmons' feet.

Like an evil bird of prey, Gambi pulled out the other

pistol from his belt and, chuckling, sighted down the barrel at the groping, lurching figure. "I'll do more than scare the hell out of him," he spoke between his teeth. And with that, he fired the pistol.

Nearly numb with horror, Gabrielle saw Simmons sink to the ground, a splotch of bright red spreading uniformly over his back.

"The bastard'll never spread his tales any more," Gambi said, satisfied.

With a demented screech, Gabrielle grabbed for his pistol, meaning to shoot him in rightful vengeance. Gambi, springing away from her grasp, delivered a stinging blow to her jaw that nearly snapped her neck and sent her sprawling backwards to land with a sickening thud in a clump of bracken. A scream of pain tore through her, and she felt as though her whole body were suddenly on fire.

"Oh, my God! Lafitte! The girl, she's been hurt!" she heard Dominque say as if from a great distance.

Her head was bursting with colored lights, and raging fires were burning in her back, in her abdomen, in her legs. Someone was picking her up, but she had no idea who. Simmons—John—her tortured mind conjured up the still figure covered with blood, obscene against the whiteness of the blazing sand. Lafitte had killed him! How could he have done it! John had protected him at a risk to his own life!

Another pain shot through her back and another, so that soon her mind refused to function any longer. All she wanted was to be free of the pain. She heard someone shouting—or were they whispering? for Hanna. Yes, yes, bring Hanna, she thought. Hanna would give her a soothing posset that would make the pain go away and let her go to sleep.

Her mind wandered, and she thought she had been caught again in the fire at Renée's. No one was going to rescue her now—Lafitte had barred the door, and Rosa was waiting outside to slit her belly if she tried to run out. She screamed at the sight of the woman's crafty black eyes.

"Help me, Rosa," Gabrielle thought she cried out, but the woman only laughed and showed her the blade of her dagger, gleaming against the heat of the sand.

The fire was closer now, it was choking her, cutting her breath off. She struggled to keep on breathing but felt the flames licking at her back, her legs. The pain surged through her, and she knew with certainty that she would not be able to stand it much longer. She told herself to relax, to flow with the pain, and it would be all right. And she was surprised when this actually seemed to help. A palpable warm spread out now from her belly and between her legs. Her legs were swimming in it, and the pain was almost gone now. She could breathe again, and she struggled back from her stupor. She must thank Mr. St. Claire, she really must, she thought. After all, if it hadn't been for him, she would have died in the flames.

She opened her eyes, and they registered the bent figure and wizened face of Mother Hanna. Now, where had she come from, she wondered, and tried to speak, to ask her, but nothing came from her working mouth. She tried to move her hand, but it wouldn't obey her wishes, and so she could only watch with a growing dread, watch the woman's hands kneading her body, the woman's face perspiring heavily, the sweat dripping down to stain her thighs.

Finally, the woman looked up at her, and there was a bitter smile on her worn face. "Now, my dear, you're going to be all right. You're stronger than I thought."

I'm going to be all right, Gabrielle thought, wondering why the woman had said that—what was wrong with me? She found that she could move her hands now, and they crept tentatively towards that warmth between her legs.

"Careful, now. You just lie back and rest. I'm going to bind you up good and tight," Hanna directed.

Gabrielle raised her hands and looked at them curiously. They were sticky and wet. The fingers were smeared with red. Oh, my God, she thought. I'm bleeding! Her mind struggled to register what had happened.

And then, with a terrible clarity, she knew. The baby!

"M-my, my baby, where is he?" she screamed, but her throat crackled so that the sound was barely a whisper.

Hanna shook her head wordlessly. "The poor little mite, he was just too small yet to make it on his own," she said slowly, a wealth of sympathy in her voice.

Dead! Her baby was dead! Gabrielle felt a large sob catching in her throat. Tears spilled carelessly down her cheeks. She wanted to cry aloud but didn't have the strength. She felt suddenly terribly weary.

Chapter Twenty-three

"It's a lovely day, ma'am, are you sure you wouldn't like to sit outside on the veranda for just a little while?" Janet cajoled, opening the shutters for the January sunshine to spill into the room and illuminate the face of the young woman who lay propped up on the pillows.

"I think not, Janet."

Janet opened her mouth, then shut it again and sighed. "All right, I won't talk of it any more today, but you can't lie there in bed forever."

She left the room, making no mention to Gabrielle of the changes that had been taking place on the island since her miscarriage. Lafitte was finding it more difficult to sleep, was drinking more than had been his custom and was going around in a fierce temper. He no longer attempted to control his men and gave them free rein on their trips to the city.

Gabrielle had kept to the confines of her room for nearly six weeks, and in this short space of time, Lafitte had grown morose and quicker to anger, more arrogant, and less caring about public opinion. He had been declared an outlaw and, it seemed, had decided to play the game to the hilt.

But Gabrielle, suffering still from her anguish over the loss of her child, knew very little of this. She only wished that that terrible afternoon had never happened. All she wanted was to forget—escape! She must get away from the island, away from everything here. The place only served to remind her of things that could never be again. She must enlist Janet's help and then make a plan.

A few days later, she approached the girl. "Janet, I must get away—leave Barataria for good. There is no longer anything between Lafitte and me to make me stay."

"It's impossible! You must regain your strength first— you could never make it through the bayous!" Janet argued.

"But Hanna said I was recovered!" Gabrielle protested, glancing imploringly at the girl.

"Yes, of course she did. But not fit for a three-day journey through treacherous swampland!"

"Please help me, Janet." The huge violet eyes were wet with tears, and Janet found herself torn.

"All right, all right. I will help you escape, but not now, not today. We must wait. Lafitte has announced an auction at the Temple and he will be busy in the next few weeks transferring merchandise to the warehouse there. After he has left, you will be able to go."

It was the first week in February, and the day had dawned overcast. The threatening rain aided Gabrielle's plans perfectly, for the weather would keep almost everyone indoors. She had decided to confiscate one of the little skiffs that was moored on the beach and use it to make her escape by water.

Sitting now in the boat, she allowed it to draw its own course from the wind and the choppy waves while she rested in the stern, only directing the rudder in order to turn the boat into Barataria Bay and away from the island.

She had no idea where she was going, or how she was going to get through the bayous without a guide, but anything was better than going back now, she thought with determination.

Towards evening, the rain was coming down so hard that there was nothing for her to do but draw her blanket over herself and huddle beneath its warmth, finally dozing off so that the harsh cry of the gulls aroused her towards dawn. She glanced quickly at the dawning sun to make sure she was still headed in the right direction, realizing that she was on the open water of the bay now, and there was no sight of land anywhere.

There descended about her an eerie silence that lasted through the close of the day, broken only by the cries of the sea birds and the splash of fish jumping in the water. That night the stars shone bright, lighting the water around her with a silvery glow. She shivered, feeling slightly spooked by the unfamiliar seascape.

A little after dawn the next morning, she noticed the beginnings of a stretch of swamp, tall reeds poking above the waterline and here and there stray logs and lumps of rocky ground sticking up. She eyed the logs suspiciously, remembering from earlier travels through the swamp how swiftly innocent "pieces of wood" could turn into the long, flat snouts of deadly, silent alligators.

The boat continued its course through the reeds, bumping once into a rock and so unnerving her that she screamed out loud, causing a flock of birds to take to the air, screeching harshly at her. She ate very little that second day, her appetite all but leaving her. As the night once more descended, she considered tying the boat to some jutting branch of a sunken tree but thought it might be too dangerous.

By the next morning, she realized that she was very near exhaustion and forced herself to eat to keep up her strength. She had passed through a small lake the night before and had been able to take only short snatches of sleep. The terrain became different again, changing from the tall marsh reeds to swamp cypress and heavy undergrowth. The vegetation was green and thick, and she realized that soon she would have to give up the boat for she was very near dry land.

About midday, she saw that she could no longer continue with the boat and tied it to a tree, eating her lunch hurriedly. The food felt like a lump in her stomach, and she tied up her pack slowly, suddenly loath to leave the relative safety of the skiff. Taking a deep breath, she stepped out of the boat, immediately sinking in mud up to her ankles. The oozing slime filled her shoes, and with disgust she pulled her feet out of the muck.

Finally she found firmer footing, and she set off in what she hoped was the direction of New Orleans. Later, it seemed as though she had walked for hours, heedless of anything but the driving force that sustained her, the need to survive. The terrain had changed once again. The ground was smoother, and there were broad-leaved trees and grass on the blessedly solid ground. With surprise, she saw that she was nearing the city's edge. Gabrielle could see cattle grazing placidly and clusters of farm buildings on either side of her. A sprawling, six-pillared plantation house topped the crest of a hill. She felt better just seeing such evidence of civilization.

Despite her harrowing experience of the past few days, she felt wonderfully alive and filled with a sudden optimism. She had beaten the swamp—hadn't she? She knew already where she would go—to Renée's, of course. Renée would look after her like a mother.

In the near distance, Gabrielle could make out buildings rising from the cobbled streets of the town, and she would have started to sing aloud, but for safety's sake she smiled secretly to herself instead. Now she must put away these last three years in the back of her mind. She would keep some of the fondest memories, and, certainly, she would never forget Lafitte. But, for the rest, it would be as though she had never existed on Grande Terre. Once again, a page in her life had turned.

PART THREE

Impasse

Chapter Twenty-four

Gabrielle picked up the *Louisiana Gazette* and read the front page absently. The paper was printed in both French and English, and she read both columns, wondering if anything had been lost in the translation.

The lead story concerned the war with England. Dispatches from Washington were alarming these days, as the war was definitely not going well for the American forces. Detroit had surrendered in 1812. The British Navy was threatening the Atlantic seaboard, and on land the English had succeeded in arousing many of the Indian nations to rally to their cause. There was a growing certainty in New Orleans that the British could not long leave alone such an important center of commerce. Governor Claiborne was beginning to drum up men who would fight in an emergency, but he was getting a surprisingly poor turnout.

She turned the page, and her eyes caught Lafitte's name in one of the articles. As always, she read the column with interest. Claiborne had issued a proclamation asking that no citizen of New Orleans engage in interaction with those lawless people who committed piracy on the vessels of nations at peace with the United States. The article went on to surmise that Jean Lafitte was responsible for these piracies and that he should carry the title of outlaw and be treated as such.

Right below the article, though, was a short notice, announcing another auction at the Temple. Gabrielle wondered if the newspaper editors had deliberately put the announcement beneath the article. These Creoles, she sighed—they saw no end to milking everything for all the amusement they could get out of it.

She laid the paper down and finished her poached eggs.

Today was March 15, 1813, and she had been at Renée's for a little over a month. It was time to start repaying her hostess for her unlimited kindness.

She got up from bed and walked to the armoire, letting her eyes go over her wardrobe with care. She had informed Renée only last night that she intended to join the other girls in the main parlor tonight and start earning her keep like all the rest. After all, she argued, she was no one who should be receiving special privileges that the others could not enjoy. And, besides, Renée could ill afford to take in someone who added not one picayune to the day's earnings. Naturally, she had expected protest from Renée, but she remained steadfast in her decision.

"But, Gabrielle, you really have no idea what this business is all about. I'm not sure you can handle it. There are all kinds of men in the city, some of them not the kind that you would look at if you met them in the street, much less invite into your bed. There are many difficult ones out there—the Jim Wests, the old men with strange ideas of love, the young bucks who demand too much for their money."

Gabrielle shook her head stubbornly. "You can't change my mind. I've known men before."

"Hmmph! How many? One, two? Good God, if it wasn't so horrifying, I might laugh out loud," Renée cried, holding her hands to her cheeks and shaking her head. "I'm telling you, Gabrielle, it just won't work."

"Would you throw me out, Renée?" As the latter shook her head, Gabrielle continued, "Then let me choose how I shall repay you, for I'm warning you that I shall leave if you don't let me earn my keep. I'm sure there are other establishments that wouldn't hesitate at using my services."

"Lord almighty, the child has lost her head. What other establishments? You'd be black and blue within a week anywhere else. At least I try to screen my clients for crazies and those with any sickness."

"Well, then?"

Renée, seeing the set look on the other's face, finally shrugged her shoulders and raised her eyes heavenward.

"All right, then. You start tomorrow. It's Wednesday and a slow night, so we can ease you in a little."

She watched as the girl started back up the staircase. "How old are you now, my dear?" she called.

Gabrielle turned. "I'll be twenty next month."

"From now on you're eighteen. You can get away with it, and the men like their women as young as possible."

Today was Wednesday, Gabrielle thought.

"Hey, can I come in?" It was Dolly, already dressed and smiling radiantly.

"You look happy today," Gabrielle commented.

"Oh, I'm nearly in transports. M'sieur de Marigny has singled me out for tonight. Ah, it is nice to have a hand-home young man for a change."

"I have met your M'sieur de Marigny before," Gabrielle said, smiling at the effect her words had on the other girl. "Only in passing, mind you. I thought he was married."

"Oh, that," Dolly replied breezily. "Everyone knows what a hateful wretch that Spanish bitch is—almost as sour-tongued as—" Here she stopped, hesitating to bring up Rosa's name.

The death of Rosa had been hushed up by mutual assent between the girls and the police in return for a few nights of free favors. But she mustn't dwell on that now, Gabrielle thought with determination. She must think of today—of tonight. . . .

"So, you've decided that tonight—is the night," Dolly said softly, bringing Gabrielle out of her reverie.

She smiled crookedly. "Yes, I'll be the first to admit I'm nervous. How did you feel when you—I mean—"

Dolly laughed with understanding. "I can barely recall now, as it must be almost five years since I came with Renée. I suppose I was a little nervous, but the man was understanding enough about it. I guess it sort of excited him to think that I was new at the game, almost as though I were a virgin all over again."

"What do you think I should wear?" Gabrielle inquired, frowning into her armoire.

Dolly shrugged. "It won't matter what you wear. Anything will look ravishing on you. I always let my mood of the evening guide me." She laughed as though at some private joke.

Gabrielle smiled back at her. "You know, Dolly, you remind me so much of a girl I used to be the best of friends with in Paris."

"Really? Who was she?"

Gabrielle grinned mischievously. "Her name was Isabel de Montfort and she married the Duc de Gramount!"

"Well, fancy that! A duchess! I never realized I had such refinement," Dolly teased, sticking her nose up in the air.

"It's not that you look like her, actually, but you act so much like her. You're brave and daring as she was, and you love men. So did she."

"Somehow I can't imagine that her husband would appreciate that," Dolly laughed, then sobered at her friend's thoughtful expression. "Oh, Gabrielle, don't start thinking back again. It's no good and will only make you weepy. One thing a man doesn't like, and that's a self-pitying whore. That's one of the first lessons you've got to learn, if you're going to make it in this business."

Gabrielle nodded soberly. The two went down to lunch, and, afterwards, Gabrielle tried to get some rest but found she was much too restless to settle down.

She supposed that after a few nights' work she would be able to discipline her routine to coincide with the normal hours for the house. But for now she stared up at the ceiling, her arms folded behind her head.

She really didn't want to think of Lafitte but found herself doing just that. Of course he had known where she would go in the event of her escape and had shown up at Renée's only a few days after Gabrielle had arrived. She had refused to go down to the parlor. She told Renée in no uncertain terms that she had no desire to see him and that she only wanted to be left alone. He had persisted for a few more days and then had gone back to Grande Terre. Perhaps he, too, had finally realized that there was no more future for the two of them together after she lost their baby. She shook her head and paced the room nervously. She should be thinking of tonight, of the drastic step she was going to take. She knew she could bow out now while there was still time, and Renée would say not a word. But what else was left for her to do? she thought dismally.

There was no one in all of New Orleans whom she could go to for aid except Renée, and she simply would not make herself a liability on the woman's shoulders. She wandered over to her dressing table and let her eyes roam over the collection of pots and brushes that Renée had lent her. The idea of painting her face held little appeal for her. A bit of coral touched to the lips and perhaps something to darken her lashes, but that would be all. As to the dress, she was still undecided when Dolly knocked on the door to call her to dinner.

"Remember when we used to joke about initiating you into the sisterhood?" her friend giggled after the meal was over. "Who would have thought that the words would come full cycle? And now here you are with us again, and this time in a very different capacity."

"Not so very different," Gabrielle whispered to herself. Then she had been the prisoner of one man, now she would be the prisoner of many.

When they returned to her room, she insisted that Dolly pick out a gown for her. They were all of dubious taste, as most of them were castoffs from the other girls that had been altered over the weeks to suit Gabrielle's lissome figure.

"I think this one should do the trick," Dolly pronounced, dragging out one of the simpler gowns, one made of deep purple taffeta. The neck was extremely low, and the sleeves reached to her wrists. The high waistline accentuated her breasts, and the dress draped into a graceful skirt that rustled pleasantly when she walked. The color turned her eyes into huge, purple violets, and, outlined in the dark cosmetic, they stood out most effectively. She pinched her cheeks to give them more color and darkened her lips with a rouge stick. Dolly piled on her head the heavy mass of blonde curls, which had become sun-streaked from her exposure on the island, making a tousled coiffure, that was held in place by a purple velvet fillet.

"You're beautiful," she announced, smiling warmly as she noted the slight trembling in Gabrielle's limbs. "I'll have to keep M'sieur de Marigny away from you tonight, or I might find myself out of a place. The other girls will be looking daggers at you all night, I'm sure. Do try to stay in the shadows for all our sakes."

Gabrielle laughed nervously. "Oh, you can be quite sure I will," she replied.

She helped Dolly with her toilet, and before she realized it, the clock was chiming nine o'clock, and it was time for them to descend the staircase.

"Renée likes for us to be in the parlor when the gentlemen begin arriving, although the crowd really doesn't get here until almost ten." Dolly shook her hair back and made a face in the mirror. "Well, I suppose I can oblige a couple of customers before M'sieur de Marigny arrives."

Gabrielle looked at her in surprise. "You mean you have to—I mean, more than one man—?"

"Not always, but if you haven't anything else to do, why not?"

"But I don't think I can!"

"It's all right, Gabrielle. Most of them only take fifteen or twenty minutes, and they're through! They usually leave the money on the nightstand or the dressing table. Everything is handled very smoothly."

Despite Dolly's jaunty air, Gabrielle hung back as she proceeded down the hall, joined by three other girls. "You go on, I'll be down in a few minutes," she called, when Dolly turned around, a questioning look on her face.

The latter retraced her steps, a frown shaping her mouth. "Look, Gabrielle, you know you don't have to come down at all."

"I know, but I will come down. It's just that I need a little more time."

Dolly shook her head and sighed. "You know, this is really ridiculous. You don't want to come down at all. You have no idea what this is all about, and I really doubt if you'd get through the evening without collapsing! Why not make it another night—or just forget it?" Dolly's voice was stern, but her eyes were pitying.

Gabrielle stiffened. "I'll be down later, I said. Now don't worry about me."

As she watched Dolly shrug and then go on, Gabrielle scurried back into her room, shutting the door quickly. Breathing heavily, as though she had just run a footrace, she wrung her hands and moved towards the window. She remembered the night when she had watched the different men getting out of their carriages and thought that perhaps she could watch for a likely looking candidate and then go downstairs to meet him. It seemed a lot easier and less whorish than simply mingling with everyone downstairs and being surveyed and pawed by all the men until one decided to take her upstairs. She congratulated herself on a splendid idea and settled down to survey the newcomers.

Perhaps an hour had passed, and she found herself yawning when she spied two men coming out of the gambling casino in order to make their way to Renée's. From the light streaming out of the casino she could make out the handsome features of Bernard de Marigny, and the thought came to her that, indeed, he would probably make a considerate lover. But she couldn't deliberately set out to flirt with the man whom Dolly was probably anxiously awaiting. The other man with him, though. . . .

Making up her mind, she hurried out of the room and down the hall, determined not to give herself time to retreat a second time. Squaring her shoulders and placing her hand on the stair railing, she began her descent, hoping to appear as inconspicuous as possible.

Such was not to be the case, however, for at her appearance one of the rivermen, dressed in buckskins, looked up and saw her slender form silhouetted against the blazing crystal chandelier.

With a rousing whoop, he called to his friends. "Goddamn, look what's coming down the stairs, men! She's a goddamn princess! Renée, what the hell you been saving this one for?"

Immediately, all eyes were turned curiously upwards, and Gabrielle felt her cheeks burning with embarrassment. She would have given anything to be able to turn and run back to her room, but it was too late now, for one of the men closest to the staircase had already caught her hand and was pulling her down. Her eyes searched the room in sudden panic for Dolly's comforting reassurance, but instead they rested on the light blue eyes of Bernard de Marigny, whose face was expressing both amusement and surprised recognition. Three or four men immediately cut off her view, pressing closely around her. This was worse than she had imagined, Gabrielle thought, aware as she was of the calculation in their eyes, the lust and greed that reflected in their faces. Hands reached out to catch her arm and drag her to some darkened corner. She stumbled blindly for a moment, then recovered herself and shook the hands off.

Thinking swiftly, she fastened her eyes directly on one of the men and said as sweetly as she could, "Would someone please get me a glass of wine? I vow it is ever so hot in here, gentlemen."

She smiled demurely, and immediately six men were hurrying away to fulfill her wishes. There, now at least she could breathe, she thought. Hesitating at what to do next, she caught sight of a small settee, set out within the circle of light. Out of the corner of her eye, she could also see Renée's huge, black majordomo, hustling the rivermen to the far side of the room.

Then, with relief, Gabrielle noticed a short, middle-aged man coming towards her. He bowed gravely and asked permission to sit next to her.

"Good evening, ma'm'selle. I am Charles Dumain. May I get you something to drink?"

Gabrielle shook her head silently, picking at her skirt with nervous fingers.

"Please, ma'm'selle, I must insist. It is very obvious to me that you are quite a jumble of nerves tonight, and I mean to put you at your ease. Will you allow me?"

"Thank you, m'sieur, but I should prefer that you not leave me quite yet." She gestured towards the rivermen who were being subdued gradually through the efforts of some of the other girls. The little man pursed his mouth and nodded with understanding, seemingly delighted to remain next to her.

Almost timidly, he took her hand in his and pressed a kiss into the palm. "Ma'm'selle, you are exquisite—you are Venus, herself, Aphrodite. . . ."

"Please, m'sieur, you embarrass me!" she protested, finding it almost like talking to one of the courtiers in Paris. She grew a little more confident and hoped that no one would come by to disturb this comforting tête-à-tête. She listened with a half-smile to more impassioned declarations from the man, nodding now and then but saying very little, which evidently satisfied him.

"You are originally from New Orleans, ma'm'selle?" he asked, moving so that he could get a glimpse of the lovely bosom that rose and fell so charmingly.

She shook her head, but declined to enlighten him further. So he launched into the subject of his own place of birth, his business, everything about him, obviously hoping to impress her with his importance.

As she listened with half an ear to his chatter, she became aware that someone was watching her. The idea rankled her considerably, so that she scanned the room to locate the man who was staring so rudely and insistently. It was nearly impossible among the press of people to locate the offender, and she tried to dismiss the matter from her mind.

Presently she looked up to see M'sieur de Marigny making his way to stand in front of her. Thinking that he had been the one staring, she gave him a cool look that held no invitation.

"Good evening, ma'm'selle," he said, bowing, still with the look of amusement on his face.

"Good evening, m'sieur." Her salutation was stiff, and she was aware that M'sieur Dumain was bristling like a bulldog about to be denied a bone.

"M'sieur de Marigny, if you will excuse the young lady and myself, we were just having a most entertaining chat," the smaller man informed the newcomer with a haughty air.

Bernard de Marigny smiled pleasantly. "Please forgive me, m'sieur, but the lady and I are old friends, and I promised her dear mama that I would have a talk with her. The dear old thing is getting on in years, of course, and she insists that I try to persuade ma'm'selle not to pursue this horrendously foolish course. I do hope you understand, m'sieur?" The glint in de Marigny's eyes served its purpose when it was coupled with the knowledge that he was one of the best swordsmen in all of Louisiana.

M'sieur Dumain got up hastily, and, with a murmured farewell, scuttled off to get himself a glass of wine. Gabrielle couldn't keep from laughing at such an ingenious plot to remove an obstacle.

Sitting down beside her, de Marigny quickly captured her hand and placed a warm kiss on the wrist, and then another further up her arm, causing a tingling sensation to run all through her.

"M'sieur de Marigny, you are indeed quite bold, I think," Gabrielle said, a little breathlessly.

He smiled. "A bold manner is the only course of action when one is dealing with a shy, young flower. It has been my experience—"

"And I presume your experience is very wide," Gabrielle interrupted, casting a sly look at him.

"Touché, ma'm'selle," he returned, keeping possession of her hand as he pressed his leg subtly against hers. "Ah, you blush very prettily," he murmured close to her ear, his words only serving to deepen the stain in her cheeks.

"Forgive me, m'sieur, but I—"

"There is no need for you to make excuses, sweetheart. You are a beautiful woman, and so anything you do is most becoming."

The flattering phrases rolled off his tongue like honey, but Gabrielle could not help but warm towards this experienced Don Juan. The thought of Dolly's disappointment caused her some momentary guilt, but now de Marigny was kissing her shoulder, his lips making warm sensations on the delicate flesh of her throat. His kisses were traveling wtih impunity up her neck and then to her face—in another moment. . . .

"M'sieur, please, I don't know what—"

"Hush, little flower, little violet flower," he murmured and took her chin between thumb and finger, forcing her to turn her head towards him. He kissed her softly but completely, with an underlying urgency that took her breath away. Indeed, he was experienced. His hand lay casually against her breast, burning its imprint through the material of her gown.

Abruptly, through her mind's eye, Gabrielle conjured a glimpse of Dolly's face watching them. With a supreme effort, she disengaged herself from de Marigny's grasp, taking a moment to smooth her gown while her cheeks flamed.

"Forgive me, m'sieur, but I cannot—I cannot continue." She turned to look at him, noting the careless lock of hair that had fallen over his brow, the look of triumph in those blue eyes.

"Nonsense, little one. Let us go to your room now. You want me as much as I want you."

She shook her head tearfully. "M'sieur, I cannot in good conscience go with you—when you have promised the evening to—to someone else."

He looked puzzled for a moment, then followed her discreet gaze, understanding showing on his face. "Ah, yes, of course. Ma'm'selle Dolly—she is a friend of yours, yes?" He grinned tightly, striving to maintain his own composure in the face of this disappointment. "There will be other nights, ma'm'selle." His eyes traveled over the exquisite face turned in profile. "At least tell me your name again."

"Gabrielle de Beauvoir."

"It suits you perfectly. I shall call you Gabrielle, and you must call me Bernard. I hope your conscience would not be affronted should I offer to take you for a drive tomorrow afternoon?"

"Oh, m'sieur—Bernard, that would be wonderful!"

"It is settled then. Tomorrow at two o'clock. You shall remain with me the entire day." He kissed her hand and then stood up to bow briskly. "Until tomorrow."

Left alone for a moment, Gabrielle took the time to cast curious glimpses about the room, noting that M'sieur Dumain had found comfort elsewhere. She decided to walk outside in the back courtyard, a charming little garden that would provide her with a breath of fresh air. It was close on to eleven o'clock by now, or perhaps later. There was the faintest chill in the air, and she would have gone in for a shawl but decided she would rather not negotiate the main parlor again. It felt good to be outside, and the freedom made her restless.

The crunch of gravel made her turn around swiftly, but it was only Renée, following her out to see if anything were the matter.

"I'm perfectly all right, Renée. There's no need for you to be so concerned. As you can see, I wasn't devoured alive tonight."

"Only because M'sieur de Marigny chose to offer you protection," the woman returned, not convinced.

"He's a very exciting man, Renée."

"Bernard de Marigny is a past master at seducing women, young and old, Gabrielle. Don't think you can handle him as easily as you might have manipulated M'sieur Dumain. He does not normally let a beautiful woman escape his clutches. Frankly, I'm surprised to find you out here alone."

"Well, I'm afraid I'm not destined to escape his clutches for long. He wants to take me out in his carriage tomorrow." Gabrielle laughed cynically. "Can you imagine,

Renée? Asking to call on me as though I were the most proper young lady in New Orleans, guarded by some forbidding duenna and an equally forbidding papa—and not just a prostitute! I could cry at the irony of it."

Instantly sympathetic, Renée put a soothing arm about her shoulders. "Now, now, Gabrielle. De Marigny is smarter than you think. He knows that you're not going to throw yourself at any man. I've an idea that he's going to want to keep you all to himself the way he looked at you tonight. I could have sworn he might eat you up like a piece of cake on a platter."

Gabrielle laughed again. "What sort of offer can a man make to a piece of cake, then?"

"De Marigny is very wealthy, Gabrielle," Renée said seriously. "He could settle you in a nice town house with two or three servants, if that's what you want. I've heard he even gives his mistresses an allowance every month. He is a most generous man."

Gabrielle had become very serious as she listened to Renée, and now she caught her hand. "Mistress to de Marigny? But he is already married."

"And of what possible significance is that?" snorted Renée. "Do you think he's going to bring you around to the house and introduce you to his wife, for goodness' sake?"

"But you said he has other mistresses," Gabrielle went on as though seeking to find a reason to refuse M'sieur de Marigny.

Renée sighed. "Knowing you, I would wager a month's earnings that within a week you wouldn't be sharing him with anyone!"

Gabrielle dimpled. "Such a compliment!"

"I've heard plenty of them tonight, given in your name. I'm afraid the other girls are not going to be too sorry if de Marigny takes you away from us. Why, I even saw Mr. St. Claire staring at you, sizing you up with as much arrogance as he'd need to throw you over his horse and kidnap you."

Gabrielle turned quickly in surprise from her idle contemplation of the star-filled sky. "How odd that you should tell me. Earlier I thought I felt someone's eyes on me, but I had thought they were Bernard de Marigny's. I must go in and pay my respects to Mr. St. Claire, don't you think? After all, I never did thank him properly for saving my life."

"He's somewhere inside, I'm sure, unless he's gone upstairs with one of the girls."

Gabrielle hurried back into the house, Renée following. For some reason, her heart began pounding in her breast, and she felt a rush of excitement at finally meeting this man who had for so long eluded her acquaintance. A memory swept through her of demanding lips, firm hands, and strong arms encircling her as she gave herself up to a whirl of passion.

But to her disappointment, Hugh, the majordomo, informed them that Mr. St. Claire had already left for the evening. Gábrielle sighed, feeling suddenly deflated. She went upstairs, alone, to her own room.

Chapter Twenty-five

Promptly at two the following afternoon, the carriage of M'sieur de Marigny rolled up in front of Madame Renée's. Glancing out the window, Gabrielle tried to control her excitement. When she felt she was sufficiently calmed, Gabrielle descended the stairs to meet him. She felt her heart's beat perk up dramatically when her eyes fell on the fine figure of this elegant gentleman.

Bernard de Marigny, for his part, could not get enough of her and congratulated himself silently for his extreme good luck in finding such a prize.

It occurred to Gabrielle that this would be strictly a union of lust on de Marigny's part, and of need on her own, with no thought of love involved for either of them.

But she pushed the bothersome thought out of her mind, determined that she would let nothing spoil a beautiful afternoon.

"Charming, my dear," Bernard commented, bowing over her proffered hand. He tucked it possessively in his arm and escorted her to the waiting carriage, aware of several pairs of curious eyes watching their progress down the street.

"I feel as though I'm on display," Gabrielle murmured as the vehicle followed Royal Street to Canal and out of the city.

"And so you should be," de Marigny returned, settling his arm familiarly around her waist.

"Ought you to be so bold in public, m'sieur?" Gabrielle asked him uncomfortably.

He laughed and snapped his fingers. "I care very little about the 'public,' as you call it. Everyone knows I'm married to a shrew, although I must admit she has blessed me with numerous children. At any rate, if you are going to be my mistress, you should get used to such things."

"M'sieur de Marigny! It is all too evident that you have little liking for wooing a lady in easy stages," Gabrielle said, smiling hesitantly.

"Life is too short to dally when you want something badly enough," he responded, his voice turning husky.

Gabrielle veiled her eyes demurely. "Where are you taking me?" she finally asked after a long silence.

"Does it matter?" he wondered, and at her startled expression, "All right, I'll tell you then. We are going to follow the river upstream a little way. I thought you might like to see the countryside around the city."

"I'm sure I would enjoy it immensely," she returned, opening her parasol to shade her face from the sun.

When they were outside the city limits, de Marigny shifted his arm from her waist to her shoulders and brought her closer against him. Bending down a little, he planted his mouth firmly on hers, forcing her lips apart so that his tongue explored her mouth while his free hand moved tentatively on her bodice.

Gabrielle broke away, panting a little, determined that he would not treat her so abusively. "M'sieur, please do not forget yourself! You may have little concern for the public, but I have my own self-esteem to consider!" She nodded towards the impassive back of the driver.

De Marigny laughed as though she had said something inordinately funny. "I wasn't aware that you had any self-esteem left. You were Lafitte's mistress for two years, were you not?"

Anger rose in her at his thoughtlessness, and, without thinking, she reached up and slapped him, her eyes blazing. For a moment, she saw brief anger in his blue eyes, but then a smile shaped that sensual mouth, and catching both her hands, he bent her backwards in the seat, moving his lips heavily on hers until she fought for breath. When he finally released her, she was very near to tears.

"You may turn this carriage around and take me back, m'sieur, for I do not care to be made a fool!"

"What nonsense," he returned, urging the driver on. "At least we both know where we stand now. It's refreshing to get that out of the way so quickly."

She looked up at him doubtfully. "I'm afraid I don't understand."

"It's very simple, really. You know now that I will not tolerate a willful bitch, and I am aware that there are certain matters that shall be considered taboo between us."

She would not reply to the dubious logic of the statement but tried to settle her hat correctly on her head and arrange her skirts that had been disarrayed by de Marigny's ardent administration of punishment.

They drove on through the sunny countryside 'and despite her ruffled emotions, Gabrielle watched the scenery with pleasure. Farther up on the crest of an elevated knoll, she could see a tall, sprawling house, gleaming white. There were a few more scattered houses, but it was obvious that this section of the suburbs had not been fully developed.

As they topped the knoll, she could see the buildings of

New Orleans perhaps ten miles away. She turned her attention to the impressive mansion, noticing the wide veranda that ran the length of the house and the two spiralling staircases that rose on either side to the second story, where a second veranda connected the two smaller wings of the house by less spectacular staircases on either side. Moss-draped trees stretched away from the house towards the levee, and cedar trees shrouded with the grayish stuff towered majestically above the white-gravelled drive. A blending of perfumes tingled her nose as they neared the drive, and she could see the crepe myrtle, roses, cape-jasmine, and magnolia dotting the well-manicured lawn.

"Why, it's beautiful—magnificent!" Gabrielle breathed, turning to de Marigny excitedly. "Is it yours?"

He laughed and patted her cheek. "I'm afraid not, my dear, although I should be extremely proud if it were. No, that epitome of grace and magnificence belongs to a friend of mine, M'sieur St. Claire."

"St. Claire? I've heard of him," Gabrielle said as she tried to keep the disappointment from her voice.

"He owns quite a bit of acreage around here but has absolutely no interest in maintaining a plantation. So there his house sits, without its master much of the time. He prefers the excitement of the city."

"I see," Gabrielle murmured, watching as they drove past the drive leading up to the splendid house. "Are you, then, quite good friends with M'sieur St. Claire?"

De Marigny shrugged. "I doubt if anyone is, as you put it, 'quite good friends' with him, my dear. Suffice it to say that we are old acquaintances, and I am fairly often in his company in town."

"I can imagine what good times the two of you must have together," Gabrielle commented wryly.

De Marigny grinned like a boy. "Ah, my dear, that goes without saying."

He broke off to point at the shell of a partially erected house a few miles down the road, closer to the city. "Another house going up. This one happens to belong to another friend of mine, M'sieur Logan, another American. This section will be fairly crowded soon and mostly with Americans!"

"It looks as though it will be very large," Gabrielle commented.

"Large! Of course, my dear—have you ever known an American without a flair for the ostentatious?" Bernard returned, a trifle snidely.

"I'm afraid I know very few Americans," Gabrielle said.

"Would you like to see the house?"

The drive was yet only a deeply rutted road of dirt, and the carriage bounced alarmingly as they made their way to the construction site. He helped her from the carriage, and they made their way through the tall grass and weeds. Bernard pointed out certain items of interest, but it was hard for Gabrielle to imagine the crisscross patterns of wood and nails as anything like a house.

Bernard took hold of Gabrielle's hand and walked with her towards the river. "I should like to build a house up a little farther along the river," he commented idly.

"How—how does your wife feel about that?" Gabrielle asked, wondering why she would insist on bringing that woman into the conversation.

"She cares little about the thought. She prefers the house in New Orleans where she can be elbow to elbow with all the rest of the population. She insists she must remain there in order to keep her place in society. Pah!" He turned to look at the girl at his side. "If she were as beautiful as you, Gabrielle, she would make a whole new society out here. More and more plantations are springing up. Why go into New Orleans when one can enjoy balls and picnics out here?"

"It seems a lovely idea," Gabrielle sighed, watching the glistening ripples on the surface of the river.

"If she were as beautiful as you," he repeated dreamily, and, taking off his coat, he spread it on the ground for her to sit on. "How many men have said that to you?"

How easily he replaces his Don Juan mask, Gabrielle thought, but answered him lightly. "Not many."

He looked at her with disbelief. "You lie, you little vixen. With whomever else can a man sink into those violet depths and never want to come out again? Who could not resist the urge to capture those golden tresses in his hands and make those beautiful lips sigh for more kisses?"

Gabrielle smiled and picked a blade of grass absently. "How pretty the words sound on your honeyed tongue," she said, her voice holding a note of teasing. "Really, Bernard, you do flatter me outrageously. There are dozens, perhaps hundreds of beautiful women in New Orleans."

He nodded his head. "Of course there are, but do they all have that special look of innocence about them? Do they blush with such ease when a man tells them how lovely they are?" He brushed her cheek with his fingers and turned her face towards him. "Do their eyes grow big with a kind of wonder when a man decides he wants to kiss that trembling mouth?"

He pressed his lips to hers, and she felt him pushing her back so that she lay in the new spring grass, her hat rolling on the ground and her parasol placed carelessly to one side.

"*Mon dieu,* beautiful lady! I could make love to you here on the grass!" he murmured passionately, placing burning, urgent little kisses on her neck and breast.

"Bernard, please, the driver—" Gabrielle cried breathlessly, pressing her hands against his chest.

He looked up. "Forgive me, I had forgotten where we were. Of course, no one else must see this perfect flesh."

He helped her to rise and retrieve her hat and parasol.

"You have ruined my carefully set coiffure," she laughed, tapping his hand lightly with the end of her parasol.

"I am delighted, then," he answered in the same vein, taking her arm once again, "for it only promises a quicker way to enjoy my pleasures." He looked down at her. "There, I have made you blush again, little innocent. I think your face will be crimson tonight. . . ."

He helped her into the carriage, and she had just begun to doze in the sunshine when de Marigny let out a cry. "Ho there, St. Claire!"

She straightened and looked in the direction of his pointing finger.

"There is my illustrious American comrade, my dear. Perhaps he will ride over this way and I will introduce you."

Gabrielle noticed the tall figure on the splendid horse, galloping over the fields, a female rider beside him. He was still perhaps a half a mile away, and she could distinguish little except that he was hatless and his hair shone a deep chestnut, nearly the same color as the satiny coat of his mount.

"He rides with experience," she commented.

"Certainly it seems he does everything with experience," Bernard returned, "but look at his companion. She is a magnificent horsewoman, too."

Gabrielle switched her attention to the woman, whose hair was flying out behind her like a silver banner. She was keeping pace with the man with seemingly effortless ease, but, as they neared the road, she suddenly veered off in the other direction, urging her horse to greater speed. With a hurried salute, the man changed directions and raced off in pursuit.

Bernard, after returning the wave, chuckled to himself and signalled for the driver to move on. "Knowing Melissa, she will no doubt lure him back to the shade of one of those old cypresses and—" he hesitated. "Of course, it is none of my business."

Gabrielle, her curiosity aroused, asked him who the woman was.

"Melissa Lawrence, another American. Her family came from England originally and settled in Virginia where her father made a fortune in tobacco. They moved here a few years ago and are one of the richest families in the state. She is an only child and, for all of her twenty-five years, is dreadfully spoiled. But St. Claire seems to be able to keep her in line very well. Of course, she's the only woman who comes close to matching his spirit and temper. Rumor has it that they will be announcing their engagement in the near future." He laughed. "I really can't imagine either of them married, much less to each other."

"I'd like to meet them," Gabrielle said, thinking aloud.

De Marigny shrugged his shoulders. "You will, for I intend to bring you out to his house one day when we can arrange a small party."

"What—what do you mean? Certainly, your wife belongs with you—"

"Anna comes out occasionally, but she has already informed me that she prefers to stay with her own breed of friend—which translates that when she grows tired of country balls and such, she will retire in grand seclusion to the Maison Marigny in New Orleans. I hardly think she would object to my having a guest to keep me company when she will not remain with me." His blue eyes sparkled devilishly.

"Oh, Bernard, but she would be furious with you and —and what would people say?" Gabrielle went on, her lovely face troubled at his audacity.

"Really, my dear, I thought you would not care so much for the gossips of the city. You seem spirited and somehow independent for all that charming vulnerability. Would you refuse me?"

Gabrielle shook her head, suddenly sad. "How can I refuse you, Bernard? If we are honest with each other, we know that you are only attracted to me on a purely physical basis, and I to you because I have nowhere else to go. It's funny—I lived those two years on Grande Terre, and yet the taste for luxury has never left me."

He took her hand and pressed it. "My poor little girl, have you not been listening to all my passionate declarations—or did you just dismiss them as the ramblings of an accomplished flirt? In spite of what you say, I do like you immensely, as a woman and as a friend."

"Oh, Bernard, you make me feel ashamed of myself," Gabrielle murmured.

"Good. It is the least I could have hoped for. And now I want you to dismiss those bothersome thoughts from your head. It's true that this will be a business liaison of sorts, but I expect more from you than just an eager, willing body. There will be times when we will discuss things and go to the theater together—Anna hates it."

They were back in the city now, and de Marigny directed the driver back to Renée's.

"Now, I want you to wait for me tonight," he whispered as he delivered her to the door. He tweaked her nose and kissed her mouth lightly. "Dress in something special for me, and I may have a surprise for you." He kissed her again. "God, I'm not sure I can wait until tonight!"

Gabrielle went inside and found Renée anxiously awaiting her return. She brought her into her office and closed the door firmly behind her. She bade Gabrielle be seated and came over to sit beside her, taking her hands in hers.

"Now tell me, Gabrielle, what are the handsome de Marigny's intentions?"

Gabrielle smiled. "Far from honorable, I'm afraid," she teased.

Renée brushed aside her levity. "I may as well tell you, my dear, that I have decided that under no circumstances are you to be subjected to the situation you were in last night. I don't care if I have to lock you in your room—you will not come downstairs any more."

"Bernard's words exactly," Gabrielle responded promptly.

Renée's face held suspicion. "Then, what are his plans?"

"He wishes to make me his mistress," she said in a quieter voice. "But I will have to remain in your house until he finds other rooms for me. I—I didn't ask him about the financial arrangements, of course, but I do hope he can install me somewhere outside the city. That's where we went today, and the countryside is so beautiful. I always did like our summers in the country in France," she said softly, "although I did look forward to being in the city again. I suppose I have had enough of that already and long to get away from so many people."

Renée sat back in her chair and laced her fingers over her stomach. "Well then, it seems that de Marigny is a shrewd businessman after all. I am happy for you, my dear."

Gabrielle smiled, and her face was at peace for a moment. Then her eyes grew misty, and she spoke in a very low voice. "Isn't life strange, Renée—that I should be so grateful about becoming the mistress of a man who, in Paris, would have had to ask for my hand in marriage or be thrown out of the house in disgrace—or worse! Sometimes, in my dreams, I remember the balls and parties—did I tell you that I was introduced to the Emperor Napoleon himself? Such an innocent I was then—so naive about the world, untouched, still a virgin until—" She frowned as though trying to remember.

"Until—?" Renée prompted gently.

Gabrielle sighed. "A man came along and changed my world."

"What else?" Renée smiled, her eyes reflecting her understanding. "Was he your lover?"

Gabrielle shook her head swiftly. "He was a very handsome man," she said half to herself. "A—dashing man—oh, you would have liked him, Renée. That's funny, I've always thought I would hate him until the day I died, but now I barely remember his face and it seems I have little hatred left."

"That's as it should be, Gabrielle. Most of us always carry a special attachment to the man who was the first. I suppose it's feminine nature."

"I suppose," Gabrielle agreed, then shook her head as though to rid it of such thoughts of the past. "I think I'll take a bath. Bernard will be here after dinner, and I may be too nervous to eat."

She hurried upstairs and to her room where she found Dolly awaiting her.

"How wonderful for you, Gabrielle!" she cried, hugging her enthusiastically. "I'm beginning to think you will get all of the luck, and I'll probably be here when I'm as old as Renée. I think she's hoping I'll take over for her, someday."

"Oh, Dolly, you'll find the right man one of these days."

"Oh, you may be right. But I don't know—even if he came along now, I might not want to go with him." She smiled. "Anyway, we're not talking about me now. When do you think you will be moving?"

"I'm not sure. I really can't think about that now. Perhaps in a few days."

A discreet knock on the door signalled Sara's entrance with towels and soap, followed by Hugh, lugging the copper tub with the help of another servant.

"Please heat some water, Sara, and bring it as quickly as you can," Gabrielle directed.

When Sara had filled the tub, Gabrielle sank blissfully into it, and Dolly handed her the scented soap. As the fragrance of a field of flowers filled the room, the girls talked on about the future, about Bernard de Marigny, and about news of the war.

"Most of the fighting has been up north, of course," Dolly was saying. "But one of my customers said that there was a good chance the British might try to take New Orleans."

"Well, let's hope it's only a rumor," Gabrielle responded.

"Unfortunately, the numerous British successes on land seem to have no effect on their naval conflicts," Dolly went on.

"Unfortunately for whom?" Gabrielle teased. "Renée seems to think that the British generals are just licking their lips at the chance to capture New Orleans. It would be quite a plum for them, considering they'd have a ready-made harbor right in the Americans' backyard."

"Whew! I hate to think of those stuffy English," Dolly commented wryly. "I doubt if we'd get any business from them."

"Always the business girl," Gabrielle laughed. "But Dolly, do you really think that the British could defeat the Americans?"

"It's not the Americans we'd have to worry about, Gabrielle, but the Creoles—you know they'd do anything to escape a war!"

The two girls agreed.

"I've heard your homeland has some troubles of her own, too," Dolly put in after a moment.

"The fiasco of Russia?" Gabrielle asked, her brow troubled. "I know that news from Europe reaches us dreadfully slowly these days, but it seems my former emperor has been neatly outfoxed by that crafty Alexander. It's hard to understand how Czar Alexander could actually order the burning of his own great city, Moscow."

Dolly nodded thoughtfully. "I suppose he knew he would have to take drastic measures to outsmart Bonaparte," she commented. "Can you imagine trudging through all those miles of snow and ice and cold? They say thousands of French troups were killed by the elements alone!"

Gabrielle found herself thinking again of Paris, recalling Isabel and her new husband, Henri, her brother, Pierre de Montfort—and Charles de Chevalier. Were all of these people who had been so close to her but now seemed so very far away—were all of them safe after such a defeat?

She found herself conjuring up pictures of Isabel huddling for warmth in a tent, waiting vainly for her husband to return. Pierre, dear sweet Pierre—so thin and somehow so vulnerable, not really made for war—could he have withstood the terrible winter and the long trek back to France? And of course, Charles—the virile, golden-haired warrior, pathetically scarred by his mother's indifference. Somehow she couldn't imagine him meeting his end on the battlefield, in the Russian snow, although she knew that that is where he would have wished to die, rather than go home to an ignominious defeat.

"Gabrielle—you're thinking of—of your friends again?" Dolly cut through her daydreaming.

Gabrielle sighed and nodded. "Forgive me. I couldn't help wondering about them. . . ."

Chapter Twenty-six

"So nice of you to join us for dinner, my boy!" said Thomas Lawrence in his heartiest voice as he stood below the candles, his bald pate shining pale in the reflected glow.

"Thank you, Mr. Lawrence, I appreciate your hospitality," replied Rafe St. Claire with only the faintest trace of sarcasm, undetectable, in his words.

"Please call me Thomas," the older man insisted, glancing covertly at his only daughter's happy face.

St. Claire nodded, and his eyes, too, went to Melissa Lawrence's face—not the prettiest of faces, he had to admit, but with an expression about the mouth and eyes that promised the most seductive of natures. St. Claire smiled to himself, and the smile was scornful.

"Do come and sit down, Rafe. It's been so long since you've dined with us," Melissa rushed hurriedly, drawing him inside the dining room, her hands laid possessively on his sleeve.

St. Claire followed her in, bowing politely to Mrs. Lawrence—Sadie, as she also insisted. He glanced about the room which spelled out wealth—new wealth—and wondered whose poor taste had gone into the decorating —probably Melissa's, as her father let her do everything around the house.

"Your ride has put a glow in your cheeks, darling,"

Sadie commented to her daughter as she replaced a stray lock of the silvery hair.

Melissa brushed her mother's hand away impatiently. "I do enjoy riding, mother. It's one of the things I find least boring—and especially when Rafe accompanies me. He does ride superlatively, don't you think, papa?"

Thomas agreed enthusiastically. "That's a fine piece of horseflesh you have, Rafe. Arabian stock?"

Rafe nodded. "I purchased him in Virginia on my last trip home. He is magnificent."

Thomas reflected his interest. "Home? Why, Melissa, you didn't tell me that Rafe had made a trip home. When was it? Did you hear anything more of the war?"

Rafe shrugged arrogantly. "It was nearly four months ago, last fall. My father was ill, and I was called home rather suddenly by my brother, Philip."

"Oh, I'm sorry. How is your father?" Sadie interrupted, looking suitably concerned.

"He's dead," Rafe said quietly, but his green eyes narrowed ruthlessly.

"Oh—oh dear," Sadie said distractedly. "I'm sorry, Rafe."

"Mother, you're repeating yourself," Melissa said with obvious irritation. "Unfortunately, Rafe wasn't all that close to his father, and the trip was more or less the conventional thing, wasn't it, darling?" She smiled at him, her blue eyes slanting at the corners.

Rafe was careful to keep the disdain out of his own eyes. "More or less," he affirmed inscrutably.

"If your father is dead, then, that is—I suppose you came into quite a great deal of—of real estate in Virginia," Thomas began, clearing his throat twice. "This damned war with the English must give you cause for grave concern as far as your holdings go. Do you have any doubts as to the safety of your home?"

The smile that shaped that sensual mouth was definitely laced with sarcasm now. "My home is here in Louisiana, Thomas. Philip got the house in Virginia, as I would have wished. Chances are it will be burned before the war is over anyway. My father's will provided very little for me in the way of real estate. What he did leave me, I converted into dollars as soon as possible."

Thomas had gotten very red in the face and now seemed to have difficulty in choosing the right words. "But, dammit, man, I mean—real estate—that land is some of the best tobacco-growing country in the world! How could you have let it go? And your brother, isn't he younger than you? As the eldest, I would think your father would have seen the title in your name instead of—"

"Papa, Rafe didn't want to go back to Virginia," Melissa put in sweetly. "He wanted to come back here with me, didn't you?" Once more those ice-blue orbs slanted upwards provocatively at him, and Rafe couldn't help the insolent grin that came to his lips.

"The truth is, Thomas," he said, "that I don't give a damn about that land, Virginia, or tobacco, for that matter. I've built Fairview here in New Orleans, and I intend to make something of it one day. My father and I saw eye to eye about my stand on that, and he was aware that Philip was hungry for the old homestead. It mattered little to me, as I saw a profit of over half a million dollars by selling out when I did. Poor Philip is trying desperately to get out now with the British advancing, and can't get a penny an acre."

Thomas' eyes had bulged considerably at the amount of money St. Claire had so casually listed. "I—I see your logic, my boy and—and I must congratulate you on your wisdom. I—I must say, it does my old heart good to see my Melissa in the company of a wise young man like yourself instead of one of those Creole dandies she used to fly away about."

Melissa shot a darting look at her father. "Papa, how you do run on! You know very well that I never flew about after any of those boys. More than likely, their fathers were the ones trying to push them into—into marriage with a rich, young American girl." She glanced wickedly at St. Claire. "Isn't it wonderful to know that Rafe would never want to marry me for my money?"

"Marry you!" Sadie burst out excitedly. "Oh, my God! Rafe, Melissa, when—"

"Mother, please," Melissa said angrily. "Rafe—hasn't asked me—yet."

Oh, Christ, in another moment she'll have me down on one knee—just for practice, Rafe thought in mingled irritation and amusement. He looked at the silvery-haired bitch and thought what a lovely whore she would make— but a wife. . . ! The thought was nearly laughable.

At the uncomfortable silence that filled Melissa's last words, Sadie rang the bell for dinner to be served. Servants glided swiftly and noiselessly about the room, serving the delicious courses, still hot from the stove. At least, Rafe thought, Melissa knew how to discipline her servants—by what means, he had no wish to find out.

"You're quiet tonight, darling," Melissa whispered as the last course was taken away.

He shrugged. "It was a wonderful meal, Melissa. I can think of a fitting dessert," he answered insolently.

She laughed and cast her eyes about the table as though to check on whether either of her parents had overhead. But Rafe was well aware that, had they heard, the Lawrences were unlikely to make any mention of it. Jesus! He could probably make love to their daughter on the dining room floor while they were sipping their cordials, and they would act as though nothing out of the ordinary were happening. Perhaps Sadie, always the polite hostess, would inquire gravely if he needed a pillow. The thought caused a dry chuckle to escape him, and Melissa, thinking she knew the reason, smiled slyly.

Was she thinking of this afternoon, he wondered? She'd nearly torn the flesh from his shoulder with her sharp nails when he finally dragged her under the cover of a magnolia tree. He had chased her for an hour, always letting her stay just a little ahead of him, but always in control. His smile thinned—except for that one moment when he heard de Marigny calling to him.

It had been peculiar how the sun had gleamed off the tousled hair of the girl beside de Marigny in the carriage, turning it to spun gold. Even from that distance, it had been easy to deduce that the woman wasn't his wife, and the rumpled air about her told too plainly that someone else had taken advantage of the warm spring afternoon to indulge in the sport of passion.

Something about that girl—it had hit him suddenly. He had been tempted to trot over to the carriage and watch her reaction as de Marigny introduced him. But Melissa, as though sensing that his attention was now focused in a different direction, had galloped off the opposite way, and he had been forced to follow.

"Rafe, you're not listening, darling," Melissa reproached him petulantly.

His left eyebrow lifted indolently. "Did I miss something important?" he inquired.

Melissa frowned. "Papa suggested I show you the new gazebo that arrived from Savannah last week. It's out in the summer garden and is the dearest thing. It reminds me of a tiny castle!" She clapped her hands like a child.

Rafe was not deceived by this display, which was put on totally for the benefit of her father. "Melissa, I'd love to see it, but I'm afraid I have engagements in town tonight, and I really should be going."

He saw the narrowed eyes, the thinning mouth. "I see. Well, if you must go, let me walk you to the veranda." She took his arm in both her hands.

Rafe bowed to Sadie. "A most pleasant meal, ma'am."

"Try not to make it such a long time before the next one," Sadie reproached him gently.

He smiled, shook hands with Thomas, whose eyebrows lifted in silent questioning to his daughter. "Business engagement in town—tonight, Rafe?" he asked striving to keep the heartiness in his voice.

"Yes."

Thomas blustered for a moment, then nodded and resumed his seat, bringing the cordial to his lips in a hurried movement. Once out on the veranda in the deepening twilight, Melissa swirled around to face him.

"Rafe, why must you go into town tonight? It would have been so easy for you to go out into the garden with me for only a moment?"

"It is never just a moment with you, sweetheart," he said laughingly. "The moment draws out to an hour and then two while you entice me into your web of ravishment."

"Oh, Rafe, you do have a way with words! You make me sound like a spider!"

And so you are, he thought objectively. A pretty little silvery spider who sucks the life out of her mate with her demands and then, when she has no more use for him, kills him with one impassioned draft of her poison.

"I must go," he said, his voice authoritative now, noting the stubborn look creeping into her eyes.

"Business engagements! Bah! You have no business engagements tonight, Rafe St. Claire. You're off to Renée's. Oh, don't think I don't know all about the 'liveliest whorehouse in New Orleans.' Do you have some special girl there who waits for you every night?"

He laughed cruelly. "Not one special girl, Melissa. There are several beauties at Renée's, all very skilled in the art of pleasing a man."

She drew herself up angrily. "I can please you better than all of them, Rafe. Don't you remember when we first met and you wanted me to—to put my mouth on you and I—I wouldn't do it—I couldn't do it! And you kept insisting, teasing me cruelly, telling me there were other girls that would do it until I—until I gave in and—"

"Melissa, for God's sake, your parents may be just inside the door!"

"Oh, Rafe, why do you do this to me? If you want me to be a whore, I'll be a whore! I can see that infuriating expression on your face now. What are you thinking? That maybe I am a whore already—that maybe I belong with your other girls at Renée's?" She was digging her nails into his arm furiously. "All right, all right. I'm a whore—but only for you, Rafe, only for you."

Disgusted with her, Rafe drew away, pulling his arm forcibly from her grip. "Christ, Melissa, save your act for your father! He's the only one who still thinks you're his darling, innocent little daughter. Why don't you admit it, Melissa? You love yourself too much and you love men even more—any men!"

Frenziedly, she began unbuttoning her bodice, ripping it open with quick, jerking movements of her fingers. Her breasts shone white as she pulled them out in her hands, cradling them lovingly, her fingers pressing slightly on the taut nipples.

"Here, Rafe, this is what you want, isn't it? Isn't it? Look at them, lover, and tell me that you have business engagements in town!"

"What's got into you, Melissa, for Christ's sake?" he said contemptuously as he tried to cover her with her bodice.

She brushed his hands away angrily. "What's got into me?" she repeated, her voice rising steadily. "I'll tell you what's got into me—lover! I practically had to come out and ask you to marry me—in front of both my parents, and you just sat there—and said nothing!" Furious, she shoved her breasts back and buttoned her bodice. "Well, don't expect me to beg anymore! I don't like to be humiliated, Rafe St. Claire—I hate it almost as much as I hate you!"

She turned on her heel and returned swiftly into the house, leaving him standing on the veranda, smiling mockingly at her bravado, knowing full well that she would come back to him when he asked for her again. She was a spirited, temperamental woman, that was true, but she was also a stubborn woman—and when she set her mind on one thing, it took a hell of a lot to pry her loose. She had still not let go of him, and he laughed to himself, imagining her standing, just inside the doorway, listening—waiting for him to come back for her.

With a silent salute, he strode briskly to where he had

tied his horse and mounted swiftly. "Good night, Melissa," he said softly to the darkening shadows.

Rafe rode at a leisurely pace into town, thinking of calling first at one of the casinos before stopping for the night at Renée's. He was riding down Royal Street when he spotted Bernard just giving the reins of his horse to Renée's stableboy.

"De Marigny, I see we both have the same idea for our evening's entertainment," he called out, trotting briskly to his friend's side and quickly dismounting.

Bernard de Marigny turned, and a smile flashed across his face. "Rafe St. Claire! Don't talk to me of entertainment, my friend, when I can well imagine how you spent your afternoon today!" he chided him, pausing on the walkway to Renée's.

St. Claire laughed and clapped the shorter man on the back. "I noticed that you seemed well set up to observe the same delightful pastime," he returned sardonically. "That *was* a young lady in your carriage I saw this afternoon—and not your wife, by the color of her hair."

Bernard winked. "You should have ridden by the carriage, and I would have introduced her to you. You'll not find such perfection anywhere else, my friend, for she is one of the most beautiful of women. She is waiting for me now." His eyes rolled upward.

St. Claire's smile deepened. "Then you and I must have a drink together, Bernard, to celebrate your unwarranted luck!"

"No, I'm afraid not. She might not take kindly to my keeping her waiting. She's never—"

"Come on, Bernard. For God's sake, I've never known you to cater to a lady's whims—especially a lady of the evening! Have one drink with me in the tavern across the street. How long can it take?"

"All right, then. You've persuaded me against my better judgement, but perhaps one drink will bolster my stamina for the night." He laughed wickedly and followed his friend across the street.

Five hours later, it was all he could do to get home without falling off his horse. His head felt four times its size, and his stomach leaped at every step his horse took.

"Bernard, I'm sorry about this, my friend. It seems we overstepped ourselves in our mutual toasting tonight," Rafe said sympathetically next to him, but Bernard did not notice that his companion rode his horse with an ease that belied the liquor on his breath.

"Just get me home where I can be sick in peace," Bernard pleaded.

"But your little friend at Renée's. Shouldn't you send her a message of some sort?" Rafe questioned softly.

Bernard shook his head. "I'll get to her tomorrow. She'll—she'll understand, I'm sure."

Rafe grinned devilishly to himself and urged his horse to a quicker step.

Chapter Twenty-seven

Dolly gazed with frustration at her friend, not knowing whether she should waste any more breath on her or land a good hard knock on her stubborn head. "I don't know why you're making such a big to-do about this, Gabrielle! Bernard has apologized profusely and has been by to see you several times these last two weeks!"

Gabrielle shook her head. "I—I just can't bring myself to make the commitment now, Dolly. I know he has explained why he wasn't able to come around until two days later after being so sick, but I still can't forgive him for humiliating me so."

"Humiliating you! Why, he's done everything he can to extract your forgiveness," Dolly exploded. "Sent you flowers, bought you presents, paid you visits. How many men would do that for a whore, Gabrielle, how many?"

"I'm not a whore!" Gabrielle flashed back angrily. And

then she immediately became contrite. "I'm sorry, Dolly, it's just that he showed so little regard for my feelings, for my nervousness, I—I just can't—"

"Well, he's a Creole, you know, and he vows he will wait for you to change your mind. Of course, he's not living the life of a priest while you're making up your mind, but you can hardly hold that against him!" Dolly shook her head again. "He's a handsome man, Gabrielle, and gay and charming. He could do a lot for you! He must like you an awful lot for him to keep paying for your keep like—"

"What—what did you say?"

"Why, I thought you knew. I didn't know—Renée didn't tell me not to say anything," Dolly floundered.

"You mean that Renée has accepted money from Bernard de Marigny in my behalf?" Gabrielle said, outraged.

Dolly caught her by the arm as she was about to fly out the door. "Don't go getting mad at Renée, Gabrielle. Will you think for a moment? You were the one who was so adamant about not being a burden to Renée!"

"Oh, Dolly, why—why didn't you tell me this before? It's so unfair to Bernard to have to pay for me when I am doing nothing for him!"

"Well?" Dolly said accusingly, folding her arms across her chest.

The two young women stared at each other, and finally Gabrielle looked away.

"Do you think you will say yes?" Dolly asked her softly.

"Oh, Dolly, I just don't know. He's married and somehow—somehow I can't help feeling sorry for his wife. I'd feel—guilty—even though I know that if it weren't me, Bernard would find someone else."

"Gabrielle, you can't think of anybody else. Think of yourself and of Bernard. He wants you, Gabrielle. He wants you enough to help you even when you've behaved so horribly towards him."

"I'm thinking of him and myself," Gabrielle answered quietly now. "I just don't know. Maybe there's something

else holding me back—something. Maybe it's the fact that
he's married, or something inside of me that's frightened
of being hurt again."

"At least see him, Gabrielle. Let him visit you," Dolly
urged persuasively.

"All right, I'll see him, Dolly. I suppose I do owe him
that much."

A few days later, Gabrielle knocked on Renée's office
door. She found her bent over the ledger sheet, pains-
takingly figuring the week's earnings.

"Gabrielle, how are things with you, my dear?" Renée
asked, smiling as she looked up from her accounts. "Oh,
yes, you told me that Bernard de Marigny is taking you
to the opening of the new casino on Bourbon Street.
Are you excited?"

Gabrielle nodded. "I—I wanted to talk to you, Renée,
about—about finances."

Renée laid down her quill and folded her hands. "Yes."

Gabrielle fidgeted with the pocket of her skirt for a
moment. "I know that Bernard has been giving you
money—for my keep."

"Yes, of course he has, but—"

Gabrielle waved her to silence. "I'm not going to protest, Renée. I know we've been through this before, and I
know that you are aware that I'm giving him nothing in
return."

Renée nodded.

"I—I just want to know—how much I owe him," she
went on.

Renée looked surprised. "Why, Gabrielle, you know
that M'sieur de Marigny doesn't necessarily expect that
you repay him. He does it on the chance that you will—"

"—become his mistress, I know," Gabrielle interrupted.
"But I am not his mistress, and I want to know how much
I owe him."

Renée sighed heavily. "Just a moment. Let me get out
your expense sheet. I keep one for every one of our girls,"
she assured her.

She unlocked the middle drawer of her desk and produced a thick sheaf of papers filed in alphabetical order. She thumbed through it for a moment.

"Here it is. March 15, 1813, through April 2—three hundred and forty-eight dollars—American money, of course."

"Three hundred and forty-eight dollars!" Gabrielle mentally calculated. "So, by the end of April, should he continue financing my rent here, I would owe him over a thousand dollars, Renée!"

The other woman nodded, replacing the papers.

"Oh, dear Lord, I can't continue to allow him to do this for me."

"What do you intend to do about it, then?"

Gabrielle gave the woman an earnest look. "Do you think—do you think I could win that much at the 'Golden Palace' tonight, Renée?"

"God almighty, Gabrielle! You'd have to be mighty lucky to win that much—and that's assuming the dealers are legitimate. You know that some of them cheat to keep the money for the house. And besides, you don't have any money of your own to begin with."

Gabrielle sent her a crafty look.

Renée frowned. "I suppose you'll be asking me for it, then?"

"Oh, please, Renée! I promise if I don't make it back for you tonight I'll—I'll get it somehow. Please give me this chance."

Renée could hardly resist the pleading in those huge eyes. "All right, all right," she said after a moment, "I give in, like I always do. It's a hell of a way to run a business, but you already know I've got a soft spot for you. But, if you lose the money, I don't want you telling me that you'll go downstairs again. I'd sooner you tell de Marigny yes before letting you do that again."

"Oh, Renée, I promise you won't regret it!" Gabrielle cried, hugging the woman with genuine affection.

"Let's just hope *you* don't regret it," Renée said softly as the girl left.

That evening, when Dolly came in to help Gabrielle dress, she found her staring down at the handful of bills on her dressing table and pressing her hands together uttering little shrieks of excitement.

"Good God, the girl's lost her wits," Dolly said, standing with arms akimbo in the doorway. "What's got into you?"

"Nothing, Dolly, nothing. I just feel that all the luck is going to be on my side tonight," Gabrielle answered, getting up to tug on a clean chemise.

"Oh, yes, I've heard that M'sieur de Marigny is taking you to the 'Golden Palace' tonight," Dolly returned somewhat sourly. "Talk about luck! I think it just follows you around, girl, looking for a chance to happen!"

Gabrielle laughed. "Don't be catty tonight, Dolly." She stopped and looked soberly at the other girl. "Dolly, it's got to be on my side tonight—it's just got to be!"

"What's so important?"

Gabrielle bit her lip. "I can't tell. It might break the spell, you know." She grinned slyly.

Dolly reached for the gown laid on the bed and slipped it over the other girl's head. The dress was of watered silk, a shimmering silver drapery that fell in soft folds around her ankles, tied with a lavender velvet sash underneath the bust.

When Gabrielle arrived downstairs, she found Bernard already waiting for her.

"Good evening, my dear," he said, taking her arm.

It was barely nine o'clock, but the April night promised to be delightfully warm, with a slight breeze that lifted her cloak as they walked outside. In the shadows of the porch, Bernard took her quickly into his arms and kissed her, pressing her tightly against him so that she could feel, even through the layers of their clothing, the hot probing of his desire.

"Come with me now, Gabrielle," he whispered. "You're more beautiful than ever, and you know how much I want you."

Gabrielle veiled her eyes with her lashes, feeling somehow guilty about her plans for tonight. Bernard was asking her to be his mistress, and here she was, trying to ensure that he could make no more claims on her.

"Bernard," she said softly, "I've been so looking forward to tonight. It will be exciting, don't you think?"

He sighed in mock offense. "Just like a woman. Here I am, laying my undying devotion at your feet, and you can only think about the program for the evening. Gabrielle, I'm convinced you let your head rule your heart much too often."

She laughed. "Perhaps, Bernard, but I think that may be a refreshing change for you."

He laughed, too, then and took her arm once more. "The evening is nice enough. Would you prefer to walk?"

She nodded. "That would be lovely," she answered.

The "Golden Palace" was one street away, and, when they arrived, it was already filled with a large crowd. Many heads turned at Bernard's arrival, and Gabrielle realized that he was a well-known figure about town and popular with the men as well as the ladies. The host of the gambling house, one Philip Paul, came forward immediately and shook hands with Bernard, openly admiring his lady.

"Welcome to the 'Golden Palace,' beautiful lady," he said, kissing her hand in most elegant fashion.

"Thank you, M'sieur Paul. I am happy to be here."

A woman dressed entirely in frosty blue, from the feathers in her brown hair to her satin slippers, came up and introduced herself as Madame Paul. After they had moved on, Bernard leaned over and whispered in Gabrielle's ear, "She's no more his wife than you are, my dear, but the real Mrs. Paul refused to accompany her husband to the opening of the 'Palace,' so his mistress must do the honors." He snickered a little to himself. "You will find, my love, that most of the women here are the mistresses of their escorts. I truly doubt that any well-bred New Orleans wife would attend amid such distressing company."

He winked, and Gabrielle hid her laughter behind her fan. "Well, then, at least I don't feel out of place."

They moved among the crowd into a room where tables were set up, piled high with an assortment of cold meats, fresh vegetables and fruits, nuts, and pastries, all of which caused Gabrielle to wish she hadn't eaten so much at dinner. Another room opened into the main gambling hall, where square tables were lined in neat rows, all covered with the same green baize cloth, and featuring a variety of card games all called in unobtrusive voices by the dealers. The dealers themselves were all fine-looking gentlemen with modestly downcast eyes and clean fingernails. They were dressed in identical blue serge suits with beige trousers.

"Do you want to try your luck, my dear?" Bernard asked, nudging her gently towards a table.

Gabrielle seemed to feel the money stuffed into her reticule as a large lump that she suddenly did not want to part with. Of course, Bernard had no idea that she had brought along her own money and was taking out his wallet, preparing to lay down money for her. Gabrielle thought it best that she let Bernard pay for her first attempts at the game.

She promptly lost twenty dollars and felt as though she had swallowed a piece of ice. Good Lord! At this rate, she could wind up owing him more money than she did already.

"Why don't you let me watch you for a while?" she asked timidly.

Bernard agreed and sat in her chair while she stood behind him watching intently. She was so wound up in the play that she didn't even notice the tall, handsome man clad in black who entered the room and gazed at her with amused recognition. A small titter passed through the ladies like a ripple on the crest of the sea. The man was soon surrounded by females and their unwilling escorts, and when Gabrielle looked up casually at the commotion, she noticed nothing unusual.

She promptly became absorbed in the game once more.

The dealer's fingers were nimble, and he shuffled the cards with practised ease. Bernard played with the conservative's skill, losing a little, winning a little, driving her half-mad with nervous excitement.

"Bernard, I simply must try it again," she said finally, gathering all her courage. She seated herself and felt his breath on her shoulder as he leaned over her.

"If you do well here, we can move to the other tables where players can compete against each other. It can get quite exciting, and I have heard everything used as ante, including a night of love or a racing horse. It really is tense at times, but I think you'll enjoy it. You won't win much at these tables," he added.

Gabrielle nodded and concentrated on the game. She used her memory to record the cards that had been played and was careful not to bet too much. After half an hour, she had a sizeable little pile next to her.

"Fifty dollars!" she said excitedly. "Oh, Bernard, now I can pay you your twenty dollars that I lost before, and I still have thirty dollars of my own."

"Bravo, my dear. Do you want to try your luck elsewhere?"

"Oh, yes, but first I must have a cool drink. It's terribly hot in here."

He took her arm and led her into the room where the food was and sat her on a small gilt chair next to the wall. Several ladies and gentlemen were talking, drinking and eating, and listening to the small orchestra set up on a dais in the back of the room. Bernard returned with a glass of chilled wine, seating himself beside her.

"Bernard, darling!"

Bernard looked up, and Gabrielle saw the small frown between his eyes. "Good God! It's Madame Bringier," he groaned. "Lord, she'll keep me for hours. *Adieu,* my sweet. Please try to amuse yourself for a few moments, and I will do my best to escape her as soon as possible."

He walked over to the other side of the room and sat down next to an immensely fat woman whose painted cheeks contrasted sharply with the rest of her pale face.

Gabrielle sat quietly, sipping the wine and fanning herself idly. After a few moments, she became aware of someone's eyes on her, and she let her own eyes roam the room uncertainly. The feeling persisted, and she began to feel a slow flush creep up her neck. She fanned her face furiously now and stubbornly kept her eyes on the floor to discourage any unwanted suitors.

There appeared before her downcast eyes two tall, black boots topped by black trousers.

"Good evening, ma'm'selle," came a voice above her head.

Angrily, her eyes flashed upwards. "Good—"

She drew in her breath, her mouth suddenly frozen, and the words died on her lips. Her eyes widened, first with incredulous amazement, then with a paralyzed dread as they took in the dark, slightly curling hair, the sun-browned face that only accentuated the cool, green hardness of the eyes, the whiteness of the even teeth behind firm, sensual lips that were just now smiling in ruthless amusement at her. She saw the broad shoulders beneath the black coat and the dazzling white jabot and cuffs, in such contrast to the brown hands, long-fingered and fine-boned.

The man moved to sit down beside her, and she noticed the pantherlike grace and agility of his finely toned body. Still unable to speak, she could only stare at him until he finally reached over to take from her paralysed hand the glass of wine, which was in greatest danger of spilling all over her gown.

She flinched as his fingers grazed her hand and snatched it away as though he had burned it. The movement seemed to bring her to her senses, and her mouth shaped the words, "You! You—here!"

"So, you do remember me, kitten. I am flattered," he remarked, noticing her flushed cheeks. With the casual air that distinguished everything he did, he leaned over and set the glass of half-finished wine on a small table next to her. "What?" he went on indolently, "no sweet embrace, no welcoming kiss? How can you have forgotten the one night of passion we shared, kitten?" He was baiting her, and with an effort Gabrielle threw off the feeling of unreality that was enveloping her.

Her violet eyes narrowed as she surveyed him coldly. "My memories of that night are only filled with rage and disgust," she got out, incensed by his mockery. "And if I ever thought I would see you again in my worst nightmares, I—"

"But however did you come to be here—in New Orleans?" he interrupted her, his left brow raised questioningly.

Stopped short in her tirade, Gabrielle stared at the man helplessly. Then, choosing to ignore his question, she posed one of her own. "And what of yourself? I knew you in France as the owner of a ship and a smuggler by trade, a despicable rogue and brigand by nature. What— how have you managed to—"

"Hush, kitten, lower your voice or people will begin to look at you. Certainly you wouldn't want to make a fool of yourself?"

Gabrielle controlled herself with difficulty, feeling an overwhelming urge to rake her nails across that amused face. How dare he—how dare he come back into her life!

"My memories of you, if you will forgive me, kitten, are somewhat foggy—although I can assure you they retain an aura of pleasant sensuality." He was laughing at her, mocking her in a way that she suddenly remembered only too well.

It was as though three years had just disappeared, and his casual, offhand manner succeeded very well in goading her temper.

"Well, I'm sorry to inform you that the memories I hold are hardly pleasant! I would rather say that they are among the worst remembrances of my life!" She shivered uncontrollably, her mind dwelling for a moment on the prison cell in Paris.

"You have not answered my question, kitten," he reminded her smoothly, observing the look of haunted fear that appeared briefly in her lovely eyes.

"What? What—?" she asked him, her voice uncertain, wavering for a moment while her mind was still held by the spell of her memories.

"How did you come to be here?" His grin turned engaging. "Come now, kitten, I promise I will confess all to you, but I am most curious. How did you happen to fall upon the most exclusive position of mistress to de Marigny?"

"Oh, yes, you can laugh very easily, can't you?" she threw at him, feeling the rage building up within her. "Especially when everything that has happened to me was *your* fault!"

"My fault? Excuse me, but now I am the one who is confused. You are telling me that *I* was the one who put you into Madame Renée's whorehouse? Who handed you over to Jean Lafitte? Who forced you to become de Marigny's mistress?" His words were uttered without a trace of concern as he saw her face go white with horror.

"You—you know all about me, don't you? How could you, how—"

He shrugged. "I'm afraid, kitten, that I can hardly remember your name, much to my extreme embarrassment, but when I carried you out of that burning house on the night Jim West tried to rape you, I looked into those beautiful violet eyes and I knew there couldn't be another woman in the world who had eyes like that."

"You! You carried me—you! But I was told that a Mr. St. Claire—" Her fingers flew to her mouth. "But you can't possibly be—"

He smiled. "Pardon me, ma'm'selle, in the excitement of the reunion, I completely disregarded my manners. Rafe St. Claire, ma'm'selle." He bowed his head mockingly, and his grin was anything but contrite.

"St. Claire—no! You can't be! I—I knew you as Rafe Savage! You're lying to me—"

He laughed as though she were a stubborn child, refusing to learn her lesson. "I can see how confusing this must be for you," he began. "You see, I couldn't use my own name in such a dangerous undertaking as I pursued in France. My name is Rafe St. Claire and has always been so, according to my birth records. Aliases are not uncommon among those who deal in undertakings not entirely legal."

Gabrielle felt as though someone had just delivered a well-aimed blow to her stomach. "My God—and it was your—your house that you took me to after the f-fire?" she whispered, memory of that night in a stranger's bed coming back in a rush of embarrassment.

He could read her thoughts by the expression on her face. "I wanted to see, kitten, how experienced you had become since my first initiation," he returned wickedly.

"Oh!" Her face was aflame, and she looked around wildly as though seeking to hide. Then she faced him, fighting for control. "But—but if you knew—if you *knew* who I was, why—why didn't you come back after—"

"I did come back, but I learned from Madame Renée herself that you had been returned to your rightful owner —Jean Lafitte—and I hardly felt it was worth the trouble to go and carry you off his island like some damned heroic knight." Again that sarcastic smile.

"If you were any kind of gentleman, you would have tried to—tried to—" she stopped suddenly and put a trembling hand to her mouth as though seeking to remember something.

St. Claire watched her movement, and he was aware of a growing desire, noticing the fair expanse of bare skin exposed by the cut of her gown. She was really a beautiful woman, he thought. At least he had remembered that much.

"Oh, what does it matter," Gabrielle was saying, her voice suddenly weary. "How could you have known that I was a prisoner in Renée's house?"

"You mean someone was boarding you in a whorehouse, for God's sake! Christ! That is a little hard to believe!" he returned disdainfully.

"It's true, I was a prisoner!" Gabrielle blurted. "I was put there—for the exclusive pleasure of one man. Why do you think Renée didn't go ahead and just let Jim West have me?"

St. Claire tried to read the expression in her eyes. "Lafitte—a man who is reputedly indifferent towards all women—you are telling me that he installed you in a house of prostitution?"

"I was not a prostitute!" Gabrielle cried. "Why is it that all of you men like to flatter yourselves that such things are all a woman cares about! First Charles, then Lieutenant Rué, Jean, and now you! I am sick to death of hearing all of your sly implications about how a woman, once exposed to the—the degradation of it, thinks only of obtaining it again! How you disgust me!" She felt herself to be on the verge of crying and tried desperately to stanch the flow of tears—she would not be humbled in front of this hateful wretch!

"Charles? You must be talking of M'sieur de Chevalier, if I can remember correctly, the son of my benefactor in France. Did he bring you to America?"

She shook her head violently. "No, no! I doubt that he even thinks of me—or cares what happened to me," she murmured, her throat thick with sobs.

"I'm afraid I'm not following you, kitten, so you shall have to shed a bit more light on this, or—"

"What do you care? Why do you bother?" she cried. "You could have saved me from those long months with Lafitte, you could have kept me from—from so much pain if only you—. Dear God! It was the least you owed me after. . . . I remember you made your profit in France and sailed away, leaving Alexandre and myself to face the authorities. I—I was arrested. But of course that wouldn't concern you at all," she gulped, her eyes wide and staring as though reliving the experience.

A flicker of concern showed in St. Claire's eyes as he leaned closer to her, and she continued. "They never told me anything—why I was being held, why I was not allowed to get word to anyone. Lieutenant Rué—hateful— he was in charge. He gave me to him—to the slave-trader!" She laughed bitterly and struggled away from the hand he placed on her shoulder. "You—you were the guilty one and you were gone, out of their reach, free! While I—"

"I finally begin to make sense of all this. You mean that you were suspected of duplicity in the smuggling venture. And our friend's son, Charles—I suppose he came away from it all with clean hands?"

"Of course, he had nothing to do with it—but then, neither did I."

St. Claire smiled. "There's no need to convince me of that," he said lazily. "I could most assuredly attest to your innocence in all things." His point was clear to Gabrielle, and she faced him, her eyes dark with fury.

"Please—do not remind me of—of things I would rather forget," she faltered.

"On the contrary," he said, his voice deepening. "Such things only serve to jog my own memory quite pleasantly."

With the smug self-assurance that only served to gall Gabrielle even more, St. Claire laid his hand on her arm and let it travel caressingly downward to her hand.

"Don't!" she said angrily, seeking to free her hand from his grasp.

"Come now, kitten, first I find you in a house of joy, then as mistress to a man whose trade is that same smuggling that you professed to loathe so much in me, and then as mistress to the most immoral dandy in New Orleans. Surely you cannot refuse a potential customer?"

"I am not M'sieur de Marigny's mistress," she hissed, her eyes blazing at him.

"If it would make you feel any better, I'll be glad to pay you what I would normally give a woman for her time and effort," he continued, ignoring the dangerous look in her eyes.

With a swiftness that caught him off guard, Gabrielle slapped him across the face with all of her strength. "How dare you! How dare you!" she breathed, her violet eyes spitting fire at him. "You put me in the same category as—as—" she stopped for breath. "I remember another time when you sought to ease your conscience, if you really have one, by giving me money. I've waited three years to slap your face for that!" Her eyes were fairly snapping now with her outrage. "Oh, yes, Mr. St. Claire, if that is really your name, you with your pompous arrogance, your disgusting self-confidence—you forced yourself on me and then thought yourself very obliging by leaving ten gold pieces for all the trouble you'd caused. Did you think the money would make me feel any less hatred towards you—or myself?" she sneered.

His face had darkened with anger to match her own. "Don't air your offended virtue in front of me, kitten," he spoke deliberately. "You are a beautiful and desirable woman, even when you're screeching and shouting like an ill-bred slut. Do you think your virtue would have lasted very long? If it hadn't been me, then some other likely young stallion would have been eager to hurdle your defenses. The question of deflowering you, my girl, is quite irrelevant. Right now, I'd like to sneak you off into the gardens outside and see what they've taught you at Madame Renée's."

"Oh-h! I hate you, I hate you!" she said, nearly beside herself with raging frustration. "How I wish I had a sword! I'd run you through!"

"Calm yourself, kitten. I see your escort coming towards us now, wondering what is causing the anger in your face. Look out, or I believe he will be only too happy to oblige you by lending you his own weapon."

Gabrielle looked up in dismay—she had quite forgotten where she was! She could see Bernard coming towards them, a questioning look on his face.

"Ah, St. Claire, I see you have introduced yourself to my friend, here, but let me make my own formal introductions. Gabrielle de Beauvoir, Rafe St. Claire. See, darling, you said you would like to meet him, and now you have!"

Gabrielle blushed agonizingly, and Rafe's smile was positively wicked.

"Miss de Beauvoir is a most charming companion,

Bernard. I wonder how you could have left her within my reach?"

Bernard smiled. "Rafe, had I known you would be trying your devious wiles on her, I would have dragged her over to sit through Madame Bringier's boring conversation. As it is, I was just about to take Gabrielle to the tables once again. Would you care to join us?"

Gabrielle looked up at Bernard with hopeless eyes, but she already felt St. Claire's hand at her elbow propelling her through the room to the gaming tables. He seated her at one of the tables, leaning over as though to whisper advice but taking the opportunity to place a kiss in her hair.

"Very sweet," he murmured in her ear, causing a shiver to run down her spine.

He seated himself across from her.

"You are going to have to play against Mr. St. Claire, my dear. See, he has placed himself opposite you," Bernard murmured.

"Oh, but Bernard, I don't think—"

"Hush, the dealer is giving instructions."

Gabrielle sat there, miserable, not daring to look at her adversary. When the dealer had finished speaking, he opened the packs of cards, shuffled them, and gave a pack to each couple at his table. There were three couples, and the woman to Gabrielle's left leaned towards her.

"My dear, you are so lucky to be playing against that devil. Just watch so that he doesn't win your petticoat!" she laughed raucously.

Gabrielle flushed and kept her eyes on the cards that were being dealt rapidly. She lost the first two hands decisively.

"Dearest, your mind is not on the game. Come now, I want you to enjoy yourself."

"Bernard, perhaps you should take my place—I don't think I'm doing justice to Mr. St. Claire."

Bernard patted her shoulder. "Nonsense, just remember what you learned before. You could bankrupt him.

Besides, I cannot change with you until the dealer calls time."

"You could bankrupt him"—the words echoed in Gabrielle's mind, and a small smile shaped her mouth. How delightful, she thought, and began to pay more attention to the cards. She won the next three hands. Boldly, she reached into her purse for the hundred dollars Renée had lent her.

"What are you doing?" Bernard protested, but Gabrielle waved aside his words.

"Renée insisted I take it," she assured him.

She saw the inscrutable smile on her opponent's face as she placed a healthy sum on the table. She dealt the cards deliberately. They smiled on her and she won again. Fifteen minutes later it was time for those who wished to do so to change partners. But Gabrielle no longer had any intention of leaving the table. She had won almost five hundred dollars. If she could double that amount, she could be her own woman and pay Bernard back the money he had given Renée in her behalf.

A curious crowd of onlookers had gathered around the table where Gabrielle and St. Claire were now the only players.

"Bernard, I'm afraid I'm bound to take your mistress away from you," St. Claire murmured, his voice holding a teasing note. But the green eyes were hard, purposeful with a determination that frightened Gabrielle, and she hesitated on the next hand.

"Afraid, ma'm'selle?" he asked sarcastically.

Stung, Gabrielle fell into his trap and gambled the whole of her winnings. The crowd watched with excitement and a sharp cry filtered through the room at the outcome of the deal. Amazed, Gabrielle could not believe that at one turn of the card he had taken her whole stake.

Beside her, Bernard was pulling gently on her arm. "Enough for tonight, Gabrielle. You're angry now, but I should have warned you. St. Claire is a devastating opponent."

"Oh, Bernard, you must give me a little more money!

I've got to win back—at least the hundred dollars that belongs to Renée!" She could picture the horror on Renée's face at the news that Gabrielle had lost that much money.

Bernard shook his head. "No, my love. I'll not have you make yourself even more furious. You'll not be in any mood to think about—my declaration tonight."

"Bernard! Please!" she cried, pulling her arm away from him.

He stopped and stared at her. "Gabrielle, what has got into you?" he wondered, his brow furrowed. "I said I am taking you home—and that is that!"

"No!" she shouted, stamping her foot on the floor. Several heads turned towards them, and voices whispered behind fans—a lovers' quarrel, how delicious!

Bernard's blue eyes flickered about the group. He shrugged. "All right then, I will leave you to his tender mercies." He placed fifty dollars in her hand. "But you shall find your own way home," he said beneath his breath, and with an angry expression on his face he walked hurriedly from the room.

Left standing in the middle of the floor, Gabrielle stared bewildered at the money in her fist. She knew that she should run after him, tell him she was sorry, make him forgive her. But her pride was involved—she simply could not let St. Claire have the last laugh.

Stubbornly, she stalked back to where he was standing at the table, scooping up his winnings.

"Mr. St. Claire, another round, if you please," Gabrielle said, her voice clear in the room.

He smiled arrogantly. "I am at your service, Miss de Beauvoir," he answered, seating himself and gesturing to the dealer for another pack of cards.

Gabrielle shuffled them herself and dealt. She smiled as she looked at her cards. Over their edges, she could see the lazy stare he was giving her. She dealt him another card—a queen.

He showed his hand.

Three queens—and she with only a pair of kings! She

blanched, and a sigh like the rustling of leaves swept through the crowd as St. Claire raked in her fifty dollars.

Furious at the calm insolence on his face, she wanted to pound the table or scream at him to vent her frustration. "Mr. St. Claire, I should hope that you are a gentleman," she began, immediately putting him on his guard as he was preparing once more to leave the table.

"I should hope so, Miss de Beauvoir," he rejoined, causing a ripple of sly laughter among the ladies present.

"As a gentleman, then, would you be prepared to lend me a small sum of, perhaps, one hundred dollars? I feel that my luck has to change, don't you agree?"

He smiled sardonically. "Not necessarily, ma'm'selle. But, as a gentleman, I will lend you the hundred dollars for one more round," he began, and she smiled with as much grace as she could muster. "But," he added, and her smile slowly disappeared, "in return, beautiful lady, you will become my mistress, should you lose."

The crowd's indrawn breath sounded like a huge rush of wind in her ears, and for a moment she could not believe she had heard him correctly. But then she knew she had. Why, the conceit of the man! To think that she would agree to such an impossible demand! She let her eyes roam the faces pressed in on her and realized they were all watching her with bated breath.

She heard him laugh confidently, a slow, haughty laughter that grated on her already taut nerves. She held her head up proudly.

"Agreed," she said, and her smile was dazzling.

Immediately, a babble of voices buzzed in her ears. She could feel the men's eyes caressing her, the women's burning holes of jealousy through her.

"Would you like for the dealer to deal the hand?" he asked solicitously.

She nodded. "I—believe that would be the fairest thing to do."

The dealer, sweat standing out prominently on his brow, shuffled the cards and dealt them nervously. Gabrielle picked up her hand—two pairs, both low. She gambled and threw away the lowest pair and another card. Across from her, she watched with maddened anxiety as St. Claire studied his cards. He shook his head—no new cards.

She breathed an inward sigh of relief. Perhaps—perhaps, after all, he was going to let her win. She picked up the new cards, and a wave of disgust rolled over her. Nothing! Well, she would have to go with the pair of nines and pray that she could bluff him.

She saw him place one hundred dollars on the table for her, along with his own ante. She stared for a long moment at the money and felt the gentle veil of perspiration on her upper lip. Absently, she ran her tongue over her lower lip, and her eyes met his for a charged moment, violet challenging green.

"Your cards, please," the dealer said, his voice breaking with tension.

Gabrielle threw her pair of nines on the pile of money and looked up at him again.

Slowly, deliberately, he placed his cards on top of hers.

She stared, wide-eyed, dismay on her face, for there were two jacks in his hand. Her eyes flew up like startled birds, the noise from the crowd deafening her. He was smiling enigmatically now, then his hand was reaching across the table to touch her limp one—possessively.

"Shall we go now, kitten?" he asked coolly.

Chapter Twenty-eight

Of course it had been her own fault—that much was quite obvious, Gabrielle thought mournfully to herself as the carriage made its leisurely way through the streets of New Orleans. Beside her, sitting far too close for her own composure, Rafe St. Claire was silent, seemingly asleep as he let his chin rest against his chest.

She risked a casual glance at him through lowered lashes, telling herself over and over what a fool she had been. What was that saying about pride that she had heard somewhere?—it seemed years ago. She remembered Pierre Lafitte telling her that pride, of all human emotions, was most likely to precede a man's downfall. How true those words were, she thought now, realizing that all of this had happened simply because she had been too proud to have Bernard pay for her keep at Madame Renée's—and then had compounded the sin by standing up to this blackguard when she knew—she knew. . . .

In disgust, she started to get up from her seat in order to move opposite him, but his hand suddenly shot out and gripped her wrist with such steely strength that she let out a cry of surprise. Her eyes flew to meet his, and she realized that he had not been sleeping at all. The moonlight shone bright on his dark hair but threw the lower half of his face into shadow so that she could not perceive the expression of his mouth.

"Sit down, kitten," he said softly, almost coaxingly.

She had little choice, and she seated herself next to him again, careful to avoid contact with any part of him. But he kept his hand on her wrist, so that she turned to him hotly.

"If you please, let go of my wrist—unless you wish to break it!"

He said nothing but loosened his hold a little so that his fingers did not probe so into her flesh.

Disgruntled, she tried to snatch her arm away from him.

"Don't be tiresome, Gabrielle," he spoke again. "Why do you insist on fighting me? I assure you that things would be a hell of a lot pleasanter for both of us if you would just decide to cooperate a little."

"You can be sure, Mr. St. Claire, that I would have no wish to make anything pleasanter for you," Gabrielle returned crisply. "As for cooperation, I'm afraid you will find yourself very disappointed in that respect, for I haven't the least intention of—of submitting to—whatever your requirements might be."

He laughed briefly, and his hand slipped up her arm beneath the cloak so that she could feel it, warm and pulsing with life, against her bare skin. She experienced a soft glow where his fingers caressed her, and she straightened up as though to ward off any weakening in her guard.

"I do hope you wouldn't consider—taking any—liberties—" she began stiffly, nodding to the impassive back of the driver.

"What's the matter with you, kitten?" he said silkily, again leaning a little toward her. "Why so stiff and straight-laced suddenly, as though we were strangers who had never met before? I've made love to you before—and I have every intention of doing so again."

"Be quiet!" she hissed, turning her head away. "Must you be so callous?"

He moved back to his original position and released her arm. "For Christ's sake, Gabrielle, you're not some wide-eyed virgin any longer. You've known men—Lafitte, Bernard, countless others, I suppose."

She faced him angrily, her voice filled with hatred. "No, I'm not a virgin any more—thanks to your initiation! You took me once and then left me without a care or a thought about my feelings! I was arrested, faced the prospect of never finding out the reason, was humiliated by men, and then witnessed the mass carnage and bloodletting when Lafitte attacked the ship I was on. He was 'kind' enough to rescue me from the wreck and promptly introduced me to the further delights of knowing a man. As for whatever 'countless others' your vile mind might dream up, I can assure you, there have been no others. Bernard—was kind enough not to press me. He—he was a gentleman!"

"A gentleman—I have an idea he was probably fattening you up for the kill," he returned sarcastically. "Your naïveté is scandalous, kitten." He seemed to study her in the moonlight for a time. "You've grown more slender than I recall since we last met," he finally said as though to himself, "and your hair looks a shade or two lighter. I suppose that's from the sun with which we are constantly blessed. Otherwise, very little about you has changed. I wonder. . . ."

"You wonder?" she repeated contemptuously. "Well, please don't bother. I daresay you didn't wonder about me even once before seeing me again tonight!"

He smiled, or she thought he did, but she wasn't quite sure.

By now the carriage had pulled up the gravel drive leading to St. Claire's house and was rounding the circle in order to set them down in front of the building.

"Welcome to Fairview, kitten," he said softly as he stepped out of the carriage and held his hand out to her.

Gabrielle tried to quiet the sudden pounding of her heart, tried to pull herself together, as she laid her hand in his and hesitated a moment, gazing blindly at the dimly lit windows of the tall white house she had admired not so many days before.

Impatient at her hesitation, St. Claire placed his hands around her waist and swung her down easily, laughing at the flash in her eyes that signalled her displeasure at his impunity.

"Under the circumstances, kitten," he said wickedly, "I think it would prove to be to your benefit if you would behave yourself."

"And what does that mean?"

"It means, simply, that you'd best calm that temper of yours before you force me to lose mine," he returned, taking her arm and walking beside her up the steps that lead to the main door.

At his knock, a very dignified black servant opened the door, bowing solemnly, as though it was not at all unreasonably late to expect him to be at his post. His eyes did not presume even to touch the woman beside his master.

"Good evening, Mr. St. Claire."

"Good evening, Solomon," St. Claire said pleasantly, drawing Gabrielle into the magnificent hallway. The majordomo closed the doors, bowed again, and disappeared down the hall, whence came very soon an immaculately dressed serving girl, hardly older than Gabrielle, who curtseyed briefly.

"Milly, please take Miss de Beauvoir's cloak." He turned politely to Gabrielle, who was finding it increasingly difficult to remain silently composed. "Will you need anything else tonight, kitten?"

She shook her head fiercely.

"Then I suggest we retire to our rooms. Milly, you will see to it that our guest has hot tea in the morning?"

The girl nodded and withdrew as silent and efficient as the butler.

"Your servants seem to work like well-oiled machines," Gabrielle put in waspishly as St. Claire guided her up the gracefully curving staircase.

They reached the second floor landing, and Gabrielle felt the first real stab of fear. He led her confidently to double doors that opened into what was obviously a man's room, and she heard the click of the lock as he closed them firmly behind her. She turned to him uncertainly, feeling horribly awkward and striving to conquer her unease. Her eyes were huge violet pools that watched him nervously.

He strode towards her. "You're shivering, kitten. You're not frightened of me, are you?"

She backed up a little. "Of course I'm not afraid of you. It's just that I'm—I'm not used to this—sort—of—thing," she added lamely, realizing how trite the words sounded even to her own ears.

"Would you like some wine—a drink?" he offered, not without a hint of irony.

She hesitated, then nodded quickly. "Yes, yes, some wine, please."

He bowed briefly to her, then turned and opened the doors, presumably to return downstairs for the claret bottle. "A moment only," he laughed softly, closing the door.

She heard his booted footsteps recede down the hall, then, without a second thought, she ran to the doors and clicked the lock to and then turned to lean against the portals, her breath coming swiftly. She could not go through with it—she just couldn't!

She let her eyes roam around the room, absently noticing articles of furniture and the tasteful appointments of the room. She moved to a low table and, because her head seemed to be ready to split in two, she began to tear at the pins that held up the heavy mass of hair, hoping that would help to alleviate the headache. She ran her fingers through the thick tresses, refusing to use the tortoiseshell comb that lay so invitingly on the polished surface of the table.

With her hair spread about her shoulders like a comforting shawl, she looked longingly at the wide bed, wishing that she could just lie down and go to sleep and dream away this terrible night. But, despite herself, she couldn't help thinking of all the other women's bodies that might have waited so expectantly beneath those same sheets—waiting for *him*. No! She would curl up as best she could in the chair, and in fact, she had just got herself comfortably situated when her ears picked up the noise of his boots in the hall once again.

They sauntered with palpable arrogance to the door, and she tensed as the knob turned. A soft laugh nearly unnerved her so that she would have sprung from the chair if she weren't sure that the door was effectively locked against her would-be suitor. She expected him to knock or call out, but only silence greeted her, and in another moment she heard his footsteps again retreating halfway down the hall. A door slammed.

She shivered, wondering just how angry he would be in the morning. Well, what had he expected? For her to welcome him with open arms, her eyes soft with desire? He'd best look to his silver-haired Miss Lawrence, she thought in a sudden huff.

She was just beginning to think herself very clever, when, suddenly, without warning, she heard a key turn, a knob click, and the door come open, letting in a soft stream of candlelight that silhouetted his tall, well-proportioned body in the doorway. She stifled a small gasp and watched helplessly as he turned to close the door once more, laying the key on top of the armoire.

"I hated to knock. I wasn't sure if perhaps you were indisposed for a moment," he said insolently, coming towards her like a stalking leopard.

She noticed in dismay that he had removed his boots and all of his garments except for his trousers, which did little to hide his expectant manhood. In the dim light, she could make out his bare chest, blurred by the curling hair that covered a portion of it. He stopped next to the bed and lit the candles in a wall sconce, which threw soft, golden light around the bed.

Gabrielle stood up and moved instinctively behind the chair she had been sitting in, like a cornered animal seeking a way out, her eyes darting swiftly around the room, hoping for an avenue of escape.

"Why so apprehensive?" he asked her mockingly. "Surely this is nothing new to you—a man coming to share your bed?"

"Leave me alone," she whispered. "I told you—"

His eyebrows drew upwards in scornful disbelief. "You didn't really expect me to believe that, did you, kitten?" he asked rudely. "A woman with your looks and spirit I cannot believe that you haven't known dozens of men, all wanting to break down those coy little defenses you are so magnificent at acting out. I'm sure you are aware that they only serve to whet the appetite?" He was standing close to the bed, his eyes watching her like a cat's, speculative and masterful.

"I don't care what you choose to believe," she declared hotly. "I suppose you think any woman should count herself lucky to find herself next to you in the same bed?" she sneered with false bravado. "Well, you can think otherwise tonight, for I'd sooner bed down with a stable-hand than—"

"Have you forgotten so soon that you owe me this night —and several more?" he interrupted ruthlessly.

Her face fell, and he could see the desperation in her eyes. For a moment he wavered, wondering if perhaps he should not judge her too quickly.

"You assured me earlier that you were a gentleman!" she countered suddenly. "Surely a gentleman would not hesitate at releasing a lady from such an odious bargain."

"Even when the lady, herself, agreed to it?" he asked. "Would you have been so obliging had I been the one to lose? Certainly you would have demanded your payment immediately." He grinned devilishly. "At least I have offered you a share in the prize." He let his eyes roam carelessly over the gleaming golden hair, the trembling mouth, the breasts that rose and fell rapidly in their silken nest. "Whether you like it or not, I want you, kitten," he said lazily, "and I mean to have you. Whether you oblige me by stretching yourself on the bed or insist that we turn this into a wrestling match makes little difference."

"I have no intention of obliging you!" she blazed, jumping out from behind the chair.

But there was no place to run—the door was locked, and it was a long jump from the long French windows that led onto the balcony. She waited in raging frustration as he closed the gap between them, reaching out to catch her arm, pulling her towards him.

Tears of fury splashed from her eyes as he pressed her against him and bent his head to kiss her. Stubbornly, she refused to warm to his mouth, pressing her lips tightly together, holding herself apart from his as best she could. In an instant, his free hand had moved to her buttocks, and he sharply pinched her, causing her to jump at such an unexpected tactic.

"Kiss me, darling, or I will have those pretty globes black and blue before too long," he murmured.

"Oh-h—you're not fair," she cried out petulantly, making him pinch her harder than before, so that she gasped.

He placed his mouth on hers once more, and, grudgingly, she opened her lips, feeling his tongue plunder her

mouth with consummate arrogance. He kissed her possessively, expertly, so that little by little her lips moved
beneath his of their own accord.

He must stop, she thought in sudden panic, he must
stop! I can't breathe, I can't think! She felt a rising tide
of pleasure somewhere deep within her, a sudden weakening that took her off guard so that she hardly realized
what he was doing to her. His hands tugged at the sleeves
of her gown, pulling them off her shoulders. A ripping
noise confirmed that he was growing more impatient, and
before she quite knew what had happened, the gown was
falling around her ankles, accompanied very quickly by
her chemise, both of which he kicked aside as he lifted
her in his arms in order to deposit her on the bed.

He straightened to look down at her, and she became
aware of her nakedness. Why must he stand there and
appraise her as though checking to see if the goods were
soiled? She had nearly forgotten the anger she had felt
when she was standing pressed so close against him. It
was as though three years had disappeared into some long
distant past, as though she had hardly been away from
him since that night when he had introduced her to something of which she had had no comprehension.

If he hadn't gone away—left France? She wondered
what would have happened to the two of them together.
But he had left her, she reminded herself brusquely, and
callously left with no regard whatsoever for her tender
feelings. He had used her then—and again after rescuing
her from the fire at Renée's—and as he was using her
now, to assuage his own need.

She watched him now, tensed to spring, as he removed
his breeches and came to join her. She steeled herself to
feel nothing as his hands fondled her breasts, his lips
caressed her cheek and moved softly to her mouth. She
invited him deliberately with her tongue, teasing his mouth,
opening her lips to draw him on—and then, with a sudden
fierce intensity, she clamped her teeth on his tongue.

With a terrible oath he withdrew and sat up to glare
furiously at her, and she was satisfied to see a thin trickle

of blood drip from his tongue as he examined it gingerly with his fingers.

"Now!" she gloated fiercely. "You see how obliging I can be, Mr. St. Claire! Should I presume you would like to see some more of my little tricks?" she flung at him.

With a movement too quick for her to escape, his hand shot out and slapped her across the face. "You little bitch!" he said in a deathly quiet voice. "So—you want to play animal, do you?" His green eyes seemed to gleam evilly in the half-light, and Gabrielle, holding a hand to her throbbing cheek, shrank back away from him with a sudden, startled panic.

She would have jumped from the bed, but his hand clamped down on her arm like a vise. She struggled to release herself, but with hardly any effort, he pulled her into the middle of the bed and brought his other hand down to hold her free arm captive. His legs straddled hers, and he effectively prevented her from turning away from the mocking gaze that seemed to cut through her.

"The kitten has claws, does she?" he laughed insultingly, as though enjoying her struggles to get free. "And she bites. You've been bad, little girl, and now you must pay the price."

He moved so that his knees could bear down on her wrists and leave his hands free.

"No, no!" Gabrielle cried, turning her head into the pillow while she strained to keep away from those encroaching lips.

His hands caught her hair and held her head steady, forcing her to face him.

"Now, you will try no more of those tricks on me, my darling, or you will be very sorry by morning. Come now, kiss me," he commanded and brought her head up to meet his so that his mouth could take possession of hers.

He kissed her long and deeply, forcing a response that she wanted to deny. But she could no longer find the will power to do so. His hands moved down her neck, lowering her head back onto the pillow. He moved with her, keeping his mouth on hers despite the feeble protesting noises that came from her throat. He slid his knees from her arms, and she felt a small ache as the blood rushed back into her hands.

She felt utterly helpless as he took his mouth away, leaving her lips bruised and throbbing. Deliberately, his hands moved down her shoulders to her breasts, massaging them roughly, without regard for her pleasure, then further down to her flat belly, stopping at the place where her legs formed a V with her body.

"I can take you now, kitten," he spoke disdainfully, "and leave you to your own thoughts, but I'm afraid I've decided not to let you off so easily."

She closed her eyes to blot out his brutal expression.

"No, my dear. In a little while, you'll be begging me to satisfy you, mewing like a cat in heat!" He laughed contemptuously. "It's no more than you deserve, my beautiful little witch!"

He bent down once again and kissed her with stimulating passion, while his hands played with her breasts until he had achieved the effect he desired. Her nipples stood out, taut and expectant, so that he could feel them like small, stiff, stabbing points against his own skin. Reluctantly he quitted her mouth, leaving her gasping for breath, and placed soft kisses on her neck and shoulders, moving downward to her breasts, which he had already readied so expertly. His arm moved underneath her back, bending her in his grasp so that she seemed to offer herself to him.

Gabrielle felt her breath coming in quick snatches, her heart pounding with violent speed, and her head whirling in a not-unpleasant sensation of excitement. She mustn't give in, she told herself, she mustn't—but she could feel her legs turning to water and her arms creeping around his neck.

She was a woman!—a woman whose desires and needs drove her to find satisfaction with a man. And, dear Lord, it had been a long time she she had felt a man caressing her like this.

She saw his dark head against the pale blur of her

skin, felt his mouth pleasuring her breasts to fine peaks
of frustration. She gasped as his teeth bit into the soft
flesh, then kissed it, as though in retribution. Without
further preamble, he slid his body down on hers so that
his hands were free now to work their miracles on her
responsive flesh.

Shyly, she closed her thighs tight, tensing her pelvic
muscles as his fingers introduced themselves.

"Let me in, kitten," he murmured, his tongue warm
on her flesh, demanding her total obedience.

Gabrielle struggled to remain firm against him, but
his tongue was a devilish instrument that flicked at her
thighs and sought out her most secret places. With a low
moan, she parted her thighs and surrendered herself to
him. Her back arched in a spasm of delight, her knees
bent against the pleasure she was experiencing.

"I didn't know," she gasped, pressing her nails into the
flesh of her breasts to keep herself from crying out in
sheer madness. She heard herself panting as though she
had run for miles, tiny rockets exploded in her, causing
delicious shivers of pleasure to run through her body.
"Stop, stop," she pleaded, clutching at his hair with her
fingers. "Oh, my God," she breathed, for he would not
stop but kept on, alternately torturing her and pleasuring
her until she exploded in a long moan that left her all but
exhausted.

Through misty eyes she saw him straighten up and
smile enigmatically, then move so that he lay stretched out
on top of her. Her mouth was open a little, her body felt
drenched in perspiration so that their bodies slipped on
each other in sensual intimacy. She didn't care that he
was achieving his ends, that he was making her want
him as he said she would. All she wanted was a release
from the exquisite torture.

She felt him poised above her for a long moment, teasing her greedily so that she wrapped her arms around his
neck, willing him to satisfy this terrifying need within her.

"Rafe," she half-sobbed in mingled shame and desire.

"Ah, you have become greedy now," he whispered

insolently. "I'm sorry I had to do this to you, kitten, but you were denying your own needs, your own body's signals. I'm afraid it was the only way to bring you to the realization that you are a full-grown woman now and should not be ashamed of your feelings."

"But—but I hated you," she said, like a child who doesn't believe that a sweet can erase the spanking received an hour earlier.

"A woman's hate is one of the most volatile emotions," he said softly. "I have an idea you don't know what to feel, but follow me now and I will show you how good girls are rewarded."

"Hurry," she whispered eagerly, seeking to bring him down to her by the sheer strength of her arms around his neck.

"A gentleman always obliges a lady," he murmured, driving downward so suddenly and so deeply that she winced at the pain.

He moved slowly then, aware of her sudden discomfort, not wanting to lose her now when he was ready to satisfy the craving of that sweet flesh. Patiently, he brought her back again to urgent expectancy, and she lost the pain of terrible wanting that had filled her. She rolled her head from side to side, and he caught his hands in her hair again to still her.

"Soon, kitten," he said, kissing her with soft, warm kisses along the jawline.

Her movements matched his now as she deliberately started to strive for culmination. It seemed that he could not get enough of her, and his thrusts were strong and hard so that she arched in a frenzy of delight, her breasts pressed flat against his chest. She wanted to scream or cry out with the intensity of her pleasure, but she bit her lip to still the sounds that rose in her throat. A delicious wave of anticipation swept over her, centering in her abdomen and spreading out to her legs and breasts. She raised her eyes to his and saw him gazing down at her, a small smile of victory on his mouth.

He kissed her again, and his movements became more

rapid, preceding the moment of release. She met his thrusts fiercely, and together they experienced a soaring sexual bliss that neither had ever known before.

Finally he was still, his face pressed into her hair, listening to her trembling cries of astonished pleasure, wondering with a sudden, uneasy pang just who had been the victor in their bout of love.

When her breathing had become more normal, Gabrielle turned her head and kissed him softly, hesitatingly, not wishing to break the incredible spell that had descended over her. Their bodies were drenched with sweat, and the sheets were soaked. His green eyes seemed to blaze down at her when he lifted his head, and the smile he gave her was truly inscrutable.

"Christ, kitten, you've done me in!" he said, laughing to himself. "I wonder if I've awakened a sleeping tigress."

She smiled impudently. To think that she had fought him like a wild woman just an hour before, had told herself she hated him! Why were women so foolish? she wondered. Why must they always hide their feelings at the expense of their own happiness?

She gazed fearfully into the handsome, satiric face above her and thought how meaningless those three years had been for her. Did he care for her, too? she wondered.

"Why so quiet?" he said in her ear, punctuating the words with a questing tongue.

She shivered. "Just thinking."

She hated the amused laughter, the mask of insolent indifference that had descended on him once more. "I hope you're thinking of keeping your door open from now on. It would make things so much easier if you would wait quietly and properly in bed for your lover to come to you instead of screeching abuse at me and stirring yourself into a lather. You could learn a few things from your friends at Renée's, although I must admit your education has been improved since that night so long ago in Paris."

"I suppose I could learn some things at Renée's," she

said, striving to match his composure, "but I really don't think I want to fight you anymore, Rafe."

He frowned a little. "This sudden capitulation has me worried, kitten. I hope," he hesitated, trying to read the expression on her carefully closed face, "—I hope you're not letting yourself feel anything foolish toward me. You know I would hate to be tied down to one woman when a constant selection is so much more palatable."

Gabrielle steeled herself to react as indifferently as he. "Of course not. What—what kind of fool do you take me for?"

He laughed. "There's only one kind of fool, little girl."

He got up and stretched, then walked over casually to look out the window. He threw open the French doors, and she could see his profile, gazing out towards the river. He stood there for so long she thought he had forgotten about her and sat up to retrieve the wild tangles of her hair and twist them into a more demure knot at her neck. She padded lightly to where her chemise still lay on the floor, suddenly feeling the need to cover herself in order to bolster her courage.

"I suppose I shall find you a house in town," he said quietly, as though speaking to himself. "Yes, I think a neat little town house close to Toulouse Street would be the best place to settle you."

Bewildered, Gabrielle walked over to him. "You're going to give me a house—of my own?" she asked.

He looked at her strangely, then shrugged. "Of course. All men keep their mistresses in their own establishments. It makes it so much easier than renting a hotel room every night."

He turned back into the room, retrieved his trousers, and pulled them on briskly, as though preparing to leave the room.

"W-where are you going?" Gabrielle inquired as bravely as she could. "Aren't you—aren't you going to stay the night with me?" she went on.

He looked surprised. "Under the circumstances, I thought you would want me out as soon as—our little business was finished. It would never do to set the servants talking," he grinned sarcastically. He stifled a yawn with the back of his hand. "Damn, kitten, I'm going to have to find a way to get you out of here before tomorrow at ten o'clock. Melissa's due to come over, and I wouldn't want her to spoil that pretty face of yours with her jealous claws."

He laughed fondly to himself, while Gabrielle, her face livid with embarrassment, stood completely still by the window, amazed at his indifference.

"I suppose Melissa is another of your mistresses?" she inquired in a wooden voice that betrayed her anger.

His expression was once more overbearing, and she fought down the fury that he could bring so easily to the surface.

"Melissa is a friend, kitten. I don't think we need to say more about her. You can stay in my room tonight. Pleasant dreams."

After he had gone, closing the door behind him, on his way to God knew where, Gabrielle flung herself on the bed and burst into tears of reaction. How could he be so horrible? He was a selfish brute—she had been right the first time. She would not deny that he was capable of arousing her body to the highest pitch of excitement, but, somehow, she must find a way to keep her mind and heart as cool and unfeeling as his own. For them, it was only two bodies, one gratifying the other. The thought should have disgusted her, but it only made her sob harder.

Chapter Twenty-nine

Gabrielle struggled out of slumber when she felt a light caress on her shoulder, her eyes opening to stare into those same green ones that she had been dreaming about.

"Good morning," he greeted her casually. "It's after

eight o'clock, kitten. I don't like my women to sleep too late, but in this case," and he grinned wickedly, "I've made an exception."

He eyed the fetching picture she made as she struggled from under the covers and stretched her arms above her head, causing her perfectly shaped breasts to lift up out of her bodice, the tips stiff and pointed. Slowly, he bent down and she felt his lips caressing her nipples. His hand sought her beneath the covers, and she shifted her legs so that his fingers caught only the stuff of her chemise.

"I've got the perfect way to wake you up," he said lazily, aware of the rebellion in her violet eyes, "but, unfortunately, I've got to get you back to town." He arose from the bed and walked over to where her gown lay still on the floor. He picked it up and tossed it carelessly on the bed. "I'll give you thirty minutes."

Gabrielle glared at the closed door and would have thrown something at it to vent her frustrations, but nothing was close to hand, and he had already gone. Sighing in vexation, she dressed in the gown, noticing that there was a large rip in the back of the bodice and that three of the buttons were missing, presumably scattered somewhere on the floor when he had pushed her dress down last night. Well, she wasn't going to look for them now, she thought, slipping into the silk stockings and embroidered garters that had been a gift from Bernard. She used the tortoiseshell comb to tidy her hair and searched beneath the bed for her other slipper.

When he returned, freshly shaved and smelling pleasantly of mint, she was ready to accompany him downstairs and outside to the carriage. "Solomon," he said to the butler, "should Miss Lawrence arrive before I return from town, please ask her to wait in the library. I may be late, so have Milly serve her coffee while she's waiting."

"Yes, Mr. St. Claire." The tall black closed the heavy oak doors, and Rafe jumped into the carriage beside Gabrielle.

"I'm going to leave you at Renée's for now, kitten. I've written down the name of a woman who rents apartments

on the south side of Toulouse Street. Mrs. MacKenzie is
completely trustworthy and will take good care of your
needs. Tell her who you are, and assure her that I will be
by tomorrow morning to take care of the financial arrangements."

Caught completely off balance, Gabrielle could only
listen to his curt instructions in bewilderment. She wondered if all men treated their mistresses like business obligations, in the same quick, concise way that this man was
treating her.

"I—I'm sure—I can manage," she said in a low voice,
"but I hope you will allow me a servant, since I—"

"All right, whatever you want," he interrupted her impatiently, his mind already on other matters.

Gabrielle leaned back in her seat, feeling unaccountably
depressed at being so abruptly dismissed. When they arrived back in town, St. Claire escorted her to Renée's
door, then kissed her swiftly and hurried back to the
carriage.

In a surge of temper, Gabrielle stamped her foot and
barged into the house, making straight for Renée's office,
without thinking to knock. An "oh" of surprise escaped
her lips as she came face to face with Bernard de
Marigny. Her startled expression caused a fleeting smile
of grim amusement to cross his mouth.

"Good morning, Gabrielle," he greeted her, casually
enough. He would have taken her hand, but she kept it
carefully within the folds of her cloak.

"Bernard! What—what are you doing—here?" she
managed, with difficulty keeping her voice from breaking.

He shrugged. "I had a few debts to clear up with the
madam. I do hate to keep creditors waiting for their
money, you know."

She swallowed nervously and scanned the room for
Renée. "But where is—where is Renée?" she asked in a
small voice.

"She'll be down directly. I've just arrived myself," he
answered as smoothly as though they were talking in the
Place d'Armes.

She sat down in a chair, her eyes jumping from one object in the room to another, anything to avoid those blue eyes that bore down on her with such accusing intensity. Finally, when the silence became oppressive, she took a deep breath.

"Bernard, I—I want to explain—about last night. I—"

"There's no need for any explanation," he said bitterly. "I have heard all about it from at least six 'sympathetic' friends already this morning. Unless you have a different version, I'd rather not talk about it now."

"But, Bernard, I swear the thing—just happened. You know, yourself, I'd never met Mr. St. Claire before last night, but—but I knew him in Paris—as someone else. . . ." She was floundering helplessly, aware of the difficulty of trying to make him understand.

"Gabrielle, there is absolutely no need to lie to me, or even to try to explain. You were taken in by the man's devilish charm. It's no crime to own up to it—many women are. I only wish you had had the decency not to make the transaction quite so spectacular.

"Bernard, please listen to me. You know I—I never played false with you. I never told you that I—that I cared for you in any other way except as a friend and companion. I realize now that the fact that you have a wife—"

"And will it make so much difference then, when your current protector is married to his Miss Lawrence?" he sneered relentlessly. "I suppose you will, in the interests of a pure conscience, leave him and move on to someone else."

Gabrielle clenched her fingers. "You wound me deeply with your words, Bernard. Why must you be so cruel?"

"I am only repaying you for your kindness to me!" he cried bitterly.

She bit her lip and raised her eyes to meet his. "It—it makes no difference to you then, that I care for this man," she said in a low voice.

"You care for him!" he laughed unpleasantly. "How could you fall in love with a man you've only known a day?" he questioned, and then as she started to speak, "Oh, yes, I forgot—you knew him in Paris too." He gazed at her for a long moment. "Let me tell you something, little sparrow. You don't care for a man like St. Claire without falling headlong into something you're not capable of handling. A man like that is not looking for a woman who might entangle him in a mesh of emotions that he has no use for. He cannot be trapped. He must be free to enjoy whatever pleasures most please him. If he had an inkling that you felt anything other than healthy lust for him, he would boot you out of his life quicker than you booted me out of yours."

He raised his hand to silence her protests. "Please tell Renée that I'll return later this week to transact my business with her," he said abruptly. "I'm afraid that, if I stay any longer with you, I just might. . . ." He stopped himself with an effort and caught her hand forcibly now. "Good-bye, Gabrielle—and should you find yourself once more alone—always remember me."

He shrugged wryly as though laughing at his own foolishness, then tilted her chin and kissed her softly on the mouth. He was out of the door before Gabrielle could think what to say to him.

She put her face in her hands. Bernard must think her truly heartless, and she supposed he had every right to have that opinion. She wiped her eyes with a corner of her skirt as Renée came briskly through the door.

"Gabrielle!" Her mouth dropped in surprise. "Child, what are you doing here?" She sat down abruptly in a chair and stared at her. "Why, I'd heard that—"

"It seems that news travels particularly fast when it involves things of such a personal nature," Gabrielle said ironically. "Yes, Renée, I lost at cards to Rafe St. Claire last night, and now I'm his mistress—or, perhaps, one of several would be more correct."

"Oh, my poor darling. You know I wouldn't judge you, child. I only want your happiness."

"This morning he brushed me off as neat as you please," Gabrielle said, "as though I were some bothersome detail that must be taken care of. I must find suitable apartments so that I can receive him without distractions and in complete privacy. Oh, I don't doubt but that he will settle a worthy sum on me, and I shall want for nothing—as long as I am good and satisfy him and—and everything is conducted on a very businesslike level. Oh, Renée, what should I do?"

Renée frowned to herself and rubbed her temples. "Do? Why, you'll do just as you have said, my dear. You will secure lodgings for yourself—where shall you be set up?"

"On Toulouse Street. He asked me to see a Mrs. Mac-Kenzie."

"Well! Toulouse Street! That's a fine neighborhood. Didn't you know that Claiborne House is on Toulouse Street, my dear? The governor himself and his lady live there! St. Claire is not doing ill by you!"

Gabrielle shrugged. "I suppose that this is his idea of a joke—installing his mistress under the governor's nose."

"You mustn't let yourself think anything of the kind. I am familiar enough with St. Claire's reputation to know that he takes women when he wants, married or single, rich or poor, and doesn't bother to make everything so private. No, I think your handsome Mr. St. Claire may feel something more for you than you think—or perhaps even he realizes."

"It'll be large enough for all of you," Mrs. MacKenzie said with evident assurance as she unlocked the door to the two-story house she was showing to Gabrielle. Gabrielle had brought along a servant from Renée's house, Jane Dell, who was more than happy to come with her.

The door of the house opened onto a spacious hall that offered a staircase to the right, leading up to the bedrooms. In the back of the house were the kitchens and a large sitting room, furnished with tasteful appointments and luxurious carpeting that sported a lively pattern of pink and gold roses.

Alice MacKenzie was not a woman to doubt, Gabrielle had decided upon meeting the tall, raven-haired woman who spoke with the slightest Scottish burr and walked with a definite swing to her wide hips. Her very blue eyes had regarded the piece of paper Gabrielle handed her and then swung round to inspect Gabrielle's own person with evident curiosity.

"So, Mr. St. Claire's wanting a house for you?" she asked unnecessarily. "I'll be damned if that stallion's not the one for surprises." She chuckled throatily, and Gabrielle couldn't help wondering in exactly what capacity Alice MacKenzie knew Rafe St. Claire.

She hadn't dared to question her though, but followed with all appearance of meekness, Jane tagging along at her heels, as the woman had walked down the street four doors to the very house where they now found themselves. Gabrielle especially liked the cool inner courtyard, a must in New Orleans for everyone who craved privacy. She knew she was going to like the place and promptly told Mrs. MacKenzie as much.

The older woman raised her black brows and laughed deeply again. "I guess I'd love it, too, if I had a man paying for it, missy," she responded brassily. "I'll warrant you couldn't afford it otherwise. But, mind you, I'll not hold that against you. Any female who can get anything but a swollen belly from St. Claire deserves my admiration." She winked and seemed amused by the slow flush that crept up Gabrielle's cheeks.

"When can I move in?" Gabrielle went on briskly.

"Oh, right now, if you like, my dear. You'd best send your girl there to market for provisions and tell her to buy some beeswax and good, strong soap. It'll need a little cleaning up since it's been empty for a few months, but it's livable now."

"Then I think I shall stay here, Mrs. MacKenzie, if you can lend us some bed linens. I'm anxious to get settled. My key, if you please?"

The woman smiled. "It's all yours, my dear. I have an extra key that I'll give to Mr. St. Claire when he comes by in the morning. Save you the trouble—and embarrassment." She winked broadly again and leaned over towards the girl in a confidential attitude. "I know these things must be handled a trifle delicately. You say he'll be visiting you often?"

Gabrielle tightened her lips. "I didn't say, Mrs. Mac-Kenzie—but of course that's entirely up to Mr. St. Claire." She took the key proffered by the other woman. "Now, if you will excuse me, as you say, there is some cleaning to be done, and I would like to get started right away. I'll send Jane down to pick up the bed linens later this afternoon."

The woman's wide mouth turned down petulantly. "Well, of course you must be anxious to fix everything up," she muttered.

When she had gone, Gabrielle leaned against the door and swallowed, glad to be rid of the obtrusive landlady. She looked around—her entire situation might not be ideal, but at least she had a pretty home.

Chapter Thirty

A week had passed, and the house was definitely taking shape, Gabrielle thought, with an inner satisfaction. Rafe had insisted that she hire a sturdy middle-aged woman to help set the kitchen to rights and two strong young men who were able to clear all the debris from the rooms and bring in new pieces of furniture as well as fresh bedding.

Rafe had not demanded anything from her except that she take his advice on certain suggestions he made for the house and, of course, that she surrender her body to his masculine demands whenever he wished. Their sessions together in the large bed upstairs were torrid and intense, and Gabrielle would find herself afterwards panting and dripping with sweat.

She found herself strangely angry that he never spent the night with her, but always left, presumably to go to the gambling halls, or, perhaps, to another lady. The thought aroused her suspicious jealousy.

His days were filled with business, and if she were to ask him about his affairs, he would shrug, and she would realize that he considered such questions not within the realm of a mistress's duties. It was humiliating in a way, and she tried to lose her anger in reading or sewing.

By the first of May, Gabrielle felt that the house was completely presentable, and she dismissed the extra servants.

Rafe had stopped by in the morning, but he seemed exceptionally preoccupied, and, although Gabrielle was wearing a new dress that beautifully accented her fair coloring, he hardly noticed her. He drank a glass of wine, inquired about commonplace things, and promptly left in a hurry as though this were a social call and she nothing more than an unpleasant distant cousin.

Striving to keep back the tears of hurt and anger, Gabrielle stayed in her room the rest of the day. She lay curled up on her bed, wondering if she had done something wrong or if he simply did not find her interesting any more. Would he soon be telling her he'd made a mistake and ask her politely to leave and return to Renée's?

At Jane's summons to supper, Gabrielle pretended to be asleep, closing her eyes tight. Certainly she wasn't hungry—all she felt was confusion and shame at her longings.

She woke up much later, realizing that she had truly fallen asleep and it was well into the evening. Yawning, she got up from bed, not bothering to light a candle, and proceeded to take off her robe. She went downstairs, checking Jane's room to make sure she was in bed and fast asleep. She hurried to the kitchen where she realized she was ravenously hungry and filched a bright red apple from the table to take upstairs with her.

Back on the upper floor, she entered her room, stubbing her toe on the doorsill and muttering an exclamation, and she bent down to rub the offended appendage. An owl hooted in the branches outside her window, then screeched abusively at the answering howl from the cat in the courtyard. Gabrielle walked to the window to shut it against the night noises, but before she could do so, something moved quickly behind her and a rough hand grabbed around her mouth.

Startled, she dropped the apple and reached up to try to pull the hand away, but another hand came out to grasp her left arm and pull it tightly behind her back so that she gasped in pain.

"Quiet!" a voice hissed behind her.

Gabrielle nodded, afraid that her arm would be broken. The intruder promptly released her, and she took in great gulps of air. Two hands on her shoulders swung her around and she tried to make out the features of the man who stood close to her, looking back at her.

"You're Gabrielle de Beauvoir?" he asked finally, dragging her towards the light of the window.

Gabrielle rubbed her arm and glared up at him, more angry than fearful now.

"I hardly think that's any of your business, whoever you are!"

He seemed temporarily at a loss. "But I thought you were Rafe's mistress. I was pretty sure this was the house."

Gabrielle ignored his words. "I don't know how you know my name, but this is my house, and, if you're not out of here in ten minutes, I'll scream loud enough to bring the watch. I might remind you that we're not too far from the governor's house, and I'm sure there are plenty of guards about!"

He laughed suddenly, startling her so that she jumped. "And I might remind you that you promised to be quiet!"

She stared at him, a little disconcerted at his complete assurance.

"If you please," she began, "tell me what you want."

He seemed to be in no hurry, and she watched with growing impatience as he backed away towards her night table to strike a flint and light a candle. He brought it over to study her face and whistled sharply.

"Christ! If you're not Rafe's mistress, I'd like to put a

claim on you for myself." He set the candle down, and Gabrielle could make out a medium frame topped by a smallish head with light brown hair and slender features.

"I don't know what you have in mind—" she began but found her words stopped abruptly as he reached over and kissed her.

His arms were stronger than she had thought, and she was quite helpless in his grasp. She struggled to free herself and drew in a sharp breath of dismay as his hand boldly slipped down her bodice to cup her breast.

"What are you doing?"

"Listen, wench, I haven't had a woman in quite a few days. Been in those goddamned swamps so long, patrolling for the governor, that I'm pretty randy right now. Hell, you must be willing. I know the likes that rents out these apartments of Alice's."

"I'm sorry, but you're wrong," Gabrielle burst out, bringing her hands up against his chest. "Now let me go."

To her surprise, he obeyed and stood watching her warily. "All right, wench. Then tell me, what's your name?"

"My name is none of your business," she returned tartly.

"I think a man who's had his hand on a lady's breast might be privileged to know that lady's name," he said calmly.

"Why—how dare you!"

He grinned. "It's just you and me here in this dark room with no one else very close by. I could dare a lot more if I had a mind to."

She sighed in resignation. "All right. My name really is Gabrielle de Beauvoir—and Mr. St. Claire is—an acquaintance of mine." She flashed him a look. "And I don't appreciate strange men coming into my bedroom and scaring me half to death."

"You don't look very scared," he said in the same level voice. "And I certainly didn't mean to frighten you, but Rafe forgot to give me the number, and I'm sure as hell not used to delivering messages to beautiful young women like yourself." He shook his head as his eyes roved slowly up and down her figure. "Should have known Rafe would come up with a woman like you."

Gabrielle felt as though she were playing some sort of game with this man and struggled not to lose her patience. "Please tell me what this is all about. Rafe has a message for me? Where is he?"

"He's taking my place for a while—searching for swamp rats, pretty lady."

"Swamp rats! Rafe is hardly the type," she said, mustering her courage, "and you don't look like a riverman yourself, for that matter!"

He laughed again shortly. "You're not the first woman who's accused me of that," he assured her. "When I go into some whorehouse, the first thing they say is I'm too thin to push those boats downstream." He grinned. "They generally don't protest, though, once the evening gets going." His eyes flickered over her and she was aware that she had on only the thin nightgown which probably didn't hide much.

"*Who* are you?" she asked tightly, abruptly.

"The name is Leigh Owens, miss. I'm a good friend of your—how did you put it—your acquaintance, Rafe St. Claire."

"If you're his good friend, why do you think you can come to my house and maul me as though—"

"I beg your pardon if I mauled you, Miss de Beauvoir. Your beauty so enthralled me that for a moment I was not myself. Rafe and I have shared a good many things in the years I've known him." His eyes twinkled wickedly.

Share! Gabrielle felt a rush of hurt overwhelm her as she wondered if Rafe had casually sent his good friend over to his mistress so that he could enjoy her while the master was away.

"Well, then," she began shakily, "if you know Rafe St. Claire so well, I'm sure you realize that he wouldn't take it kindly if I told him about your boldness tonight. In fact, I'm—I'm expecting him to come home any minute now. He should be here—"

Owens shook his head with a smile. "I'm afraid I don't believe a word of it, wench. It's well after one o'clock, and Rafe is probably up to his hips in swamp water, hoping to catch some of those pirates with their goods on their way to New Orleans."

"I—I don't understand, he never told me anything about—"

"Forgive me for keeping you in suspense," he began, taking off his shirt to reveal a dreadful scar that reached from his right shoulder to his left armpit. "Rafe wanted me to inform you of his whereabouts and to tell you that he won't be seeing you for, perhaps, a week or more." He turned towards the bed. "Now come on, wench, get over here and hop into bed. I haven't talked this much to a woman in all my twenty-five years, and I don't particularly care for so much conversation before a good roll in bed."

Gabrielle hesitated, and they stood confronting each other, he with the knife still held carelessly in his hand. After a few moments, he shrugged, placed the knife under the pillow, and sat down on the bed to remove his boots and trousers. She modestly kept her eyes from his nakedness as he padded around the room to douse the candles.

When the room was once more in darkness, she heard the bed creak and heard him sigh deeply. "Christ, are you going to stand there all night? If you're that set against it, I'm not going to press you. After all, maybe Rafe wouldn't like it if I had a bit of fun with you— although you're only his mistress, after all."

The words bit cruelly into Gabrielle's brain, and she wanted to shriek with the pain of Rafe's indifference. She waited until she heard Owens' snores filling the room and her eyes had grown accustomed to the darkness again. She could see him against the whiteness of the sheets, his arms flung out carelessly and his legs tangled in the bedclothes.

She felt unbearably weary herself, and angry towards the man who had had the audacity to send this rogue to her house in the middle of the night, knowing, perhaps, what the outcome might be. Oh, what did it matter—he hardly seemed to care about her anyway and was surely not thinking of her now.

It would certainly have surprised Gabrielle to know that Rafe St. Claire was huddled in the long marsh grasses, hidden behind a bald-cypress tree, cursing the mosquitoes that seemed to be eating him alive.

His eyes pierced the darkness and the murky fog that seemed to get thicker by the minute, trying to make out the form of Rob Martin who had set up his vigil next to a thick clump of seagrass that completely hid him from view of the muddy bayou that ran slowly through the swamp to make its way down to Barataria Bay.

Rafe cupped his hands to his mouth and let out a deep-throated hoot. Five seconds passed, and the call was answered in kind. Then silence. There were only the night noises, the swishing of the muddy water, the hushed breathing of himself and the six other men who had come tonight, waiting for Lafitte to make the fatal mistake that would send him to prison.

He thought briefly of Gabrielle, the woman he had made his mistress through a quirk of fate, the woman whose lovely face had stayed in his mind long after others had receded to the furthest regions. Jesus, she was beautiful, he thought, considering her in his mind's eye. He hoped that Leigh had been able to give her the message. And, thinking of Leigh with Gabrielle, he suddenly had an uncomfortable stab of jealousy. He shrugged it off quickly. It wouldn't do to sidetrack his thoughts now.

He'd promised Claiborne he would lead the hand-picked crew who would wait night after night, hoping to catch Lafitte's men unawares. His thigh muscles began to ache a little from squatting so long, and he could imagine how the others felt. After all, the job should have belonged to the customs officials or the militia, but Claiborne had got nowhere with the city council, and so he had had no other choice but to call on his long-time friend, Rafe St. Claire, to try and carry off this little coup.

Rafe glanced upward through the shrouding mist and

saw the moon, full and bright, hanging in the far western sky. It looked like another worthless night, he thought with disgust and was just about to give the signal to disband when the sound of stealthy oars slicing through the thick water caused his skin to prickle with anticipation.

Christ, it had taken the bastards long enough, he thought. Leigh had waited two weeks without a sign of them. He reminded himself that his participation in this business was by no means wholly objective, since his recently purchased shipping firm was suffering losses at the hands of Lafitte's renegades. And the damn Creoles thought it all so amusing, he thought bitterly. The fools couldn't even comprehend the disastrous results on New Orleans commerce, results that would stretch to every one of their own concerns unless Lafitte could be stopped soon.

He listened as the sounds of a boat splashing with muted oars came closer up the bayou, listened for the voices of the men speaking low among themselves. He wondered if Lafitte would be among them and thought, probably not. From the sounds it seemed there were two boats involved, and, a moment later, his guess was confirmed as he peered through the grass to make out two hulls, lit eerily by yellow lanterns.

The first boat slid almost within an arm's reach of him, and he could see quite clearly the weatherworn faces of the four men who manned the oars—rough, dangerous men who would kill to keep from ending up in the calaboose. The boat went on slowly past him, and now he could see the second skiff, heavily loaded and low in the water, piled high with barrels and crates destined for Lafitte's secret warehouse so that they could be auctioned to the highest bidder another day.

He noted that a length of thick hemp joined the two boats, and he could see only two men on the second boat. Good, the odds were even. He waited until the boat passed him, and then, stealthily, he crept from behind the marsh grass and waded into the slimy water. They had chosen this place to attack since the stream was barely five feet deep and narrowed into a sort of bottleneck so that it would be impossible for the skiffs to turn about and run the other way.

His hand brushed the barnacled side of the boat, and his fingers clung to the thick rail. He strained unconsciously for the sounds of discovery, but none came. He knew the others had by now maneuvered into their positions, and he took a deep breath before swinging himself in one fluid motion over the side of the boat. At the same time he uttered a high-pitched yell that was answered as his men launched themselves from their positions.

The Baratarians were, at first, too surprised to react. But as soon as they realized that their attackers were small in number, pistol muzzles smoked, and the sound of gunfire added to screams, yells, and curses.

Rafe saw the two men on the first skiff coming towards him—big, barrel-chested men with knives gleaming and mouths screaming foul abuse at him. He aimed his pistol at one and shot him clean through the chest, causing a great gout of blood to spill out onto the deck, but the giant kept coming, grinning menacingly as he grunted an instruction to his companion.

Swiftly, Rafe drew a dagger from his boot, tensing on the balls of his feet as they came for him.

"Over here, you renegades!" It was Rob, brandishing his sword and jumping onto the boat.

The two brutes hesitated, and Rafe dove for the one who was already wounded, bringing his knife up to plunge into his throat. But the man was quicker than he had thought possible and twisted away so that the knife found his shoulder blade instead. The jarring movement of knife meeting bone caused Rafe to lose his footing and slip sideways.

He felt a knife slice through the air close to his face and hurled himself in the opposite direction, noting at the same time that Rob had engaged the other ruffian with his sword. The wounded giant roared in outrage at missing his target and plunged again with his knife only to find empty air.

Rafe struggled to his feet and tacked about behind the

man, circling him warily now, aware that his quarry was not unlike a wounded bear who would fight even more fiercely when cornered. The brigand was puffing now, and Rafe could see the blood still spurting all over the deck, streaming down the man's big belly. He backed away as the man swiped through the air with his free hand, then followed it with slicing motions of the knife.

Rafe was aware of the dangerous footing on the slippery deck and crouched close to a barrel, waiting for the other to make his move. He could hear, above the shouts and clang of steel, men screaming in agony, and he hoped that they were not his men. He risked a quick glance behind him and saw Rob fighting in close combat with the other man, their knives catching the moonlight as they searched for an opening.

Rafe turned his attention to his opponent, who was bellowing curses at him, clutching his chest now and eyeing him with hatred.

"I'll castrate you, you son of a bitch!" the man screamed and charged him, death on his face.

Rafe sidestepped behind the barrel, and the man flailed the air and lost his footing in his own blood. Quickly Rafe bent down, his hands closing around the man's throat. The river pirate made horrible gurgling noises that nearly sickened him, but the fat giant refused to die, and with all his remaining strength, he rolled over and brought up his knife.

Rafe felt a white-hot stab of pain against his ribs, and, gritting his teeth, he caught at the fat wrist and pressed down with all his strength until the knife clattered heavily to the deck. His hand reached for the weapon and closed over the rough-hewn handle. The point drove downward into the creased, sunburned neck, and, finally, the ruffian lay still.

Rafe stood up and clutched at a barrel, feeling the dizziness wash over him in waves. He picked up the knife and made his way to where Rob was still struggling with the other riverman.

"Help me, for Christ's sake!" Rob was screaming at him.

Rafe could see the long gash on his forehead and the streams of blood that were wetting the deck, but he couldn't tell which man was the worse wounded. His right arm was beginning to feel like a dead weight, but, making the effort, he plunged the knife into the river pirate's broad back and was surprised to see him slump immediately to the deck. Jesus, he was glad this one lacked the stamina of his dead friend.

Rob looked at him with a crazy light in his eyes. Both of them turned to the sounds of the other boat and then looked at each other wearily. Out of the corner of his eyes, Rafe saw a furtive figure disengage himself from the fighting, jostling group on the other boat and slip stealthily into the water. He waded towards their boat and the light of the lantern lit up his face briefly.

"It's Lafitte! Goddammit, it's Lafitte!" Rob cried in disgust, clutching at the useless leg that had been cut by the pirate's long blade.

Rafe watched the man move away from the boat and then disappear into the tall marsh grass. He could have spit—or wept. Lafitte had been here—in his hands—and he had got away.

"Goddammit!" he swore deliberately. "The bastard's escaped!"

The two wounded men sat down on some crates, listening to the lapping of the bayou waters against the sides of the skiff, waiting for the fighting to end, their eyes hard and disheartened, staring at nothing.

Chapter Thirty-one

Rafe St. Claire turned restlessly in the bed, gritting his teeth against the painful ache in his side. He had an idea that that damn doctor had been half-drunk when Melissa had summoned him in the grey dawn.

He could barely make out her clear, cool voice ordering

one of the servants to fetch a basin of cold water and some fresh towels.

"Dr. Bernais assures me he will be fine, governor. He had to stitch the wound in his side, but thank God his ribs served to deflect the blow, and nothing internal was touched. There may be a slight fever, but I'll make sure cold compresses are applied."

Rafe wanted to grin but found his mouth wouldn't function for him. How like Melissa—methodical, precise, and so practical when practicality was needed—but, God, she was an animal in bed.

He struggled to open his eyes and saw the pleasant, rather round face of Governor William Claiborne leaning over him, the candid eyes registering his sincere concern.

"You did well, Rafe," he was saying in that level voice of his. "We've been able to tie some of the names on those crates to certain ships that have been reported missing for the last few months. This gives us additional evidence against the Lafittes."

Rafe felt the anger surge up within him. "But the bastard got away," he muttered.

Claiborne shrugged, a habit he had learned from the Creoles. "No matter, we'll catch him another day. At least we've shaken him up." He smiled. "When your friends brought you back into town, I had them cart you to Miss Lawrence's house, since I knew that here you would receive the very best of care."

Rafe nodded. He was at the point where he wouldn't have given a damn if they'd taken him to the worst whorehouse on the docks. All he wanted now was to sleep. Before he could do so, he knew there was a question he must ask.

"What of the others?"

Claiborne frowned. "Martin will mend, although I'm hoping that leg doesn't continue to give him trouble." He seemed suddenly uncomfortable. "The only casualty was Bruce Fairchild—pistol wound in the throat. I've—I've already informed Mary."

"Oh, Christ!" Rafe groaned, recalling the sweet, dimpled face of Mary Fairchild as she had kissed her young husband good-bye. He closed his eyes and let their voices drift hazily over him.

Sometime during the night, he awoke, sweating with the fever, and he felt cool, soft hands placing a damp cloth on his forehead, pressing him back to the bed. He could see long, golden-blond hair, could feel it brush his arm as the woman leaned over, could see those wide, violet eyes watching him with concern.

"Kitten?" he whispered hoarsely.

"Rafe, honey, you must be dreaming," came Melissa's soothing voice through layers of cotton wool that seemed to surround his head. "It's Melissa, darling."

"Melissa," he sighed, then closed his eyes again and went back to a fitful sleep.

In the morning, he was much better, the fever abated. Melissa carried in hot cornbread, molasses, and gumbo, hoping to tempt his appetite.

"Jesus, I hate being in bed," he grumbled, then grinned mockingly at her, "except, of course, when it's serving its true purpose."

She smiled back. "Rafe St. Claire, I do believe you're going to be recuperating a lot faster than Dr. Bernais thought possible." She placed a cotton napkin on his lap, letting her hand linger softly as it explored the proof of his well-being.

Rafe caught her hand in his and pressed it hard. "I wouldn't be doing that, 'Lissa, my dear, unless you're fully prepared to take the consequences," he said insolently, his free hand moving to slip itself inside her open gown.

His fingers caressed the responsive flesh, and he thought absently that Melissa's breasts were really too big to fit a man's grip properly.

"Rafe! I do declare you do surprise me, lover! If I hadn't seen the length of that wound in your side. . . ."

"I suppose the doctor swathed me like a goddamn baby," he replied with a touch of temper. "It feels like I have ten pounds of gauze going around my middle."

She took his hand from her breast and fidgeted with the

silver. He ate the soup slowly, favoring his wounded side and drank deeply of the wine she had brought.

"You make an excellent nurse, 'Lissa," he said affectionately. "You should apply as a volunteer to the Sisters of Charity for work in their hospital."

Melissa, giving him a wry grin, shook her head. "I'm doing this for you, darling. Anything I do for you has to be perfect."

His answering grin was devilishly wicked. "Anything?"

She nodded, and he thought she looked as though she would have liked very much to pounce on him.

"You enjoy men too much, Melissa," he said, his voice losing the teasing note, and her face seemed to freeze for a moment.

Her full mouth trembled loosely and she folded her hands tightly together. "You're cruel, Rafe," she rebuked him softly. "You know very well that I—I do love you deeply. I can't help that I—that I enjoy that part of it, too."

"I can't help it either, dearest—especially now," he added, mocking her again.

"Why don't you call me what you did last night?" she said, letting her hand work its way beneath the bedcovers once more after she took the tray from his lap.

His brows arched into sardonic black crescents. "Pray tell, what was that? I'm all ears, as there's no telling what might have spewed forth in my delirium," he replied.

"You called me 'kitten'," she said, her hand finding what it sought and closing possessively.

Rafe frowned. "I must have been delirious," he said. Her fingers squeezed him, then he felt her sharp fingernails bite deep, and he jumped. "For God's sake!" he cursed her. "Gently, you little silver-haired bitch!"

Her blue eyes were narrow and reminded him of cold, perfect sapphires.

"I can't help being jealous, Rafe," she said quietly, passing the tip of her pink tongue over her upper lip.

He laughed shortly. "A tigress—jealous of a kitten?" he drawled mockingly.

Then he gasped suddenly as she flung herself wordlessly against him, pulling back the counterpane so that her experienced mouth could bring him back to her. His hand came down hard against her head, and with a violent motion, he jerked her by her hair.

Spitting like the tigress he had likened her to, she slithered out of his weakened grasp and pulled her skirts up so that she could straddle him. Her determination was so comical that Rafe couldn't help laughing. The effect on her was instantaneous, and, with as much dignity as she could muster, she rose from the bed, smoothed her skirts, and lifted the tray.

"You enjoy pushing me to the limit," she muttered, "enjoy hurting me, using me for your own ends." Unexpectedly, he perceived the tears coming to the surface. "I only hope, Rafe St. Claire, that someday, some woman will have the strength to put you through the same kind of hell." He stopped laughing and watched her thoughtfully as she flounced out the door.

Five days later he was ready to leave although he was still a little stiff and sore. He shook hands with Thomas Lawrence, who still had that hopeful look about him, and was mounting his horse when Melissa flew off the porch to throw her arms about him and kiss him one last time. He kissed her fully in the eyes of her parents and couldn't help laughing to himself at the sudden flush that suffused Thomas' face.

Then he was off on his chestnut stallion, riding to Fairview, his mind full of business, dismissing the memory of Melissa's face as though she were nothing but a passing addiction. He must see his attorneys this afternoon. His shipping firm needed constant supervision, and although Rafe trusted his lawyers implicitly in business matters, they needed a firm hand to keep them from letting things slide.

He also wanted to see Bernard as soon as possible. De Marigny was a good friend, and he wasn't about to let a girl come between them now. At the thought of Gabrielle, he smiled to himself. He'd neglected her far too long, he thought, and it was high time he paid more than just a cordial visit to her. Tonight, he would let her know that she would have to resume paying him for her keep.

Chapter Thirty-two

Gabrielle was just sitting down in her customary chair next to Jane in the sitting room when she heard the front door open and close. Straightening up, she looked at Jane, then hurried to the hall to peer down towards the door. Her breath left her in a small gasp as she perceived the tall, muscular form striding confidently towards her.

"G-good evening," she said in a small voice.

He nodded to her, then strode past her into the sitting room, ignoring Jane who was attempting to pass unnoticed as she slipped out of her chair.

Jane left, closing the door behind her, while Gabrielle walked back to her chair and sat down carefully, her eyes riveted to that broad back. "I was expecting you earlier today," she began uncertainly, wondering at the darkness of his face as he turned to her.

"I've seen Leigh Owens today," he began tightly. "He was drunkenly informing everyone who cared to listen that he was privileged to spend one night in your bed— with my wholehearted approval!" He stopped, waiting for her to confirm or deny his statement, but when she was silent too long, he continued, "I'm away a few days and I come back to find my mistress is dallying with one of my best friends!" he said between his teeth, but still appearing to lean indolently against a large armchair.

Gabrielle, feeling justifiably angry, shook her head quickly. "He was here on *your* orders, if I remember correctly. He was most eager to inform me that you both shared *everything*—was I supposed to believe that included *me*, too?"

Rafe watched her eyes flashing up at him, and his fists tightened. God, how he hated the beautiful little bitch! He had not seen her in so many days, and then he found that she had been entertaining another man in his absence! It was too much.

"Mr. Owens did sleep in my bed that night," Gabrielle continued. "There was very little I could do to dissuade him—I'm only sorry now that I didn't join him! I can see, though, that you are determined not to believe me!" She hesitated. "If you have no wish to continue this—affair—I will have my things packed and will be out of here as soon as you like, but—I will need some time to find suitable living arrangements for myself."

He laughed, his dark brow arched sarcastically over his left eye. "Suitable arrangements?" he mocked her. "Perhaps, ma'am, you were thinking of the Hôtel de la Marine, or maybe even a place on the waterfront, for surely those would be the only quarters you could afford—and that only if you gave yourself as down payment." He eyed her with a brutal contempt. "But then, I suppose you wouldn't flinch too greatly at the indisposition?"

Her face turned pink, and she lowered her eyes. "You really don't think I—"

"—would stoop so low?" he finished caustically. "Why, yes, in all truth, I do. Surely you realize that no one is going to be obliging enough to give you a room free of charge, do you—unless he is as big a fool as I was!"

Gabrielle's hand whitened as she grasped the arm of her chair. "You act as though I'm ungrateful, but I—"

"Oh, for Christ's sake, Gabrielle! Please, no pretty speeches. I'm afraid I'm not in the mood for them right now."

She straightened up then, her pride rescuing her from the degrading situation. "I fail to see how your sarcasm and bullying is supposed to make you less a fool," she countered impudently. "If you think that I am going to sit here and let you treat me this way, I'm afraid you're terribly mistaken. I am not obliged to listen to your insulting remarks!"

He applauded briefly, then she saw his eyes narrow

slightly, and the green blazed at her like the fire in an emerald. "Oh, my dear mistress, I'm afraid you are the one in the wrong. You see, you are obliged to listen to whatever I may take it in mind to say to you. You're obligated to do even more than that, actually." He moved closer to her and smiled wickedly. "You forget, kitten, that I own you now. You are my personal possession—a woman paid for already and greatly in arrears in the debt she owes me."

Gabrielle stood up, her violet eyes matching his in anger. "What do you mean? I belong to no man—my spirit and my soul are my own and I shall do with them as I please!" she returned, breathing harder.

"And your body?" he questioned her softly. "I suppose you consider that your own, also, but you are wrong, my dear. I am the only person who has any rights over that."

His arms reached for her, and she flinched as his fingers bit into the flesh of her upper arm.

"Let me go," she said, between her teeth, struggling to move away from him.

He laughed insolently. "Come, come now, kitten. Surely you did better than that with Owens. I want to hear you say sweet, welcoming things to me. I want your hands to caress me. I want. . . ."

"Oh, you're hateful!" she cried out, pushing at his chest with her hands. "You only want to insult me!"

He held her still and deliberately bent down and kissed her, hard and bruising, forcing her mouth to open to him. His hands left her arms and pressed against her back, so that her body was crushed to his.

She felt dizzy and somehow pliant in his arms, telling herself that she hated him, that he was only using her, but unable to stop the warm yearning at his touch. When he finally released her, she gazed up at him, her eyes huge and darkened, her breath coming in short gasps.

He looked down at her, and his smile was commanding. "Now, I want you to come with me upstairs, kitten, and we'll see about paying back that debt you owe me."

"Oh, you—you make it all sound so businesslike, so impersonal," she flung at him desperately.

"But that's all it is, kitten—business. You wouldn't have it otherwise, would you?" he mocked her, following her to her bedroom and swinging the door shut. "Take off your clothes, kitten," he said, a sardonic look on his face.

Gabrielle watched him in disbelief as he pulled off his coat and proceeded to lay his shirt over a chair. She stood silently, trying to swallow the lump that seemed to be stuck maddeningly in her throat. How could he do this to her? If only he would show one ounce of tenderness or a bit of affection, she would do anything for him—anything but this. He treated her like a whore, like some nameless hussy off the street, hurrying to get things done so that he could pay her and be on his way. It disgusted her, and she would not be abused in such a manner.

When he was naked, he looked up expectantly and frowned to see her staring at him so accusingly. "What's this? Don't tell me you're going to balk now?" he asked impatiently. "It's too pretty a gown to rip," he added with a menacing note in his voice.

"I'll not behave like some courtesan no matter how much you try to force me into it," she replied, her voice breaking disconcertingly.

He eyed her speculatively for a moment, then, with a sigh of impatience, he strode over to her and hooked his fingers in her gown. "You're a stubborn woman, kitten," he muttered, "but you're no less desirable because of it."

And with one wrenching pull, he ripped the gown down the front of her bodice so that the two halves lay open over her skirt. His hands cupped her breasts, and his thumbs pressed hard against the nipples.

"That's a pretty fast-sounding heartbeat—for a woman who professes no interest in what's coming," he laughed scornfully, bringing his hands down to her waistband.

Gabrielle bit her lip so that she wouldn't cry out involuntarily as he tore the skirt away from her. She would not go along with his disgusting game, she thought, but she found it increasingly hard to keep her promise to herself to remain uncooperative when he carried her to the bed and began to caress her flesh with the touch of a master. Her only defense was to fight him, and she began to slap at his hands and kick out at him with her feet.

His laughter only increased her fury, and she tried to bite his hand, her eyes spitting at him. He wrestled with her as a cat plays with a mouse, letting her use up her strength so that his ultimate goal would be all the easier.

When she stopped for a moment, breathless and tired from her useless exertions, he moved his body on top of hers and smashed his mouth over her lips, kissing her with an abusive mastery that she hated. She wriggled beneath him, curving her fingers into claws to rake at his face. He caught both her hands and moved his mouth downward to her tender breasts, biting at the smooth flesh until she entreated him to stop.

"I hate you! Oh, how I hate you!" she sobbed, even as he drove fiercely into her.

A cry escaped her lips as he moved in her mercilessly, and, despite herself, she felt the burning heat within her, filling her entire body with a sweet, delicious pleasure that made her back arch to meet his thrusts and her arms entwine themselves around his neck.

He recognized her surrender and slowed his movements, taking his time now that her resistance had been shattered. He watched her face, noting the struggle taking place within her between the desire that was suffusing her and the mental pride that made her continue to resist him.

"Relax, kitten," he murmured softly, nuzzling her hair with his lips. "Enjoy it."

A moan trembled in her throat, and she turned her head away from him so that his mouth grazed her chin and moved down her throat, seeking those high, rounded breasts that pressed provocatively against his chest.

"Impudent little things," he commented, nibbling at her flesh.

His movements were increasing in rhythm now as her stirrings beneath him excited him beyond belief. Her hands moved on his back now like gossamer wings that stroked him and added to his own pleasure. They climaxed together, lifting each other to the pinnacle of pleasurable delight, and, afterwards, he lay on her, gasping as the shock waves rolled over him and finally receded.

"Jesus, kitten," he said laughingly, "you must be the best piece ever to grace my bed."

Gabrielle, whose eyes had been cloudy with desire, flinched at his words and looked up at him bitterly. "Is that all you can say?" she demanded, catching at the sob in her throat.

He shrugged and rolled off her, drawing her against him. "I meant it as a compliment," he returned nonchalantly.

She would have said more, drawing on her anger to fire her words, but it was so nice to be held close against his lean, tanned body and have his fingers idly caressing her. She shivered in his embrace and moved her hand so that it lay, small and white, against his chest.

The next morning she awoke still clasped in his arms, and she revelled for a moment in the comfort and security. Her hands moved along his chest, stroking his side. He winced and awoke instantly, glaring at her as though wondering how he came to be in her bed.

"Christ, kitten, can't you be a little more careful?" he asked her.

"What—what do you mean?"

"Open your eyes, dammit! I'm still a little sore there."

She followed his pointing finger and gazed in surprise at the pinkish scar that looked to be the result of some sharp object—a knife?

"How did it happen?" she asked, touching it gingerly. He shrugged. "A fight."

She moved up on her elbow and looked down at his face. "A fight? And you were hurt? Why didn't you come to me? I would have—"

"No need, kitten. I already had a nurse," he replied, grinning arrogantly. "It's just a knife wound, nothing serious," he explained, observing the hurt look in her eyes. "I was actually on a mission for the governor—

trying to catch your old lover." He could see now the carefully closed expression.

"Did—did you catch him?" she asked.

He shook his head, angry suddenly and not quite understanding why. "No, the bastard got away, but we were able to get some evidence against him—although I really don't know if Claiborne will be able to use it. Seems a damn shame when you consider that a good man died because of it."

"How awful," Gabrielle murmured, her mind far away.

Rafe looked into those violet eyes and wondered what lay behind them as they stared at nothing. Was she thinking of him? Abruptly, he pushed her away so that he could pad over to the window.

"It's going to rain," he said absently. "I guess I'd better get dressed. I don't know if Lafitte recognized me, but if he did, I'm sure I can expect increased retaliatory action directed against my shipping firm."

Gabrielle shook off her reverie and faced him, sitting up in the bed, the sheet drawn over her breasts. "Must you leave already?" she said a little wistfully, at which he grinned at her lazily.

"Why, kitten, am I to believe that you actually want me to stay with you? And all the time I thought my presence was—distinctly unsettling to you."

Gabrielle pinkened and looked away from those penetrating green eyes that seemed to bore into her head. "Well, it's just that—that I do get lonesome sometimes, and I—"

He frowned. "So I've noticed, and, when you get lonesome, you must have someone to while away the hours with—no matter who it might be," he said sarcastically.

She jerked her head up and glared at him. "That's not true! Why won't you believe that I—"

He walked over to her and pulled down the sheet. His fingers played with her breasts for a moment, then swooped lower down over her belly. Her breathing quickened, and her arms were beginning to reach for him when he stopped and his mouth shaped itself into a cruel grin. She looked up at him, not understanding.

"You see how it is with you, kitten. You're a very sensuous young woman—a man's touch on you, and you're instantly in heat, ready for satisfaction."

Her cheeks blazed in her embarrassment, and, with a cry of anger, she pushed him away and drew the sheet over herself again. "Oh, you're the most—the most—" she searched for a word to describe aptly her feelings for him. Her violet eyes narrowed, and she glanced a sideways look at him. "Did it ever occur to you, that yours is the only touch that has that particular effect on me?" she asked him.

He smiled wickedly. "You flatter me, kitten, but I'm sure you have more sense than that. You already know my feelings when it comes to our relationship."

"I do?" she countered quickly. "Please inform me afresh, for I think I must have forgotten."

His smile disappeared as he gazed into those eyes that had suddenly become seductive and teasing. Her small hands reached out to caress him, moved over his flesh so that in a very few moments, the proof of his readiness was apparent to both.

"It seems that a woman's touch has much the same effect on you," she said softly. "Am I to assume that every woman you go to bed with has such powers?" She let the sheet slide away from her as she brought her body up, fastening her arms about his neck.

"Are you trying to seduce me, you wanton bitch?" he asked her, but he didn't move away.

She nodded. "My education has improved vastly since you first took me all those years ago in Paris," she informed him softly, interspersing her words with kisses on his mouth and neck.

She felt his hands bringing her closer and then pushing her back into the mattress, his body following hers. She kissed him deeply, moving her mouth deliberately, lingering as her hands flew over his body.

"You're terribly excited, my darling," she whispered, her eyes meeting his and noting the wary expression on his face.

She could hardly believe what she was actually doing,

behaving like a whore, seducing a man, trying to relax him enough for the pleasure to come. She hated herself for the deception, knowing what she would do, but she continued caressing him, licking his shoulder, biting hard into the iron-muscled flesh, waiting for the right moment. He groaned and caught her head between his hands, kissing her face passionately now, responding to her abandon. She waited, positioning her body, gently pressing him away from her so that he would roll over onto his back on the bed. Her hands pleasured him, bringing him surely to the peak of excitement, and then—she sprang up from the bed and stood, trembling a little, looking down at him.

Her smile was anything but contrite. "So!" she said trimphantly, flushed and breathing hard, "it seems we both have some power!"

He looked at her, not believing for a moment what she had done. Then she saw those green eyes go dark, and the fury in them made her step back.

"You scheming little whore!" he said savagely, furious at himself for believing that she—for allowing his iron control to slip for a moment, furious at her for so blatantly destroying any trust he would have had in her.

His movements were supple as a panther's as he slid from the bed, his eyes dangerously hooded as he watched her step- back.

"I was only trying to make you see how unfair you were being when you—"

"I don't give a damn what you were trying to do, you teasing bitch!" he said between his teeth. "But this is not the time to stop what you've started. I expect you to finish this delightful little seduction scene."

"You—you don't seem to understand. I was trying—"

"Shut up and get back in that bed!"

He reached for her and, as she turned to escape him, caught at her long hair, wrenching her head back painfully as he pulled at a fistful of the thick, soft silk. She cried out and dug her nails into his hands, struggling to get away. He pulled her back towards the bed and threw her on it, springing on top of her and wasting no time in gratifying himself. When he was finished, she lay still, her cheeks wet from her tears, her face turned away from his probing eyes.

He looked down at her, disgusted by his own actions that would have been better suited to some conquered town. He slid from her body and stood up, noting with surprising regret the marks he had made on her breasts with his ungentle fingers. Regretfully, he lifted a lock of her hair and brought it to his mouth.

"I'm sorry, kitten," he murmured softly.

She refused to say anything. He donned his clothes and was moving towards the door when he realized she was sitting up now, watching him. He blew her a kiss and grinned with that devilish expression.

"I'll see you again tonight, kitten," he said briskly. "You will keep the sheets warmed for me, won't you?"

"Oh-h-h!" she exploded, reaching for something to throw at him. Her fingers closed over a small crystal vase, and, with contained fury, she threw the fragile glass at the point where he had been standing, but he was gone and the vase hit the door with a loud tinkling crash. From the hallway, she could hear his insufferable laughter, and she pounded her fists into the pillow.

When the sound of his boots had vanished down the hall, she got out of bed and paced restlessly back and forth across the floor, devising all manner of schemes and plans to get even with him for this last affront. But she stopped suddenly, realizing that anything she might devise would only be ably repaid in kind.

She sighed. Why not admit the truth, she thought wearily—that she loved him. In spite of everything—or perhaps because of it—she loved him. She sat down abruptly and closed her eyes, but his face came too easily to mind.

She stood up and called to Jane that she would be taking a walk within the hour, and soon the two young women made their way down Toulouse Street and headed for the Place d'Armes. They moved through throngs of people, many of them blacks, the women with calico dresses and the ever-present tignons wrapped around their shorn heads, and the men naked to the waist and accompanied by watchful overseers taking them for duty on the docks.

It was as yet too early for many of the Creoles to be taking the air, and Gabrielle was thankful that she could think without the usual accompanying crowd noises. She looked up at the tall spires of the Church of Saint-Louis and touched Jane on the shoulder.

"I—I haven't been in church for so long—would you like to come with me?"

The two moved into the cool, shadowy vestibule where convent girls waited in pairs to walk down the aisles, the ever-watchful nuns forming them into neat rows with waves of their white-clad arms. Gabrielle and Jane walked around them and into the high-ceilinged church, past the rows of pews, polished and waiting.

Gabrielle genuflected at the first pew and knelt on the velvet kneeler, folding her hands. The half-forgotten words she had learned as a child came tumbling back. She prayed for so long that her knees began to ache at the unaccustomed position, and her head sagged in her hands.

She rose with Jane and made to leave. Outside the church, the light was brilliant, the air filled now with sounds of the milling crowds of people, all taking their promenade around the square.

"Gabrielle!"

The masculine voice came to her through the crowd, and she smiled to see Bernard de Marigny coming towards her, his blue eyes alight with pleasure.

"Gabrielle, to find you here after all these weeks of not seeing you! *Sacre bleu!* You are more beautiful than ever, my dove." He kissed her hand.

"Bernard, you look the same—handsome as always," she smiled, glad that this occasion of their first meeting was void of strain.

"I never change, Gabrielle. But I've missed you, my dear. I didn't realize that a woman could have such an effect on me, but it seems you have made a lasting mark on my heart." He took her hand and led her around the square as they talked. "Now, I want you to tell me how you have been. Has—has St. Claire been treating you decently?" He looked at her sharply.

"Yes, Bernard. Of course, Rafe has many things to keep him busy, and his business interests are quite varied —but he is very good to me," she ended lamely.

Bernard clucked his tongue. "And I suppose that he considers you just another of his business interests, allotting so much time for you in his schedule."

"Bernard, please do not pry."

"Gabrielle, I cannot stand by and see you hurt by a man who knows of no other way to treat a woman. Let me, at least, come and visit you."

Gabrielle shuddered, remembering the coldness in Rafe's eyes when he had learned of Leigh Owens' visit to her. "No, no, Bernard. You must not. It would be difficult." She felt the urge to leave him suddenly, to escape those knowing eyes.

"Ah, Gabrielle, if only it could have been different between you and me," he said regretfully. "I would have worshiped you, my angel." His voice became deeper. "I would have made love to you every night with tender passion—does your Rafe behave so admirably?"

"Bernard, please!"

He shrugged. "All right—you must forgive the troubling stabs of jealousy, my dearest."

A tall, dignified black servant bowed in front of them and proffered a silver basket to de Marigny, who accepted it gravely and riffled through the small cards stacked inside.

"What is it?" Gabrielle asked in some curiosity.

Bernard grinned at her and pointed to the card bearing his name. "An invitation to a party. Miss Melissa Lawrence requests the honor of my presence at eight-thirty in the evening on July 20 to help celebrate her birthday."

Gabrielle paled visibly as Bernard casually fingered the edges of the other cards, flipping them forward until he stopped at the card addressed to Rafe St. Claire. She shrugged as Bernard dismissed the servant.

"I would expect Rafe to be asked to such an affair. After all, he is influential in the city and—"

"And just happens to be on Miss Lawrence's list of most eligible bachelors—probably '*the* most eligible,'" Bernard interrupted smoothly. "Oh, Gabrielle, it does wound me to see you hurt by a man who deserves you even less than I. You don't think he will not attend just for the sake of your smile?"

"Of course he will attend, Bernard. Do you imagine that I am some simpering fool, thinking there is nothing that can tear him away from my company?" Her voice was wary. "If, as you say, he is going to ask for a betrothal, there is very little—in fact, nothing—that I can say or do to stop it." She pressed her skirt with her hands nervously. "And now, I really must go, Bernard."

"Of course, my dear," Bernard answered, taking her hand and holding it tightly for a moment. "But please remember what I said before, Gabrielle. It was no idle offer, and I make it again with my whole heart. If you ever need me—I'll be there."

Chapter Thirty-three

Melissa Lawrence stretched delightedly, like a contented cat, and let her fingers slide softly across her lover's chest, stopping to twine the dark, curling hairs around her little fingers. She laughed huskily and bent to kiss the sensuous mouth that could arouse her like that of no other man she had ever met. Rafe St. Claire reached up lazily to imprison her face and press her lips firmly against his.

"Oh, darling," Melissa sighed, "I'm so happy today. We do go well together, don't we?"

She heard his small mocking laugh and felt some of her happiness drain away. "My dear 'Lissa, you go well with any man," he returned dryly, letting his hands slide from her neck to her breast, lingering there.

Melissa pouted and moved away from him, moving his head from her lap. "Why must you always spoil a perfectly lovely afternoon?" she asked him regretfully, standing up to let her toes dig into the softness of the earth. Her eyes casually roamed the secluded little copse of trees where they were lying and out to where the shimmer of the Mississippi River was brightened by the July sun.

"I didn't think I was spoiling it," he commented lethargically.

"Oh, you know very well what I meant," she returned, picking idly at the leaves of a mulberry bush. "You always find a way to destroy the mood after we've made love together. When it comes time for you to be gentle and loving and whisper sweet things to me, you come out with something hateful."

"Hateful? 'Lissa, you know very well I don't mean to be," he laughed lazily, sitting up now and brushing twigs and leaves from his hair.

"Well," she hesitated, then went on, "you could at least —tell me you love me." She waited for some reaction, and when there was none, she plunged on more boldly. "After all, if we are to announce our engagement at my birthday party tomorrow night. . . ."

He turned now and eyed her with his familiar arrogance, so that her voice lost its strength and died away uncertainly. "Our engagement?" he questioned her disdainfully. "I wasn't aware of such an important event." He glanced sharply at her. "Is this some new little scheme you've cooked up between your parents and yourself? If so, I'm afraid I'm the least likely candidate for the position."

Melissa opened her mouth, then stamped her bare foot on the ground in a growing temper. "Rafe St. Claire! You're not going to embarrass me after—after. . . ."

". . . after you've told half the city that I've asked you

to marry me, and you knew perfectly well that no such thing ever occurred, nor is it likely to. Melissa, I've told you before, I just don't want to be married—I don't want to be tied down to one woman just yet." He saw her eyes brighten with tears and stood up. " 'Lissa, 'Lissa, why must you be so like other females? I thought you and I were having a marvelous time together—surely you can't deny that?"

"A marvelous time," she repeated bitterly. "You don't even give me the distinction of being your mistress, or at least you don't bother to honor me with the official title! I suppose you save that for that young woman whom you keep in town!" Her voice rose in a crescendo and her eyes blazed furiously through the tears. "Do you think, Rafe St. Claire, that I am blithely going to continue offering myself for your service any time you please? Do you think I care so little for my reputation that I would continue indefinitely as your plaything while the rest of society shake their heads and pity me?"

Rafe threw a piece of grass on the ground and reached for his trousers. "I wasn't aware that your 'reputation' has ever been a major concern with you, Melissa," he said sternly. "As for 'that young woman' as you call her, I've never tried to conceal that I was keeping a mistress. Christ, after the episode at the 'Golden Palace,' I would have been surprised if you hadn't known about her! But she has nothing to do with the reason why I don't want to marry you."

With shaking hands, Melissa was struggling to get into her chemise, succeeding only in ripping it dreadfully in her anger. With a wail of despair, she sat on the ground, her fury turning into a torrent of tears. "If—if you think that—that I can't get anyone else to m-marry me, I'm afraid you're wrong, terribly wrong," she got out breathlessly between sobs. "Why—why Charles Landon or—or Nicholas Beauville—either one would jump at the chance to make me his wife!"

Rafe, buttoning his shirt and avoiding the reddened eyes of his paramour, smiled to himself. "In that case, I suggest you quickly go to one of them and try your wiles on him—but you will have to hurry since you plan to announce your betrothal tomorrow night."

"O-oh, I'll kill you!" she cried, flying at him with nails bared and her hands curved into claws.

He caught her wrists, bruising them with the pressure of his hands. Tears splashed down her cheeks as she struggled helplessly in his grasp.

"Oh, Rafe, I—I didn't mean that. I couldn't hate you, no matter how hard I tried!" she said, her voice coming slowly through her tears. "Please, please forgive for my terrible temper. Of course, you will still come tomorrow, won't you?"

He felt suddenly sorry for this tear-stained young woman and angry at himself for what he must do to convince her that he would not marry her. "Of course, 'Lissa," he said gently, releasing her wrists. "You know I would like nothing better than to toast your health, and to see some man who is worthy of you—"

"Oh, God!" she laughed wildly. "Don't—don't mouth those same platitudes that have been handed down to women for centuries!" she said. "You will suggest that I concentrate my efforts on Charles or Nicholas now—anything but continue to harass you with wild pleas for marriage, I suppose?" She shook herself and stared at him sadly. "Rafe St. Claire, you're a bastard," she said slowly. "A handsome, exciting bastard—but a bastard nonetheless."

Her eyes were harder now and as impersonal as though he and she were strangers. She began putting her clothes on, and they both completed dressing in silence.

"I suppose," she began casually, as they walked to their horses, "that your mistress must be a most understanding woman—that, or blinded by love to all of your faults."

He laughed drily and cupped his hands so that she could mount her horse. "Understanding hardly describes her, 'Lissa. No, I would say that she is much like yourself, my dear. Unfortunately, I seem to be attracted to the wrong type."

"Well, in any case, I should like to meet her," she said with bravado. "Perhaps you should bring her to the party. At least that would keep tongues from wagging over me, I daresay."

He glanced sharply at her, then grinned in disarming aplomb. "What an original idea, 'Lissa," he laughed. "A man bringing his mistress to a social function graced by the élite of the city—your idea certainly appeals to me."

"I thought it might," she replied woodenly. They rode on unto they came to the crossroads. "Bring your painted whore, then," she said brusquely. "One more woman to humiliate would most likely serve to bolster your male ego! I can only pity the little fool!" And she whipped her horse and galloped madly away, her silver hair flying out behind her.

"The witch!" he thought, but not without some admiration for the way she had attempted to recover herself. He had no doubt but that she would still entertain thoughts of marriage with him, and the idea rankled in his brain, for he realized now that he had grown tired of the woman's constant tirades and selfish claims on him.

"Bring your painted whore then!" she'd said.

He laughed out loud. Now, that really did appeal to him. Why not take Gabrielle to the party? He spurred his horse to an even trot. Those stuffed shirts of old men and their shriveled-up wives would certainly have to sit up and take notice of a woman like Gabrielle. Christ! After all, hadn't she been born into that very kind of society? And what more effective way to rid Melissa of any lingering idea of marriage?

As he spied Fairview coming closer, he smiled to himself and slapped his booted thigh. Damn! He'd do it after all!

Gabrielle faced Rafe across the length of the room, her face determined, her mouth tight with disapproval. "I'll not go with you tonight, Rafe, I don't care what you say. I'll not be made a laughingstock in front of all those people—and *her* least of all." She folded her arms across her breast.

He merely watched her, amused, knowing that he would get her to accompany him even if it had to be by force. "Put your clothes on and fix your hair, Gabrielle. I would hate for you to arrive looking like what they will have all already labelled you." He smiled in mocking disdain and threw her dressing gown at her. "I'll call your servant to fix your hair."

She picked up the dressing gown and threw it back at him in a fury. "I'll not go, Rafe, and I'm not going to change my mind!" she said firmly.

Slowly, he closed the half-opened door, then turned to face her, noticing her slight trembling as she stood and watched him. He offered a thin smile.

"I've had all I can take from sassy women," he said lightly. "You're my property, Gabrielle, and you will do as I tell you, or punishment will be meted out."

She laughed, but with little conviction. "Punishment! What am I? Some dog or animal you must apply the switch to, to make me obey?"

His green eyes flashed dangerously. "An excellent idea, ma'm'selle," he said silkily, crossing the room with his arrogant saunter and grasping her by the arm. "Rest assured, I shall be careful where I place the marks so that they'll not be discernible beneath your gown." Like lightning, his hands ripped off her robe and caught her against him. "Christ! You're beautiful naked," he whispered, his hand chafing her breast as he lowered his mouth to hers. This kiss was long and artful.

Bravely, Gabrielle tried to resist his power, but her hidden longing and love for him made her weak in his arms, and she pressed herself against him ardently.

"Now then," he said, releasing her slightly, "could it be that you have changed your mind, kitten?"

She opened her eyes to stare at him, then backed away. "Why must I accompany you?" she asked. "There should be no invitation to a man's mistress—and—and besides, is this night not to be the announcing of your—your betrothal?"

"I'm not going to marry Melissa Lawrence, kitten," he said firmly, "and I have said as much to the lady. But this is hardly a concern of yours."

"You're not going to—" she repeated, puzzled. "But Bernard told me—"

"Bernard? When have you seen him?" he asked quickly, his aggressive features becoming overbearingly arrogant.

She blushed. "I see him occasionally when I attend Mass and during my walks to market," she murmured defensively.

"Oh, Christ! My mistress consorting with yet another former lover! Soon I suppose I shall have to keep count!" he said in an explosion of anger. "I suppose Bernard is laughing up his sleeve."

She seemed genuinely surprised at his attitude. "Consorting with—?" Her eyes flashed at him in anger. "Bernard and I have conversation, and that is all!" Gabrielle could not understand his fury but supposed it had something to do with a man's ever-expanding pride. "If you are so angry with me, surely you have no intention now of taking me with you tonight," she said, reaching for her robe with a gesture of finality.

Immediately, she regretted her words, for her arm was drawn back painfully, and she was thrown onto the bed. She could not see his hand dart out for the riding crop that he had flung carelessly in a chair when he had entered her room, but in the next instant, a sharp pain seared her buttocks. She screamed as he repeated the action and then did it again.

Rafe brought the quirt down once more on the firmly rounded flesh. Four diagonal stripes crisscrossed the rapidly swelling area and finally he threw the crop down, breathing hard, hating himself and her at the same time.

"Now will you go with me, goddamn you?" he breathed. His answer was a muffled sob and a quick nodding. "Good! I'm going to call your servant now and I'll expect you to be ready to leave by eight o'clock. That gives you at least two hours!"

He stalked out of the room, ignoring the young woman who still lay on the bed, one arm flung outward over her head. After he had gone, Jane rushed into the room, her eyes dilated and her mouth forming soundless words of outrage.

"It's—it's not very bad—really," Gabrielle assured her, struggling to her feet. She winced slightly and found that she was trembling.

"Oh, ma'am! My God, I can't believe a gentleman would do such a thing!" June exclaimed, studying the cuts cautiously. "He's a brute, a brute!"

"All this for a silly party!" Jane went on heatedly. "And you with a baby on the way! Oh, ma'am, why didn't you tell him?"

Gabrielle flushed and looked away. "I doubt it would make any difference with him," she said quietly.

She laid a hand lightly on her belly, remembering that day some weeks ago when she had felt nausea rise in her throat and had been terribly sick all morning and for several mornings afterward. The dizziness, the tiredness, the absence of her monthly flow—all these had told her what she had dreaded to believe—that she was pregnant! For a few days, she had been sunk in gloom, remembering that other time when she had found herself with child. How excited Lafitte had been! She recalled the plans he had made with her, the promise that one day she and the child would leave with him and start a new life. And then—she had lost both of them. . . . How would it be with this innocent young life, newly started within the secret confines of her body—what would St. Claire say when he found out?

As well as Jane and she had been able to figure out, she had conceived that first night when Rafe had taken her to Fairview—would that please him, she wondered, to know that this child was begun in the beautiful house he had built for himself? She was nearly three months along now, and the baby would be due some time in January, but she had refused to tell Rafe, despite Jane's alternating pleas and scoldings. He would know soon enough, she thought miserably, recalling how she had ballooned in the middle stages of her first pregnancy.

"Lie on your stomach and let me apply some ointment," Jane suggested, returning from her room with a soothing poultice.

Gabrielle fought down the temporary nausea that threatened to engulf her and allowed Jane to smooth the ointment, then stood up and walked to the window to breathe deeply of the warm, honeysuckle-scented air.

After washing, Gabrielle donned a clean chemise and sat down on the pillow while Jane arranged her hair in a becoming coiffure of loose curls and picked some fresh blossoms from the rosebed to settle among the glistening coils. Jane buttoned up a gown of soft green watered silk with a rounded neckline that set off Gabrielle's breasts superbly, and she was ready.

Picking up her gloves and fan, she hurried downstairs as well as she was able. Rafe had already returned and was waiting for her in the sitting room, dressed handsomely and staring out the window absently.

Gabrielle felt a small thrill as her eyes went over the broad shoulders encased in the finest black broadcloth, the tall, highly polished black boots, and the silver-and-blue embroidered waistcoat that fit snugly over the creamy silk shirt. Surely, she thought, his child would be beautiful.

He turned, sensing her presence, and bowed. "I see you mean to be biddable this evening? Mind that you behave properly, kitten. I wouldn't want to repeat tonight's earlier performance."

"Miss Gabrielle de Beauvoir and Mr. Rafe St. Claire!" the majordomo announced.

Gabrielle smiled mechanically at the crowd, some of whom looked up at her in curiosity, others completely ignoring her, their eyes fastening on her companion. One of the latter detached herself from a small group of people and came forward quickly, her silver hair telling Gabrielle immediately that this must be her hostess.

"Rafe," she crooned, her ice-blue eyes sweeping over the young woman at his side with calculated indifference. She took his arm possessively and began to escort him to the group she had just left.

"Wait, Melissa, I want you to meet Gabrielle." Rafe introduced the two women, and Gabrielle could see his amusement at the distinct coldness between the two of them.

The other woman's eyes seemed to freeze into icy chips, then she smiled and indicated the crowd. "Please feel free to mingle among the guests, Miss de Beauvoir. I'm sure you will enjoy yourself this evening," she added in a tone heavy with disdain. She turned back to Rafe who was watching Gabrielle with a speculative look in his eyes. "And now, my dearest, will you come with me? Papa has been wanting to discuss a few things with you, and my cousin, Cynthia, is over from Savannah and simply dying to meet you!"

She hung on his arm, and together they left Gabrielle standing rather distressed on the edge of the step. Bravely, she scanned the group, some of whom were staring at her rudely, and hoped that she might find someone who might at least look friendly enough to speak to.

With some hesitation, she made her way towards one of the side alcoves, trying not to notice the curious stares of the women and bolder glances the men gave her. Oh, no, she thought in sudden panic, they all know! She sat down on one of the settees, folding her hands in her lap to keep them from trembling, and determined to keep her eyes on the floor until Rafe came and took her home.

Such was not to be the case, for a familiar voice sounded close by and Bernard de Marigny leaned over and whispered. "You look beautiful. Stand up so everyone can see you!"

Gabrielle looked up quickly. "Oh, Bernard, I feel so freakish. Everyone keeps looking at me as though they expect to see two heads growing on my shoulders."

He smiled. "Sweetheart, don't bother yourself with them. Come with me. I want you to meet someone."

He took her hand, and, reluctantly, she followed him into the crowd. She saw a woman perhaps ten years older than she, seated in a chair and laughing with two or three other people standing around her, obviously entranced by her dark-haired, vivacious beauty. As Bernard drew her forward into the small circle that surrounded the woman, Gabrielle immediately sensed the hostility directed at her, but at least it did not come from the hub of the circle, and so she smiled with all the charm that made up part of her French heritage.

"Madame, I would like you to meet a friend of mine, Gabrielle de Beauvoir. Gabrielle, may I present Madame Suzette Claiborne."

The governor's lady! Gabrielle immediately executed a flawless curtsey. "I'm honored, madame," she murmured softly, her eyes meeting the dark ones that studied her thoughtfully for a moment.

A small hush seemed to settle over the group as though everyone were waiting for the woman's reaction to this invader to their circle. Then, with a dazzling smile, Suzette Claiborne stood up and took the younger woman's hand, pressing it lightly.

"Miss de Beauvoir, you are, like all Frenchwomen, impeccably well mannered. Please sit here next to me and tell me all about yourself, yes?"

Gabrielle breathed an inward sigh of relief and listened with half an ear to the murmurs and comments that flew about the group. She held tight to the small white hand that brought her up to the center of he circle. Briefly Bernard's hand squeezed Gabrielle's for reassurance, before he disappeared into the crowd again.

"And now, ladies and gentlemen, if you please, I should like to have conversation with Miss de Beauvoir—if you will excuse us?" Madame Claiborne said lightly, her dark eyes flashing around the group.

Politely, the people who had been pressing closest withdrew to a respectful distance, and Suzette turned to this young woman whom she had heard was nothing more than a lowly prostitute—but she had been surprised by the girl's obvious presence and bearing. Surely that rascal, St. Claire, had stepped well past the bounds of etiquette and common decency by bringing such a woman to a gathering like this, a party where it had been rumored he would announce his betrothal to Melissa Lawrence. Of course Suzette, true to her Creole background, had always felt a certain disdain for these upstart Americans who besieged New Orleans with their uncultivated ways and uncivilized manners, but as the governor's wife, she was obliged to mingle with all levels of society, just as her husband, a native Virginian, had to do.

She had known instinctively that this young woman who sat so anxiously next to her was not a stranger to such gatherings—and surely the name was French and possibly of ancient lineage. Yes, the girl aroused her lively interest, and, being Creole, she was determined to delve into her background.

"May I call you Gabrielle?" she inquired politely, her eyes studying the fine bone structure, the candid, violet eyes, and the slightly trembling mouth.

"Of course, madame." Gabrielle murmured.

"I must admit, you don't fit my picture of you—I mean, what I had been led to believe," Suzette began, noticing the rush of color to the girl's face.

"Pardon me, madame, but if you asked me to sit beside you only to delve into personal matters, then I must ask you to excuse me," Gabrielle returned stiffly.

Suzette smiled even wider this time, her eyes dancing. "Just as I thought, Gabrielle. It seems you have the breeding of an aristocrat, for I hardly think a woman of the streets would be so touchy about my words." She laid a hand gently on the other's arm. "I'm sorry, I would not want to pry." She hesitated. "But you are from France?"

Gabrielle nodded. "My father was André de Beauvoir, Marquis de Molisse. I was born in Paris. Both my parents are dead, madame."

"I'm sorry, Gabrielle, but it is hard for me to understand how such a girl as you would find herself living as mistress to a rascal like St. Claire. Oh, yes, he is certainly handsome and virile enough to arouse any woman's interest, but you—"

"Please, madame."

"Of course, my dear, I'll not question you any further. But I daresay I should scold M'sieur St. Claire severely for bringing you here tonight, knowing how embarrassing it would be for you. I shall have to speak to my husband about it."

"Oh, no, madame, I—"

"Child, you're not afraid of him, are you?"

"No, madame, but I'm afraid that Mr. St. Claire would not find it very agreeable to be scolded on my account."

But Madame Claiborne was not to be deterred, and Gabrielle watched in distress as she signalled to a plump, fair-haired man of medium height and middle age, who was standing with a group of men off to one side. Gabrielle watched Governor Claiborne as he approached, noting the pleasant face devoid of any dramatic vigor and the candid, bright eyes that returned her look without rancor.

"My dear, you wished to speak with me?" he said, bowing over his wife's hand. It was easy to see that he adored her.

"Oh, William, I must insist that you reprimand that scoundrel, St. Claire, and do it immediately, for bringing his charming mistress into such an embarrassing situation."

"What—what did you say? St. Claire—brought—whom?"

"Forgive me, dearest. May I present Miss Gabrielle de Beauvoir, the Comtesse de Molisse. Gabrielle, my husband, Governor Claiborne. Now, William, perhaps you will understand better when I relate the details which I have just learned. . . ."

Gabrielle listened, distraught, as Madame Claiborne launched into a conversation with her husband who listened with a look of astonishment on his face. She then concluded, "St. Claire has an obligation to—to marry this young woman after he has used her so ungallantly for his own purposes! Surely you might suggest to him—"

"My dear, please do not press me on this affair. It is assuredly a private matter between St. Claire and Miss de Beauvoir."

He looked completely uncomfortable now, and Gabrielle felt a trifle sorry for him and was at a loss as to explain Madame Claiborne's sudden and intense interest in her problems.

They were all three distracted by the sound of a gong proclaiming the entrance of the birthday cake, aflame with candles. There was a generous round of applause as Melissa Lawrence, resplendent in blue satin, her hair alive with tiny brilliants, stepped over to cut the first slice. With the aid of a servant, she knifed out a portion and, turning, boldly crossed to St. Claire and offered him the price of cake. Everyone smiled knowingly, and titters passed among the ladies. The cake was wheeled to the far wall, while the orchestra tuned up for the first dance and the servants began cutting the cake and wrapping the pieces in cloth napkins.

Madame Claiborne was still looking a trifle thunderous, and Gabrielle was only too happy to accept Bernard's proffered arm as he led her to the ballroom floor.

"Oh dear, I'm afraid Madame Claiborne is quite a remarkable woman," Gabrielle whispered to him as they joined the other dancers.

"—A trait she shares with only one other woman in this room," Bernard whispered back, gliding her smoothly across the floor.

"No, no, you don't understand," Gabrielle went on, ignoring the compliment. "She seems to think that I have been treated so shabbily by Rafe St. Claire that he should immediately make amends by marrying me!" and she shuddered at the thought.

"And what is so remarkable about that?" he asked her.

She looked directly into that blue gaze. "He would hate me, Bernard! You know as well as I that Rafe St. Claire will not have someone tell him whom he will marry. And

besides—I'm not sure that I should enjoy the prospect of
being his wife."

Bernard gazed at her, a smile of amusement playing
about his lips. "Ah, now, we aren't being truthful, are we?
You're in love with him, my darling." While she averted
her gaze, Bernard chuckled. "It's just too bad that the fool
doesn't realize what a prize he owns now."

Gabrielle would have said something in return, but she
felt suddenly the force of someone's eyes on her, and, as
Bernard swung her around, she encountered Rafe's arrogant glare reaching across to her even as he tightened his
hold on Melissa. She remembered suddenly their earlier
argument over her conversation with Bernard—and now,
to have him dancing with her must be making him very
angry indeed! Well, what would he expect her to do? she
wondered defiantly, just sit meekly against the wall for
the rest of the evening while he pawed over his lady
friend?

She tilted her chin and matched him look for look,
infuriated to see his glare turn into a look of amused calculation. She concentrated on the steps of the dance, determined not to think of him anymore. Afterwards, she was
thankful for Madame Claiborne's patronage, for she did
not lack for partners, much to Melissa's fury.

"Your little mistress hardly seems lonesome without
you, darling," Melissa egged Rafe as they sipped chilled
wine on the terrace.

He frowned slightly. "No."

Melissa watched the movement he made bringing the
glass to his lips, then touched him on the shoulder, pressing
her breasts against him. "Let's not think of her, my darling. Why not go inside and—and surprise everyone with
news of our betrothal? I should think that declaration
would at least cause her impudent smile to disappear,"
she said craftily.

He shrugged. "I should think it very stupid of myself
to trade one bitch for another," he said brutally.

At first, Melissa could not believe the harsh finality of

his words. Then, as her mind finally acceped them, she drew back her hand and struck him as hard as she could, enraged that he should speak to her so. She noticed someone walking down the steps leading into the garden and was about to call out when she saw that it was none other than "that young woman" herself, escorted by Bernard de Marigny. She turned back in triumph to where Rafe was staring at her with disdainful contempt.

"Look for yourself, for I believe your mistress is planning to dally with a mutual acquaintance," she pointed out, noticing the look of anger that suddenly encompassed his face. For a brief moment she almost regretted her action, but there was nothing she could do as he stormed past her.

Gabrielle and Bernard had not noticed the couple standing above them on the balcony when he had suggested they get some air. Gabrielle had been glad to accept this suggestion after the last dance, for she had felt a little dizzy, a timely reminder that she was three months gone with child. She took Bernard's arm, and they walked to the far exit that led to the gardens, revelling in the unexpected coolness outside on this normally hot July evening.

They walked through the neatly groomed trails winding through the trees and bushes, all emanating a well-cared-for air. She hugged his arm spontaneously, causing his heart to quicken unaccountably at her nearness.

"Madame Claiborne is very kind," she said absently, bending to sniff at a blossoming jasmine. She felt Bernard's arms going around her, lifting her up to him, and she turned with a start of surprise to see his eyes soft with desire.

"Did I tell you already how lovely you look?" he said in a husky voice, pressing his face into her hair and breathing in the fragrance of the blossoms pinned there.

"Bernard, please, you mustn't," she said.

He sighed. "I mustn't—that's all you seem able to tell me," he said ruefully, looking down at her. "Every other woman here tonight would protest very little, if at all.

Unfortunately, it is my own fault that they all seem to compare so unfavorably with yourself. You're bewitching me, Gabrielle. If I were free, I'd marry you myself!"

"Oh, Bernard, sometimes I wish——"

"What would you wish, you little bitch?"

Both of them turned to see Rafe St. Claire standing in the middle of the path, his face carved from stone. "I'm truly surprised that you didn't accept his offer, as it seems you enjoy his company so well."

Bernard stepped easily in front of Gabrielle, his eyes taking in the fury on Rafe's face. "Now, St. Claire, you and I have been friends for a good many years. It seems to me that you are reading Gabrielle wrong in this situation. If anyone is to blame, it is myself."

"I blame you both equally," Rafe said scornfully. "I would expect this little scene from you, de Marigny, as you have a propensity for bringing agreeable ladies out into a garden for a quick roll in the grass, but——"

"I resent that!" Bernard said quickly, his Creole temper beginning to surface. "I suggest you return inside, m'sieur, and leave me to escort Miss de Beauvoir home. I will tolerate your rudeness only on the grounds that you may have drunk a bit too much wine tonight in honor of our hostess's birthday."

"And I would suggest you leave the lady, and I use the term loosely, and myself alone, de Marigny. This is none of your affair. I will dismiss your earlier remarks."

"M'sieur, I think it is my affair. I don't doubt but that you will unleash your temper on Miss de Beauvoir, and I will not tolerate it. Now, if you will excuse me, I am taking her home."

St. Claire barred the way effectively, and Gabrielle, seeing the naked rage in his eyes, felt a coldness within her. "De Marigny, you will quit us at once," he spoke savagely. "Do you think I'm fool enough to think you'll obligingly take her home and leave her to her own bed?"

Gabrielle stared in horror at the two men. She must stop this at once! They were both being dangerously stubborn. Quickly, she stepped from behind Bernard.

"Please, Rafe, don't forget that Bernard is your friend. He only—"

With a movement too quick to be detained, Rafe's hand shot out and struck her across the face. "Whore! You'll come home with me, and I warn you that what you experienced earlier today was mild compared to what you'll get tonight!"

He made a lunge for her arm, but Bernard, enraged now, caught him fairly on the jaw with his fist. "You would strike a woman, so I believe you have very little honor, m'sieur. But what is left should be obliged to meet with me tomorrow at dawn beneath the Oaks. I trust you will be there?"

Gabrielle, her hand to her bruised cheek, realized that Bernard had just challenged Rafe to a duel. "No, no! Bernard, please—you can't do this."

"Quiet, Gabrielle, please," Bernard said, striving to regain his composure. He glanced at the other man. "Do you accept the challenge?"

Rafe shrugged with amusement. "Do you expect me to fight you over a whore? I'll forget what you said, and you will leave us alone now."

"She's not a whore, St. Claire, as you well know. She's a lady, and yet you treat her little better than a servant. You're worse than a cur!"

By this time, several others had gathered, disturbed by the commotion outside. Among them was the governor himself, with Madame Claiborne close beside him. Melissa, who realized that her goading had achieved results far beyond what she had intended, laid a timid hand on Rafe's shoulder.

"Please, Rafe, take me inside now. Let's—"

He shook off her hand as he would a bothersome insect. Realizing that now she had truly lost him, Melissa stared at his back for a moment, then buried her face in her hands and sobbed uncontrollably.

"Now, see here, Rafe, and you too, Bernard, I think we should all go back inside and reason this out in a calmer atmosphere," the governor was saying.

"There is nothing to reason out," Rafe said coolly now, his anger under control. "This woman is going home with me, and M'sieur de Marigny is going to go home to his own wife."

"You'll meet me at six-thirty tomorrow morning, St. Claire, or everyone here is witness to your cowardice," Bernard seethed.

Gabrielle saw Rafe's face pale and his jaw tighten. A thick silence seemed to muffle the group—then in a low voice and bowing slightly, Rafe accepted his challenge. "All right then, shall we say swords?"

Bernard inclined his head quickly. "And as to Miss de Beauvoir—"

"I shall see to her," Madame Claiborne spoke up firmly. Leading a trembling Gabrielle back into the house, the two women left the terrible scene.

"Oh my God!" Gabrielle wept, "I can't let this happen. I—I don't understand—"

Suzette patted her hand. "We can never understand the pride and unreasoning stubbornness that cause men to kill each other in the name of honor," she said, "but unfortunately, it's part of our world, Gabrielle." She took her upstairs and helped her to calm herself.

"But if Rafe is killed—I'll—"

"He won't be killed," Suzette soothed her. "Bernard is the best swordsman in New Orleans, but he's not a vindictive man. He'll most likely wound him just enough to call an end to it. I've never known him to duel to the death. A spurt of blood—this will satisfy him. And perhaps it will put some sense into the man you so obviously love."

"But Rafe, is he not an excellent swordsman?" Gabrielle demanded.

Suzette shrugged. "He is," she admitted reluctantly. She smiled suddenly to herself. "I must admit, it should be an entertaining match."

Gabrielle stared at her in astonishment. How could she be so carefree about it? Somehow, her thoughts turned

back to something someone had said a long time ago.
What was it?

Almost unwillingly, Lafitte's voice came to mind. . . .
"I hear his sword is nearly as swift as de Marigny's. Ah,
now that would be a duel to watch. . . ."

Chapter Thirty-four

Gabrielle lay sleepless in the bed in the Governor's
House on Toulouse Street, not even a block away from
her own house. She looked at the clock—five-thirty. She
rose from the bed and paced the room frantically, conjuring up thoughts of Rafe lying dead on the ground—the
father of the child whose life quickened beneath her breast.
Or Bernard! Could she live with the thought that she had
been the cause of his death?

Making up her mind quickly, she threw off the nightgown that Suzette had given her and hurriedly dressed in
the clothes she had worn the previous evening. With
stealthy swiftness, she slipped down the hall and downstairs, out into the kitchens where the cook and two
maids were already awake, yawning sleepily over coffee.

Once out in the street, Gabrielle raced towards her
house, praying that Rafe would still be there. She arrived
breathless and with a stitch in her side, gasping as she
pounded on the door. A yawning Jane opened the door
and stared at her mistress in surprise.

"What—what time is it?" Gabrielle asked hurriedly as
Jane helped her inside and off with her cloak.

"Just a little before six," Jane answered.

"Where is Mr. St. Claire? Has he not been here at all?"

Jane shook her head. "No, should he be? I thought you
had decided to stay at Fairview when you didn't return,"
Jane said, watching Gabrielle don her cloak once again.

"What am I to do, Jane?" she demanded of the girl. "The father of this child may be killed today. I've got to stop the duel!"

Jane, struggling to understand the situation, came up with an idea. "Hitch the wagon, Will!" she called to the stableboy, then turned to Gabrielle. "The wagon is a lot faster to hitch up than the carriage, and Will can still drive you to The Oaks in twenty minutes."

"All right, but hurry, for goodness' sake!"

Gabrielle ran after the boy, her cloak flying out behind her. Jane watched them go with a worried frown and a few minutes later heard the wagon rumble through the carriage gate.

"Can't you go any faster, Will?" Gabrielle asked presently.

He shook his head. "Not through the streets, but we'll make better time when we hit open country. Just keep your patience, ma'am."

After what seemed an eternity, she asked, "Are we getting close?"

He glanced warily at her. "Pretty close. Another couple miles, and you'll be able to see the tops of the oak trees."

And what would she see beneath them? she wondered unsteadily. A thin ray of sunlight parted the fog, and then another, until the grey shroud had completely disappeared. Now they were in a field of long grass. Off to the right, she could see a copse of oak trees and six or seven figures moving around. Oh, God, she was in time! They hadn't begun yet.

Will pulled the wagon to the edge of a large oval of hard-packed earth, and Gabrielle jumped down quickly, nearly losing her footing in the still-slippery grass. She found better traction on the oval of earth and ran, lifting her skirts. She could make out the tall, unmistakable figure of Rafe St. Claire and the shorter one of Bernard de Marigny, both standing as though at attention while a man between them was saying something in a low voice. Nearby, a short, stout man with a decided paunch and a large bag appeared to be a physician. Two other men stood close to the duelists, listening to the man in the middle. After he had finished talking, both men looked at each other and shook their heads slowly. Gabrielle was close enough to call out, and she stopped for a moment to catch her breath.

"Rafe, please wait!"

She could see his green eyes, mocking, indifferent, graze her quickly before turning back to Bernard and the other man. He was handing them their swords now, and the stronger rays of the sun glanced off the points of steel as the two men grasped the weapons.

"No! Please wait," Gabrielle sobbed, feeling tears streaming down her cheeks.

Bernard whispered something to the mediator, and he nodded, then glanced at the sky as though reminding him that the duel must begin soon. Bernard walked to where Gabrielle stood, staring at the scene in disbelief as she struggled to pull herself together. He caught her arm and brushed back the tangled hair that blew about her face.

"*Chérie,* you should not be here! Get in my carriage immediately and pull the blanket around your shoulders."

She shook her head. "I'm all right, Bernard, but I must stop this duel at once. I won't have you both duelling over me. Please, you've got to understand, Bernard!"

He shook his head firmly. "I'm sorry, Gabrielle, but my honor is at stake as well as your own, now. I can't back out."

She looked at him piteously. "Please, Bernard, if you care for me—don't do this thing."

He would not answer her. "I must go back now, my dear."

She caught at his hand, forcing him to look at her. "Bernard, I—I must tell you—I must ask you. . . . You won't—Is it over at the first sign of blood?"

He looked at her impatiently now. "Do not ask foolish questions, Gabrielle. This is a matter between men, and they are waiting for me."

He was going and she must tell him—no matter the cost of her own pride.

"Bernard, listen to me," she whispered quickly even as he walked away from her. "I am going to have his child, Bernard!"

He stopped as though jerked by invisible strings, then turned and looked back at her in disbelief. "Gabrielle, are you sure? You are carrying his baby?" He was holding her arms now, shaking her a little.

She nodded. "I'm three months pregnant."

He paled noticeably, and then she saw the anger flood his face and the steely quality come into the blue eyes. "Why didn't you tell him, Gabrielle?" She could not look at him then. "You couldn't tell him because you were afraid to, weren't you? Afraid he wouldn't believe the child was his?"

Still she would not look up, and she felt him release her. There was nothing more she could say, and he walked back to where the others were waiting. Her eyes met Rafe's green gaze and their coldness chilled her to the bone. She could see murder there and something else that she couldn't quite fathom.

Her heart nearly stopped beating, and she stood there silently, unable to tear her eyes away as the mediator placed the two men some paces apart. They both took off their coats and stocks, handing them to their seconds, then poised themselves for the signal to begin. A pistol shot rang out in Gabrielle's ears, and she watched as the two men came closer, circling each other warily as the others hurried to get out of their way.

They parried and thrust in slow rhythm that resembled an exercise drill, and she realized that they were both merely getting the feel of their swords, gauging the other's strength and weakness. Every fiber of her being cried out to these two men, and she felt as though she must run between them and stop this carnage. But of course she could not run to them—all she could do was watch and wait.

The sun was getting higher now—it was going to be

another hot day. The clang of steel rang out faster and louder—or was it just her imagination? She heard the wheels of a carriage in the distance, and then another. Two more men with their puffed egos ready to do battle for some imagined slight to their honor, she thought in disgust.

Now, in the clear light, she could see the soaked shirts of both men clinging to their backs. They were well matched—neither would give ground. It would be a duel of stamina, she thought, for surely one of them would slow soon. They both appeared to size each other up, and then a particularly fierce thrust by Bernard was parried by Rafe, and both men were shaken by the force of their clash. They backed off again, circled, and came together and again backed away.

Bernard suddenly seemed to spring to life as he executed a series of thrusts, fences, and parries that caused the waiting duellists to murmur approvingly. Rafe's agility was the only thing that saved him as one of the thrusts whistled close to his side, and he sprang away with lightening speed. Bernard thrust again, and Gabrielle could see Rafe flinch as the tip of the other's sword nicked him at the shoulder. A fine point of blood beaded on his shirt and then streaked down his sleeve. The mediator held up his hand and stood between the two men.

"Blood has been drawn. M'sieur de Marigny, M'sieur St. Claire, do you wish to call the duel satisfied?"

Rafe gazed coolly at his adversary and shook his head. Bernard shrugged and did the same. The man backed off and once more gave the signal to begin.

Again the watching, the search for an opening began, and Gabrielle could only look on, asking herself why they had not stopped the duel. I love you, Rafe, she screamed soundlessly. I want you to see your child one day and be proud of him. She was unaware of the tears splashing on the ground in front of her, or of Will, who had come up silently behind to offer her comfort should she ask for it.

The duelists continued, and the sunlight was steaming now, causing Gabrielle to shrug off the cloak that she wore. How many minutes had gone by—perhaps fifteen, twenty?

The whole of Rafe's left sleeve was red with blood, and still he fought on, coolly, logically, waiting for an opening in his opponent's guard. The moment came when Bernard slipped after a thrust that caught him off balance, and Rafe struck his sword deep in his shoulder, jarring off the collar bone. A spurt of blood instantly dyed the front of Bernard's shirt, and, once again, the mediator stepped between the two to ask them if they should call their honor assuaged. Once again, both men shook their heads.

As they circled once again and continued the graceful, almost elegant movements, Gabrielle felt as though her mind would no longer accept this tragedy that was unfolding. She could see that Bernard was slowing down, his fluid movements becoming clumsy, less true—and Rafe, too, was becoming tired, missing his thrusts completely too many times.

Rafe stepped forward quickly with a sudden snakelike movement that caught Bernard by surprise and his sword only just came up in time to deflect the other's blade, but then Rafe disengaged before Bernard could adjust his grip again, and the point flew downward ripping into Bernard's thigh.

Bernard screamed with pain, and anger suffused his face as he thrust hard at Rafe who had half-turned, waiting for the mediator to break them apart again after this third drawing of blood. The point of Bernard's saber struck Rafe's shoulder blade, and, in surprise, Rafe looked back at Bernard for an instant before falling backwards to the ground. Bernard was instantly on top of him, his sword pressed to his opponent's throat, his arm tensed.

Gabrielle could see the almost eager wildness in his face as he pressed his sword closer. No one moved, and Rafe still wore a look of cold disbelief on his face. Gabrielle heard a woman scream and realized that the sound came from her own throat.

"No! No! Bernard, you must not kill him, for God's sake!"

She was running now, disregarding Will's frantic attempt to grab her by her skirt or the other men's disapproving looks. Gabrielle was beyond coherent thought—all she knew was that, with one more stroke, the man who had awakened her to womanhood, who had made her his mistress, who had planted a part of himself within her, would be dead!

Rafe was looking at Bernard's face still, completely disregarding the woman, who stopped three steps away to implore Bernard to withdraw and call his honor satisfied.

"Gabrielle, you should not have come. Now go away," Bernard said, not taking his eyes off the man on the ground, or his sword from his throat.

The other men were all staring at Bernard now, waiting for him to end it, but still Bernard hesitated. Finally, in a voice hard with anger and pain, he said, "I could kill you now, St. Claire. I could run this sword through your throat and that would be an end to you—but, unfortunately, we have been friends a long time and—I have never before killed a man in a duel. Then, too, there is the woman to think about."

Rafe's green gaze did not falter as he looked into Bernard's face. "She has nothing to do with the outcome of this," he said quietly.

"She does!" Bernard cried out, pressing the point of his sword so that a bead of blood appeared at the tanned throat. "She carries your child, you fool!"

Not by a flinch or a movement did Rafe signal what he felt at this announcement, but Gabrielle saw his eyes darken incredibly so that they seemed almost black.

"I could kill you, but I won't," Bernard began, "if you will promise to marry Gabrielle de Beauvoir immediately."

A harsh laugh broke the tense stillness in the air, and Rafe's amused expression infuriated Gabrielle. "Marry her? For Christ's sake, de Marigny, have you lost your reason? She's nothing—she'd sell her favors to any man who knocked at the door. Jesus, how do I know the little bastard she's carrying is mine?"

He was stopped abruptly by increasing pressure on the

sword, and a trickle of blood rolled down his neck and pooled slowly on the ground.

"You'll marry her, St. Claire, or say your prayers—if you believe in God!"

It seemed that the scene was frozen for a moment, with no one moving or making a sound. Gabrielle was aware only of Rafe lying on the ground—willing to die, incredibly, before honoring her child with his name. It seemed that an eternity went by, and she could see the sweat pouring from Bernard's face. Rafe's in comparison was cool and detached as both men stared at each other.

Finally, Rafe's voice broke the silence. "I hardly see that marrying her will assuage your conscience, de Marigny. But neither can I see forfeiting my life for such madness."

"You will marry her, then?" Bernard pressed.

"I'll marry her."

Looking relieved, Bernard took the blade from his throat and stood up with difficulty, his leg obviously paining him greatly. The doctor bent quickly to examine it.

Meanwhile, Rafe rose unsteadily to his feet.

Gabrielle started to go forward timidly to offer whatever service she might be able to render, but was stopped abruptly by the look of withering contempt Rafe gave her.

"It seems you are to acquire a husband, mademoiselle," he said, his voice scornfully mocking her. His eyes swept over her figure as though seeking the truth of her pregnancy. "And I," he went on, his face showing amusement now, "am acquiring a family."

Gabrielle thought she had never seen his eyes so like twin emeralds as he gazed unwinkingly at her, and she wondered what Bernard had done to her.

PART FOUR

Destiny Fulfilled

Chapter Thirty-five

Suzette Claiborne stroked the rosy cheek softly as she leaned over the bassinet, then straightened up and smiled at the infant's mother. "He is beautiful, Gabrielle," she said, noting the appropriately proud expression on the other's face. "And motherhood agrees with you, my dear," she went on, her dark eyes sweeping over the curving hips and upthrusting breasts.

"Thank you, Suzette," Gabrielle said, tucking the blanket around the sleeping infant. "Little Paul does love compliments, and at only a month old!"

Suzette sighed and slipped into a chair. "It's hard to believe he's already a month in this world. It seems only a few days ago that you and Rafe were attending the Christmas Ball at the Governor's House and I looked up to see your white face as you clutched the table. Goodness, that's a memory that will stay with me for a long time, I grant you!"

Gabrielle smiled, too, at the memory. "I just refused to believe that he was going to be early," she said as though to herself—and another memory pushed itself into her thoughts, of another baby born before its time. "It was rather frantic that night, wasn't it?" she laughed deliberately.

"Of course, I should have known that Rafe would be his cool, practical self even in the face of such an unexpected situation. There he was taking you upstairs and directing one of the governor's aides to fetch a doctor! Poor Dussault never did get over the imagined slight."

Gabrielle remembered the hours of interminable waiting and the pain that encompassed her totally before Paul André St. Claire finally made his appearance on a chilly Christmas morning. She had been surprised at Rafe's insistence on staying beside her, his gentle encouragement when she was in the worst throes of despair. It hurt her to think that, even after that, he could still be sarcastic and mocking with her at times, almost indifferent. But at least he had never questioned the paternity of the little boy, who from the first had looked just like his father.

"How are things going in the city?" she wondered aloud, realizing that she was neglecting her guest.

A thoughtful frown crossed Suzette's lively face. "Things aren't really good, Gabrielle," she began in a subdued voice. "I worry about dear William sometimes for he works hard enough for two men, and that group of idiots called a senate is openly hostile to any suggestions he has for trying to catch Lafitte and throw him in jail. You've heard about the terrible news at the Temple?"

Gabrielle shook her head.

"Well, the first of the year, handbills were distributed all over the city announcing another auction at the Temple. The auction was to be held on January 20, and over four hundred slaves were being offered for sale. William nearly had apoplexy when he heard about it and appealed to the customs office to do something about it. The collector of customs sent a small force to stand guard at the Temple, and we all thought that Lafitte had finally been outfoxed."

"And? He was—captured?"

Suzette shook her head violently. "Word came only two days ago that Mr. Stout, who was temporarily doing duty as an inspector, was killed and two others fatally wounded during a foray with Lafitte and his companions!"

"Oh, no!" Gabrielle said, wondering just how far Lafitte would go.

"But what's worse," Suzette continued with the air of one imparting rather sensational news, "is that the auction was a complete success! All the slaves were sold, and Lafitte made enough money to continue greasing the palms of the legislature! I tell you, William nearly smashed his fist through the wall of our bedroom when he heard the news! If things go on as they are now, this mess will be the death of him."

"Oh, I'm sorry," Gabrielle said. "Is there nothing that can be done?"

"William wants to call a meeting with some of the American merchants and bankers and select a friendly grand jury to send out indictments against both the Lafittes and their lieutenants. I don't know if it will work, but something has to be done. Lafitte sends armed men with every consignment of contraband goods now, it's said, and there is absolutely no way to stop him, given the lackadaisical air of the legislature."

"And as though this thing with Lafitte weren't bad enough," Suzette continued, "the English have convinced the Indians to display hostility. William has sent repeated requests for assistance, and they have gone virtually unanswered. General Flournoy says he can afford no more than seven hundred men to concentrate in the entire state! I'm telling you, my dear, if it weren't for our brave General Jackson, I don't doubt we'd have been scalped before now!"

"Rafe told me about his routing of the Choctaws at Horseshoe Bend," Gabrielle said swiftly.

"Six hundred Indians were killed and the rest scattered," Suzette said proudly. "Ah, they say Andrew Jackson is a real man. Tall and lean, and a fearless warrior!"

"Let's hope he can help us with the English if it comes to that. The governor needs all the support he can get now."

"I must say, my dear, your husband may be a scoundrel when it comes to women, but he is one of William's staunchest friends, and sometimes I just don't know where we'd be without him."

Gabrielle felt pride blossom in her breast. "He believes in what the governor is trying to do," she put in. "I only hope they can both come through this trying time in one piece."

Suzette echoed her hope fervently. She got up, loath

to leave her friend, but saying that she had guests coming for dinner that evening and had to get back to the city. "I'll expect you to visit and bring little Paul the minute you're allowed out of the house," she said fondly, drawing her cloak about her as Gabrielle accompanied her downstairs and to the waiting carriage.

Gabrielle was sitting near the window, the baby at her breast, when she heard her husband's familiar step outside the nursery. She turned her head to welcome him, her heart beating faster as always when he entered the room.

"Rafe, you're back early tonight," she said, feeling awkward as his eyes travelled to the suckling babe.

He sauntered over to her chair and bent down to take her lips, his mouth drawing every ounce of sweetness from her so that she closed her eyes in abandon.

"Christ, I feel jealous of my own son," he said with feeling, letting his eyes fasten on the round globe of her breast.

Gabrielle flushed, thinking that it had been a long time since they had been together in the big bed.

"Tonight, kitten, I'm not taking no for an answer. I have an idea your doctor enjoys seeing husbands suffer." His eyes flashed down at her and his mouth twitched in sarcasm. "I didn't marry you just to be the mother of my son," he said wickedly.

His maleness was so powerful, Gabrielle thought she could melt in her chair. He desired her and made no bones about his wanting her physically, but he had never told her that he loved her, and she was certain that he had amused himself in other arms when she was confined with the baby. The thought caused her waves of jealousy, but she swallowed her pride painfully and made no mention of it to him.

The first few months of their marriage, he had treated her like a whore to be used at his pleasure with no thought as to her feelings, but his anger had finally worn down when her belly began to swell with the child. When Paul was born, Bernard de Marigny had visited the manor, and there was a tenseness in the air when the two had met, but it did not take long for them to settle their differences, and Gabrielle had breathed a sigh of relief when Bernard left, smiling merrily in true Creole fashion and shaking Rafe's hand with genuine fondness.

"I had to forgive him," Rafe had laughed later that evening, "after all, he came away from the duel with a limp from the wound in his thigh, and I had nothing but a few more scars to show for it." Then he'd looked at her wickedly, "And an obstinate wife, of course."

Now as his gaze bored into hers, she thought she would never love him more than she did at this moment. Words choked in her throat, and she lowered her eyes so that he couldn't read their expression. If only he would tell me he cares for me even a little, she thought wistfully, planting a light kiss on her son's forehead. When she had laid him back in his crib and had spoken to his nurse, she followed Rafe to their room.

"Suzette Claiborne was here today. She told me that things haven't been going well."

His face born an enigmatic expression. "She told you about Lafitte's latest exploit?" he asked. "He's got to be stopped. As it is, legal trade and commerce in this area are virtually at a standstill thanks to his illicit smuggling." He strode around the room, his hands clasped behind his back.

"I'm sure—I'm sure he'll not escape much longer," Gabrielle said soothingly. "Lafitte may be clever, but—"

"Ah, yes, you of all people should know how clever he really is," he interrupted sardonically.

Gabrielle paled but brought her chin up. "That was a long time ago, Rafe, and I don't see how bringing up the past will—"

"Christ! I'm sorry, kitten," he apologized unexpectedly. "It's just that I'm so wound up in this whole damn mess, and when I think that he and you—" He stopped and was at her side in four quick strides. "Damn you! You're surely the most beautiful woman I've ever known—and the most maddening!"

He caught her to him and pressed her backwards in his

arms, kissing her almost savagely, hurting her mouth so that her lips felt bruised when he released her. Her head whirled dizzily, and she clung to him for support.

"God, I want you, you little witch!" he said passionately, his hands going to her shoulders to pull down her dress.

"Rafe, dinner will be ready soon. The servants—"

"To hell with the servants, woman! You're as ready for me as I am for you! Dammit, now be an obedient wife for a change!"

She was powerless to resist the expert hands, the masterful kisses, and she let him undress her, then lay her on the bed, her whole body awakening to sensations she had not known for a long time. He was not gentle with her, and she did not want him to be. His mouth and tongue evoked shivers in her flesh, his hands caressed her, stroked her. Her nipples grew taut in his lips, and her whole body felt on fire. His knee parted her thighs and she arched upwards as he entered her, driving so hard that she gasped in pain.

Her arms clung to him, and she was unaware of the room or where she was—she knew only this man whom she loved more fiercely than ever, this man who could make her whole body scream with desire, he who was her whole being. The pleasure washed over her in waves, and she heard herself moaning, calling his name. His mouth tortured her sensitive breasts, and she rolled her head from side to side, her nails digging into his back.

She opened her eyes to find his gaze on her, cloudy with desire, intent on achieving his own ends, but willing to bring her along on the crest of his pleasure. He prolonged the act until she could barely stand it, trying helplessly to stifle her passionate cries so that her teeth sank into his shoulder. Her hair was damp on the pillow, her whole body a white-hot core of passion that built to an incredible crescendo as her movements grew faster, willing him to assuage the ache in her.

There was no one else in the world for her at this moment, only this man whom she hated and loved and fought for and against, who knew how to draw every drop of reserve from her nature and reduce her to a half-mad, passionate woman, as abandoned as any whore, and just as shameless in her need. He brought her to the peak of frenzy, and she cried out in fulfillment as the culmination was reached.

He lay on top of her, breathing rapidly and planting kisses on her cheeks and neck. She lay silent now, trying to put her disordered thoughts back into place. Her eyes flew open, and she pulled his head down to her mouth, kissing him with a sweetness that was exquisite in its simplicity. When he moved away, she saw the inscrutable expression on his face as he gazed down at her.

"Christ!" he said a little shakily. "If motherhood does this to you, I've a mind to keep you with a full belly every year!" He was teasing, but there was a serious note in his voice that disconcerted her, and she flushed in embarrassment.

"I—I just wanted to make up for lost time," she said with a trace of impudence.

He grinned lazily, his head supported on one elbow as he played with a tendril of her hair. "Kitten, you certainly did just that!" The curl felt like heavy silk as it slid through his fingers, and, unexpectedly, he pressed his lips to it in a gesture that nearly unnerved her with its gentleness.

Her mind screamed her love for him, and she fought against the need to tell him, but she folded her lips, and the moment was all the more bittersweet for having been lost.

He got up from the bed, grinning. "All this exercise has made me shamefully hungry," he said, laughing a little as he put his breeches back on.

Gabrielle sat up, pressing her hands to her hot cheeks. "I—I don't know if I can face the servants after what they must have heard!"

At the dinnertable, Rafe resumed his talk of Lafitte and the governor's troubles. Gabrielle listened dutifully enough although her mind kept slipping back to the passionate interlude in their bedroom—an episode that Rafe seemed so easily to put out of his mind.

"Kitten, if you're bored by all this talk of war, please don't sit there as rigid as a soldier and pretend to be interested," she heard Rafe admonishing her sternly.

She shook her head, blushing at being caught. "I am interested truly, Rafe, but I—I had something else on my mind."

She thought he must be able to see her thoughts, for a wicked grin shaped his sensuous mouth as he leaned towards her, his eyes sparkling. "You're blushing, Madame St. Claire," he whispered insolently. "Are you already hoping, perhaps, for a sister for Paul?"

"Perhaps," she answered boldly.

He sat back with a wide grin on his face. "Ah, woman, you are lucky to be married to a man who is fond of children."

"And you are lucky," she said impudently, "to be married to a wife who enjoys making them."

He laughed uproariously. "You're getting as bold as that handsome Suzette Claiborne," he said arrogantly. "I've a mind to keep you out of her company!"

He continued to smile fondly at her; then, as though with an effort, he set his mind once more on other things. "Word came today," he began seriously, "that Napoleon has lost a big battle, you could say a crucial one. The battle was fought last October at Leipzig, and he was defeated decisively by as many as two-hundred thousand allied Prussians, Austrians, and Russians. I'm afraid it looks as though this is truly the beginning of the end for the 'Little Corsican'." He frowned as his fingers began a soft drumbeat on the table. "The worst of it, unfortunately, is yet to come. More and more French are fleeing to New Orleans—the fools don't realize that we're fighting the same enemy they are! New Orleans will be glutted with refugees in a few more weeks. Shanties and makeshift houses are going up faster than anyone believed possible, and all that miserable humanity jammed into such squalid surroundings bodes ill for the other citizens. Looting, robberies, even murder are steadily increasing—not to mention disease and filth. The sewage canals can't handle everything that's being dumped into them." He shook his head. "Claiborne's got a bigger problem than Lafitte and even the British on his hands unless he can convince some of the people to move out of the city. By summer, the pestilence could reach epidemic proportions."

"All those poor people—perhaps I could do some volunteer work for the sisters of the Ursuline Convent. I could distribute food or clothing—or just give comfort to some of those poor women." Her violet eyes looked hopefully at Rafe, but he shook his head deliberately.

"If you think I'd let you put yourself in danger for them, you're crazy," he said. "No, you'll not offer your services in that area. I don't want to see you hurt."

She veiled the emotion that showed in her eyes as he went on aggressively, "You're the mother of my son, kitten, and in spite of everything else, I care enough about you to protect you from as much unpleasantness as possible."

When she looked up, their eyes locked for a moment, each of them trying to read what was in the other's.

Chapter Thirty-six

"They've arrested Pierre Lafitte!"

The words were on everybody's lips, muttered in the streets and in gaming rooms and whorehouses. A platoon of dragoons had been sent to scour the usual haunts of the Lafittes and their lieutenants, and Pierre had actually been arrested in the street near the Place d'Armes! Orders had also gone out for the arrest of Jean Lafitte, Renato Beluche, and Dominique You. The Creoles could not believe that the governor had actually been so bold as to carry out his threats.

"He's asking for trouble!"

"Lafitte won't stand for having his brother sent to jail!"

"Sauvinet's money will get him out before the week is over!"

The populace could not believe that this man, the brother of the powerful and terrible Lafitte, could actually have been arrested and locked in the strongest cell in the calaboose. Bail had been denied, and everyone waited, wondering what would happen next.

What did happen shocked nearly everyone—or at least everyone in the governor's retinue—for a few days later, John Randolph Grymes resigned from the office of district attorney and announced that he and Edward Livingston, an attorney highly regarded in the city, had undertaken the defense of the Lafitte brothers. The Creoles, not to be caught napping, smiled slyly to each other as though to say I told you so, for it was common knowledge that although both men were among the most distinguished members of the Louisiana bar, both were Americans— and Americans would do anything for gold.

Gabrielle was aware of the burning anger in her husband, noting the strained tenseness in her face, the impatient attitude he took with everyone, including herself.

"Damn Grymes!" he muttered one evening in August while he was dressing for a dinner at the house of Bernard de Marigny. "And damn Livingston! I can't believe he would do such a damn-fool thing, despite the money! Well, dammit, they'll not get Pierre Lafitte out of prison with their honeyed lawyers' phrases!"

Gabrielle dressed carefully, willing herself to keep silent, knowing how easily the slightest careless word might set fire to Rafe's volatile temper. She looked curiously at herself in the mirror, wondering if she was still as attractive to Rafe as that day almost five years ago when they had first looked at each other in the hallway of Alexandre de Chevalier's house. Certainly, in the eight months since Paul's birth, she had regained her supple figure, the waist as slim as ever, the stomach flat and smooth, the breasts still impudent beneath her chemise. Why, then, when Rafe looked at her, did she sometimes see anger, distrust in his eyes? Did he think he had been cheated?

It still nagged her that he was more often than not ungentle with her, and tenderness was a rare thing between them these days. She supposed that she could attribute most of this to the worries of the war and Lafitte, but it rankled that she could not tell him of her love for him.

Rafe looked over at his wife from his position by the window and saw her looking reflectively at herself in the mirror. What was she thinking, he wondered? He shook his head and turned back to stare outside. He had always been a man sure of his women, but this woman who was his wife—she was the only one who could make him feel as though he were not getting the last word. His feelings towards her had undergone a change that he could not comprehend.

Christ! He wasn't going to fall in love with her and make an ass of himself! And then there was this mess with the Lafittes and his new position as aide to Governor Claiborne, a post he would not have accepted if he hadn't been urged by his wife. His shipping business was stagnant, anyway, with the war going on, and so Gabrielle had reasoned that it would be a good thing to keep him busy. Goddammit! Behind those wide, innocent eyes lurked a woman of iron, he had begun to suspect.

When they made love, he always felt that she was holding something back, keeping something from him. Oh, yes, he was satisfied, more so than with any other woman he'd ever known, but with his sixth sense, he knew that she held back just the tiniest bit—that she was forcing herself to hide something from him.

His conflicting emotions had driven him away from Gabrielle, it seemed, and, on top of everything else, Melissa had shown up. The silver-haired witch was married. She was Mrs. Nicholas Beauville now—and a more dull or boring husband wasn't to be found, she complained. Rafe and she had accidentally met on Royal Street, and she had persuaded him to come to her town house for a drink. One thing had eventually led to another, and it had taken considerable restraint on his part not to skewer the bitch in her own bed, but his conscience had won-out, and poor Melissa was left, panting abuse at him while he made quick his escape. She was a sly little weasel, though, and they seemed to run into each other too much for it to be mere accident. It was hard enough not to give in to her wiles without this jumble of emotions he felt for Gabrielle stirring him up.

Hell! He'd almost give up the whole mess and return to the life of an outcast if it weren't for his son. He smiled proudly to himself, hardly believing that he could feel this strange outpouring of love for one individual. Love was somehow alien to him, a thing reserved for children to feel towards their parents before their disillusionment twisted the feeling to pity. There were times when he would walk into his son's room and see Gabrielle bending over him affectionately, playing with him, laughing at his attempts to talk back to her, and a feeling like none he'd ever known would wash over him so that he would nearly start to shake from its intensity. Because of this unfamiliar weakening, he knew that he was even more brusque and sarcastic with his wife afterwards and he hated himself when he brought that hurt, uncomprehending look to her face.

"Rafe, I'm ready."

Gabrielle's voice, cool and composed, floated over to him and he turned to look at her as she waited for him in the doorway. Christ, she was beautiful! Her blonde hair with just that touch of red in it gleamed in the curled coiffure, sparkling with tiny brilliants. The perfect figure, outlined so maddeningly in the exquisite gown she had had made especially for tonight, was shown to full advantage, from the low neckline to the draped skirt that fell so gracefully from the sash beneath her breasts. Her eyes, dark-violet and slightly tipped at the corners, looked back at him steadily.

He bowed and made his way to her, bending so that his lips brushed the swell of her left breast. "Lovely, kitten. I'm proud of you—very proud, Mrs. St. Claire."

Gabrielle felt her heart quicken. Why, why was it that he could topple her reserve with just one word or gesture? She trembled when he took her arm possessively and hoped he wasn't aware of it. At the bottom of the staircase, they waited a moment for the carriage to be brought around, and she looked up to see his eyes on her, speculation in their green depths.

"It—it should be a lovely party," she said to dispel any uncomfortable silence.

He nodded. "I'm sure Bernard is as proud as a peacock to be chosen chairman of the legislature's defense committee. He's a good man—they chose well."

The ride was relatively short, and in no time, Rafe was handing her out of the carriage and escorting her into the Maison de Marigny where lights shone in every window and the gay music of the Creoles sounded pleasantly in one's ears. Bernard's face seemed aglow with pride and laughter, and Gabrielle waited to greet him, her eyes glancing quickly off his wife, Anna, who stood like a sour scarecrow next to him, her dark features pressed into an impatient expression.

"Gabrielle, my dear, allow me to present you to my wife, Anna," Bernard was saying, clasping her hands and pressing a kiss to her cheeks.

"How do you do, Mrs. St. Claire?" Anna replied formally, her hand as cold and lifeless as a dead fish.

"A pleasure to meet you, madame," Gabrielle murmured, hurrying to move on. Goodness! No wonder Bernard looked elsewhere for pleasures of the flesh!

Behind her, Rafe was clasping her lightly about the waist, guiding her farther into the room full of milling, buzzing people. She could barely breathe in the heavy, moist air and sought refuge next to a window, where she fanned herself energetically while Rafe disappeared in order to greet some acquaintances.

"Lord, it's hot in here!" Suzette Claiborne exclaimed, coming to stand next to her friend, her dark hair damp with perspiration. "What a dreadful night for a party, no?" she said fitfully, nearly collapsing on the bench next to

Gabrielle. "Such a shame that Bernard couldn't have been appointed in the winter."

Gabrielle nodded agreeably. "He's so pleased with himself, I haven't the heart to tell him how stifling it is in here."

After a time the orchestra began tuning up, and, as though that were a signal to the heavens, it suddenly started to pour down rain. Within a few minutes a heavy deluge had begun, cooling things down considerably.

"I'd better get back to William. I'm sure we'll be expected to begin the dancing."

Gabrielle watched the brilliant red of her dress disappear into the mingling throng, and she searched impatiently for Rafe's tall figure. A flash of vivid blue appeared at the corner of her eye, and she turned slightly, frowning a little, to see the figure of Melissa Beauville approaching on the arm of her new husband.

"Oh, Gabrielle, my dear," she trilled, deceptively sweet. "Are you looking for your handsome husband? I'm afraid the poor darling's been bombarded by the governor and his other aides, all talking the same thing—war and Lafitte." She laughed again, irritatingly. "Goodness knows I tried to get his attention, but it look as though he prefers the company of those dreadfully boring men tonight."

Nicholas Beauville, who seemed terribly ill at ease, bowed swiftly to Gabrielle, then negotiated his reluctant wife over to another part of the ballroom. Gabrielle watched the couple with anger and pity, wondering idly what kind of marriage they must have together. She maneuvered her way through a score of people who sought to detain her for a moment until she reached her husband's side.

"Rafe, the dancing—it's about to begin."

Rafe seemed not to hear her as he listened eagerly to the news being imparted by another of the governor's aides. For lack of anything better to do, Gabrielle hung onto the group, catching snatches of conversation.

"Pierre Lafitte's been sick for days now—dysentery. Christ! His cell smells like a nigger pen. The guards have to slosh it down with buckets of water every night, or else gag from the odor!"

Gabrielle blanched at the conversation, her mind recalling the happy, gay Pierre she had known a long time ago—a Pierre who hid his wisdom and his sadness behind the cloak of the buffoon, in deliberate contrast to his younger, smarter brother.

"And what of his brother, Jean?" Rafe wanted to know.

"In hiding. We've checked at Pierre's mistress's house, but those *griffes* are close-mouthed about the whole thing. Look at us like we're the criminals."

Dear, sweet Marie, Gabrielle thought, pretty, young, and so kind to her. She was soon to bear another child to Pierre, their second, and she must be overcome with fear and grief to see her lover in such a horrible place. The memory of her own stay in a prison cell brushed her mind with frightening black wings for a moment, then it receded as she fought down the encroaching nausea.

"W-why must you keep him in heavy chains?" she asked in a small voice.

Several curious pairs of eyes turned to look at her. "What, madame?" one of them asked politely.

"Pierre Lafitte—if he is ill, helpless—why must you keep him manacled inside his cell?" she asked again, carefully avoiding her husband's cold gaze.

Dussault shrugged. "Why, madame, Pierre Lafitte is a dangerous prisoner, a man capable of murder to free himself from his cell. We must keep him chained for the protection of the guards."

Dussault cleared his throat uncomfortably and would have spoken again, but Rafe suddenly pushed his wife away from the group, nodding his apologies for her interruptions. Once in a fairly secluded corner of the room, he grasped her arm and turned her sharply to face him.

"What in hell is the matter with you?" he thundered, nearly shaking her in his anger.

She glared back at him. "I can't help it. I think it's terrible, disgusting, to keep a man in chains when he is obviously ill! How can you treat him like an animal?"

Rafe gritted his teeth and stood still for a moment, obviously trying to regain his control. "Listen to me," he began carefully. "It is none of your goddamn business what we do with prisoners of the state. It comes as no surprise to me that you choose to stand up for your former lover's brother so bravely, but, for God's sake, must you make a fool out of me in the process?"

Gabrielle eyed him warily. "What are you talking about? No one has the least idea that I—"

"Well, I don't give them long to suspect something with your ill-timed remarks, madame!" he interrupted savagely. "Why—why can't you be like other women," he continued caustically. "Why must you have a brain that can work against her own husband—a tongue that's too busy wagging to realize what she is talking about! Kitten, I think I could cut off your head and do very nicely with the rest of you!"

"I'm sure you could, Rafe St. Claire!" she cut in quickly, shaking with anger at his crudeness. "But, then, any woman would do!"

He glared ruthlessly at her. "Exactly," he said with a cold finality. Then bowing, he walked away from her.

Feeling suddenly drained, Gabrielle experienced a sinking sensation as she watched him walk away. Oh, how she hated him when he acted so superior to her—as though a woman couldn't think as well as a man! Well, she would certainly show him that she could do just as well without him, she thought, and, in a huff, she moved towards the center of the crowd which had begun to part for the dancing.

Bernard and Anna and the governor and Suzette began the first dance. The music soothed Gabrielle's high-strung nerves and she found herself gradually relaxing. When the dance was over, she eyed the man to her right rather boldly and hoped that he would ask her to dance.

"Mrs. St. Claire?" the light-haired man bowed smartly over her fingers.

"Another American, how charming!" she said lightly, letting her eyes glance at him teasingly.

"Why, don't you remember me, ma'am? Leigh Owens. I'm a great friend of your husband's." There was amusement on his face now.

Gabrielle carefully concealed the surprised embarrassment in her reaction and smiled engagingly. "Well, Mr. Owens, are you going to ask me to dance or not?"

When the music stopped, Bernard claimed her, and she settled back to let him guide her through the next figure.

"Where is Anna? I don't see her," she wondered idly.

He shrugged, and she could feel the tensing in his arms. "She went upstairs, complaining of a headache—an excuse she seems to rely on more and more lately."

"She—she did look a little unwell," Gabrielle put in quickly, hoping to soothe his injured feelings.

His smile returned. "Gabrielle, you're sweet," he whispered in her ear, taking the opportunity to tickle it with his tongue.

"Bernard!" She tapped him lightly on the arm. Then more seriously, "You must be terribly excited about your new commission."

"If I'm terribly excited at the moment, it isn't because of that commission," he put in boldly.

She couldn't help laughing.

"A Creole never gives up," he admonished, releasing her when the dance was over.

She looked for Rafe in the crowd and frowned to herself to see him dancing with Melissa Beauville, the two of them seemingly engrossed in their own private conversation. Why must he insist on hurting me, she wondered, knowing how I dislike that woman?

As the evening wore on, the champagne began to flow more freely, and several of the youngest couples slipped out into the gardens to pay homage to the goddess of love. Gabrielle kept a sharp eye on Rafe, who had gone back to his conversation with the other aides, and she breathed a sigh of relief. Melissa, however, not to be turned away so easily, was hovering near him, her ice-blue eyes intent with purpose.

It was quite late when Rafe felt her hand slide softly

into his. "You promised me another dance, dearest," she said lightly, pulling him away.

"'Lissa, where's your husband?" he asked her, even as he let her bring him out to the dance floor.

"Oh, Nicholas doesn't care too awfully much for large gatherings," she said airily. "I believe he's in Bernard's study with the governor and a few others, talking about the war—what else?"

"If so, then I suppose I ought to be in there with them," Rafe said musingly.

She laughed. "Don't be silly. There must be someone left out here to amuse the ladies."

At the end of the dance, she fanned herself energetically, glancing towards the double doors that led into the gardens. "The rain has stopped, darling, and I'm dreadfully hot. Would you mind awfully escorting me?"

She looked all promise, all invitation. Rafe gazed at her boldly, then let his eyes sweep the room, noting Gabrielle's absence from the gathering.

"I believe your wife went upstairs at Bernard's request to look in on his wife," Melissa said, following his eyes. "Are you worried she might berate you for strolling through the gardens with me?" she challenged him brazenly.

The green eyes hardened. "Of course not," he said and led her through the doors, feeling the warmth of her breast against his arm.

Gabrielle, coming downstairs from her errand, saw the two of them just as they disappeared into the velvety darkness outside. It took her a moment to recover her composure before she purposefully strode towards where Bernard was lounging against the wall in conversation with Suzette.

"Anna seems genuinely not feeling well, Bernard," she said quickly. "I made a cold compress for her and directed one of the servants to press it on her forehead and temples."

"You're an angel," Bernard said approvingly. "Suzette and I can both agree on that."

Suzette laughed. "You know how hard I've been trying to get her to join in some of the volunteer work," she said. "We can use an extra pair of hands, filling the soup bowls and binding up sores for those poor refugees. So many of them pouring in and living in such ghastly conditions—it makes me sick to dwell on it." She shuddered.

"I promise to talk to Rafe again," Gabrielle said quickly.

Suzette pressed her hand and took her leave as one of her other friends beckoned her toward a small group of ladies.

"Where's your husband?" Bernard asked casually.

She shrugged. "Somewhere about," Gabrielle responded just as casually.

They stared at each other for a moment.

"I saw them, too," he said finally, and Gabrielle bent her head. "They've been out there long enough," Bernard continued, taking her hand. "I think it's time you reminded your husband of his obligations."

"Oh, no, Bernard, I—"

"Nonsense. I'll come with you."

He steered her inconspicuously towards the garden doors, and they walked outside, where the air after the storm was once again thick and damp. They passed several couples clasped in varying degrees of embraces, and Gabrielle's eyes began to search in some alarm.

"Rafe, Rafe, please don't stop now, lover. I need you."

The urgent cry brought both of them to a sudden halt, and Gabrielle seemed turned to stone. She and de Martigny were hidden from the unsuspecting trysters by a screen of mulberry bushes, and Gabrielle stepped forward blindly to peer through the leaves. The vivid blue dress had fallen discarded, crumpled in a heap in the grass. A white body lay on the ground, squirming beneath her husband, who was still dressed, his breath ragged after the struggle with Melissa.

"Goddamn you, you bitch! Get your clothes on before someone comes out and finds us here," he panted, trying to trap her flying arms. "I don't fancy a duel with your suitably outraged husband."

"You could kill that milksop with a single stroke," she flung back at him. "You can't fool me, Rafe St. Claire— you're worried about that whining whore of a wife of yours!"

The smack of his hand across her face sounded inordinately loud in Gabrielle's ears.

Melissa laughed sarcastically. "She's got you—you!— wrapped around her little finger," she spit at him. "Wagging your tail like a dog when she's near—don't you think she has her own lovers?"

"Shut up, Melissa, shut up!"

Gabrielle saw him fumble with his breeches, and she closed her eyes.

"Damn you for a bitch, but there's only one way to shut your filthy mouth!" he snarled.

"Yes, yes. Oh, yes, Rafe! Harder, harder!"

The sound of their sweating bodies moving against each other nearly made Gabrielle sick, and she turned away, leaning against Bernard.

"Gabrielle, let me—" he began in a low voice.

She shook her head. "Don't say anything, Bernard. Leave them alone," she managed as they walked away.

She felt as though she would faint or just stop breathing, anything to wipe out that horribly animal scene. Bernard led her to a secluded bench away from the house and took out his handkerchief to wipe her face.

"Men are bastards sometimes," he said quietly.

Gabrielle was silent, her head resting on his shoulder as she took deep breaths of the sticky air. They sat there, unmoving for a long time, until Bernard made a move to rise. "Come on, my dear, I'd best get you back to the house."

She looked up at him and her expression was curiously soft. "Bernard," she said steadily, "kiss me."

Bernard stared at her. He was an old hand at these games, but he didn't like playing them with this woman. She would only be using him to assuage her anger at what she had just witnessed.

"Gabrielle, let's go inside," he said gently, taking her hand.

But she slipped away from him and then faced him squarely, her face close to his. Her arms went about his neck, and she brought his lips down to hers, kissing him slowly and thoroughly—the embrace aching in its sensuality. Bernard pressed on her shoulders, aware that this was dangerous ground and that very soon he would not have any control over his actions.

"A Creole never gives up," she mocked him, softly. "Show me how the Don Juan of the city misbehaves with a willing woman," she breathed in his ear, interspersing her words with flicks of her tongue.

"I'll not have you using me or shaming yourself like this, Gabrielle," he said, but the sternness was no longer in his voice, and his arms were drawn around her now, pressing her hard against him so that she could feel the proof of his interest.

In one fluid movement he was pushing her down to the wet grass, his hands going to her bodice, slipping beneath the gown to cup her breasts, which were hardened with desire. He kissed her again, taking the lead himself now, giving himself up to this woman-flesh that he had so long desired and hungered for.

She let him lead her breathlessly through a sensual haze, aware of his hands peeling her gown from her shoulders, his mouth enveloping the tips of her breasts, his maleness probing at her thighs. In the back of her mind, she could picture again the white female body and her husband's above it, kissing, caressing.

She hated Rafe! She hated him, and she would pay him back twice over for his infidelities!

The moist air felt heavy on her thighs, and she realized that Bernard was raising her skirt so that it lay crumpled around her middle. His lips and hands on her caused a low moan to escape her throat, and she arched towards him, impatient.

"Soon, soon," he murmured, his face close to hers now, his mouth taking her lips with practiced artistry.

Sudden, raucous laughter close by nearly caused her to

jump up in alarm, her mood effectively shattered. Both
she and Bernard heard the crunch of boots on the gravel
and watched through the enveloping leaves as a man and
woman walked by—Dussault and some lady friend, chattering merrily about some inane experience.

When they had passed, Gabrielle looked at Bernard,
stricken at what she had allowed to happen. "Oh, Bernard," she sobbed suddenly, "I'm so—so ashamed!"

Bernard, struggling against his sexual urge, took a few
moments to gain control of himself, then stood up, settling
his clothes into some order. "Nothing happened, Gabrielle,
nothing," he reminded her.

"But I forced you—I—we almost—oh, my God!"

He laughed harshly. "You didn't force me into anything, my love. It will be my eternal regret that that fool,
Dussault, happened by when he did, and that he is the
owner of such a penetrating laugh." He wiped his sopping
brow and reached down to pull her skirt over her legs.
"A sight too lovely to bear," he said jerkily, helping her
rise and straighten her gown.

Gabrielle was nearly incoherent by this time, and Bernard looked around helplessly, unsure of how to deal with
this woman's tears. "I'll find Suzette," he said, patting
her hand awkwardly and hurrying out.

Gabrielle sat down on the bench sobbing heartily until
Suzette rushed up with Bernard close on her heels.

"Here she is, Suzette. You—you must do something!"

Suzette strove to keep the laughter from her voice.
"Gabrielle, are you crying because you have been left un-
assuaged, *chérie?*" she questioned. "For Bernard has
already told me that the—um—culmination did not tran-
spire. Come now, pull yourself together. Goodness, if
every woman did this after a flirtation, we'd have all the
women in the city going around nervous wrecks!" She
proffered her handkerchief, and Gabrielle wiped her face
gratefully.

Bernard exited gracefully, and Suzette put her arm
around Gabrielle. "Come. I'll take you upstairs through
the kitchens, and we'll see what we can do about pressing
your gown."

"Oh, you don't understand, Suzette! Rafe—I saw him—"

"Hush, my dear. There's no need to relate your personal matters to me."

They entered the house and hurried upstairs, where Gabrielle undressed and Suzette called for a servant to press the wetness from the gown.

"I can't believe I would do such a thing," Gabrielle murmured.

"You'd been hurt," Suzette interjected. "A woman whose feelings have been wounded as yours had knows no ease of mind until she has paid back the debt in full."

It was several minutes before the servant returned with the gown, fairly crisped and almost completely dry. Gabrielle donned it quickly, checked her hair, and wiped her face, drying her eyes before the two women prepared to return downstairs.

At the landing, they could see a knot of people, Claiborne and Bernard among them, questioning a stranger who, by the look of him, had ridden furiously from far away. Cries, frenzied questions, and loud voices had turned the ballroom into a hubbub of noise.

Suzette, with Gabrielle in tow, made her way to her husband's side. "What—what has happened?" she asked fearfully.

William Claiborne looked pale and terribly concerned. "My God, Suzy, the bastards have fired the Capitol! Washington City is destroyed—President Madison fled just in time! God help us now."

Chapter Thirty-seven

Gabrielle wiped her brow and stretched the muscles in her back, then glared up at the sun that remained so pitiless in the cloudless sky, shining down with an intense heat that was enough to drive anyone to the closest stream.

Her eyes returned to the ground and jumped from one anxious face to another, all those faces turned towards her and the few other women volunteers, seeking comfort from them when they were nearly too tired to give it.

In the week that she had been helping Suzette's small task force in their volunteer work, she had come to know some of the women refugees, watched their tight faces sorrowing over a sick child, crooning to a husband depressed by an endless day of seeking work or lodging.

The day after Bernard's ill-fated ball, she had informed Suzette that she would be glad to do whatever she could. She had not told Rafe until the following day when he questioned her where she was going. His face had nearly exploded in rage.

"I told you—I don't want you down there with that filth and disease. Do you care so little for your son?" he demanded angrily.

She flushed for a moment, then jerked her chin up in determination. "I'll be careful," was all she said, and she hurried out to the waiting carriage, leaving Rafe to nurse his anger alone.

But he hadn't too much time to do so, for it wasn't long before British vessels appeared in the Gulf of Mexico, boldly parading the waters, like stalking tigers waiting for the right moment to spring on their prey. The naval threat had the whole city in an uproar, and Claiborne was hard put to keep order in the streets. An armed guard followed the women volunteers now, for many people would not hesitate to rob them of the food and clothing they carried with them.

Gabrielle gazed, exhausted, at the nearly empty basket of produce she carried on one arm. A few more oranges and celery stalks remained, and she signalled the men to follow her down the road to where a tiny village of hovels had sprung up in the months since the refugees began arriving. She stopped first at the shanty of a woman she had come to know.

"Hello, Céleste. How are the children today?"

"They complain always of the heat," she laughed, "as

though they had never before felt the sun on their backs. I tell them to go fishing for their dinner and take a swim." She selected a piece of the celery, her fingers pressing knowingly for the tenderest stalk. "This will be good in the soup, no?"

Gabrielle agreed. As she was about to leave, the woman caught her sleeve. "We have some new arrivals," she said. "A highborn lady by the look of her. Poor thing, she was too proud to accept my invitation to dinner, and her looking as though she's about to drop that baby in her belly pretty soon. I fairly begged her to have just a little, but she smiled and said that she was sure her husband would find something for them to eat." The woman sniffed disdainfully. "That one she calls her husband—I saw him this morning, daydreaming in the grass while she tried to collect firewood. If he were my husband, I would kick his backside and tell him to do the work!"

"Where is she?" Gabrielle asked, steeling herself not to flinch from the duty that was more painful to her than any other. Talking to ladies of the aristocracy depressed her almost unbearably, for inevitably they would talk about their days of pomp and riches, going back over and over to remind her that they were titled folk and couldn't understand why they were treated in such slovenly fashion in America.

Wearily, she walked down the road in the direction Céleste had pointed out, to where she could make out a lean-to propped up against a young sapling. A woman crouched over a fire, blowing softly on it. There was no sign of a man anywhere.

"Good afternoon, madame," she said in the cheeriest voice she could muster.

The woman did not look up, obviously thinking the greeting was for someone else, and Gabrielle moved closer, noting the dullness of dark hair that had once been soft and shining. Even seen in her crouched position, the woman was clearly far along in her pregnancy, possibly eight months or even more.

"Madame," Gabrielle began again, putting out her hand gently. "Let me help you."

The woman started, looked up, dark eyes slowly widening in her pinched face. Gabrielle dropped her basket, and she felt as though a hand was squeezing her chest. Tears appeared in the woman's eyes, and she struggled to stand up.

"Gabrielle! Gabrielle! Oh, my God, Gabrielle!" the woman babbled, crying and swaying as she leaned forward.

"Isabel!" Gabrielle could hardly believe her eyes. "Isabel, is it really you?" she cried, clasping her in her arms.

The two women wept unashamedly for some moments before Gabrielle finally recovered herself. "Isabel, I can't believe that you're here! How—when—?" Her eyes darted from the woman's thin neck to the woefully distended belly, beneath a dress that was none too clean and had been torn in several places.

Isabel looked as though she were about to collapse at any moment, and Gabrielle helped her to a stool, the only piece of furniture that she could see.

"Gabrielle—what—what are you doing here?" Isabel gasped. "How did you come to be here? I thought—they told us that you—"

"Hush now," Gabrielle soothed her, realizing that Isabel probably hadn't been told the truth about her departure from France so long ago. "I live here, Isabel," she said simply. "I'm married."

Isabel seemed not to hear her, for her eyes had sharpened perceptively as they stared at her gown and the fine-kid shoes she wore. "You—you didn't come over with the others," she said. "You don't live in this wretched place, as I do?" Her tears were bright and uncomprehending as she looked up at Gabrielle, confused.

Gabrielle, her heart breaking at her friend's grief and ignorance, placed a comforting hand on her shoulder and made a quick decision. "Isabel, I'm going to take you home with me. Where is your husband? Where is—Henri?"

Isabel seemed to jerk forward, and then her face broke into little pieces as she once more let rain a torrent of tears. "Henri, oh, Henri!" she sobbed into her hands.

Gabrielle looked at her uncomprehendingly. "Is he all right?" she asked quickly.

Isabel shook her head violently. "He's dead, Gabrielle. He died on board ship during the Atlantic crossing," she said, struggling for control. She wiped the tears from her face with a corner of her skirt and took a deep breath. "Henri and I left France when Napoleon abdicated in April," she began quietly now. "We left with friends and tried to take as many valuables as we could, but it was hard to get organized because of the frenzy of people scrambling to get away before the Prussians and the British took over completely. I was quite—quite ill during the voyage, as I had recently found out about my—pregnancy. Then—" and here her voice shook again and tears threatened to spill down her cheeks, "then a bad storm hit us. The captain was very brave and managed the crew spectacularly, but everyone was so frightened. Some of the passengers—the men—were asked to help relieve the crew at their watches during the night. Henri—Henri was k-killed by a falling mast on the second night of the storm." She gulped and for a moment her eyes were stricken by the remembrance. "We came to New Orleans and lived near the docks for a few weeks, but—but one night a man tried to break into our room and besides— our money was—gone."

"Oh, my poor Isabel," Gabrielle said. "My dear Isabel." Where was the vivacious, laughing girl she had known in Paris? "Your parents?" she asked, dreading the answer.

"My father was killed at Leipzig. He insisted on fighting, despite his age. Maman died shortly before we left France. I'm glad she wasn't here to see this."

There were so many questions that Gabrielle wanted to ask her. What about Aunt Louise? Was she well? And her husband—she *had* a husband, yet Henri was dead. The question formed on her lips when a voice broke through her inner turmoil.

"Isabel! What are these soldiers doing here? Christ, don't tell me we're in trouble with the law now!"

Gabrielle turned, and her eyes met astonished grey ones. The blond hair, the athletic build—it couldn't be, but, yes, on top of everything else—it was Charles! He was looking from her to Isabel who stood now and was smiling almost happily.

"Oh, Charles, look who has found us. It's Gabrielle, it really is!"

"Gabrielle!" the name came out on an explosion of sound. "Gabrielle de Beauvoir? But—she's dead!"

Gabrielle found herself shaken by the words and the deliberate way in which he said them. "Of course I'm not dead," she said quickly. "I'm here in New Orleans. It really is me, Charles."

He still looked dazed, distrustful. "But word came that your ship, the *Lillias*, was sunk. No survivors were reported."

Gabrielle didn't stop to wonder how he knew of such a thing but concentrated on convincing him that it was truly she. "You're both coming home with me," she said matter-of-factly. "I'll not have Isabel, in her condition, exposed to all—all of this."

"You live here?" Charles frowned, and Gabrielle could see the cold look in those grey eyes. "I suppose you'll be taking us to some new little hovel, as wretched as all the others we've been in." His voice was sarcastic, "Please, don't do us any favors."

Gabrielle grew angry at his hardheadedness. "Then stay here if you like. Isabel is coming with me, Charles. I can make her comfortable and put some good food into her. What can you offer?"

She gazed contemptuously at him, and his knuckles tightened as his hands balled themselves into fists.

"I'll find work. I've already applied at the Cabildo for a job in the governor's guards. I'm sure they can use a fine soldier."

"And what is Isabel to do in the meantime—have her baby here on the grass?" Gabrielle wondered disdainfully.

Charles looked almost murderous, and Gabrielle was amazed at the animosity that had so naturally sprung up between them. Isabel was getting to her feet, pushing her way between them. "Enough of this nonsense," she said sharply. "Charles, Gabrielle is an old and dear friend! I love her like a sister, and she is offering us her help." She gazed at Charles with a beseeching look, and he shrugged.

"Do as you like, then."

Isabel glanced back at Gabrielle. "It seems I do remember that you and Charles never did get along," she said musingly.

"I'm not going to let that stop me from taking care of you," Gabrielle said firmly. "Get your things together, and I'll come back in a few minutes with my carriage."

When she returned, Gabrielle saw that Isabel had tied into neat bundles what pitiful belongings they had. On perceiving the elegance of the carriage, Isabel's eyes grew rounder.

"My goodness, Gabrielle, it seems you have done quite well," she said softly. "Whom did you marry, my dear, the governor of Louisiana?"

Gabrielle smiled and shook her head. "Not quite."

Their belongings were strapped to the carriage, and Charles and Isabel climbed in to sit opposite Gabrielle, Charles' face anything but friendly, and Isabel still looking rather dumbfounded.

"It seems like years since I've ridden in a carriage," she said, a hint of her old humor returning.

"Well, don't get too excited," Charles put in sourly. "It's not as though it's yours, my dear."

Gabrielle hated to see the effect his words had on Isabel's countenance. How in the world had Isabel ever married Charles de Chevalier? Why had she chosen him?

As they drove away from the city, Isabel filled her lungs with air. "Lord, I've gotten so used to the stench of that canal, I hardly realized what clean air smelled like."

"We live out a little from the city, but Rafe says that fairly soon the city will expand to meet us," Gabrielle replied. "He's probably not home now—he has duties as one of the governor's aides, but he'll arrive in time for supper. He'll certainly be surprised to see you!"

Surprised was probably not the word, Gabrielle thought. She wondered just exactly what his reaction would be. Surely he would recall Charles as the son of the man who had financed his smuggling venture in Paris. She wondered what kind of reception Rafe would give them.

"It's—it's really breathtaking!" Isabel exclaimed, her eyes bright with growing excitement as the carriage rounded the drive and stopped in front of the door to Fairview. "You must be quite wealthy, my dear," she added archly.

Charles was silent, his eyes going slowly over the graceful architecture.

"Come inside," Gabrielle urged. "We've plenty of room, as there are only Rafe and I and Paul—"

"Paul?" Isabel wondered, taking the steps slowly.

Gabrielle blushed for a moment under Charles' surveillance. "Paul is my son. He was born last Christmas."

Isabel pressed her hand delightedly. "Congratulations! So you're a mother before me!"

They walked through the impressive hallway and into the sitting room, where Isabel seemed rather loath to sit on any of the chairs. Charles immediately sprawled in the nearest one and looked for all the world as if he belonged there.

"For God's sake, Isabel, it's not as though you've never known a house like this before. Christ, we've only been away from France for six months!"

Isabel's face tightened. "That's true, of course, but even in France we—that is—poor Henri was in some rather dire financial straits," Isabel returned.

"Can I get you something to drink?" Gabrielle intervened, fearing an outburst.

"Some tea would be Heaven," Isabel answered.

"I could use a good, stiff whiskey," Charles added.

When she returned with the tea, Gabrielle could sense

the tension in the air. She handed the cup to Isabel, whose eyes were reddened considerably.

"Gabrielle—you've been more than kind—bringing us here—and—offering your help, but—but Charles insists that we cannot accept your charity," she got out with difficulty.

"Charles, you're a pompous fool!" Gabrielle spat at him, her violet eyes dark with frustrated anger. "Because of some silly pride, you would put Isabel's life in danger!"

A nasty smile appeared suddenly on his face. "And you, my dear, are still the little spitfire, defying me every step of the way." He looked over to Isabel significantly. "I've missed that in a woman."

Gabrielle fell silent, watching him with mingled rage and repugnance. Charles walked about the room and finally came to stand next to the window, looking as though he were surveying the property for a price.

"All right, then," he said finally. "If you are so insistent, we'll accept your hospitality, but only until I find employment and am able to find our own lodgings."

"Of course," Gabrielle managed, hating him for the way he had invariably twisted things so that it seemed she had been obliged practically to beg him to stay. She beckoned to Isabel who had sat silently through the discussion. "I'll show you to your room."

The two women left Charles, who watched them speculatively for a moment, then shrugged and walked back to the sideboard to refill his glass. Once in Isabel's room, Gabrielle called for a maid to bring hot water, towels, and soap.

When the girl had gone, Isabel turned to her friend, a weary smile on her face. "I keep thinking that any moment I'm going to wake up and I'll be underneath that little tent, slapping those damned mosquitoes and willing to give anything for a cool drink of water," she said soberly. "It really is true, isn't it, Gabrielle?" She hesitated. "It really is you?"

Gabrielle nodded. "Yes, it really is me, and you're here

with me in my home now. I'm going to take care of you until that baby makes its appearance."

Isabel sank into a chair, feeling its material idly with her fingers. Her dark eyes were cloudy with memories, and she looked up at her friend almost warily.

"It's not going to be the same—is it?" she said wistfully. "I'll never again be able to picture you as that innocent little girl, blushing at my ribald stories of love and dreaming about balls and escorts. I'm not the big sister any more, the strong one, leading you around by the nose on all my little escapades." She stopped and shot a look that was part grateful, part pleading. "You were the best friend I ever had, Gabrielle. When they told us what happened—that you had been charged with treason! I didn't know what to think! I knew you were incapable of so foul a deception, but—but—when Henri and I arrived in Paris after his campaign, there was—nothing—I—could do." Her voice slowed as she relived the frustration and anger she had experienced. "I grieved for you and asked Henri if there was anything to be done, but we found that you had already left France, exiled forever. We—we didn't even know where they had taken you! But, then, I had so many things to occupy my mind," she ended. "I—I suppose you blame me for not—for not trying harder to find out what had happened to you?"

Gabrielle lowered her eyes. "I hated you for a while," she said simply. "I thought about everything you had—a home, wonderful parents, a devoted husband—everything you could have wanted, and I pitied myself for having nothing."

Isabel's laugh was harsh. "And now justice has been done," she said wryly, "for the tables have surely been turned." She looked at the other girl steadily. "And did you think I had completely forgotten you?" she half-whispered.

"I didn't know what to think. Everything was so hushed up and done so quickly."

"Well, at least everything has worked out well for you."

"Yes—it has," Gabrielle responded quietly, thinking of

the *Lillias*, Jean Lafitte, Barataria, and Renée's whore-house—everything that had brought her to this point.

"I must admit—I am looking forward to meeting your husband, who must love you very much."

Gabrielle blushed and turned away. "Your bath should be here momentarily," she said to hide her sudden discomposure. "I'll leave you to relax while I search for something for you to wear."

She half-fled from the room and the whirl of emotions that Isabel's sudden words had evoked. ". . . who must love you very much. . . ." How easily the words sounded on the tongue, but how very different it was in the world of reality! she thought sadly, her mind unwillingly remembering the whiteness of Melissa's body in the dark. She had never mentioned the incident to Rafe, hating herself for her cowardice, but even to say that hateful woman's name made her cringe.

She called one of the maids to go up to the attic and bring down to Isabel the trunk that held the clothes she had used during her own pregnancy. The maid dispatched, Gabrielle went downstairs, remembering that she had left Charles alone in the sitting room, a disquieting thought somehow, as though she had invited a burglar to dine with them.

As she expected, Charles was still lolling in the chair, his shirtfront stained where he had spilled a little of the liquor. Obviously, he had been imbibing freely, for his manner was loose and his mouth already a little slack.

"I think, perhaps, you would like to see your room now, Charles. You can bathe and rest before dinner, if you like."

He eyed her blearily. "Are you my mother to order me about?" he inquired nastily. "I'll thank you not to give me orders, madame."

Gabrielle gazed at him worriedly. Perhaps she ought to call the majordomo to help her with him. She had turned to go when she felt Charles' hand on her arm, pulling her down to sit beside him.

"The years fall back quickly, don't they?" he wondered.

"This could be my father's house and you and I in the sitting room there, the old antagonism stronger than ever. I would ask you if you were frightened of being alone with me here, and it would goad that fiery temper of yours. We would have a battle with words, both of us knowing how easily I could silence those tempting lips, close those candid eyes—"

"Charles, you—you can't look backwards now. This is not your father's house. It is my house."

He laughed again. "So it is, so it is. And so you may order me about as you wish and tell me to go to my room when I displease you. You could lock me in my room for disobedience, or send me to bed without my supper."

Gabrielle stared at him, at a loss to explain his words. "Charles, don't be silly. You're a man, and I—"

"Am I a man to you, Gabrielle?" he cut in savagely. "I haven't experienced the feeling for a long time, you see. After Leipzig, after I saw my men cut down like dogs, there was nothing I could do, you do understand. I was a great soldier, a brave man—but I ran. I ran like the worst coward. I ran because I didn't want my shining brass buckles to be shot off, my new white uniform to be soiled by my own blood. I ran from the enemy! I let my men be killed by those cursed Prussians!"

He was nearly in tears now, but still his hand was hard on her arm, forcing her to listen to his agonized tale. "I ran until I came to a wagon of wounded men, and I pushed one of them out to make room for myself." He glanced fiercely at her. "He would have died anyway, and, I reasoned, wouldn't it be better to save an officer—a man who could lead them into battle once more? After all, men in the rank and file could be had anywhere—could be bought for the price of a pair of boots. But the funny part about it was that the man was not a footsoldier, and he didn't die, you see. He lived, and he was not one of those toads whose guts are spilled on the battlefield every day. He was a captain, my dear, and he was determined to see me thrown out of the army in disgrace!"

Gabrielle couldn't bear to listen anymore. "Please, Charles, you don't have to—"

His fingers pinching into her flesh silenced her. "Oh, I do have to tell you, I must tell you! I was disgraced, kicked out of the army! People shunned me, and only dear old Henri kept on supporting my case, doggedly determined that there must have been some mistake! Henri really was a fool—I told him so enough! So you see, there was really nothing else for me to do when he died on board ship—I had to take care of his wife—a woman whom I cared for very little, but in this, at least, I thought I could regain my manliness."

"Charles, it was a wonderful thing you did!" Gabrielle soothed him. "Isabel needed protection and you—"

His grin was sour. "Isabel would have done all right, maybe even better, without me. Isabel is a woman who can get what she wants easily enough. She's a whore down to her bones. What do I care about the child she has in her belly—it's not mine—and sometimes I wonder even if it is Henri's."

Gabrielle wrenched her arm angrily from his grasp. "Charles, how dare you say such evil things! Isabel was very much in love with Henri. She was heartbroken when she told me of his death!"

"Oh, a guilty conscience can just as easily cause a broken heart, my dear," he said, downing the rest of the liquid in his glass. He sighed. "Hell, what does it matter anyway. I married the bitch and will do my duty by her. Of course, I never thought you would show up like the little angel of mercy to lend a helping hand. My God! I thought I was rid of you, and now you're back to throw everything in my face!"

"Charles, I—I don't understand you. I only want to help Isabel. She's my friend and—"

"—and I am not," he finished abruptly. "Did you ever think we would meet again, my fair lady?" He stood next to her, so close that his whiskey-laden breath fanned her face.

"I never even thought about it," she returned, icy-calm.

He laughed as though she had said something terribly funny. "I'm very hurt, my darling, for, you see, you were always with me—the woman in my dreams, the woman around the corner, the whores I went to for pleasure. And I thought to myself, you're a fool, Charles, how can you fuck a dream?"

He sat back in his chair and began laughing crazily. Gabrielle stared at him in consternation, wondering if he had gone mad.

He held out his glass to her. "Another drink, if you please, little sorceress!"

She ignored him and hurried from the room to fetch Solomon to help her get him upstairs. When she returned, she found him snoring loudly, sprawled in the chair, his mouth open like a fish out of water.

Chapter Thirty-eight

"You remind me of the good little shepherdess, welcoming the lost sheep," Rafe drawled sarcastically, leaning against the bedpost as Gabrielle finished explaining the events of the day.

"Isabel would have done the same for me," she said staunchly.

His smile was overbearingly insolent. "Would she?"

Gabrielle blushed indignantly. "Of course she would. I suppose you never had a friend close enough to feel that way about you!"

He laughed. "I've had enough women to worry about feeling 'that way' as you call it, without counting on my male acquaintances."

"Oh, please, don't throw your casual flings in my face!" she shot back, her anger sparked by his smugness. "Don't you think I can guess at your disgusting habits when you're away?"

He looked infuriatingly amused. "Of course, madame. I hardly think you have to guess at my habits, as you knew all about them before we were married." His green eyes were hard as emeralds now. "I even had the notion that some of those habits weren't all that disgusting to you." His mouth quirked into a lazy grin, as he moved closer to her. "Take off your gown, wife, and let us see just how disgusting we can get."

Her eyes blazed furiously at him, twin violet stones that narrowed in outrage. "How can you possibly think that I could—"

But his hands were already on her shoulders, forcing her to him so that his mouth closed over hers, stopping her protests effectively. She fought him angrily, her mind burning with the thought of the other women he had held like this, subdued to his will—perhaps even earlier tonight! Her hands curved into claws to rake his face, and he caught them in his, his face dark with excitement as he pulled her towards the bed. She scratched and kicked, but he finally succeeded in peeling the nightgown from her shoulders so that he could push her onto the mattress.

"You—you think you can come to me," she cried out in fury, "after seeing that—that woman!"

His movements slowed as he looked down at her scornfully. "I don't know what you're talking about, damn it! You're my wife, lest you forget, and you practically arranged the marriage yourself, my dear. Now, you'll be a good girl and lie quiet, or I'll thrash you for your disobedience!"

She snarled like a tigress. "I'll not be made a fool of and then welcome you on my back with open arms," she spat at him.

He shrugged and laid his body over hers, holding her hands with his as his knee sought to gain entrance between her thrashing thighs. "Goddamn it, kitten, if I wasn't so hot with wanting you, I'd leave you for a more biddable piece!"

But she would not stop fighting him, and her movements excited him to the point where, despite himself, he forced her roughly, knowing that he hurt her, although he was aware only of his own throbbing senses.

Afterwards, breathing heavily and feeling her warm, slippery flesh beneath him, he heard the sound of her sobs, stifled by the back of her hand. He looked up, his brow lowered, not for the life of him knowing what the matter with her could be.

"Look at me, kitten," he commanded, "and tell me what the hell is troubling you!" His green eyes gazed into hers.

"H-how can you be so unfeeling," she sobbed. "You know very w-well what is the matter with me! I'm sick of y-your exploits with other women!"

He looked dumbfounded for a moment, then a guilty look stole over his face. "I suppose I should have guessed," he said quietly. "Jane couldn't keep her lip buttoned forever, but—"

"Jane!" she said, rolling from beneath him and sitting up to stare at him. "Jane!"

His face wore a disdainful expression. "Hell, kitten, it wasn't as though I raped the wench! She took to it willingly enough and from what I could tell wasn't so loath for another round!" He saw her face go livid with fury.

"You had the—the audacity to consort with a girl hardly seventeen—my servant! You're even lower than I believed," she flung at him.

"I didn't plan it," he said. "You had stayed the night in town, and I came home, a little drunk, and there she was—"

Gabrielle could hardly believe her ears and then heard herself laughing. "Jane—never told me anything," she managed.

Rafe caught her hands and jerked her still, his face brutally disdainful. "Don't be an idiot!" he said roughly. "I'm sorry, but you wouldn't have known about it if I hadn't thought—"

"And how many others do I not know about?" she

questioned him viciously. Then her expression changed, grew calculating. "I do have a lot of catching up to do with you, don't I? Dear Bernard, I'm sure I can count on him to make a cuckold out of you!" Her head snapped back with the force of his hand on her cheek, and tears started in her eyes.

"Christ, woman! You act as though I spend all of my waking hours planning which woman to take next."

Gabrielle dashed the tears from her eyes and her mouth tilted upwards. "Oh, but it would be perfect, wouldn't it, darling? Bernard and I—and then you and Melissa. I've heard how popular it is among the decadents to exchange partners and indulge in bedsport. It would make everything a lot simpler, wouldn't it?"

He flung her away from him. "You're talking nonsense, kitten," he said, making an effort to quiet his voice. "I'm sorry about Jane, but you can't blame her. I'm sure she was as surprised as I when it happened. Neither of us has ever felt the inclination to make the relationship permanent, I can assure you. As for other women—"

"Don't bother to lie," she said dully, her head in her hands. "I saw you, Rafe. I saw you with her—with Melissa."

To her surprise, she looked up to see an angered look on his face instead of the one of shock she had expected. "The woman's a bitch, Gabrielle," he said. "Her demands are insatiable. I feel sorry for her husband."

"So sorry that you feel obliged to make love to his wife behind his back?"

"I didn't make love to her," he replied in a tight voice.

"But I saw you!"

He shrugged. "I subdued her. Her temper nearly matches yours and she threatened to go to you and tell you that we'd been having an affair all the time you and I had been married. Knowing how easily you'll believe anything said against me, I assured her silence in the most effective way I know." His smile was sardonic. "But I haven't touched her since, though God knows, with your tantrums, I've been tempted!"

"You blame *me*! You can actually blame me! Don't think I believe your tale for one minute," she said quickly. "You don't love me, Rafe St. Claire, and you never will!"

He caught her in his arms. "Love? My dear wife, I never thought that had entered into our contract. Did you expect that with a few words mumbled by a priest and a gold band slipped on your finger the emotion could suddenly spring into existence? I never led you to believe that I loved you, for God's sake!"

"I'm sorry, how stupid of me," she flung back at him, feeling tears gathering in her eyes once more. "I had hoped —that is, I thought that we could at least come to care for each other for Paul's sake." Tears spilled onto her cheeks and dropped on his arms, and she could not look at him. "All these months—all this time," she sighed softly. "I should have known better—I should have realized."

Rafe, gazing at the bent head, feeling the tears on his skin, suddenly wanted to enfold that shaking body in his arms in a tender gesture that would bring her back to him. Damn! Had the girl actually fallen in love with him? A funny way she had of showing it, practically clawing his face and fighting him with all her strength when he desired her. She was a wildcat, a temptress, a mother, a regal courtesan—all of these things combined to drive a man mad with desire. Other women paled beside her, but he must fight that feeling that was threatening to engulf him—or surely, he would no longer be free if he allowed it to overcome him. But if he didn't love her, why did he have this overwhelming urge to press her against him and comfort her, to kiss away those tears and make her moan for him with that soft, keening sound that caused a man's blood to quicken in passion?

His strong, sun-browned hand came up to stroke her silky mane of hair, to push it back from her face, as his other hand tilted her chin up so that he could look into those violet pools that made a man want to drown in them. God! she had a beautiful mouth, made for a man's kisses, trembling now as she looked at him, her face wet. His two hands cupped her face between them and drew her towards him so that his mouth pressed into hers, feeling it part softly beneath the pressure. The kiss grew deeper and whirled them both into a swimming sensation that turned slowly into blissful oblivion. God, he could go on kissing her like that forever, revelling in the warm, pliant mouth that was responding so sensually to his unspoken demands. His hand swept from her hair down her arms to her breasts—such beautiful breasts, firm and uptilted, the peaks hardening with desire even before his fingers touched them.

Gently, he laid her down on the bed, letting his hands go farther down to caress the flat belly and silken joining of her legs. He thanked the heavens that she did not protest or question him now, but let herself be swept along willingly on the wave of his desire. It did not seem amazing to him that the two of them could be now so utterly joined, so fully in tune, when, just moments before, they had faced each other in mutual fury and distrust. All that mattered was this—the coming together of two splendid bodies, the soaring of two spirits, seeking an emotion, a pinnacle of shared feeling, that was surely the most exquisite music two people could experience together.

Neither uttered a word, so afraid were both of breaking the spell. And then, when she was stretched taut with desire and he could prolong his excitement no longer, they knew a rising tide of joy that brought both of them surging together in the culmination of pleasure. Several minutes passed, during which neither was sure that they should speak.

Rafe touched her cheek gently and gazed into her eyes. "Surely you know that no other woman has ever done that for me," he murmured.

She smiled almost shyly. It was not what she had wanted to hear, but it was a beginning.

Gabrielle awoke the next morning, noticing that Rafe had already risen and dressed and was probably downstairs meeting their guests. She smiled to herself, knowing that little by little she would win him now.

She called Milly to help her dress and, on a whim, chose a bright gown of yellow muslin, sprigged in tiny violet flowers. Her face was radiant as she looked at her reflection and blew herself a small kiss in salutation, then swept into the hall and down the stairs where she found Rafe and Charles seated in the library.

"Good morning, kitten," Rafe drawled lazily, letting his eyes travel thoughtfully over her shining face and sparkling eyes.

"Good morning, darling. Good morning, Charles. I do hope you slept well?"

He nodded and his satirical smile seemed to guess at the reason for her high spirits so that she blushed unwillingly. "Where is Isabel this morning?"

"Still in bed," he responded, his grey eyes jumping from her mouth to her bosom.

"Then—then I suppose I should go up and see how she is," she said uncertainly, disliking the lack of respect in his gaze.

"Charles and I were discussing the possibility of finding him a position in the city guards," Rafe cut in smoothly, aware of the tension between his wife and this man, whom he had remembered only vaguely. The man's manner irked him, and he could easily see the effect it had on his wife.

"That would be wonderful," Gabrielle replied lamely. She made her exit swiftly and went to Isabel's room.

"How are you feeling, Isabel?"

"Much better, thank you." Isabel stretched. "I'm truly ravenous, Gabrielle. Could we breakfast together here in my room?"

Gabrielle smiled. Isabel's face was still pinched and a little sallow, her hair still not shining as it once was, but these were things that would be easy to change, especially after she was delivered of her child.

"When do you think the child will be born?" she said after the maid had brought a breakfast tray.

The other shrugged. "As soon as possible, I hope. I

believe I shall have perhaps another two weeks of this, and then the little rascal should make his debut."

"It seems I was only just in time, then," Gabrielle said, sipping her tea.

Isabel nodded. "What I would have done without you I really don't know," she confided. "Oh, I'm sure Charles would have taken care of me, but—sometimes—I really wonder if marrying him was the best course of action.

"It seemed the only possible thing to do, I suppose," Gabrielle put in.

Isabel noticed the look of pity in her friend's eyes. "Oh, don't think I presume that Charles is in love with me, Gabrielle. I found out soon enough that he can't love any woman—except maybe his dead mother, who, from all accounts treated him abominably."

Gabrielle nodded. "I remember his father telling me about it." She looked at Isabel with sudden curiosity. "Did you ever find out what happened to his father?"

"I think Charles told me he died in Italy—poor man!"

Gabrielle echoed the thought, then decided to turn the conversation to something else. "They say that General Andrew Jackson is due to come here sometime in the winter. Let's hope he's not too late to stave off the British."

"He must be a brave man and a grand fighter," Isabel said. "From all reports—and news travels fast in the shanties—if anyone can beat the English, he can."

"I'm sure Governor Claiborne hopes the rumors are accurate. Suzette tells me that he is nearly beside himself with worry."

"You know the governor and his wife?"

"Of course, didn't I tell you that Rafe is one of the governor's aides? You really must get out of bed and meet my husband."

Isabel agreed and rose from the bed, dressing herself with Gabrielle's help in one of Gabrielle's maternity gowns. The two women found the men still in the library, talking of war.

"Rafe, I would like you to meet Isabel—de Chevalier. Isabel, my husband, Rafe St. Claire."

"Charmed, madame," Rafe said, pressing a kiss to the hand she extended.

Isabel's dark eyes danced. "Oh, but he's so handsome. You didn't tell me," she exclaimed laughingly.

Rafe's smile mocked her excitement, and Gabrielle saw Charles watching his wife with a cold contempt.

"Why don't you sit down, Isabel, before our host has to fight you off with a club," he said nastily.

Isabel crimsoned, then seated herself next to him, fairly subdued by his unkind words. Gabrielle cleared her throat in embarrassment, then suggested a glass of wine for everyone. They seated themselves, and Rafe resumed the interrupted conversation.

"So, we received word just yesterday that the British had asked Lafitte and his crew to join them in return for various rewards and the like. I must say I was surprised when the scoundrel wrote to Claiborne himself, asking him what he might counter with to induce him to refuse the British bribe. The man has gall, certainly, but to expect Claiborne to drop all charges against him is a bit hard for the governor to swallow."

"I can almost admire a man like that," Charles put in, draining his glass.

Rafe glanced at him with mocking contempt. "Lafitte's clever, there's no denying that, but I've an idea that he's not going to win on either side this time."

"What makes you so sure? The British might keep their promise and allow him free passage, with a trunkful of gold besides. This man Lafitte must be able to command a good deal of respect from his men, else why the longevity of his reign on Barataria?"

Rafe smiled scornfully at Charles as the man made his way to the wine bottle. "Lafitte is a murderer, a smuggler, and a robber. He makes a great deal of profit illegally at the expense of lawful business concerns in the city."

Charles turned quickly. "You have little room to talk, St. Claire, when it comes to illegal trafficking, for I do recall that you enjoyed your own large profit from smuggling—at the expense of my father's good name."

Immediately, Gabrielle's muscles tightened. This was dangerous ground, and Rafe's lids drooped over his eyes to cover the menace in their green depths.

"As you say, the profit was large, and part of it helped to finance this house—the hospitality of which you are now enjoying," he put in pointedly. "May I remind you, de Chevalier, that it was your father who came to me and asked me to help him in that particular venture."

"With the money procured from the very same woman who is now your wife, m'sieur!" Charles cried involuntarily.

"I didn't even know your father had taken the money!" Gabrielle was standing up now, determined to defend herself, but, at a scowl from Rafe, she resumed her seat.

"It doesn't matter where your father received the money," Rafe went on smoothly. "The fact remains that your father had conceived the plan some time before. The smuggling was profitable, as has already been established, but, as I am sure you will agree, it did not put a stranglehold on the commerce of France, nor did it endanger the people to whom it was shipped in the West Indies. It was Napoleon, himself, who diminished his own trade by putting up the blockade."

It was obvious that Charles was struggling within himself, and, for a moment Gabrielle saw the gleam in Rafe's eyes as he anticipated a fight. But Charles recovered himself and poured another drink calmly enough, carried his glass across the room and resumed his seat. "Well, admittedly, all this is in the past," he got out.

"We are not discussing the legality of smuggling, assuredly," Rafe went on, "but the effect Lafitte's tactics have had on the business growth of the city. He has got to be stopped before it's too late!"

"And what has Claiborne decided to do about his letter?" Gabrielle asked quickly, her curiosity overcoming her.

Rafe glanced speculatively at her, and she knew he was

thinking of a time past. "The governor has decided to give him no answer but wait it out for as long as possible. He hopes the British will get tired of waiting and be moved to action."

Charles studied his fingernails thoughtfully. "The British have greater manpower and armament strength—why don't you surrender before people are needlessly killed?" He glanced meaningfully at Gabrielle and Isabel.

"As a soldier, de Chevalier, I'm surprised to hear you say that," Rafe answered him quietly, and a dull flush crept over Charles' face.

He was about to say something, then thought better of it.

"I—I think I should go back to bed and rest awhile," Isabel said to break the silence.

"I'll escort you, my dear," Charles returned, falsely solicitous, and Gabrielle perceived the shrinking movement Isabel made at his approach.

He hates her, she thought to herself, and Isabel is afraid for herself and the baby. The thought strengthened her resolve to help Isabel in any way she could, and after they had gone upstairs, she turned to Rafe, who was eyeing her wickedly.

"You've invited a hornet's nest into our happy little home," he mocked her. His expression turned grim. "I only hope your friend produces her offspring as soon as possible and that I'm able to get a post for her husband, although with his attitude, I'm not sure I want to." He came over to her and bent to kiss her lips. There was no trace of his tender mood of the night before, and Gabrielle's heart sank.

"I'm off to the Governor's House, kitten, but I should be home for dinner."

He was out the door and mounting his saddled horse before Gabrielle quite realized he was gone. She glanced toward the upper story and wondered if, perhaps, it had been unwise to invite Charles back into her life.

Chapter Thirty-nine

Events were taking place so rapidly that Gabrielle found little time to wonder about Charles or his strange behavior. Isabel was nearing her time and was so tired these hot days of September that she could hardly move from her bed. She slept restlessly, and Gabrielle stayed up many a night soothing her hot flesh with cool compresses.

"Oh, I hate it! I hate it!" Isabel would moan, glaring at the mound of belly that was making her so uncomfortably hot.

"Hush, Isabel. I know how you feel, but it will be over soon enough."

Rafe was busy most days at the Cabildo, and he spent many nights away from Fairview, a situation hardly to Gabrielle's liking, with Charles continuing to baffle her with his actions—he drank himself to sleep many nights, and she kept her door locked.

In mid-September, Pierre Lafitte escaped from his cell, although how he could have done so was hard to explain, considering his ill health and the tight security. There was more money to grease more palms, the governor declared. Had Lafitte actually accepted the British offer?

A few days later, the question was answered in grand fashion. The British destroyed Barataria, bombarding it with the big guns on their ships. Word came that Lafitte had died in the foray. Other rumors maintained that he had escaped and was already on his way south. Still other stories circulated saying that he was in hiding somewhere in the city.

A close watch was posted on the house of Marie Villars, who was the avowed mistress of Pierre Lafitte, and all the comings and goings there were carefully observed. Marie lodged formal complaints at the Cabildo, stating that her

right to privacy had been breached—all in words too formal for anyone to doubt that they had been written by
Grymes or Livingston. So, the watch was increased, and
the complaints were filed away to be forgotten.

Gabrielle could imagine the fear and worry that must
engross Marie. She had only recently been delivered of
another daughter, and her lover, father of her two children, ill and defeated as he was, was still being hounded
by the authorities.

"Lafitte is in quicksand up to his neck now," the governor informed his aides confidently. "With the destruction
of his base of operations and his men scattered, his hand
has been played out. We only have to wait for him to
make a false move, and we'll haul him in with our own
net, gentlemen."

The citizens of New Orleans were relieved, but it
seemed sad that such an ignominious end must come to
the romantic pirate. Still, Jean Lafitte had not been captured yet, and who could tell what might happen with
the British vessels arriving, new ones daily? The poorly
equipped Americans watched with slowly descending
hope, noticing that the seasoned men of the enemy were
beginning to outnumber them three to one.

Gabrielle waited impatiently for the coming of Isabel's
baby, and she sensed her friend's growing fear. The heat
hung heavy in the city, but the atmosphere was not nearly
so bad at Fairview, where there was a breeze off the river
at twilight that served to cool the nights somewhat. Rafe
had been chosen to do some surveillance work off the
Louisiana coast with two or three volunteers, and Gabrielle clung to him anxiously, wishing he didn't have to
leave her. He would be gone on this mission nearly five
days, and the thought of enduring the heat, Isabel's pleas,
and Charles' strange looks weighed nearly unbearably on
her shoulders.

Rafe, sensing his wife's dread but not realizing the
cause of it, kissed her affectionately and caressed her hair,
assuring her that everything would be all right. "I'll be

back on Monday, kitten. I'm sure you'll do your best while I'm gone."

"Oh, but I will miss you," she said wistfully. "I'm sure you're right, but it's just this horrible heat. If it would only rain—everyone's on edge." Through misty eyes, she watched him leave, straddling his stallion and riding off down the road.

She went to Paul's room and played with him until lunch, dreading the inevitable meeting with Charles at table. As she had expected, Charles was his usual taciturn self.

"So, the brave warrior has gone riding off to save the whole city," was his first ugly comment.

"Hardly, Charles," she began in exasperation. "He has merely gone to try and find out how great the British strength actually is."

"Rather unnecessary, don't you think? After all, it's common knowledge that they outnumber us ridiculously, and our arms are sadly in need of replenishment."

"You sound so smug about it," Gabrielle returned hotly. "It seems that you are only too glad to run again from a confrontation." She regretted the words instantly.

Charles' face turned white, then red. "A low blow, madame, but worthy of your kind," he finally managed between his teeth.

"Charles, I—"

"Please don't say anything more, madame. I believe I follow your drift—you suppose, and correctly too, that I am a disgrace as a soldier, that I am a coward, hardly fit to tarnish the name of your brave husband with my tainted barbs." He shrugged. "At least cowardice has its rewards, something I was unaware of during my days of honor and glory. You see, your husband has gone off to the heat and dust and mosquitoes, while I can bask in the coolness of the veranda, enjoying female company and sleeping in a comfortable bed." He leaned towards her, his eyes gleaming. "Of course, that bed does get lonely at times due to the—incapacity—of my dear wife.

I can only hope, madame, that you, too, feel something is lacking while your husband's mind is so busy with martial affairs?"

Gabrielle blushed to her hairline, aware of the complete lack of propriety that Charles had just exhibited. "M-my husband is more versatile than you suppose, then, Charles," she responded with spirit.

He laughed, amused by her retort. "Bravo! I shall look forward to another excellent repast at dinner," he said, getting up from the table. He came to stand next to her and bowed so close that his lips brushed her forehead.

Gabrielle started back, and he smiled cruelly. "I have waited a long time."

Then he was gone, and Gabrielle sat in her chair, shocked at his behavior and supremely nervous because Rafe would be so far away tonight. Well, she would eat dinner in her own room. At least she would spare herself the ordeal of Charles.

The heat was all-powerful now, and everyone prayed for rain. Sitting in the library, trying to concentrate on her reading, Gabrielle felt a drop of perspiration roll down her neck. Rafe would be back tomorrow, and she would be so happy to see him.

Isabel was acutely miserable and this morning had been groaning softly, complaining of pains and a backache, which signaled the coming of labor.

"Mistress, come quickly—Miss Isabel—come quickly!" It was Milly, her eyes white and round in her dark face, and Gabrielle hurried upstairs to Isabel's room.

A shriek of pain erupted from that tormented face, and Gabrielle realized that the pains this morning had been actual labor and that Isabel's baby would be arriving this very night.

"Stay with her, Milly, and give her sips of water if she asks for them. Rub her back if she complains about it."

Isabel's hand grasped hers. "Don't leave me, Gabrielle, please don't leave me. I'm—I'm not very brave right now."

Gabrielle patted her hand. "There's nothing to having a baby," she assured her. "It just takes a little time, and I'm going to find Charles to ride over to the city to fetch the midwife. I'll be right back."

Isabel nodded, trying to smile, but a fresh pain seized her, and she twisted away.

Gabrielle, with a warning glance to Milly, hurried to Charles' room. He was not there, and she ran downstairs, calling him, but he did not appear. She looked out a window and saw the black storm clouds building up in the distance. She took a moment to thank God for the promised rain and then hurried to the stable.

"Good afternoon, madame." It was Charles, an empty bottle in his hand and a drunken smile on his lips. "How goes it with my sweet wife?"

"Charles, get up and throw some cold water on your face," she said angrily. "Isabel is ready to deliver, and you must fetch the midwife. Oh, I knew I should have had her stay with us this last week!"

". . . no condition to ride, I'm afraid," Charles was mumbling stupidly, eyeing the empty bottle pathetically.

"Dear Lord!" Gabrielle exclaimed, feeling the urge to smash the bottle over his head. She would have to go herself.

Leaving Charles propped up against a stack of hay, she called for the stableboy to hitch up the light gig. After one last glance over her shoulder, she was out the door and urging the horse to greater speed. She had prayed for rain for weeks, and now it looked as though the floodgates were going to let loose at any moment! She eyed the storm clouds warily.

It took her nearly an hour to get to Mistress Lila's house, and she jumped from the wagon seat just as the first drops of rain began to fall. Breathlessly, she told the woman that Isabel was in labor and needed her immediately.

"All right, all right. I'm sure she'll be fine until we can get there. Just calm down, Mrs. St. Claire, before you stir yourself into a lather."

Gabrielle waited in a chair as patiently as she could while Lila gathered up her things and tied on her bonnet.

"Mighty wind beginning to blow," the midwife said. "I hope you can get me there—and yourself—in one piece, Mrs. St. Claire."

Gabrielle nodded and helped Lila into the seat, then climbed up herself and grasped the reins. The rain began pelting down now, steaming as it hit the sun-baked earth. Then, all at once it seemed they were running through a curtain of rain. Gabrielle peered through the water, trying to avoid trees and holes in the road. It seemed hours before she barely made out the yellow lights in the windows of Fairview, just ahead. A few more minutes, and she was helping Lila Brown into the house, guiding her to the stairs and into Isabel's room from which there issued screeches and yells of pain that made her shiver.

"Get hot water and towels—and a fresh nightgown for her to change into afterwards," Lila ordered briskly.

Isabel was nearly beyond recognizing them, and her hands and feet were pounding the mattress, seeking a way to make the pain leave her.

Gabrielle dispatched Milly to the kitchen for the hot water and towels while she rummaged through Isabel's armoire for a nightgown.

In a few minutes, Milly was coming in, holding a steaming kettle in one hand and a large basin in the other, with a stack of towels laid over one arm. Gabrielle took one and positioned it as Lila instructed under Isabel's thighs.

"This one's going to be easy," Lila assured her as she leaned over and wiped Isabel's face with a wet cloth. "Ah, that's a good girl," she praised Isabel when the latter pushed again. "Yes, I can the little skull now. Harder, my dear, and we'll get a look at the angel's face."

Isabel, eager now, realizing the ordeal was nearly over, pushed again, and Gabrielle watched with a kind of awe as the wrinkled red face appeared in Lila's hands, remembering how she had beheld her son's face in those same hands not too long before. Then the shoulders appeared, followed by the narrow trunk and the fat little legs.

"Give me a towel dipped in water," Lila ordered. She used it to wipe the baby's face and mouth, and immediately a shrill wail issued in the room.

"Oh, Isabel!" Gabrielle declared, laughing and crying at the same time. "You have a little daughter!"

Isabel smiled weakly. "After all that waiting—and only a girl," she murmured. "I'll call her Henrietta, after mama."

Lila sponged Isabel's body after performing the necessary ministrations, while Gabrielle wiped little Henrietta, who was now letting out a veritable squawling.

"Hush, little one," Gabrielle murmured, "or you'll be waking Paul, and I don't think I could put up with that right at the moment."

When Isabel had been dressed in a fresh nightgown and was resting comfortably, she held out her arms for her daughter and pressed the baby to her breast.

"The milk will come in a few days," Lila assured her. "You have big breasts, and your daughter will grow fat and pink."

Gabrielle showed their guest to a room where she could spend the night, then went downstairs to inform the servants of the new arrival. She hesitated over whether or not to tell Charles. Outside the wind had become fiercer, and the rain was driving furiously. She hurried out to the stable, glad of the warmth inside.

The stableboy had already taken the horse out of the gig and had put her in her stall. Gabrielle measured out two cups of oats and poured them into the animal's feedbag. "You're a good girl, Vanity," she said, rubbing the sopping flank.

"Madame?" A hand on her arm made her spring about in panic, but she breathed easier at sight of Charles' face. "You're quite soaked," he said, his voice less drunk than she had anticipated.

"Of course I'm soaked! You would be, too, if you had

been able to ride for the midwife!" she snapped back irritably. "Now, if you'll excuse me, I'll go in and look in on your wife and daughter once more before retiring. I only came out to tell you that they are both in good health."

"A daughter? Ah, Isabel will like that. She can mold her into the image of herself."

Gabrielle wasn't sure she caught his meaning, but she made to leave him. His hand detained her.

"Don't go in yet, my dear. Can't you share a drink with the new stepfather?"

Gabrielle gazed at him narrowly. "I doubt you need another drink," she said, "and I have better things to do."

"Not before I'm finished with you," he said softly and pulled on her arm so that she stumbled against him.

"Charles, you're drunk, and I'm tired. Now, if you don't mind—"

"I told you before, I've waited a long time for this," he said ignoring her, pulling her along behind him into the farthest recesses of the barn.

Gabrielle tried to pull away from him, but his strength was much the greater. The wind was howling outside, rising in a crescendo to crash with a sudden shudder against the walls. Her cry of alarm was easily lost. Charles was pushing her into a carpet of new hay, pressing his hands to her shoulders to pin her down.

"Charles, Charles, you don't know what you're doing! Let me up instantly! Isabel will be wondering where I am!"

He laughed mockingly. "Isabel has just had a baby. I doubt that she will be wondering about anything else."

"Charles, let me up!" Her voice shook the slightest bit, and the last word was sounded on a shrill note, as his hands began tearing at the sodden cloth of her gown.

"So, you're beginning to feel fear at least. Aren't you?"

Gabrielle brought up her hands to pummel Charles' face, but this seemed to have no effect on his sureness of purpose.

"I must have you naked, my dear, I simply must,"

he said as though apologizing for ripping the front of her gown.

She cried out as his teeth bit into the flesh of her breasts, her hands trying to cover them from his seeking mouth. His fingers pinched a nipple cruelly, and she gasped at the pain.

"Charles, listen to me. You—you can't do this!"

"I'm going to have you," he repeated as though reciting a lesson. "I must have you. I must. For many years, you've tortured me, looking out at me from every woman's face I've seen, teasing me with your eyes and mouth." His hands were pushing her skirt down, inexorably easing it from her hips.

"Oh, God! No!" Gabrielle screamed again, and Charles' hand balled into a fist and came crashing down on her temple, effectively driving her into oblivion.

She came to some minutes later and felt as though the side of her face were swelling up to twice its size. Her tongue seemed to loll in her mouth like a wad of cotton, and she opened her eyes to try and focus. Images swam dizzily, and she thought she saw three images of Charles' laughing face. She shuddered and closed her eyes again. Something warm and soft was moving on her stomach and she opened her eyes again, finally able to focus them. She could see the top of Charles' head, with his face pressed into her flesh, his tongue avidly seeking.

"No, please, stop!" she said in a whisper.

"Quiet, whore! You are a whore, and I'm using you like one! I've always known what you were, you bitch! Father never knew—you had him fooled, didn't you? Trotting off to your parties and your lovers, leaving him alone, leaving me alone—but you didn't care, did you? Did you?"

Horrified, Gabrielle realized that he was seeing her as his mother, and she struggled against the nightmare that was surrounding her.

"You like this, don't you?" he asked harshly, dipping his tongue downward, forcing her thighs apart with rough hands. "This is what you want, isn't it? You greedy bitch!"

His fingernails were digging into the soft flesh, hurting her cruelly, and she thought she, too, must be going insane. She had to get away, get away from this madman! Struggling to her elbows, she tried to stop the dizzy whirling of her head.

"Charles, listen to me! For God's sake, listen to me! I'm not your mother. I'm Gabrielle St. Claire—Gabrielle, Charles, Gabrielle!"

He looked up at her, and the look on his face caused a chill to pass through her. "Gabrielle. Lovely, violet-eyed Gabrielle! I hated you for a long time," he said slowly, bringing himself up so that he could stare into her eyes. "I've hated you because you reminded me of her—just the same. I hated you so much, I wanted to kill you!" he breathed raspingly in her face. "But I couldn't destroy such beauty. I had to find another way to make sure I would never see you again."

His eyes were crafty now, as though he knew a secret that he wasn't quite sure he would share with her. He forced her back on the hay, and she could not look at those mad, staring eyes any longer.

"I thought you were gone. I thought I had finally found the way when I told them about you."

She opened her eyes. "You—told—?"

He nodded, and oddly his laugh was almost a chuckle. "Yes, you're clever, my dear, but not clever enough, it seems. I was the one who informed on you—I did!"

Gabrielle shook her head, trying to understand what he was talking about.

"Come now, don't act so stupid! I'm telling you how it happened! I was the one who told the police that you had given my father the money for the smuggling! I planted the story in their minds and added a small amount of gold to testify to its integrity. Oh, I was sure I had you then!"

Gabrielle looked at him with new loathing. "You mean you—you informed on your own father!" she said in disgust.

He nodded. "Ah, now you're catching on. Of course—oh, I admit, it was distasteful, having to relate the fact that it was my own father who was involved, but I had to do it in order to get to *you!* There was no other way." He was smiling now like a teacher who is delighted with his pupil's progress. "You see, I found out about it quite by accident. The other man who had gone in on the venture with my father had come to see him to try and talk him into rejoining after my father had decided to get out. I happened to be in the hall, and they were in the library, carelessly forgetting to close the door tight. I must admit, I almost denounced my father right there, I was so shocked that he could commit treason against Napoleon! But then I thought—what a perfect way to incriminate that little bitch who settled herself so impudently in my household, making my father jump to her pleasure in the same way my mother used to do! This was my best chance! Oh, I had to leave first to pretend to rejoin my troops, but it was easy enough to get in touch with the Paris chief of police and apply for a furlough. It took a considerable sum to get you out of the country, but it was worth it—it was well worth it, knowing the degradation I was putting you through! I even came to the prison that night—a farewell gesture, you may say! Then you sailed away from France, and I thought everything would be all right."

He stopped and she could feel the force of his hatred. "When Lieutenant Rué told me he had received word the *Lillias* had been sunk somewhere in the Caribbean, I couldn't believe my good fortune! I believed you dead!" Gabrielle shivered at the exalted tone of his voice. "But, dead, you were more devilish to me than in life! I saw you everywhere. I heard your voice. You haunted my dreams and taunted me unmercifully. I even tried to kill myself in battle once, but the wound only gave me a fever in which you came to me all the time. The hate festered in me and made me less than a man. I no longer knew how to fight, I couldn't concentrate on my maneuvers. I couldn't command my own men any more. And then, when I couldn't stand it any longer—I ran away, ran away from everything. But even then, even after my disgrace, when I thought your taunting would be satisfied, you were still with me! Four years, my dear, you were with me!"

He paused for breath, and his hand sought her breasts again, stroking them as though enjoying the texture of the firm flesh. "So you can imagine my pain and distress when I saw you again a few weeks ago! Something snapped inside of me, and I knew there was only one way to rid myself of you!"

Gabrielle felt her fright choking in her throat. He was going to kill her! She could almost feel his hands encircling her throat! He laughed, noting the fear on her face.

"No, I'm afraid I can't kill you, my dear. It does no good, you see—I've already found that out. I must possess you, possess that lovely, teasing body that I have dreamed and lusted after. For, once I know your body, you will no longer have the power to haunt me with your mystery. You will be a woman, nothing more, like any other!"

Gabrielle gazed at him with horror-filled eyes. Oh, God, she couldn't endure this madman thrusting himself into her, abusing her—she couldn't! He was fumbling with his trousers now, intent on achieving his purpose without further preamble.

With a quickness that caught him off guard, she rolled from beneath him and got to her knees. His hand slipped from her shoulder, and she stood unsteadily, willing the rolling ground to cease its movement.

But it was too late then, for he was beside her again, knocking her once more to the ground, where she began struggling against him, kicking, scratching, her nails making long gouges in his face. They struggled silently, like wrestlers, Gabrielle realizing it would do no good to scream in the face of the howling wind and driving rain. His fingers dug painfully into her ribs, her legs were tiring, and she was nearly out of breath. She was slipping gradually, she knew, but she must fight on.

Charles sensed her weakening and laughed victoriously, pressing down on her like a band of iron, squeezing her rib cage until she nearly lost consciousness again.

"Now, now, I will have you, my dear," he whispered, and in the next moment, she felt an agonizing driving deep within her, hurting her so dreadfuly that she choked on her own scream.

"I'll ride you, you whore! I'll ride you until you beg me to stop!" he said through his teeth.

"You—you animal!" she cried out, her thighs burning from the scrape of the trousers that still hung around his legs. "I curse you to hell! I hate you, I hate you!"

His hand tore across her mouth, and she tasted blood while her head whirled once more in a vortex of pain and fire.

"Damn you, bitch! I'll make you plead with me! I want to see you beg!"

It seemed he could go on forever, and she felt blood, warm and sticky, trickle onto her legs. He was going to kill her, she thought through the mist of pain. And then she thought she must be hearing things, for a voice was calling her name in the darkness of the barn.

"Here! Help me!" Her voice cracked on the last word, and Charles' mad laugh filled her ears.

"Are you crazy, bitch? No one is going to help you now! You're mine!"

She couldn't stand it anymore. The pain was surging all around her, her whole body bruised, and still he punished her.

"Gabrielle!"

It was a man's voice, heavy with pain and shock. It was the last thing she heard as she went sinking slowly into welcoming darkness.

Chapter Forty

Images flickered behind her closed eyelids. Voices far away called to her, but she didn't want to wake up just yet, she thought. If she woke up, she would see

Charles' mad face staring down at her, the apparition of
Satan himself, filling her with pain and laughing at her
misery. Pain still enshrouded her, and it hurt even to
move the fingers of her hand. Somewhere she could hear
a voice calling her again, a face moving into view, the
horrified expression mirroring her own.

"Rafe," she said softly, "how can you be here?"

But her lips didn't move with the words, and she didn't
want them to move—they hurt too much. Just let me lie
here, please, she thought. She crept back thankfully to the
waiting darkness. Still he called to her. Shut up, shut up!
Let me sleep! But he would not, and no matter how
tightly she closed her eyes or how hard she willed her
ears not to listen, his voice reached out to her—as it always would—reached her and drew her towards him.

I'm coming, damn you!

And then her eyes opened, and, before she was conscious of the pain once more, she gazed into the coolness
of green depths, and, because she was sure this was the
last time they would meet, and it no longer mattered
anyway, she whispered, "I love you, Rafe."

The green depths deepened and became darker. His
eyes did not mock her now.

"Is she conscious? Did she say something? My God,
our prayers are answered!"

What in the world was Renée doing here? Gabrielle
wondered through the pain that was rolling in waves over
her again.

"No, you're not going back again, Gabrielle," Rafe said
gently to her, supporting her head while another gentleman gave her a spoonful of bitter-tasting liquid. She
coughed once, and the movement made her ribs throb with
a bruising pain.

"Well, it looks as though we might be able to get some
soup down her. Renée, if you'll feed her, Jane can hold
the bowl," the physician was saying.

"I'm tired," Gabrielle protested, and this time her
voice was louder.

"Of course you are, my love," Renée said gently, her

eyes moist. "But you must try to get some of this broth down. It will help."

The warm liquid did feel good going down her throat. Four, five, six spoonfuls, and that was all. "Let her rest," the doctor was saying.

It seemed a long time later that she opened her eyes once more. She wondered how long she had been in bed. Her thoughts were lucid now, and, although the pain was still there like a familiar companion, she seemed to be able to bear it. Her chest still ached if she moved, but her limbs no longer sent shooting pains to her spine.

"May I have a drink of water?" she whispered, and in an instant Renée was clucking over her, offering the glass to her lips.

"Oh, my dear, I'm so glad to see you awake today. It's been nearly two days, and we've all been terribly worried about you. Is the pain still bad?"

"No. You said two days, but how—"

"Don't think about anything right now but getting well, child."

"Renée?" Her voice was still infuriatingly weak, but Renée heard her and smoothed back the hair from her forehead and looked anxiously into her face. "I'm hungry, Renée."

She clapped her hands together, and her smile of delight seemed to encompass her whole face. "Did you hear that, Dolly? She's hungry!"

Then Dolly's face was close to Renée's, and she was smiling too, her hand taking Gabrielle's and pressing it in relief. "Oh, Gabrielle, I always did say that, behind that delicate-looking exterior of yours, you were as strong as a horse."

Gabrielle watched them both with tender affection and was overwhelmingly grateful for their presence. One of the servants entered with a steaming bowl of stew, and she ate every bit that Dolly spooned into her mouth. Afterwards she felt strong enough to sit up in bed and asked that little Paul be brought to her. Holding her son's wiggling body in her arms was harder than she had anticipated.

"Where is Rafe?" she asked happily.

Renée and Dolly looked carefully at each other. "He—he was called back to the city, Gabrielle," Renée said gently. "He stayed until everyone was sure you were out of danger, but he had to go back this morning."

Gabrielle felt a cold, hard lump settle in her chest, a pain that had nothing to do with her bruises. He hadn't even said good-bye to her, she thought morosely. She was a fool, she really was a fool! In spite of everything, he didn't love her. Well, he had certainly told her not to expect it—why had she gone on believing that she could make him love her? She hugged little Paul closer to her.

Two weeks had passed since the rape, and the October air brought a blessed coolness that expressed itself in the balmy breeze that sighed through the slats in her windows. Gabrielle sat at her vanity while Dolly arranged her hair. She had mended rapidly, and now only a greenish-black crescent on her temple remained from that horrible memory. Through her conversations with Renée, she had been able to piece together the events that had occurred after she fell unconscious.

It was luck that had prompted Rafe to come back to Fairview from the city, despite the driving rain—luck, and a nagging remembrance of his wife's anxieties. As he was leading his horse into the stall, he had heard a thrashing about in the back of the barn and thought, at first, that it must be two of the servants enjoying some sport. But then he had caught the sound of a woman whimpering in pain and the demoniacal laugh of Charles as he bragged of his exploit. He called Gabrielle's name, and then he recognized her voice beneath the piercing screams of the wind and discovered the odious deed.

"You were unconscious," Renée told her, "but de Chevalier was continuing his crazed passions until Rafe jerked him backwards by his collar. He was stronger than Rafe reckoned and landed a blow along his jaw that dazed him long enough to enable de Chevalier to escape into the rain. It was impossible to find which way he had gone, and Rafe realized that your safety was more important. He rode like the devil for the doctor, who happened to be staying the evening at my house, so naturally I insisted on accompanying him. It took all our strength to keep Rafe from riding out to find that bastard Charles and strangle him."

"And—what happened to Charles?" Gabrielle whispered.

Renée told her the rest. His body had washed down river to the city where it caught on a wharf piling and was dredged up from the water. No one questioned the cause of death, for so many bodies were thrown into the river from quarrels among the boatmen, but either Charles slipped along the muddy bank or threw himself in the water in order, finally, to escape his demons forever.

"Isabel?" Gabrielle wondered, feeling an ache in her heart for the friend who had already lost two husbands.

Renée shrugged expressively. "Her only concern was for you. That girl's been brought up proper not to show her feelings, but I think she'll get over it. As far as I could tell, there was no love lost between the two of them, and I might add there was almost a sense of relief on her face."

Gabrielle nodded. Perhaps, now, Isabel could grow to be her old self again.

Then, as Dolly's skillful hands arranged her thick hair, Gabrielle sighed deeply. "Things are changing so fast, Dolly," she murmured. "Sometimes I feel as though my whole life has been one long upheaval. How much longer can I endure it?"

Dolly smiled. "Now, don't go feeling sorry for yourself. You're luckier than most, Gabrielle, with a wonderful son who adores you, a husband who can give you anything."

Gabrielle was careful to keep the emotion out of her face. The two women made some final touches to their toilets and walked downstairs together where Isabel and Renée were waiting for them with the children.

"I'm not sure I'm doing the right thing by taking this drive with you," Isabel confided, "but I just couldn't stay in that stuffy bedroom any longer. Oh, I'll be so glad when I'm able to get around as I used to," she added ruefully, gazing pointedly at her still-swollen belly beneath her gown.

Despite her complaints, though, she was very much in awe of her new daughter, whose slightest wish was her command. She had taken to calling her "Ria," and the name seemed to suit the dark-haired pixie, who was sure to look exactly like her mother as she grew older.

The four women clambered into the carriage, and Gabrielle directed the driver to drive along the bank of the river. She sat back with Paul in her lap to relax in the healing sunshine.

"It's funny how quickly a woman can bounce back from an experience like the one you had," Isabel commented thoughtfully, smoothing the unruly down on Ria's head.

Renée shrugged. "I'm sure many women go through practically the same thing some nights with their drunken husbands, she put in grimly.

Isabel nodded, and her shiver indicated her own aversion to Charles' attempts at lovemaking while he had been her husband.

"I suppose the governor is starting to muster more men," Gabrielle commented, changing the subject deliberately.

Renée nodded. "The turnout is dreadfully poor. Bernard de Marigny, as chairman of the legislature's defense committee, is nearly ready to tear out his hair at the lack of response. He's had notices printed up, urging citizens to do something to protect their own interests." She leaned towards Isabel. "The Creoles are notoriously lazy, my dear."

"It's a shame, really," Dolly put in. "After all, many

of those men will be hurt the hardest because their businesses have been here for years. The Americans have a good deal less to lose as far as private business is concerned."

"Ah, but the Americans are fighting for their country, Dolly, not just the business concerns of New Orleans," Gabrielle put in quietly. Then, more briskly, "Rafe is trying with the governor's help to set up training camps. The men who have volunteered are, for the most part, green recruits, he tells me, and they don't know the first thing about warfare. They'll have to be trained in a matter of weeks, since no one really knows when the British are going to make their move. The question is—will they have enough time to make a smooth-running military machine out of this jumbled melting pot of human beings?"

Then, too, there was still the question of Jean Lafitte and his men to think of—Lafitte was like a thorn in Claiborne's side. He had still not been captured, and Claiborne's boasts of the tightening net were a thing of the past. Lafitte still wrote to Claiborne, and Pierre now added his own letters, asking him to make a decision. But what decision was there to make? Surely Lafitte did not still hold the belief that the British would accept him on their side after they had destroyed Barataria! Was there another card that the pirate held up his sleeve, some trick that the governor and his aides did not yet know about? It was a frustrating puzzle for Claiborne, and meanwhile, his men still watched the house on Rampart Street, waiting for a chance to catch the pirate unawares.

Edward Livingston had detached himself publicly from Lafitte after the pirate's escape from Barataria, and, although Claiborne still suspected he was sympathetic to the privateers, the governor accepted him back again. John Grymes still worked openly for the Lafittes, tossing his hat in the ring with their cause. His letters came weekly to the Cabildo, and he, himself, requested audiences with the governor—they would be shut up for hours. Rafe talked scornfully of these meetings, repeating his own opinion that Lafitte was only trying to buy time until he could figure out a foolproof escape plan.

"More and more men seem to be coming in, according to the latest reports. I swear, don't those English have anyplace else to go?" Renée asked peevishly.

They all fell silent, each lost in her own private thoughts. Gabrielle couldn't help the concern she felt for Rafe who seemed to be working hard enough for two men these past few days. She wondered if he tried to forget his cares in the arms of the prostitutes of the city. He had visited her often while she was recovering, but was not allowed in her bed, under the doctor's orders. And God knew, her husband was a man of lusty appetites. How could she expect him to remain faithful to her now?

When the carriage had turned back and was approaching the white pillars of Fairview once more, Gabrielle leaned forward eagerly to see Rafe's chestnut stallion being led around to the stables. He was home! The warm feeling that rushed through her told her that her face would be transparent as glass when she greeted him—but it didn't matter—he knew now that she loved him. There was nothing more to hide. She stepped down eagerly from the carriage, handing Paul to Renée, and went rushing to the library where she knew he would be.

"Rafe!" she swung open the door, her eyes alight with welcome—but the look on his face stopped her midway.

"Two more ships sighted in the Gulf today," he muttered dejectedly. "It seems as though the British are determined they will get a foothold here and use New Orleans as a base for their naval operations. It's really brilliant military strategy. I can't blame them for that."

"Oh, darling, surely more help will arrive for us before—"

"I'm afraid not," he cut her short. "Claiborne received word just today that no more troops can be spared from the North. We'll either have to recruit more from the surrounding areas—or go in with what we have."

"How—how much longer do you think—?"

"Who knows? We have their ships under constant surveillance, and they don't seem to be making a move towards land as yet. Still patrolling the waters, the damned
bastards, defying us with their standards waving in full
sight of land."

"What do you think they're waiting for?" she asked.
"Perhaps their orders have gotten mixed up."

He laughed savagely. "No more than our own, kitten.
The communication is terrible. We haven't heard any
word in the past month on the condition of Washington
City, or even if the president has been captured! It's a
damnable mess!"

Gabrielle looked at the tired disgust in his face and felt
the urge to wrap her arms around him and hold him close
against her. But she fought it down. "Would you like
something to eat?" she asked instead.

He nodded carelessly.

She hurried out of the room and noticed Isabel walking
up to her room. Renée and Dolly stood in the hall waiting
for her.

"We know you have too many things on your mind,
Gabrielle," Renée began. She noted the impatience on the
young woman's face as she and Dolly stopped her in
midflight. Her heart was still with her husband. Renée
smiled understandingly. "I just wanted to tell you that
we'll be borrowing your carriage to take us back to the
city."

"Oh, Renée, Dolly! Forgive me! I—"

"It's all right, dear. As I said before, you have other
things to attend to now, and Dolly and I have to get back
to see how the business has been running itself while we've
been gone." She chuckled.

Gabrielle ran over and kissed them both. "I'll visit you
when I can," she promised. When she returned to the
library, she found Rafe pacing up and down. He turned
and smiled in amusement upon seeing her flushed face
as she set down a tray. His eyes seemed to bore into hers,
and Gabrielle felt her whole body weakening. He stepped
over to her swiftly and clasped her hungrily in his arms.

His mouth was warm against hers, and she returned the kiss with an ardor that astonished him.

"I needed that, kitten," he said in her hair, and she was content to stand there with his arms around her.

Chapter Forty-one

October passed slowly as each day the citizens of New Orleans waited for the British to move. But the blow never came, and, by mid-November, nerves were stretched to the breaking point. It was with relief that news finally came—General Andrew Jackson was on his way from Mobile. Would he bring more soldiers with him? The people fervently hoped so, for their own force, despite more volunteers, was still pitifully small compared to the British.

Gabrielle's days had been full of volunteer work. She spent three days a week sewing uniforms for the soldiers. Rafe was gone much of the time, but she made an effort to be home when he returned. They made love passionately, as though each time would be their last, and Gabrielle gave herself so that Rafe would have no need for other women. Sometimes, as they lay together in the big bed, he would hold her close and kiss her so tenderly that her heart would go out to him, and she would have to turn her face away to hide the tears.

One evening after they had exhausted themselves and lay, not speaking, each deep in his own thoughts, Rafe talked of his worries.

"God, Gabrielle, we've not nearly enough arms, and here it is almost the end of November. It's obvious that the British have planned well, for there is no way a ship can get through their lines with the needed guns and ammunition. Our overland routes let only a trickle in, because the Indians are thick along the Natchez Trace, and the British still hold some of our northernmost forts."

"What of General Jackson?" she asked in concern. "Surely he is bringing help with him from Mobile."

Rafe shook his head. "I'm afraid not. We learned today that the general should be arriving the first or second of December, and he will have only six officers with him and perhaps a wagonload of materials—but that's all." He turned towards her and his hand played idly with a gleaming tendril of hair. "Sometimes I don't know why I ever got involved with all this worry and headache," he admitted grimly. "I could have been free, not troubling myself with the problems of others and a city like this. I probably would have continued on west after a time, but I let myself get too involved, and now I find I care too much what happens." He tilted her chin and looked into her eyes. "I've an idea that you contributed greatly to this change of character," he chuckled. "Perhaps it was even because of you that I—" He stopped and kissed her. "I'm starting to sound maudlin."

"I didn't think you were sounding maudlin," she said spiritedly, cuddling closer. "I'm sure I would have liked what you were about to say."

"I'm sure you would have, kitten. Most women enjoy hearing a man make a fool of himself for their benefit."

Gabrielle touched his shoulder with her lips. "I don't think it's foolish to tell a woman you care for her," she said boldly.

His hands drew her away from him, and he stared at her. Then an inscrutable smile played about his lips. "You've trapped me," he said lazily. "Yes, I do admit it. I care what becomes of you, kitten. It seems that between you and that son of mine—of ours—I can't go on acting as though things don't matter to me."

Gabrielle pressed her body joyfully against his. He loves me, he loves me! Oh, why doesn't he say it? she thought happily. But neither of them was able to say another word, for a few moments later they were once again whirling in a well of pleasure.

"Weapons—guns!" Rafe stalked up and down the room like a caged tiger, his face a mask of ruthless aggression. "Damn Lafitte's black soul! Damn him!"

Gabrielle looked at him in confusion, sitting down unobtrusively with a cup of tea still in her hand from dinner. He hardly noticed her as he continued to rage about the room.

"Christ! Jackson will be here in three more days! Three more days! The British are bound to know about it, and they're not going to be wasting too much more time."

"Have you—have you found out something new?" she asked him uncertainly.

He stared at her, and his eyes were black with frustrated fury. "The bastard's been holding that ace for long enough! Damn him! He's got a cache of arms hidden somewhere and is in no hurry to tell us about it! Demanding to receive a written document, signed by Claiborne himself, granting him full pardon—or he'll destroy the arms himself before escaping into Mexican territory!"

Gabrielle couldn't quite see the cause for such agitation. "Well then, it seems simple enough. Why doesn't the governor give Lafitte what he wants? We need the munitions, you said as much yourself."

Rafe swung around to her, a scornful contempt on his face. "Do you think the governor is about to trust a renegade like Lafitte to keep his word?" he asked accusingly.

"But wouldn't he have escaped if he weren't going to keep his word? Why would he even bother to mention the arms?"

Rafe, completely exhausted after a night spent at the Cabildo, tried to regain his patience. "Don't you see, Gabrielle? Lafitte could be using this as another ploy to gain time. While Claiborne talks his offer over with the legislature, Lafitte could use the time to get away! Then we'll have lost both the pirate and his weapons. If Claiborne should decide to send him the signed pardon, he could use that to get out of the United States and into Mexico!

"If only we could be sure that he was telling the truth!

If only we could trust him! Jesus, what I wouldn't give to be able to hand out a few more guns among the recruits! And ammunition would be a godsend. Do you realize that we can't even use real ammunition for target practice? Now, how the hell is a man going to learn to shoot when he has no idea where his bullet is going?"

Gabrielle's heart went out to him. If only there were some way she could help him, she wondered desperately. A dark, secret answer welled up and entered her brain . . . she couldn't do it, she couldn't! Rafe's words interrupted her thoughts.

"A general like Jackson deserves more than we can offer, kitten. What good are brilliant military strategy and brave men when one has no guns? Bravery and intelligence don't make the enemy back away."

His face looked anguished, and Gabrielle closed her eyes, wondering at the twists of fate that had once more put a horrible decision in her hands. Would she do any good if she went to Lafitte? He could lie to her just as easily as to the governor, or, worse, he could hold her hostage once she got there. No, Rafe would never allow her to go—and could she do it behind his back? Would he understand? Oh, God, what should she do? His next words seemed to make the decision for her.

"Since General Jackson will be arriving soon, Gabrielle, I'm afraid I'll have to stay the week in the city. The governor is putting up all of his aides in his own house so that we can plan our strategy from there. When Jackson does arrive, I'll be on call for a few days. I'll be back as soon as I can, sweetheart." He kissed her quickly, then went upstairs to make ready for the journey.

Gabrielle chewed her lip nervously. What she was about to do was foolhardy to say the least! It was a dangerous plan and one she wasn't even sure the governor would go along with. And it would have to be carried out in the strictest confidence between Claiborne and herself. If the plan went wrong, she would have only herself to blame. She sat down in a chair to think of how to go about it and was still sitting there when Rafe came back downstairs.

"Don't look so worried, kitten," he said, regretting his careless words before. "I shouldn't have said anything to you, but I was upset, myself. There's absolutely no need to concern yourself with these things. You stay here and take care of Isabel and the children, and I'll see if perhaps we can arrange a dinner for General Jackson when he arrives. That should keep you occupied." He brushed her lips regretfully, thinking of the long, weary nights without her to warm his bed.

Gabrielle saw him to the door, then went upstairs to compose a letter to the governor. Sealing the envelope, she hurried to order one of the stableboys to take it into the city. All she could do was wait now. She went back inside and found Isabel waiting for her in her sitting room.

"You look tired, Gabrielle," she said gently. "I'm afraid these past days have been a trial for you."

"As they have been for everyone," Gabrielle added.

Isabel shrugged. "You always did seem to feel things more intensely than others," she went on. "Gabrielle, you are unfortunate enough to be different from most of us empty-headed coquettes who have but one aim in life—to catch a man and persuade him to marry us." She laughed sardonically. "I always did envy you that special quality."

Isabel sighed deeply, then went on. "I've been thinking lately how my life has changed since I was that spoiled débutante in Paris, and then Henri's wife. I've known some difficult times, some degrading experiences—much like yourself." Her dark eyes were sharp in the knowing face. "But I'm not asking you to compare notes with me," she said with a husky laugh. "I guess what I'm leading up to is—well, we've both got our own lives to live now. We're women with different needs and desires from the goals of those two schoolgirl friends in Paris. We'll always be friends, time has been the test of that, but—now it's time that we part. I've realized that it will never be the way it was before."

Gabrielle nodded, her mind far away in Paris for a moment.

"So, I've come to a decision. I'm going to take up residence in the city with Ria. I've already discussed this with Renée. Now, don't get that wide-eyed look. No, I'm not going to prostitute myself or bring up Ria in the wrong kind of environment. I'm going to be a seamstress for Renée, and she'll lend me enough money to find a place to live until I can pay her back. Who knows, with the contacts I'll have, next week may find me with my own sponsor!"

"Next week . . . ?"

Isabel nodded firmly. "I'm leaving tomorrow, Gabrielle. When I come to a decision, I've got to stick to it, or I might not be brave enough to follow through later."

"I—I know what you mean," Gabrielle responded thoughtfully.

Isabel hugged her. "Don't think I'm not grateful for— for all you've done for me. If it weren't for you—well, things would never have turned out like this, would they?"

"No," Gabrielle agreed with a shade of bitterness in her voice.

When she had gone, Gabrielle sat down, gazing out of the window at the gathering dusk. Isabel, she had always told herself, had a propensity for taking care of herself. She loved the company of men, and Gabrielle had the idea that she was growing a trifle bored having no one to flirt with at Fairview. Isabel was like a bright, flickering jewel that needed just the right setting to be shown to best advantage. Objectively, she would make the perfect mistress. Isabel must do as she thought best and she, Gabrielle, must do. . . .

She glanced anxiously at the clock and wondered if the stableboy had reached the governor yet. God knew, Governor Claiborne had enough on his mind without catering to the strange fancies of one of his aide's wives. She only hoped he would not show the note to Rafe. That night she went to bed keyed up and was unable to sleep.

It was quite early the next morning when one of the maids told her that a soldier from the garrison was waiting downstairs to conduct her to the Cabildo. All traces of sleep vanished, and Gabrielle jumped out of bed to dash some water on her face. The time had come, she thought, with a lump in her throat.

She was ushered into the governor's private quarters in the Cabildo and then was obliged to wait nearly two hours, cooling her heels in the anteroom. Her fingers clasped and unclasped in her lap, and she jumped when William Claiborne walked in, his plain face heavy with concern and sopping with perspiration.

"Mrs. St. Claire, I am sorry to keep you waiting, but we've been busy preparing for the general's arrival. I take it your husband does not know of your visit?"

"No, governor. It is a matter of the greatest importance and I did not wish for him to interfere." She hesitated. "Could we sit and talk in private?"

The governor, looking a bit flustered, complied.

"Through my husband I've learned that you are in dire need of arms for our soldiers. I've also learned that you have received various communications from Jean Lafitte, hinting at a store of guns and ammunitions which he would exchange for a full pardon."

"That is so, madame, but how this concerns you—"

"Governor, I know that I can count on your discretion in this. What I am about to tell you must be held strictly in confidence." She took a deep breath. "I—I was captured by Lafitte aboard a ship bound from France for the West Indies. I became his mistress." She held up her hand as Claiborne was about to intervene. "Please let me finish. I became his mistress for reasons that may or may not be called justifiable. Let us say, he served as a protector and I was alone in this new land. I lived with him on Barataria for two years, and during that time I believe that he came to care for me. I know that he is in hiding now, and I hoped to go to him and persuade him to give you arms in exchange for his freedom. I realize that you don't know whether you can trust him or not, and I thought—I thought perhaps I could obtain his word on it. If he would tell me where the arms are being stored—"

Claiborne had risen from his chair and his face was

bright red. "Madame! You must forgive me, but I believe you have lost your reason! Of course you can count on my silence where your confession is concerned, but I cannot—I simply cannot follow the course you have outlined. It would be sheer madness! Do you think for one moment that, supposing he even remembers you—that he wouldn't have you killed on sight? This man is not some fine gentleman, as you seem to suppose. He is a criminal, a fugitive from justice. What is even worse, he is a *desperate* criminal! No, madame, I thank you for your good intentions, but it is impossible!"

"Governor, please! I am willing to risk my life to do this. You would be losing nothing by it. And what if he would tell me where the guns are hidden? Think what it would mean for you!"

For a moment, the governor's eyes were greedy, then he swept the feeling aside. "No, madame, I'm afraid I will have to remain firm. You'd be taking your life into your hands, and I would be responsible. If anything were to happen to you, I would hate to have to face your husband." He mopped his brow and prepared to take his leave.

"Wait, governor! Please, let me try! I realize that the plan is not foolproof, but I have an idea. Let me go to Marie Villars' house with an armed escort—disguised, of course. Let me talk to Marie and see what she will tell me. I knew her during my time on Barataria, and I think I could persuade her to listen to me. Very soon the British are going to begin their attack, and we need more guns! If I can help you get them, let me try. Lafitte will grow tired of waiting soon. I'm sure you find it hard to believe that he has waited this long. When he leaves, your hopes for more arms go with him."

The governor reseated himself and thought about her words for what seemed an eternity. "And what if you find he has already left, madame? You will be endangering yourself for nothing."

Gabrielle shook her head. "I do not think he has gone, governor. Please let me go to the house of Marie Villars, and let me at least attempt to reach Lafitte. You could give me a paper, signed by your own hand. A paper granting him full pardon."

Claiborne shook his head. "I cannot do that, but I could give you something informing him that proceedings will be slowed if he will tell where the guns are. If he gives us their whereabouts, then I will issue the pardon, but not before."

Gabrielle sighed. Lord, men were stubborn, when so much else was at stake besides their damned pride! She nodded. "Then you will let me go to Marie?"

"I'll never understand your reasons for doing this, madame. You need not have told me about your past life, and yet you risked it, to do something that holds no gain for you."

Gabrielle smiled. "If I can take some of the worry from my husband's face, it is gain enough for me."

He threw up his hands. "All right then, I agree to your plan."

Chapter Forty-two

As Gabrielle walked down the street toward the house that she vaguely remembered, she found herself, much to her own self-contempt, feeling a strong inclination to turn around and run. She knew she was no martyr, and certainly she had no wish to consciously put herself in any real danger. Her fingers were shaking, and she experienced a bit of difficulty smoothing her skirt and straightening her bonnet. She could feel, she was sure, several pairs of eyes on her, peeking curiously through the windows, and her feet moved less quickly as she neared the house that belonged to Pierre Lafitte's mistress.

Dear God, let me be doing the right thing, she thought for the hundredth time. Let him not have forgotten me!

Her steps slowed in front of the trim, neat little cottage that faced her with a frightening silence. Hesitantly, her fingers curved against the wooden door, and, with swift finality, she knocked. No answer came from within, and she waited, still fighting the urge to run away. A second time she knocked, and the response was the same. She was beginning to feel a little ridiculous, standing there on the porch, facing a closed and silent house, when she caught a movement at the window. Someone was home, that was certain—refusing callers, no doubt. She knocked harder.

"What do you want?" The voice was soft and husky, and it took all her strength to stay on the porch and answer.

"I want to see Jean Lafitte."

Silence. Then the voice came again with a perceptible hardening. "We here have no idea of Lafitte's whereabouts. Leave us alone and go back to the governor from whom you came. Tell him that we have done nothing wrong."

"Then why do you keep your shutters barred and your door locked against callers in the night?" Gabrielle asked, knowing for certain that she was not speaking to Marie Villars.

"That is none of your business. Good night."

"No, wait! I have not come from the governor," she lied. "I am Gabrielle St. Claire. I—I knew Lafitte a long time ago. I visited this very house when Marie's first child was born."

Her voice was desperate. Was she not even to see Marie because of some spiteful woman refusing her entrance? A sudden hush seemed to settle inside the house, and now the female voice held a note of jealous hostility.

"I don't know what you're talking about, or who you are. I am telling you to go away—now."

Gabrielle ground her teeth in frustration at having to deal with such an impertinent individual. "All right, then," she said quickly. "If you don't want to hear what I have to say—if you don't care what happens to Lafitte, then I am certainly not going to stand here and make a fool of myself." She had turned to go when the sound of a latch being drawn caused her to pause.

A different voice called, "Come in then, Gabrielle, if you truly want to help us."

"Marie!" Gabrielle stared at the girl. The soft glowing skin was blotched and mottled from constant crying and worry. The deep, liquid eyes were ringed in circles. "Marie!" Gabrielle said again. Involuntarily, she swept up the steps and hugged her.

"Gabrielle! You—here! What has happened? After all these years—why have you come here?" Marie ushered her into the house and closed the door.

"Marie, I must speak to Lafitte. I want to get a message to him. If I could meet him somewhere else, perhaps?"

"Gabrielle, listen to me. We are watched constantly here, and there is little doubt that you have been observed. Lafitte is coming here tonight with Pierre and Dominique. He will—"

"No! Marie, don't be a fool! Can we trust this woman?"

Gabrielle turned and saw the woman whose voice she had heard from behind the door—hardly a woman, really, a girl of perhaps seventeen years.

"Catherine, I'm sure Gabrielle has no wish to bring harm to Lafitte," Marie soothed her.

Catherine—the little sister! The one who had adored Lafitte even then and had hated Gabrielle because she was his mistress—a girl no longer, and, by the protests she was making, still faithful to Lafitte. Was she, perhaps, his mistress now?

"But how can you be sure she hasn't been sent to trap Jean?" Catherine was arguing vehemently.

Gabrielle saw the shadow of doubt cross Marie's face.

"On my word, Marie, because of everything we once shared, I swear to you that I only want to help!"

Catherine's pretty face was still suspicious, but Marie sighed. "We need help now, Cathy. Lafitte can't go on like a hunted animal forever."

Suddenly the younger girl's face crumpled into a half-sob. "All right, then, but if anything happens to Jean—I'll—I'll kill myself, I swear it!" she wailed.

Marie drew Gabrielle inside and led her to the main living area, where a little girl, no more than three, was playing with a cornhusk doll. A fat, calico-clad black woman hovered protectively over her while holding a tiny infant, who was sleeping peacefully.

"Now listen carefully. Jean and Pierre will both be here tonight to meet with Mr. Grymes," Marie began.

"Grymes must not know of this," Gabrielle interjected quickly.

Marie nodded. "They will meet around eight o'clock for about an hour. After Mr. Grymes has gone, I will ask Lafitte if he wants to see you—and, if he agrees, I will send Cathy for you, but you must not wait at your home. It is too far away."

"You know where I live?" Gabrielle asked helplessly.

Marie smiled. "You are a woman married to a man often in the public eye. You, yourself, draw much attention, my friend. It has not been hard keeping track of you."

Gabrielle blushed, realizing that all this time, she had barely spared a thought for this woman. Marie's dark eyes shone with understanding.

"Where will I come for her?" Catherine prodded. "That is—if Lafitte will see her."

Marie's face grew blank.

"Renée's. Madame Renée's," Gabrielle said quickly. "It's not too far, and Catherine can come around back. I'll be waiting in the kitchen."

The three women stood, and Marie led Gabrielle to the door. "I can only pray that your efforts will bring about good news for us, Gabrielle," she said, waving farewell.

Gabrielle hurried to the waiting carriage. "Drive to Madame Renée's," she ordered.

The driver shook his head. "No, ma'am. The governor gave me express orders to bring you straight back to his quarters when your task was finished."

"But it's not finished! Now, please!" Gabrielle said, cursing Claiborne for thinking of everything.

"I'm sorry, ma'am, but you'll just have to bring that up with the governor."

Gabrielle was silent as she sat in the coach. It would not take long before she was once more facing Claiborne. And she had no news for him—yet! But he would get angry and think he had been duped—and that would be the end to all her hopes! The carriage turned into Toulouse Street, and then the driver was holding the door for her.

"Through that door, ma'am. The governor is in conference now, but he will be with you as soon as he can."

Gabrielle thanked him stiffly and watched him as he led the carriage back to the stables. She eyed the soldier guarding the pass gate and wondered if she could persuade him to let her through. Boldly, she sauntered over towards him.

"Good evening, soldier," she laughed, forcing her voice to be gay.

He started and turned around suspiciously. "Hey, what are you doing here?"

She shook her head. "I don't know, myself. You see, the governor sent for me, but he didn't have time to see me." She cocked her head and came closer to him.

"What business would he have with you?"

Gabrielle was delighted at the response, for at least the soldier did not suspect her to be Mrs. Rafe St. Claire, but some hussy. "Don't know," she grinned. Then, shrugging her shoulders, "Oh, well, if the governor decided he has no further use for me, I suppose I'll have to make up the night's coin elsewhere."

She started to go through the gate, holding her breath. The soldier's hand detained her.

"Say, honey, I get off my shift in another hour. Would you care to wait for me?" His hand fumbled over her breast. "I'll make it worth your while."

"Oh, sir—I don't know. You—you say an hour?" she said breathlessly.

"Yes. Wait for me down the street, sweetheart, and

we'll have ourselves a real good time." He winked, then released her.

Once outside the gate, Gabrielle breathed easier, and, when she was out of the soldier's sight, she broke into a run for Renée's house. It wasn't too far, but the dark streets scared her, and she kept thinking of reports of murders and robberies. Her feet barely touched the ground as she ran, not stopping when a voice called drunkenly to her or a man stepped out of the shadows, a whiskey bottle in his hand.

By the time she reached Renée's, she was thoroughly rattled and took a moment to compose herself. She remembered that she had told the driver of the carriage where she wanted him to go, and it was very likely he would remember it when they realized she had got away. They were sure to come to Renée's house, but there was nothing else to do but hope the governor would be detained a long time in his meeting, so that her escape would not be discovered too soon.

In a few minutes she was sitting in the kitchen, drinking tea and babbling her story to a shocked Renée, who kept shaking her head in amazement.

"If I had an ounce of sense in me, I'd march you right back to the governor's quarters, Gabrielle," she said sternly. "Why don't you go back there, child? I'm sure he'd listen to you."

Gabrielle shook her head. "He won't, Renée. He was very firm in saying that he wouldn't allow a second chance. I had to lie to Marie, for I really don't think she would have told me anything if I had said I came from the governor. But now is my chance—don't you see? Lafitte will be there tonight, and I can speak with him—persuade him to—"

"Gabrielle, do you have any idea of the danger you're putting yourself through?" Renée interrupted. She grasped the girl by the shoulders and shook her slightly. "I remember the day when Lafitte brought you to me. I could see in his eyes that you were special to him. Gabrielle, Gabrielle, the man was in love with you—in his own way, he loved you! And now you're throwing yourself in his path again. You might as well be jumping into his bed! A man like Lafitte is not a man easily given to loving a woman. I've never heard him to care for any female! Do you realize what you may be stirring up again by putting yourself in his hands?"

Gabrielle shook her head stubbornly. "It doesn't matter, Renée! You must understand. I'm doing this for Rafe and the governor and everyone in this city! If jumping into Lafitte's bed would get those guns for us, I'd do it ten times over!"

Renée looked at her sadly. "Gabrielle, think of Rafe! Would he want you to do this? Could he forgive you if he learned of it?"

"He won't learn of it, Renée. Claiborne gave me his word!"

"And you gave him your word to abide by what he said—and you didn't! Do you think Claiborne will keep his promise? Perhaps not intentionally, but still Rafe is bound to find out!"

"Renée, please let me do what I have to do! Please don't give me away now!"

"Still a child you are, my dear, despite the fact that you've borne a babe. You won't listen but must go your own way. All right. If the officials come, I'll not say a word, but if Rafe finds out you've gone to Lafitte, he'll not rest until he tears this place apart!"

"Thank you, Renée, and—don't worry."

Gabrielle watched the clock run its course with agonizing slowness. Nine chimes struck, and still Catherine did not make an appearance. She grew fitful and began to pace the kitchen restlessly, each minute that passed feeling her resolve slowly begin to crumble. In the rear distance, she could hear a lone horse moving close to the house, and her heart quickened, but it was only another customer.

Ten o'clock! Surely the governor knew of the deception by now!

"Gabrielle St. Claire?"

Gabrielle turned quickly, making out Catherine's face pressed to the window.

"I'm ready!"

Gabrielle slipped out the door, and together they crept around the house and out into the street. Catherine's mood seemed gloomy, and Gabrielle kept silent as they hurried through the streets of New Orleans. A small company of soldiers passed them, and Gabrielle wondered if they were on their way to Renée's house to find her. Certainly the police would not expect the wife of Rafe St. Claire to be jaunting about in the dark with a quadroon girl, on her way to see Lafitte! She almost giggled at the look of disbelief on their faces should they catch her, but instantly sobered, thinking of the consequences.

Catherine was going away from Rampart Street, and Gabrielle touched her tentatively on the shoulder. "Are you going the right way?"

"Yes. We must avoid being stopped," she hissed back, not breaking her stride.

Gabrielle was breathless before long, and she gazed doubtfully at the fence that Catherine was urging her to slip through—the girl took malicious pleasure when Gabrielle tore her skirt on a nail. They hopped over a water trough and slid around the brightness of open windows. Gabrielle felt as though this obstacle course was hardly necessary, until, when Catherine pressed her into a crouch, she caught a glimpse of a city guard quietly patrolling the street.

Now, Gabrielle could smell the river close by. They padded through an alley, and Gabrielle nearly twisted her ankle as she stepped into a jagged ditch cut into the brown cobblestones.

"Quiet!" Catherine hissed as Gabrielle let out a small whimper.

They squeezed through another fence, then turned a sudden corner so swiftly that Gabrielle didn't see the man looming up in front of her until she bumped squarely into

him. Thinking they'd come upon a city guard, Gabrielle
tried to pull away but was held fast by strong, encircling
arms.

"Let me go! I'm on my way—"

"You've arrived, Gabrielle," came a voice she instantly
recognized, and, before she could exclaim, a warm hand
closed over her mouth.

"Hush, no joyous cries of reunion, please," Lafitte cau-
tioned her harshly, "or you'll have the watch on us for
sure."

She nodded swiftly, and the hand was removed—did
she imagine the fingers caressed her cheek for an instant
before glancing away?

"Jean—is—is everything all right?" Catherine murmured.

Lafitte shrugged. "Nothing has been right, sweetheart,
since those cursed English arrived," he returned bitterly,
but he walked to where the girl stood anxiously and em-
braced her.

Embarrassed, Gabrielle moved away and bumped into
still another man. In the moonlight, she could barely distinguish the features of Dominique You.

"Lord, girl, what happened to you?" he whispered ex-
pansively, noting the torn gown and tumbled hair.

"Nothing. I guess I'm not used to such dangerous short-
cuts. Where—where are we? Why haven't we met in Rampart Street?"

Dominique coughed uneasily. "Lafitte suspected that
you might be the bait for a trap, my dear. Oh, no offense
against your integrity, but you can never be sure about
that old fox, Claiborne."

"Then, you'll not tell me where we are."

"Close to the river, minx. Now, no more questions.
Come inside, and I'll light a candle."

Gabrielle obeyed and found herself in a small room
in which bales of dry goods had been stored. The floor
was swept clean, and a table and chairs had been set up.
There was no other furniture except for a makeshift bed
made of bundles of cloth.

"A glass of wine?"

Gabrielle took it thankfully and was a little uneasy when Dominique started to leave. "Aren't you going to stay?"

He laughed. "Your business is with Lafitte, puss."

Gabrielle seated herself at the table and waited for Lafitte to come in. When he did, she noted that Catherine was no longer with him. Her eyes passed briefly over the tall, slender figure, the long, black hair with a trace of grey at the temples, the snapping black eyes in the still-lively, brown face.

"So—you've come to me, Madame St. Claire. I am deeply honored indeed," he began sarcastically, savoring a glass of wine himself. "I must say I'm surprised at your husband for allowing his wife to come into the viper's den alone."

"He—he doesn't know I've come," Gabrielle said, her eyes darting away from that penetrating black gaze.

"What? You've come on your own?" he exclaimed in mockery. "Then you were not afraid to put yourself into my hands?"

Gabrielle frowned. "I've come to help you, Jean."

He was unbending. "How is it that *you* can help me," he demanded, "when the best lawyers in New Orleans cannot seem to do so?" He leaned closer. "Do you hold the governor's ear so that with one sweet word—and perhaps a few bouts in his bed—he will pardon the terrible villain? Come now, madame. I must confess my curiosity got the better of my good judgement, but I find the amusement wears thin when it is my life at stake." He got up and walked to the door, staring out moodily. "Of course, now that you're here, I suppose you'd make a priceless hostage." His eyes gleamed as he came back to her.

Gabrielle drew away uncertainly, and he laughed at her nervousness.

"I couldn't kill you, Gabrielle, so don't look so stricken, but the threat might just work." He seemed to consider for a moment, and Gabrielle's face pinkened.

"I've—I've not come to be bullied by you," she began. "I wanted to—"

"Why did you want to help me, Gabrielle? Why? If I recall correctly, you ran away from me a long time ago. Didn't you hope never to have to face me again?" His voice rose with remembered rancor.

"Jean, you must understand that I—"

"Christ, woman! You ran away from me after—after the death of our child, and now you expect me to welcome you for your trouble!" He had moved around the table, and his face was close to hers.

Gabrielle steeled herself not to jump away but returned the stare as steadily as she could. "Jean, I know that you have had correspondence with Governor Claiborne and that you've both reached a sort of stalemate. Neither of you will budge. . . ."

"I never did trust that old fox!" Lafitte interrupted. "I told him that I'd not go over to the British if he'd drop all the charges against me, but he wouldn't answer. The sly son of a bitch waited it out so long that the British grew tired of waiting and blew my island to hell, damn them! Well, Lafitte isn't a man to be treated shabbily, by God!" His face was crafty now—the face of a cat who has his mouse cornered. "I happen to know that Claiborne is in desperate need of men and weapons. The fool could have had my men, who can fight a hell of a lot better than those milksops of his—they can do nothing better than parade in the Place d'Armes with their fancy dress uniforms! And weapons! Claiborne needed guns and ammunition. He must have them if he's to have a prayer against the fighting machine the British have assembled."

"And you have these weapons, don't you, Jean?" Gabrielle put in softly.

The man slumped to a chair warily. "Perhaps, my curious little temptress, perhaps—but I've a notion to sell them to the British for good solid gold. I'd have more than enough to sail away and rest easy for the rest of my days—and damn Claiborne to the British firing squad!" He pounded his fist on the table in emphasis.

"But what if—if Claiborne were willing to pardon your crimes, Jean? What if, in exchange for men and arms, you could walk the streets of New Orleans—or anywhere— a free man, a man no longer hunted and hounded by the law?" Her voice was hopeful as her eyes looked into his and saw the spark of consideration in them.

Then he shook his head. "No, I've come to the conclusion, madame, that Claiborne is an ass, too proud to forgive the man who has exposed him too often to public ridicule."

"No, Jean, you're wrong. It's true, he's proud, but he has been sullied and scoffed at so many times because of your exploits—how can you blame him?" She reached inside the neckline of her gown and pulled out the precious letter signed by Claiborne himself and passed it to Lafitte to read. "Here, see for yourself."

Lafitte scanned the paper quickly, then sat back in his chair. "So, in public Claiborne swears his vengeance, but in private he employs a woman to bring me words of reconciliation. I must give him credit for his cleverness, the damnable crook!" He glanced at her. "And tell me, how it is that you are the bearer of such important tidings? Don't tell me you have opened your life with me to public perusal?" His dark brows slanted downwards.

Gabrielle's cheeks were hot as she replied, "I confided in Governor Claiborne only—and he has given me his word—"

"It would be shameful, wouldn't it? The wife of Rafe St. Claire, a respected man in the city, to be known as the one-time mistress of the pirate, Lafitte!" His face was almost cruel. "Your husband would be forced to sue for divorce if word spread, wouldn't he?"

"Jean, please, the past is over—and I am not sad to see it so."

He laughed mockingly. "But let's get back to business, shall we? Claiborne tells me that he will grant my men and me a full pardon if I will tell him where the munitions are hidden. How can I trust his word?"

"His signature is on the paper—and my being here is proof of his good faith," Gabrielle cried, vexed at this game he continued to play with her.

He rubbed his jaw thoughtfully. "I suppose you persuaded him as to my own integrity?"

She nodded. "Jean, please be sensible. This is a way out for you without having to suffer an ignominious surrender! General Andrew Jackson is going to be here in another two days. If he knew you had supplied arms to the troops, you would have his support too, I know it! Everyone says he is a just man."

"God, I never realized that you could be so loyal to a cause!" he laughed scornfully.

"Jean Lafitte, you have just as much to gain."

"Did you think of that when you embarked on this perilous mission?" he asked her, placing the paper on the table and standing up to look down at her.

She averted her eyes.

"Gabrielle, sometimes I wonder what might have become of us if—"

"Jean, please. You know that I am married now and that I have a son."

"He is your second son," he reminded her softly, and Gabrielle could not help the mist of tears that covered her eyes.

"Gabrielle, Gabrielle," he repeated and she felt his hand smoothing her hair. "I had such plans for the three of us—such wonderful plans! I had enough gold to take us far away from this place, to where we could have started over again. It would have been different."

She shook her head. "No, Jean. It would never have worked. You must know that, yourself, deep inside. You would have grown tired of the sameness of life after a while and become angry with me for being the cause of the loss of your freedom. It would not have been long before you would have started the old ways again. It's in your blood, Jean."

"Still—it was a wonderful dream, while it lasted," he said and his voice seemed to come from far away. The hand brushed her shoulder and then rested softly against her cheek. "It's funny, looking back on it," he murmured. "You fought me for so long that I wasn't sure what you would say if I—" He stopped and shrugged. "As you say, that's all over now, but I've learned something, Gabrielle. Love is a magical thing that comes and goes so quickly sometimes that you can miss it because you're not looking for it. Instead, your mind is filled with petty things—money, success, hatreds and jealousies, pride."

His hand tilted her chin up, and his eyes burned darkly into hers. His dark head bent, and, in another instant, she felt his mouth on hers, and her lips trembled. He tasted the tears on her face, and, very gently, he kissed her—so gently it was almost a sigh.

"I could make love to you now," he whispered. "There is nothing to stop me from taking you by force—nothing except yourself, you see," he finished sadly. "I know you could never come back to me, Gabrielle."

She shook her head, her eyes swimming with tears so that she could hardly see the expression on his face. He kissed her once more, infinitely tenderly—so sweet, so sweet—and her heart lurched in her breast. I could almost have loved him, she thought, watching him pick up the paper once more.

"You had best get back to your husband, my love, for I've an idea he will not take kindly to what you have done."

"And—and what about—"

He smiled at her and folded the paper. "Tell the governor that I will hand over the arms. When General Jackson arrives in New Orleans, I shall call on him myself and tell him where they are hidden. I will tell you, Gabrielle, that I have hidden them in the storehouse not far from the Temple, so that you can be assured of my promise."

She got shakily to her feet and thanked him, but his hand brushed aside her words. "I'm not doing this because I have any great love for these United States or for Governor Claiborne, or even Andrew Jackson. You are probably right, and, after this is all over, I'll not be content with my pardon and a place of honor in the city. I'll be moving on again, somewhere new and exciting, raw and ready for exploitation." He laughed cynically at himself. Then he took her hand in his and pressed a kiss into the palm. "But I shall never forget you, my lost love."

"Oh, Jean!" she whispered brokenly and began to weep silently.

He made an effort to shake off his mood, and his voice was once more brusque. "Come now, spitfire. You'd best be off. There are soldiers all around this place, and any one of them will be honored to show you back to the governor's, I'm sure." He took her arm, and together they walked out into the night.

Chapter Forty-three

On December 2, 1814, General Andrew Jackson reached New Orleans, accompanied by six of his officers. The citizens of New Orleans clamored to greet him, and they cheered at the sight of the tall, gaunt man who rode his horse skillfully, despite the long illness that he had suffered. His hair was iron-grey and he wore it long, drawn back from his famous hawklike features, and his complexion had grown sallow from his sickness. He was far from well as he rode into New Orleans after fighting one long campaign, and now he was prepared to face another. Governor Claiborne had prepared quarters for him in Royal Street, and these were to serve as the headquarters of the entire campaign. Jackson worked with a feverish energy that left others dazed.

Gabrielle was among the throng that cheered him as he rode into the city. She was staying in town for the duration of the campaign, as there had been alleged sightings of British scouts combing the areas south and west of New Orleans. Suzette had opened her doors to her, and it soothed Gabrielle to accept her company. She still thought with a mixture of guilt and dread of those events that had resulted from her visit with Lafitte.

As Lafitte had foretold, one of the patrolling soldiers had seen her walking alone and immediately offered his assistance and took her quickly to the governor's quarters. There, a stern-faced Claiborne awaited her, and, to her shock—her husband watched as she made her entrance.

"So, now that you have played the whore with your old lover—and told the world—you come slinking back to make your report. I'm not surprised, madame!"

"Please, Rafe, there's no need to be so brutal," Claiborne intervened quickly. He asked her to be seated, and Gabrielle took the chair thankfully.

Why—how had Rafe found out? She cast an accusing glance at the governor, but his manner did not soften.

"Why is it that you directly disobeyed my orders?" he barked.

Gabrielle could barely speak after her emotional ordeal with Lafitte and especially now, with her husband's eyes ruthlessly searching her. "I—I knew what I had to do," she began.

"Spread your legs for that renegade!" Rafe said through clenched teeth.

Gabrielle flushed deeply and Claiborne, himself, went a dull red.

"St. Claire, if you continue to bully your wife, I will have to ask you to leave the room," he warned, but there was a trace of guilt in his voice that he had allowed the woman to go at all, against his better judgement. "Tell me what happened."

Gabrielle told him how she had waited at Renée's for the girl to arrive to take her to Lafitte. She described the meeting in detail, omitting only the kiss that Lafitte had given her. "And he has given me his word that he will reveal the hiding place of the arms to General Jackson himself!"

"His word! The word of a pirate!" Rafe laughed cruelly. "What did he ask in return, my honorable wife? Can you look your own husband in the face and tell me truthfully that he didn't touch you?"

Gabrielle's cheeks were on fire, and she could not bear to look at those burning green emeralds.

"See for yourself, governor. She has accomplished only her own humiliation—and mine."

"St. Claire, I'm asking you to leave the room. You've scared her to death with your accusations!" Claiborne got out.

Rafe hesitated, murder in his eyes, but he shrugged finally and left them alone.

"Now, I realize that this is all damnably messy, madame, but I must insist on the truth from you."

"I'm telling you the truth, governor," Gabrielle said with sincerity. "Lafitte told me he had considered selling the arms to the British for gold, but I believed him when he told me he would honor his word to me—and you. He—he even told me where they are hidden as a sign of his good faith."

Claiborne jumped up from his seat. "Then tell me, madame, for the love of God!"

She shook her head slowly. "I can't. He must tell the general himself and receive his pardon."

"What!" Claiborne's eyes nearly popped out of his head. "You mean you know where these vital arms are, and you won't divulge their hiding place? Madame, I could have you arrested for consorting with the enemy!"

Gabrielle tried staunchly to stop the flow of tears, but it was useless, and she began sobbing, her shoulders shaking uncontrollably. "Please, why can't you trust me?" she asked him, beseechingly.

In spite of his convictions, Claiborne found himself softening. "All right, all right. I've a mind to have you thrashed for your impertinence, but Suzette would never let me hear the end of it. As it is, you will stay in my house until the time—if he actually does it—Lafitte calls on General Jackson. If he does not, then I will expect you to tell where the hiding place is. I don't think that is being unfair."

Gabrielle agreed tearfully, and the governor signalled for the soldier to escort her to his wife's rooms. In the passageway, Rafe loomed up in front of her, and she shrank away from him.

"I'll take the woman the rest of the way. Thank you, soldier."

The soldier saluted, and Gabrielle faced her husband's rage alone.

"Damn you for a lying whore!" he exploded. "You couldn't wait to get back to him, could you? With your soft words and melting eyes, I actually believed that you loved me. I should have known better. No woman who truly loves her husband runs off to another man and throws herself in his arms." His hand shot out and closed about her throat, shaking her like a chicken. "I ought to strangle you myself," he ground out. "I ought to shut that lying throat forever!"

It seemed he was quite capable of carrying out his threat, and Gabrielle clawed at the hand that was throttling her. "Rafe, please, Lafitte didn't—didn't touch me," she gasped.

"He didn't touch you! You lie, madame. I can see it in your eyes!" He threw her against the wall, where she crumpled to the floor. He stood there, staring at her for a long moment, his chest rising and falling rapidly as he struggled to control his fury. "Don't ever come near me again," he said in a deathly quiet voice. "If you do, I'm not sure I'll be able to stop myself the next time!"

And he was gone down the hall, leaving her to grope against the wall and relieve her tortured throat. My God, she had truly lost him! She wept bitterly and huddled against the wall until a soldier found her and led her away.

Now, as she cheered along with the populace, Gabrielle's hand went to her neck in remembrance. She knew, through Suzette, that Rafe was working at a feverish pace, drowning himself in papers and orders—anything to get her out of his mind.

Next to her, Suzette put a comforting arm around her. "Don't worry, Gabrielle, he'll come back to you once he's had time to cool down."

But he didn't come back. Later, the day of Jackson's arrival, the general met with Claiborne, Commodore Patterson, Edward Livingston, John Grymes, and Nicholas Girod, the mayor of New Orleans. As the governor's most trusted aide, Rafe St. Claire was also present at the meeting, carrying dispatches and keeping himself busy. The men discussed the military strategy of the British and the numbers of their troops.

The next day, General Jackson rode on an inspection tour to the American encampments. Despite the jaundice that plagued him, he was witty and charming among the men. The troops immediately took to him, and his popularity was widespread. "With a man like that leading us, how can we lose?" they shouted to each other.

In a rather surprising move, Jackson appointed Edward Livingston as his military secretary, and Mrs. Livingston gave a dinner for the general. Rafe noted Jackson's ease of manner among the ladies, and the Creole women were really quite captivated with him.

"The general does have a way with the populace," Dussault commented acidly, standing next to Rafe as they sipped champagne.

"It's easy to see that he'll have no trouble keeping the rank and file together," Rafe agreed. "His face looks so tired, though, it's a wonder he can still stand up!" He set his glass down and moved towards the general, who greeted him cordially.

"St. Claire, I hope you approve of my staying up late," he laughed merrily.

Rafe started, aware that a frown must have marked his face. "Forgive me, general, my first concern is for your welfare," he responded quickly.

Jackson clapped him in friendly fashion on the shoulder. "But where is your beautiful wife, St. Claire? I vow I have heard of no one else from everyone tonight. They are wondering why she is not here."

Jackson's sharp eyes did not miss the stiffening in the man's jaw.

"She was not able to join us this evening," he managed.

"I see. Well, in any case, I'm sure I shall have the pleasure soon. I must say I am looking forward to meeting her!"

"Thank you, general," Rafe replied coolly and bowed in silence.

What, he wondered, would the general say if he knew his beautiful and charming wife had thrown herself into the very arms of the enemy! Rafe ground his teeth together in controlled rage. How could she do it to him? How could she—knowing how he had fought against Lafitte all these years! And now, to have his own wife go willingly to him—Lafitte must have enjoyed the moment immensely!

"Good God, St. Claire, you look as though you're ready to go out and murder someone!" Leigh Owens commented at his shoulder. "What's the matter with you?"

"Nothing, Leigh. Nothing that a long night in a spirited whore's bed couldn't cure," he answered, with an ugly twist of his mouth.

Leigh laughed uncertainly. "Christ, man, you don't need a whore! Your wife—"

"Shut up, Leigh, shut up before I put my fist in your face!"

Leigh blanched and backed away. "Jesus, I didn't mean anything dishonorable by it, Rafe. I only meant that there's no need for you to consider—"

But Rafe had already stalked off, and with nervous reservation Leigh watched his tall, dark form disappear in the crowd of guests. What in the hell was the matter with him? he wondered. For the past couple of days, no one had been able to talk to Rafe for fear he would lash out at them in his black mood.

Working his way through the guests, Rafe saw no one. His mind was filled with pictures of his wife—Gabrielle and Leigh, Gabrielle and de Chevalier—how did he know she hadn't encouraged the pitiful bastard? And now she had cuckolded him a third time with the very man he had cursed and stormed at for so long. A woman's voice called flirtatiously to him, but his eyes would not focus because of the red mist in front of him. Goddamn her! If it was rape she wanted, he would certainly give it to her!

His strides lengthened as he neared the door, and then he was through it, out in the street where the cool air helped somewhat to clear his head. A soft, feminine giggle made him turn around, and he was aware of Melissa Beauville's face turned up to him in obvious invitation.

"Rafe, darling, I've been wondering where that sweet little wife of yours has been lately? No one's seen her at all the parties in honor of the general."

"Where is your husband tonight, Melissa?" he asked her sarcastically, his eyes going blatantly to the neckline of her gown.

Melissa giggled again, and her mouth parted. "I haven't the slightest notion, Rafe. I suppose he's somewhere about." She shrugged her shoulders and threw him a challenging look from beneath her lashes. "You look as though you could use some company, darling."

He laughed savagely, frightening her a little. "Yes, you're quite right, Melissa. I could use some company at the moment." He gestured to one of the waiting carriages.

Melissa clapped her hands, amazed at the ease of her conquest. "Oh, Rafe, where shall we go? I know of an adorable place where we could rent a room and—"

Before she could finish, Rafe had caught her hand and was pulling her towards the nearest carriage. He had no idea whose carriage it was or if they were likely to come looking for it soon. He only knew he must punish *her*— punish that bitch who had made a fool out of him. Without gentleness, he pushed Melissa into the carriage and closed the door.

"But, darling, you'll have to find the driver first. He—" But Melissa's words were cut off abruptly by the force of his mouth on hers. "Oh-oh, Rafe—"

He was already pushing her skirts up, crumpling them around her waist, fumbling with his trousers.

"My goodness, lover, you are impatient tonight," Melissa crooned, delighted at such primitive tactics. She didn't mind that he was not gentle with her—was, in fact, not even touching her except for his hands tearing at her undergarments. "Not so fast, lover," she cooed softly. "If you're worried about my husband arriving, don't. Nicholas is a fool, and—"

She stopped in mid-sentence, aware of the sudden stillness in him. "Darling, what's the matter?" she questioned him, beginning to squirm against him with desire. "Rafe?"

He was moving away from her now, straightening his clothes and looking down at her with such contempt that she closed her eyes.

"I'm sorry, Melissa," he said unexpectedly, "but I have no wish to punish your husband simply because he's a fool."

And then he backed out of the carriage and was gone, leaving Melissa lying, stunned, her skirts still up to her neck and the cool air chilling her legs.

Gabrielle enjoyed a quiet dinner that night with only the Claiborne servants for company. It soothed her not to have to smile and converse politely with everyone when her heart was breaking inside. She ate in her room and then went to the nursery where Paul was sleeping along with two of the Claiborne children.

She kissed her child softly on the forehead and tucked the sheet around his chin, then walked back to her own room. She supposed that the Claibornes would not arrive home until very late and started to undress when she felt a sudden uneasiness, as though someone was watching her. Her eyes searched the room, but in the light of the single candelabrum, she could not see into the recesses that were hidden in folds of darkness. Uneasily, she slipped out of her dress and reached for the nightgown that the maid had folded neatly on the chair.

"You'll not be needing that tonight, madame." The male voice caused her to jerk around quickly, her eyes widening as she perceived a man's tall figure outlined against the window. "I've heard," the voice went on mockingly, "that you give your favors freely, madame, and I have come to claim you this night."

Gabrielle let out a sigh of relief. "Rafe, it is you, isn't it?"

What kind of game was he playing with her? He didn't answer but moved into the circle of light. He reached over and extinguished the remaining candles, and in a moment the room was filled with bright moonlight.

"Rafe, are you all right?" she whispered in some alarm.

His scornful laugh seemed to echo in the darkened room. "I have never felt better, madame. I am looking forward to our night together."

She backed away a little, her hand still clutching the nightgown against her. "You—you did give me a scare," she began hesitantly.

He laughed again, and she could imagine the amused mockery in his eyes. "Why should a man scare you— I had heard you were quite used to them in your bedroom."

"Rafe! Stop it! I—I don't know why you're playing this silly game with me, but I don't like it!"

"I am not your husband tonight, madame. Just think of me as a man whom you must do your best to please. You're my woman now. Come, don't be coy with me!"

He strode across the room and caught her by the shoulders. She waited in trepidation for his kiss, but he only pushed her backwards toward the bed. She floundered helplessly for a moment, then fell onto the mattress. Her heart began a slow thudding as she felt his body press down against hers, and her arms went about his neck instinctively.

"Ah, that's better. A man must get his money's worth," he murmured, his lips teasing her breasts.

She ignored his words. They didn't matter. All that mattered was that he was here with her—he couldn't keep away from her, despite what he thought! He was caressing her thighs and her belly, and she welcomed him gladly, moving under him in a way that she knew would excite him even more.

"Oh, Rafe," she said gently, happily, "I do love you so!"

He stiffened against her, and his tense body seemed poised for a fraction of a second in the air as though she had wounded him.

"Whores mustn't talk of love!" he hissed ruthlessly, and his body slammed down hard against hers now.

Confused, not knowing what she had done wrong, Gabrielle couldn't help the cry that escaped her as he entered her flesh. In another moment, his hand had clamped down on her mouth, bruising her lips with the pressure. Oh, God! No, please, her mind screamed, don't do this to me, Rafe, please! She struggled against the suffocating hand, but he didn't seem to notice, and soon the lack of oxygen began to play on her mind.

This was not Rafe who was raping her so indifferently. No, this was Charles! My God! She was screaming inside at the violation, her eyes seeing the blond head on her bosom, feeling the hurt he was inflicting on her muiltiplied ten times over in her dazed mind. No, no, no! Please, don't hurt me any more, her eyes beseeched him as tears spilled down against the hand on her mouth.

Then, suddenly, the hand was pulled away, and she took in great gulps of air. The whirling in her brain slowed and then stopped. Rafe's face hovered above hers, and there were pain and self-contempt mixed in those green eyes.

"Jesus Christ, Gabrielle! Forgive me!" he muttered brokenly.

Willing herself not to tremble, she reached out and touched his cheek gently, so unnerving him that he collapsed against her, his whole body shaking.

"Rafe, I don't blame you, my darling. I don't blame you," she whispered. "I love you too much."

He raised his head again and looked into those wide,

candid eyes, and he turned his head away. Silently, he raised himself from her and stood looking down at her. Then, without a word, she saw him walk towards the door and pass through, closing it gently behind him.

Chapter Forty-four

New Orleans was in an uproar over the latest news. Lafitte had gone to General Jackson! The newssheets were scattered over the streets, proclaiming that Governor Claiborne had issued a full pardon against both Lafittes, their lieutenants, and the men of Barataria! This, indeed, was an exciting day, for Lafiitte had told Jackson where he would find a large supply of ammunition and weapons, stored close to the Temple. All proceedings against the Baratarians had been dropped by official decree, and, to top it off, because of their artillery skill, Dominique You and Renato Beluche had been made captains!

How the Creoles loved it! Oh, they had known all along that Lafitte was a clever fox—but this was far more than they had ever imagined. He had, without the loss of an ounce of his own pride, neatly turned the tables so that he was practically proclaimed a hero for his part in adding to the supply of arms. No one knew quite how it was done—or why.

Well, no matter the reason, leave that to Lafitte's own discretion. At least now they had something to use against the British!

Very quickly, Jackson put the whole city under martial law, an irksome situation to the freedom-loving Creoles, but one they knew they must accept under the difficult conditions.

Gabrielle had not seen Rafe again since the night when he had come to her room at the Governor's House, and she had not made mention of it to Suzette, although it troubled her that Rafe had seemed, if anything, even further away from her than ever. Governor Claiborne gave her a formal apology, and he added his sincere thanks for her part in bringing about Lafitte's meeting with General Jackson.

"Are you sure—er—you wouldn't want me to let it out that it was you—"

Gabrielle shook her head quickly. "No, governor. Let it be a secret between you and me and Lafitte." And Rafe, she thought, wondering if this news had caused him to think more dispassionately about the meeting she had had with Lafitte that night. Probably not, she thought dejectedly. The bulletins doubtless only served to strengthen his opinion that she had gone to bed with the pirate in order to insure his cooperation.

She was thinking such gloomy thoughts as this one morning when Suzette came rushing in, obviously distracted.

"Oh, Gabrielle, my dear! The general, I should have known he was ill! The poor, brave man is suffering from malaria, of all things. How in the world can he expect to lead our men into battle when he should be in bed under a physician's care?"

Gabrielle stood up in surprise. "General Jackson is ill? But—but it can't be—you told me he has attended every party given for him and has been working until late at night with the governor on military planning. How could a sick man—"

"That's just it! I don't know, myself! The man can't be entirely human—anyone else would leave the strategy to one of the others and try to get over the fever before the battle begins. Oh, William is in such a state as you've never seen! He even snapped at me this morning!"

She burst into tears, and Gabrielle put her arms around her to comfort her. "There, now, Suzette. If Jackson believes he can do it, there's really nothing anyone else can do to stop him."

"Oh, but Gabrielle, you haven't seen him. His face

is positively haggard, and sometimes his eyes look as though they will glaze over at any minute. It's horrible to watch him put himself through such torture."

Gabrielle bit her lip. Lord, everyone's nerves were on edge—if the people found out that Jackson was a sick man, how could their hopes continue to soar? It would be disastrous if they thought he was incapable of leading the attack! "There is nothing you can do," she repeated, "except to keep control of yourself."

"Oh, that will be harder than you think! Jackson will be here for a small supper tonight, and I—I don't think I can stand to watch him without breaking into tears."

"Suzette, you've always been the perfect hostess. Your upbringing is not going to let you down now. You must pull yourself together. How many will be attending tonight?"

Suzette sniffed, but she seemed to draw some strength from the other's words. "Only about twenty. Jackson and his staff, of course, and William and his immediate staff. No ladies will be present except myself—and you—you must come, too. William told me expressly that you should be invited because of your—your contribution." She stopped and shot a look at her friend. "What contribution is that, my dear?"

Gabrielle thought quickly. "I have no idea, unless it has to do with the uniforms I helped to sew."

Suzette smiled. "Yes, I suppose that must be it. William is a kind man, deep down, but lately I'm afraid we've all been at odds, trying to outguess the British and get ourselves in shape."

Gabrielle agreed. "Come, now, why don't you rest and think about what gown you are going to wear tonight? I'll be glad to look in on the kitchen and see what sort of menu to prepare."

"Oh, I can't expect you to do that, my dear," Suzette sighed. "I'll go speak to the cook immediately. I only hope Jackson doesn't have some certain preference—I must try to please everyone, you know."

Gabrielle smiled, recognizing the years of training coming back instantly to the harassed woman. "Well, at least let me see to the table settings."

"Oh, you are a dear, Gabrielle. I don't know how you can do it with—with your own problems."

Gabrielle hurried out of the room, forcing her mind to stay with the difficulty at hand. Rafe will be here tonight, she kept whispering to herself like a refrain. He'll have to speak to me. I'll make him! He won't dare to make a scene in front of the general. I'll make him understand—I must try!

With that determined thought, she set out at a furious pace, ordering the servants about with a briskness that surprised them. She had the best white tablecloth brought out and aired. Fresh flowers, anything that was in season, were gathered in fragrant bundles and arranged in vases throughout the dining room. Suzette's family china was brought out of the cupboard and washed and polished until it sparkled as brightly as the crystal. New candles were placed on the table in tall, silver candlesticks that had also to be polished, and the best linen napkins were washed and pressed into shape.

It was already late in the afternoon when Gabrielle finally found time to sit down and cast an experienced eye over the dining room. Everything shone brightly or glowed darkly with the richness of cherrywood. The draperies had been aired, and the tall, many-paned windows had been washed twice over. She would go upstairs now and rest, herself, before it was time to dress.

She chose a gown of violet-blue silk with a flounce of white lace around the hem and more lace trimming the full, double-tiered sleeves, and she picked up her fan confidently. She had just joined Suzette at the foot of the stairs when a servant announced the general's arrival.

Her first impression was mixed. The man was tall, certainly, but painfully thin, and his bones seemed to stick out through the dress uniform he was wearing. His face was kind, though, despite the sharpness of the features, the drawn, sallow skin, and the sunken look in the intelligent eyes. His hair was thick and grey, and his brow was furrowed, indicating the many worries that plagued him. She could see in that straight, tight-lipped mouth a firmness of purpose that in some part explained his desire to continue even in the face of his illness. His eyes seemed to lighten as they touched hers, and he was taking her hand firmly in his, and she noticed in his palm the heat that spoke of his fever.

"Madame St. Claire, I am deeply honored to meet you after so long a time in the city."

She blushed a little, which seemed to delight him thoroughly. "Thank you, general. I am delighted to see you here tonight. I do hope we can take your mind off the depressing events of these days, if only for a little while."

He grinned. "I'm afraid that would be a monumental task, my dear, but you are certainly welcome to try."

He kissed her hand and went on to greet Suzette, who seemed to be bearing up a good deal better after her nap. Gabrielle went through the rest of the introductions with only half an ear, as her eyes kept returning to the door, waiting for *him*. Even before she saw her husband, she knew he was about to enter, and her eyes locked into his. Her heart began beating so quickly that she felt the urge to press a hand against her breast. Then he was coming towards her, and she couldn't fathom the look in those green depths. Her whole body trembled as he took her hand, and she knew he must be aware of it.

"Good evening, madame. You are looking exceptionally lovely tonight."

He kissed her hand and went inside the room. Gabrielle could have screamed her impatience. That was all! Those few trite words that could have as easily been said to any other woman! Her eyes glittered with her anger, but she schooled herself to remain calm for the sake of her hostess, who was looking at her uneasily.

"I'm all right, Suzette," she assured her as they walked into the room and sat down at the table.

She found herself between her husband and the general, a situation ill-timed for her riot of feelings, but she did her best to carry on light conversation. Rafe ignored her and appeared to be deep in important conversation with the gentleman to his left. Gabrielle seethed through the various courses of the dinner and was more than glad when it was over, although her stomach was fairly tied in knots.

"We will leave you gentlemen to your port and cigars," Suzette said, rising. "I have planned a little entertainment for later on, general, if—if you are not feeling too tired."

Once alone in the sitting room, Gabrielle faced Suzette, her face enraged.

"Did you see him? Did you see him! He ignored me grossly throughout the entire meal! General Jackson must be mightily confused as to whether he is truly my husband or not! He's deliberately set out to humiliate me!"

"Oh, Gabrielle, perhaps he is—he is just not sure what he feels right now," Suzette put in, hoping to alleviate some of her friend's anger before the gentlemen joined them. "For goodness sake, he must feel something! He loves you!"

Gabrielle snorted at these words. "He doesn't love me, Suzette, he never has loved me! I tried to make myself think that someday I could make him love me, but how can I fight indifference! If he would only talk to me, treat me like a person instead of a fixture in the room! No, it's impossible! I'm sick of being treated like a stranger. As though—" She stopped suddenly and leaned her head against the window. "I—I can't go on like this, Suzette, with my heart twisted and battered by his casual attitude. I simply can't go on."

"Gabrielle, you must remember that Rafe has many, many things on his mind. You've got to try to understand what a burden this whole thing has been for him. I—I don't know the circumstances of your quarrel, but I'm sure it was caused by tenseness over the campaigns. Look at yourself! Would you be acting this way if you weren't affected, too?" She reached over to the sideboard and poured her a small glass of wine. "Now I want you to drink this and pull yourself together. We still have the rest of the evening to get through, and I'm not about to face it alone." Her words seemed to have the desired effect, and Gabrielle drank the glass of wine. "Now I must look to the dessert, my dear, so you wait here for me, and, if the musicians arrive, please show them to their places."

Gabrielle nodded without enthusiasm, and, feeling the need of some fresh air, she opened the tall French doors leading onto the balcony. She could hear the men talking through the other door which led from the dining room to the balcony. She leaned her elbows on the stone railing and gazed out at the garden, her head full of memories.

"Madame?"

She didn't hear the word the first time and continued her sad reverie, her chin propped up on her hands.

"Madame St. Claire?"

She turned around, embarrassed, and found herself facing General Jackson.

"I saw you from the window, standing out here alone. It was beginning to get a little stuffy inside, and I hoped some cool air might lend a hand in sharpening my senses."

Gabrielle noticed the tiredness in his eyes. "You're not well, general. Perhaps you ought to lie down for a while."

He chuckled. "Perhaps I should, but I can't."

"Why not? This party is only your staff and the governor's aides. Surely they would understand. It is easy to see that you are ill."

"No, I'm afraid they expect more than that of me," he said, sighing a little. "You see, they look at the troops and see their ill-fitting clothing, their greenness, and they shudder to themselves, wondering how in the world such men can win a battle. If, on their other side, their leader becomes incapable of supporting them, they would be lost in the middle, able to rely on no one."

"But, whom can you rely on, then?"

"I must rely on myself, madame, and, of course, the good Lord. So you see, I have many people who look to me for support, chief among them, myself."

"But—but it is impossible to drive yourself to the point of exhaustion and then—then expect to lead men into battle!"

He patted her hand. "You know, my dear, you remind me of my wife, Rachel. She's a strong-willed woman like yourself, always wanting to tell me what to do."

Gabrielle blushed. "General, I didn't mean to presume—"

He waved aside her words. "It's quite all right, my dear. We could use more women like yourself. I must admit I was prepared for a lovely face, an enchanting smile, and an empty head, but it is easy to see that you are an intelligent woman. Mr. St. Claire is a lucky man."

He saw her face grow sad and realized that, as he had suspected, all was not well with these two. He took her hand in his. "You know, my dear, I've been through a lot in my forty-seven years. I've been in battles that hung by a thread, have had bullets go through me, have been tomahawked and knifed more times than I like to remember, but I don't dread anything more than having to face Rachel after a quarrel. It's funny how a man can be the bravest one on the battlefield, but when it comes to affairs of the heart, he's turned into jelly at the mere thought of patching it up. Oh, pride enters into it, I grant you that, and sometimes it takes quite a while to figure out the right words to say, but it never fails—there comes a moment when I'll look in Rachel's eyes and we both know we don't have to say anything."

Gabrielle could easily see the love and tenderness that seemed to reshape the tired features. He must have been a handsome man in his youth, she thought.

"It's easy to see you love him, my dear. It's all over your face when you look at him. And I have an idea that, no matter how he might think he must struggle against it, your husband is very much in love with you.

He was as nervous coming over here tonight as a boy going to his first dance. Give him time. It's hard to fight two battles at once."

Gabrielle sighed, and her eyes were bright. "For a general, you are awfully romantic," she murmured shakily, and Jackson laughed.

"And I do tend to stick my long nose into other people's affairs, eh?" He shrugged. "Well, someone's got to keep up morale. Now, before Mrs. Claiborne begins to wonder what's become of me, I suppose I'd best get in and endeavor to enjoy the entertainment."

He rose and took her hand, tucking it into his arm. Gabrielle had found a good deal of comfort in his words, and her heart ceased its wild crescendo and began to beat normally again. She held up her head proudly as they entered the salon.

"Ah, there you are, general. I see you are enjoying one of the fairest flowers of our city," Governor Claiborne said gallantly.

"Mrs. St. Claire and I have been having an informative discussion."

Gabrielle caught the eye of Bernard de Marigny, who had arrived late, and went over to greet him. "Bernard, I haven't seen you for ages!" she exclaimed.

"Gabrielle, my dear, seeing you is better than a good stiff drink!" he said, kissing the hand she extended to him. "I see you have already worked your charm on the general."

"I would say rather that the general has worked his charm on me," Gabrielle returned, smiling. "He is truly a wonderful man, Bernard. I can see how the men have taken to him so."

"His health has many of us worried, though," Bernard frowned. "He'll keep going until he drops from sheer exhaustion."

"I think he will make it," Gabrielle said soberly. "His determination is boundless, and his concern for the troops quite remarkable."

Suzette was clapping her hands now for their attention,

and Bernard and Gabrielle moved in closer to the others.
"Everyone must be seated. General, if you please," she
said, indicating the chair next to hers. "I have a little
evening music and a singer whom I think will please you
all greatly."

Everyone took their seats and Gabrielle was careful
to sit as close to her husband as she dared. He had only
to lean forward a little, and she would be able to feel his
breath on her neck. During the course of the evening,
she was sure she could feel his eyes on her, and, when
she dropped her fan accidentally, a familiar brown hand
brushed hers as he handed it to her. Their eyes met and
she smiled shyly at him, watching his eyes change expression. For a moment, she thought he was about to
say something, and then he sat back in his chair, his
face carefully closed once more against her. She had to
cling tightly to the general's words in order to keep herself from weeping once more with frustration.

When the evening came to a close and everyone was
saying their farewells, Gabrielle walked deliberately over
to her husband. "Will I be seeing you later tonight,
darling?" she asked sweetly, keeping her voice low.

He acted as though she had stung him for a moment,
but when he looked at her his eyes were almost teasing.
"I'll see what I can manage, madame," he said wickedly,
"but please do not wait up for me."

She waited expectantly for his kiss, and, when he
would have only brushed her mouth, she put her arms
strongly around him and molded her lips to his. Her eyes
were sparkling seductively, and it took all of his strength
to leave her there.

"Your wife is an exceptional woman, St. Claire,"
Jackson commented as the men walked outside.

Rafe nodded absently, but his mind was recalling the
texture of her mouth when she had kissed him, the slight
pressure of her impudent breasts against his coat, the
way her eyes tilted upwards when she smiled, revealing
the dimple in her cheek. Why must he continue denying
himself the pleasure of that sweet, vulnerable body that

he dreamed about at night? Why did he keep on resisting the urge to tell her—to tell her. . . .

He frowned to himself. He couldn't allow such thoughts to keep thrusting themselves at him. He must concentrate on the battle against the enemy. It would take all of their cunning and strength to pull a victory out of their situation. He knew it as well as Jackson and Claiborne and the rest of them. Lafitte's stockpile had helped, that was certain, but the question remained—would that be enough?

Thinking of Lafitte, he shifted uneasily in the coach. She had at least been telling the truth as far as his integrity was concerned, but what of the other? What had she done to actually make the pirate help the Americans? Could he believe that they had only talked of arms and battles and the enemy? Objectively, he had been aware of the man's good looks and abundance of charm. It would have been easy for him to seduce her, the two of them alone in the dark, their memories of their time together brought back to them.

He shook himself to clear his head and for a moment thought of slipping back to her tonight. No, he wouldn't go back just yet, he decided firmly. He looked forward with a groan to the hard bunk he would be using once again tonight.

Chapter Forty-five

Rafe waved away the hand that shook his shoulder.

"Get up, St. Claire. Get dressed. The general wants to see you!"

"Christ, man! I've only just gotten to bed," Rafe mumbled irritably, turning over in his bunk.

"The British have landed only a few miles east of New Orleans in a surprise assault. We've no time to lose!"

Rafe came awake instantly then and looked up into Leigh Owens' pale face. Grabbing his boots and jerking them on swiftly, he splashed some tepid water over his face and hurried after the other man. Jackson's headquarters on Royal Street were aswarm with militia, everyone talking at once. Rafe was ushered into the room and presented himself to Jackson with all speed.

"Sir, I've heard the news," he said as Jackson shook his hand and asked him to be seated.

"Yes, it's lucky we've had men posted in strategic spots, or they might have slipped in unnoticed." Jackson shuddered at the thought. "We've got to attack now, during the night when they least expect it. They'll be regrouping after their landing and won't know what the hell's hit them!"

"Right, sir, but how can I be of service?"

"As the governor's aide, I know that you have led several surveillance missions, St. Claire. I am aware that you are not a military man, but from all accounts you can fight like the best of us." Here the general offered a craggy smile. "I suppose I'm drafting you into the damn thing, but I've got to have someone who can carry this out without blundering. Do you think you can do it?"

Rafe nodded quickly.

"Good. I'll give you the best men among the troops. Now here is the plan. You've got to come up on them by surprise while it's still dark. No doubt they're confident enough to leave a few small fires going, and these will help to guide you. You will attack swiftly and do as much damage as you can, then withdraw to our defensive lines. I've drawn them along the map here." He pointed to the paper spread out over his desk.

"But, general, your defensive lines are barely five miles from the city limits!" Rafe exclaimed in disbelief.

The general nodded. "I'm aware of that, St. Claire, but it is the best place to make our stand. The ground is not so soft or swampy as it is further south and west. I'm told an abandoned canal runs along this line and it will be the perfect place to construct our breastworks. I've already had men working on the parapet, throwing up logs and mud. I suppose cotton bales might be used also."

Rafe shook his head. "The bales would be useless, general. The British could set them afire too easily."

Jackson nodded. "You're right. Christ, that could have proved our downfall!"

Jackson ordered the troops singled out for the mission to be readied. "God go with you," he said to the man he was sending into battle. For a moment he hesitated, thinking of accusing violet eyes and a trembling mouth, but he shrugged the image aside. He watched as Rafe hurried off and hoped he had chosen the right man.

In his own mind, Rafe was aware of the danger and of the trust Jackson had shown in him by selecting him for this job. He assembled his men in an encampment close to the defense line. He was glad to see Leigh beside him. His orders were quick and given sharply with no time for questions. The men silently checked their weapons and waited for the signal to move.

"Do you think they have an idea what they're in for?" Leigh asked Rafe as they marched in loose formation towards their goal.

"I don't think it will be as bad as you think," Rafe returned. "The British will probably have posted a few sentries around their camp, but most of them will be asleep."

He directed the men to split up into small groups as they neared the shoreline so that they could surround the encampment on all sides. They crouched among the weeds, the smell of the swamp sharp in their nostrils. Above him, on a slight crest, Rafe could make out the figure of a sentinel, silently pacing back and forth, his gun cocked and ready to sound the alarm.

Rafe signalled to Leigh to stay where he was and indicated the sentry. Leigh nodded and crouched further back as Rafe made his way through the rushes towards the lone figure. He knew that at the three other corners of the camp there would be other guards, and three more Americans like himself were crawling towards them, hoping against hope that no shots would be fired to alert the garrison. His eyes never left the figure which continued its clockwork pacing.

Carefully, he inched himself up the hill until he could smell the new leather of the sentry's boots. He would have to wait until he made a turn, the better to catch him off guard. He could feel the dampness creep into his trousers and was vaguely aware that he was sweating profusely. His muscles began to ache as he waited, hoping to catch an opening. He wondered if the others had been silenced yet and knew they would wait until he gave the signal to attack. His arms felt awkward and he slipped his hand back to where the knife lay heavy against his calf.

Off to his right, a night animal scurried into the darkness, and the sentry ceased his pacing for a moment to peer into the night. He levelled his musket, and Rafe held his breath, cursing the bad timing. If the man fired, he would awake the others in time for some of them to put up a fight. He waited, tensing on the balls of his feet, as he readied himself to spring. The guard, thinking better of it, decided not to pursue what he had obviously deduced was only some animal. Rafe heard his sigh settle in the air and watched him put the gun down at his feet for a moment while he took out his handkerchief to mop his brow.

Now! Like a spring uncoiling, Rafe jumped out, then ran a few steps, his knife held ready in his hand. The guard had time only to see a flash of metal and a man's merciless face before he was silenced forever.

Rafe stood panting, wiping his blade on the ground and checking for other sentries. He picked up the primed musket and waved it high over his head. Down in the rushes, Leigh saw his silhouette in the moonlight and signalled his men up the hill. Below them, the enemy camp lay peaceful with a few fires still glowing but untended. Rafe signalled two men to tell the other blocks of troops to attack when they heard the first shot. Crouching low to the ground, the men moved carefully down the hill, closer to the tents. Rafe nearly tripped over a sleeping soldier, and they were close enough to hear the snores coming from the tents.

"Now!" he yelled and fired a shot that felled the alerted soldier.

Swarms of men came down from the hill and surged around the tents so that many of the enemy were killed before they were even aware of what had happened. Rafe fought through the smoke and smell of powder, directing some of the men to destroy the johnboats the British had used to land. Screams, yells and, savage warcries issued from Americans mouths, and Rafe found himself yelling abuse at the enemy who had dogged them for months.

It seemed to be all over in a matter of minutes, and Rafe was already signalling his men to retreat, not to waste ammunition. They backed up the hill, their eyes taking in the scene of complete surprise they had carried out. British soldiers rushed to and fro, hauling in their wounded, lighting smothered fires, and cursing at the Americans who had outfoxed them.

The American troops withdrew to the defense line as Jackson had ordered, and Rafe hurried to headquarters to inform the general of the success of the mission.

Jackson sat back in his chair and smiled reflectively. "That will give them something to think about," he chuckled. "We've pricked them a little, aroused their anger. It won't be long now, gentlemen, before we have our battle." He looked around the table at the excitement in their faces. "The British will be bringing up reinforcements now. We're still outnumbered, but I think I know the way to beat them."

"We've been able to secure additional men, sir," one of his officers said. "I believe we can count nearly four thousand men in our ranks now."

"Good news, Morgan, but it won't be superior numbers that win the day this time." Jackson's long face grew crafty. "During my years in battle, gentlemen, I've learned quite a bit about different techniques of fighting. You recall during the War of Independence, we beat the enemy simply because we employed Indian tactics, hitting them from behind trees and ground cover, while the British continued to march in orderly formation, clearly making themselves sitting ducks." He slapped his thigh exuberantly. "Well, that is exactly what I propose we do again. The British haven't learned a thing from that war, and I've observed they still march in formation, shoulder to shoulder, making a sort of wall of flesh. Anyone, gentlemen, who can hit the broad side of a barn should be able to make a dent in their ranks."

"It should work," Claiborne said hopefully. "It makes sense."

"Of course it makes sense! Didn't I just tell you I've seen too many battles not to know it works?" Jackson repeated. For a minute he looked at St. Claire, who was watching him with a new regard. "St. Claire, you've done us a great service. You've earned some sleep, man!"

The mud-and-wood rampart stretched along the canal from the Mississippi River to the swamp to the west. All along it, men waited, guns ready. Some laughed and joked, others held quieter conversations, still others gazed out onto the field of Chalmette, whence the enemy would come.

On December 28, five days after the surprise rout, the British attacked, but they were easily driven back by cannon fire. Still, Jackson warned his men to hold their rejoicing, for these skirmishes were only a test of their strength.

On New Year's Day, the Americans watched in dismay as the British set up cannon from their warships. A huge bombardment began, and for hours the field was a haze of cannon smoke and the roar of firing weapons.

Rafe, walking along the defenses, looking for any weakening in the line, came upon a group of Baratarians, and he easily recognized Dominique You's swarthy features and broad-shouldered body, manning his gun with little effort. Unwillingly, Rafe stopped for a moment to observe as the men loaded, primed, and shot the cannon with smooth efficiency.

"I'd say you knew your way about a cannon," he said during a lull in the firing.

You shot him a look. "You could say that, sir. I can outshoot those artillerists of the English any day. I've had enough experience, if I may say so myself."

"I'm sure you have," Rafe returned grimly.

You's brows drew down in a puzzled frown. "Hey, now, you'd not be looking for a fight would you?"

Rafe shrugged his shoulders. "And lose the best artillery man we've got?"

You burst out in a roar of laughter. "That's right, sir, that's right as rain." He went back to his gun, chuckling at the man's audacity.

Rafe continued his inspection of the troops and gave words of encouragement to them when he could. More men were called up to patch breaks in the earthworks, and it was during one of these repair sessions that he saw Bernard, slapping mud determinedly into a crack.

"Bernard, what in hell are you doing here?" he said curiously.

Bernard smiled ruefully. "I hesitate to say it, Rafe, but as a swordsman I may be the best in New Orleans, but a gunman I am not. I've got to make myself useful, don't I?" He winked conspiratorially. Rafe slapped him on the shoulder and continued on his rounds.

Later in the day, when it became evident that the line had held, there was a general rejoicing among the troops, and a round of whiskey was given to each man.

"The British are finding it harder than they thought to crack our defenses," Claiborne said with some relief when Rafe met him back at the Cabildo later that evening.

"Let's hope they give up fairly soon," he responded drily.

Claiborne nodded. "God, it is getting colder, isn't it? Do all the men have blankets?"

Rafe nodded, his mind recalling the thin, bedraggled pieces of cloth that passed for protection against the cool night air. "Excuse me, governor, but have you seen my wife? I'm afraid I've not had time to visit her."

"She is well and asks me about you constantly. I say, you could use a little time off. Why don't you go over there tomorrow and look in on her?"

Rafe shook his head silently. "I've got my duties to perform," he said. "Is it fair that I should be able to visit her when the troops are stuck day after day in the lines?"

Claiborne flushed a little at the reproach. "Do as you wish, then, Rafe," he muttered, "but if I were you, I'd be more careful of my possessions. A girl like that, there just aren't that many around, you know."

A girl like that? Back in his bunk, his arms crossed beneath his head, Rafe wondered just what kind of girl Gabrielle was. Had it been only a little over five years ago that he had first seen her, standing at the top of the steps when he'd brought de Chevalier home that night? He recalled the alarm in those eyes and the tempting view of her legs as she rushed downstairs and into the sitting room.

Even then he had been drawn to her and had barely kept himself from seducing her in de Chevalier's own house! Oh, she had hated him for a while—had even conceived the notion that he was trying to blackmail her guardian! He had to laugh at that, but then he grew restless thinking of that night in France when he had carried her up to the room and took her for the first time.

She had been innocent, as he'd expected, and afraid, but still she had kept on struggling against him, cursing him and promising she'd kill him if he ever came near her again. It had been a brutal gesture, he admitted now, to leave the gold pieces under her pillow. He could imagine the humiliation and pain on her vulnerable face. But he had done it simply to make her keep her place in his mind—he couldn't let this one night be any more special than others. He had consciously tried to cheapen the memory by leaving the money behind. He couldn't admit to himself that she had struck a chord deep within him that kept her face in his memory long after he had arrived back in Virginia.

God, when he had recognized her the night of the fire at Renée's, he could barely believe his eyes. But before he could convince himself to make himself known to her, Lafitte had come and taken her away. He remembered with bitterness her long months with the renegade and how he had even gone to Barataria once on the pretext of buying slaves when he really wanted to see if she was happy.

Their paths had crossed again at Renée's and once more when he had seen her with Bernard de Marigny. Naturally, he had assumed that she was his mistress, for it was common knowledge that de Marigny never let a fish get away once caught. But he had been wrong, he realized that now, and too damn proud to tell her so.

When he had seen her at the Golden Palace it had been all he could do not to sweep her off her feet and carry her away with him. She was even lovelier than he remembered, but he had kept lying to her, like a fool, telling her that their night together in France had meant nothing to him and that he could barely recall it.

Their first night together at Fairview had shown him her maturity, and he had known then that he wanted her with him. But he was too proud, always too proud, to admit it to her. What strange wickedness in him had caused him to treat her so cruelly after they were married? He could kill any man who came near her, and yet he fought her constantly when they were together.

Then Charles de Chevalier came back into her life with his poisonous thoughts, his distorted brain. God, hadn't she suffered enough without that? And then her eyes, looking into his, soft and tender as he had never seen them before, had whispered that she loved him! Christ, it unnerved him so badly he had ridden away before she had come to full consciousness. He wouldn't blame her if she hated him now. No woman should have to put up with what he had given her. But still, and his face showed his astonishment, still she went on loving him. Why, why didn't he tell her . . . tell her he loved her!

He could look in her eyes and kiss her sweet mouth, and his heart would open so that he nearly choked with the emotion. Why couldn't he say the words that would make her eyes light with happiness? After this battle was over, he promised himself he would tell her. He'd tell her he loved her—that he'd always loved her and had been a fool for too long.

Chapter Forty-six

At dawn on January 8, 1815, the British made their all-out attempt to flatten the impudent Americans. It was a cold, foggy dawn, but the sun soon dispelled the wreaths of mist and shone gloriously on the red coats of the enemy as they marched forward in an unbroken line across the field of Chalmette.

General Jackson rode along the line, shouting encouragement to his troops and urging them towards victory. He had positioned his best frontier marksmen in strategic positions, and he shook his head at the stupidity of the enemy's mass formation in battle.

Rafe St. Claire rode close to the general, and the breeze lifted his dark hair as he bantered with the gunnery sergeants. Jean Lafitte had been sent to guard the American rear in a vessel which could sweep down on the longboats of the British should they decide to attack from the Gulf. Bernard de Marigny sat on a fallen log, his sword in hand, hoping that they would get close enough so that he could prove himself in battle.

And in the city, Gabrielle bit her lip and waited with a mixture of fear and impatience. She had been among the ladies who stood on their balconies and threw flowers to the men who were marching off to the uncertainty of battle. From her lips had sounded the words of "Hail, Columbia" and "La Marseillaise," and she had added her prayers for a victory to everyone else's.

"Oh, God, this is the worst part, for the women," Suzette sighed, pacing up and down the room. "This interminable waiting."

"The men have to wait, too," piped up another lady, and a ripple of agreement floated through the room.

Gabrielle glanced around at the hundred or so ladies who had gathered together last night at the house of Madam Porée and spent the night, praying and talking, encouraging each other. She glanced at the clock on the shelf and saw that it was just a little past six o'clock—surely it would begin soon.

As if in answer to her thoughts, a dull boom sounded, shaking the house as others quickly followed it. The cannonading had started! Many of the women began shrieking in hysteria, and Madame Porée rushed about the rooms administering smelling salts to those who had fainted. Close beside her, she could feel Suzette's trembling, and Gabrielle grasped her hand in comfort.

"We must be brave," she said aloud. "We must be brave."

Suzette nodded, although her hand still shook.

The booming of the cannons and the popping of guns seemed to go on and on until Gabrielle almost became used to the noise in the background, coming as it did at neatly spaced intervals.

"Mrs. St. Claire, you look as though you're holding up all right," Madam Porée said, a little breathless from her rounds. "Do you think you might be able to serve some coffee and tea to those ladies who would like some? I should appreciate your help, my dear." Gabrielle nodded, squeezed Suzette's hand, and followed their hostess into the kitchen.

"What do you think, madame?" she wondered as the other woman poured hot coffee into delicate china cups.

"What can I think?" she responded. "I think that we will win."

Gabrielle smiled at her. "My husband is out there in the battle, and I, too, feel sure that we will emerge victorious!"

Fate would not be so cruel as to take him away from her before they had discovered their love, she thought. She had had many days in which to think of him and their life together. She loved him—of that she was sure, for no matter what he could do or say to her, she would still care for him as fiercely as she did at this moment. She would try hard to understand him, to listen to him—she must, if they were going to make their marriage work.

As she passed out cups of coffee and tea to the ladies, her mind was far away from this stuffy room and all these frightened women. She was thinking of the way his hair grew long at the back of his neck and the way his eyes could look so mockingly amused when she got angry with him. She remembered the way his mouth could curve into a bold smile that quickened her heart and made her realize that she would follow him wherever he went.

How long had she loved him? she wondered idly now. How long had she known that he was the only man who could make her senses swim and her whole body yearn towards him? Was it as long ago as that night in Paris? God, it did seem long ago, now. Other men had come between that first night and this moment.

She thought of Lafitte's dark, snapping eyes and rakish figure. He had loved her in his own way, she knew that, and, deep within her, she knew also that he had touched a corner of her own heart. She smiled to herself, recalling those days at Renée's, when Bernard de Marigny had paid her way and got nothing in return. He had certainly been gay and charming, but he could never have offered her what Rafe had been able to give. Oh, it wasn't that Bernard was married—he was like a bee, flying from flower to flower, getting his fill of the nectar before moving on. If she had let him take her, she was sure he would have grown bored with her, too, after a time. Now, they were good friends, and she was glad of it.

It was good to know that Bernard and Rafe had patched up their differences, too. Rafe, so stiff and unyielding when it came to matters of pride—unbend just a little, my darling, she thought. Rafe, Rafe, why do you put us both through this torture? she wondered.

How many men would be killed? Would the battle end today? Her thoughts were echoed in the minds of every woman present. But they must wait—wait for word before they could breathe again, before they could smile and laugh and look forward to their men coming home.

The candles sputtered and went out, were lit again, and through the slats in the window Gabrielle could see the high shadows of midday. Still the noises of war continued. The women began to sing a psalm—it would help to strengthen their spirits.

Suzette had recovered herself and urged the women to make themselves useful during the time of waiting. "Some of us can fold blankets and others can begin rolling bandages for the wounded."

With relief the women agreed. It would be something to do. They worked wordlessly and with renewed determination, and the hours began to creep by. At last, someone heard the sound of a horseman in the street, galloping madly. Did he bear good tidings, or would he tell them that the British were on their way to the city?

Madame Porée hurried to one of the windows and opened it, peering out.

"Victory! Victory!"

Everyone inside could hear the words shouted at the top of the young Creole's lungs. With a glad cry, Madame Porée flung the window open wide now, and other women hurried to follow suit. Shouts and joyous cries filled the air as the news spread swiftly through the city. Women hugged each other and cried together. Suzette and Gabrielle hurried out into the street, eager for more news. They could see the first stream of men returning from the battlefield, waving their hats high in the air and shouldering their guns proudly despite their fatigue.

"We routed the whole lot of them," one of the soldiers cried in answer to Suzette's question. "Hurrah for General Jackson!"

The cry was taken up everywhere as the men trooped back into the city. Wine flowed, and women laughed through their tears.

Once their safety was assured, Suzette ordered her carriage and, along with many of the other women, drove at once to the battlefield, laden with bandages and bedding for the wounded.

Seated beside her, Gabrielle knew a moment of uncertainty. What if she should find Rafe on that battlefield, his blood seeping slowly into the greedy earth? She quickly brushed the thought from her mind.

She and Suzette descended from the carriage and walked among the wounded, strewn helter-skelter in the grass. Many—far more than the Americans—were British, and Gabrielle felt a well of relief rise up in her. She set to work with Suzette on her errand of mercy, and, when the bandages they had brought were exhausted, she tore her petticoats to make more. Many of the women worked far into the night, tirelessly bringing comfort to those who had not escaped from injury.

It was almost dawn when Gabrielle rose from her crouched position over a dying British soldier and glanced behind her.

He leaned forward on his horse, his green eyes reflecting the joy in her own, and his mouth curved into that exasperating lazy grin. They stood looking at each other, and she felt her heart leap at the tenderness in his expression.

She would have gone on staring at him forever, if his voice, slightly mocking, shaded with pride, hadn't asked lovingly, "Madame, is that how you would greet your husband, home from battle?"

Was she dreaming the same dream over again, she thought happily, or was this truly real now? She stood in a white dress, waiting for him by the river, sheltered from prying eyes by a copse of old, gnarled oaks. Her heart quickened as she heard the hooves of his horse galloping towards her, and in another minute he would walk through

the trees and take her in his arms. She shook back her hair
in the morning sunlight, and it caught and held the reflected glory in golden tresses. Her perfect mouth was
smiling, showing the single dimple in her cheek, and her
eyes were filled with love and a tiny secret that was hers
alone for the moment.

She heard his boots crunching the twigs under foot, and
then his tall, strong figure was coming towards her. The
green eyes flashed for a moment with the intensity of his
love, then twinkled into amusement.

"The majordomo told me I could find you here, kitten,"
he said. "I've got news for you! Official word has just
reached New Orleans that the war is over. The peace
treaty was signed two months ago!"

Gabrielle laughed in delight. "That is wonderful news,
darling." And I have news even more wonderful for you,
she thought—but not yet, my dearest. Her hand patted
her stomach contentedly where a new life had already begun.

"You look like the cat with her cream," he teased her.

Then his arms went around her, and he was holding
her close against him so that she could feel the pounding
of his heart in rhythm with hers. Her eyes were incredibly
clear as they gazed into his, and he felt a stirring within
him at her nearness.

Gently, he lowered her to the ground, which would
serve as their bed, its spring-green grass as soft to her as
any silken cushion. Their kiss was long and deep as each
questioned the other and knew the answer to their new-
found love.

Gabrielle sighed deeply, feeling the response to him
begin to fill her with a delicious anticipation as he began
to caress her.

"Oh, Rafe!" she whispered suddenly, "think of all the
time we wasted."

He smiled at her and planted a kiss on the tip of her
nose. "I shall endeavor, madame, to make up for all lost
time." He sensed her complete abandon and traced a
finger over her lips. "I'm a stubborn male, aren't I, darling?

But once I've been made to see the light, there's no turning back."

His green eyes deepened, and she thought she could drown in their depths.

"I love you, kitten," he whispered tenderly.

She laughed with an overwhelming happiness, her arms wrapped tightly about his neck, knowing they had the rest of their lives together.

About the Author

Theresa Conway is twenty-six years old, married, and the mother of a four-year-old daughter. Ms. Conway worked as a secretary for five years during which time she researched and wrote GABRIELLE. Ms. Conway has been writing for her own pleasure since the age of fourteen, and she is among the elite few who have had a first effort published.

Ms. Conway enjoys traveling, tennis, competitive sports and the Mother's Club at her daughter's Montessori School. She lives in St. Louis, Missouri, and is currently at work on her second historical romance.